"WILDLY IMAGINATIVE, ENTIRELY ORIGINAL, AND AS QUIRKY AS A TEQUILA WORM.
It's drawn on a very large canvas, and Mr. Childress, as always, stretches his enormous talent into new and amazing shapes. This book is part magic realism, part Peter Pan as told by Truman Capote to Antoine de Saint-Exupéry."

—*Pat Conroy*

"Childress is great with myth and magic, treating them as part of every-day life most people overlook. . . . *Gone for Good* finally pulls out all the stops, climaxing with machine guns, explosions and superhero battles. There's not one American author in 1,000 who could pull it off. Childress does, proving that in this book, he's the real magician."

—*Seattle Post-Intelligencer*

"Proves once again that Mark Childress remains one of the most origi-nal and imaginative writers of our generation."

—*Fannie Flagg*

"If you like *either* rock and roll, rhythm and blues, jazz, bluegrass, cir-cuses, state fairs, or volcanoes, then you'll love *Gone for Good*. And beneath the fine music, fabulous rides, and bright lights of this book run the warm currents of home and love. The magic of this book is that Mark Childress somehow does it all together."

—*Clyde Edgerton*

"Like Lewis Carroll taking us with Alice as she falls down a rabbit hole, Mark Childress leads readers of *Gone for Good* into an alternate world they never dreamed existed. . . . The end is a dizzying montage of action and revelations. Hats off to Mark Childress for a thoroughly good read."

—*Lincoln Journal Star*

"Crackles with originality . . . Quirky ingredients, boiling together, cre-ate a spellbinding potion. . . . [Childress] gives muscle and sinew to his stowaway cast, grit and green to his beach and jungle setting, and heart and soul to the fantasy plot of this multilayered tale."

—*Southern Living*

Please turn the page for more reviews. . . .

Gone *for* Good

ALSO BY MARK CHILDRESS

Crazy in Alabama

Tender

V for Victor

A World Made of Fire

CHILDREN'S BOOKS

Joshua and Bigtooth

Joshua and the Big Bad Blue Crabs

Henry Bobbity Is Missing and It Is All Billy Bobbity's Fault

MARK CHILDRESS

Gone *for* Good

Ballantine Books • *New York*

A Ballantine Book
Published by The Ballantine Publishing Group

Copyright © 1998 by Mark Childress
Ballantine Reader's Guide copyright © 1999 by The Ballantine Publishing Group,
a division of Random House, Inc.

All rights reserved under International and Pan-American Copyright Conventions. Published in the United States by The Ballantine Publishing Group, a division of Random House, Inc., New York, and simultaneously in Canada by Random House of Canada Limited, Toronto.

Owing to limitations of space, acknowledgments for permission to reprint previously published material may be found on pages 371–372.

Ballantine and colophon are registered trademarks of Random House, Inc.

www.randomhouse.com/BB/

Library of Congress Catalog Card Number: 99-90083

ISBN: 0-345-41453-5

This edition published by arrangement with Alfred A. Knopf, Inc.

Manufactured in the United States of America
Cover design Cathy Colbert
Cover illustration by Josef Sumichrast

First Ballantine Edition: July 1999

10 9 8 7 6 5 4 3 2 1

For Hoke and Charles,

partners in crime

Adventure is a plan gone wrong.

—RICHARD EVELYN BYRD

All things are full of gods.

—THALES

PART ONE

PART ONE

1 / *Superman Considers His Obligations*

1972

SUPERMAN AMBLED ONSTAGE in his flip-flops, old holey jeans, the tattered sky-blue work shirt. He squinted into the blaze of lights with an uncertain grin, like a stagehand who has wandered past the wrong curtain to find ten thousand people standing and cheering for him. Superman Willis was famous, and so was that shirt. He had worn it for years, at every concert, in every album-cover photo. It was part of his image, indelible as the ink stains under the breast pocket.

His fans thought he must have a whole closet full of sky-blue shirts, identically tattered and stained, but in fact he had just that one. He never took it off unless his wife made him wash it, then he'd hang around bare-chested in the laundry room waiting for it to dry.

One time after a show in Milwaukee, a moon-eyed young girl offered him five hundred bucks for the shirt. "Sorry, darlin'," he said, "Superman's got no powers without his shirt," but when he saw her little-rich-girl disappointment he put on his most charming smile. "Tell you what, though, I believe we could make a deal on these pants."

He was part of the folk-rocker wave that rolled over America in the years just after the Beatles, when rock and roll wore itself out and people started buying the poetic crooners like Jackson Browne, Jim Croce, James Taylor, Joni Mitchell, and . . . Superman Willis. He got his big break at Monterey, 1969. For three years now he'd been hot, hot, hot. The single of "Superman's Revenge" sold four million copies, a triple-platinum smash. "When Time Stands Still" won the Grammy for Song of the Year. *Newsweek* put his face on the cover with the words THE NEW SUPER-POET OF POP spelled out on his cheek.

His nickname came from "Superman's Revenge"—not his best song, but the biggest hit of his career so far. The fans had started it, chanting

"Su-per-man!" between encores. The name carried its own momentum. Entertainment-page editors couldn't resist writing headlines like "SUPER-MAN" SOARS AT SOLD-OUT COLISEUM SHOW.

He bought a mansion in Encino and a Beechcraft Baron B58P twin-engine six-seater airplane. He went to pilot school and began flying himself on his concert tours, high over America, one show at a time.

At first he loved being famous, loved the money and applause and drugs and girls and the fun. After a while it got to be the same fun over and over, and then it became the opposite of fun. There were only so many drugs and girls you could do in one lifetime—at least that was the theory, and Superman had been testing its limits for quite some time now. The only thing that got him truly high these days was to be up in the sky by himself, flying.

He would fly to someplace like El Paso, ride a limo to town, get up onstage in his sky-blue shirt with his Gibson twelve-string around his neck, and sing his twenty-two songs. When he was done, the local promoter would hand him a paper sack with ten or twelve thousand dollars in cash. Then it was back to the limo, fire up a doobie, and ride to the airport on a cloud as big as his head.

His real name was Ben Willis, but he wasn't Ben anymore—he was Superman, even in his own mind, when he was alone. Hadn't he learned how to fly? Wasn't he certain, on nights when the show went well, that he could deflect bullets with his bare hands? On those nights he felt invulnerable.

Tonight was not one of those nights. Superman had been on the road for six months without a break, riding the wave of his momentum. He was exhausted. His songs sounded forced and juvenile. He sang them with about one-tenth the effort he had put into writing them. He cheated his audience, and they didn't even notice. They danced in the aisles and sang along with the hits as if he were putting on one hell of a show up there. They transformed the darkened arena into a star field of cigarette lighters, each flame signifying the enthusiasm of one human being.

The only one not having fun in the El Paso Civic Auditorium was the man in the pool of white light at downstage center.

His life would be perfect, he thought, if he could disappear right now—keep the money, give up the career, and walk away from all the people: the fans, the band, the producers and handlers, promoters, roadies, groupies, hangers-on. His wife.

He knew it was a cliché to work so hard all these years and finally hit the big time, only to find himself with this restless desire to get the hell out of Dodge. But stardom was not at all what he thought it would be.

When he started out, he was Ben Willis, a solo act. Each day contained at least one private moment of joy, a glimmering instant when he paused to reflect on his growing good fortune. Now, after all the years of hard work, those moments were much harder to come by. He was Superman, with an entourage of thirty-three people—always a crowd around, never a moment alone unless he was up in his plane. Even then he'd be sailing along at nine thousand feet, over the heads of white clouds, and just about the time he got to feeling nice and alone, he'd remember the busload of obligations trundling along the highway, toward the next gig.

His wife Alexa was on that bus. Her fear of flying was one of the main reasons he had learned to fly. Alexa was a beautiful woman, a blond Louisiana beauty queen who had turned herself into a hippie-chick to please him. She would never win a prize for intellectual achievement, but she was lovely and long and so very blond. Everyone said they made a great-looking couple, which meant Alexa looked great and Superman looked better standing beside her. She had been at his side for most of his long grinding climb to the top, so she considered it her duty (and her reward) to be present for every moment of glory. She followed him to every city on every tour—always *there,* always watching him sing from just beyond the speaker tower. He rarely had a moment out from under her relentless gaze.

Alexa wore Puma Indian beads and tiny Janis Joplin glasses. She had this earnest way of nodding her head while you were talking, as if she agreed with every single molecule of what you were saying. Every so often Superman would gently suggest that she go home to Louisiana, take care of Ben Junior awhile, give her mother a break. That would start her crying—he didn't really love her, if he loved her he would ride on the tour bus with her instead of flying when he knew how it scared her, on and on like that nag nag boo hoo until deep in the night.

He knew this was only one of her acts, and not the best one. Underneath the sensitive hippie exterior, Alexa would always be Doris Marie French, the former Miss Southwest Louisiana, a woman of unanswered ambitions and strong jealousies. She was convinced that the moment she let Superman out of her sight he'd be helping himself to one of the succulent young things at the stage door. And she was right about that.

The Baron burst through a layer of fleece at ten thousand. Superman tweaked the dial. "Phoenix center, Baron four nine four Alpha Delta."

A burst of static was the only answer.

The popping and snapping warned of a big fat thunderstorm straight ahead to the west, in the ominous darkness beyond that curtain of blue velvet light.

Superman worked through the low-band frequencies, announcing himself to thin air. In this lonely corner of New Mexico, nobody seemed to be home.

The first flicker of lightning brought his eyes up from the panel. He stubbed out the joint, squared his shoulders, filled his chest with the air of serious purpose. Flying in weather was not the way to have fun. More than once he had put down at some hicksville airstrip and disappointed an auditorium full of fans to keep from flying through weather. He considered himself a good pilot, but down deep inside he was not absolutely certain of his invulnerability. Twenty minutes in a serious thunderstorm can make any man wonder about that.

Flight service in El Paso had not mentioned weather along the route to Phoenix. Or maybe they had, and he hadn't been paying attention. He'd been in a hurry to get out of there. There was a girl waiting for him in Phoenix. A waitress in the coffee shop at the Airport Hilton. Becky. Red hair. A mouth like molten lava.

"Phoenix center, Baron four niner four Alpha Delta. . . ."

Lightning unfolded a spidery hand across the sky. Airspeed one hundred eighty-five knots. In five minutes Superman would be swallowed by that towering darkness, surrounded by pitching thermals and lightning and sheets of rain. He eased the nose down to take a look below.

This part of New Mexico was a wasteland, not a road or a glimmer of light anywhere. He fished a chart from the pocket behind his seat, smoothed it out on the panel.

The air through the vents became suddenly cooler. A green smell of rain.

He could turn around and let the storm chase him back to El Paso. Or try to plow through it, west toward Phoenix. He could go north a hundred miles and land at a dot of a town called Sanderson, where the chart showed an unlighted thousand-yard strip. Or he could turn southwest over the Mexican border, toward that clearer patch of darkness, and try to fly around the line of storms.

He thought of Alexa on the tour bus, peering anxiously up at the clouds. She was always talking about Buddy Holly and the Big Bopper and Patsy Cline, all of whom fell to pieces at the height of their fame. She was always having bad dreams about Superman in his plane, relating them in vivid detail—as if she didn't know that was the worst kind of luck.

He banked over south, into Mexico. He hoped he wouldn't have to put down there, didn't have a passport, never had felt the need to leave the good old U.S. of A. But he had the cash gate from the last three nights, forty thousand dollars in a Kroger sack under the seat, and that should be enough to get him out of any situation....

Except maybe this storm. Big mama. Lightning revealed a huge line of thunderheads rising to twenty-five, thirty thousand feet. He flew south for a long time, skirting the eastern edge of the storm wall, trying to find some place to punch through. The VOR signal faded. It was humbling to fly along in smooth air, hardly a bump or a wiggle, while all that vast energy churned the sky off his starboard wing.

For the first time in a very long time, Superman was the only one on earth who knew where he was.

His spirits began swelling up like the heads of those clouds. Flying south to Mexico, flying away from you.... He felt a tingle in the back of his neck. A song coming on, or something major about to happen. He remembered this sensation from his early years on the road: this is how it feels to have an adventure.

Now and then a cluster of lights slid under his wing, some lonely hamlet. He was surprised to see that the Mexicans had electricity. He'd never thought about it before, but if he had, he'd have guessed they all lived in mud pueblos lit by candles or something.

He flew over a ridge of high mountains into a valley spread with the lights of a fair-sized city—and hello there thank you Yes, in the top of the windscreen, glowing blue about five miles ahead, a nice little airstrip all lit up and glowing for him. He tuned to 122.8 and keyed the mike. "Howdy, Mexico, Baron four niner four Alpha Delta, how y'all doing down there, over."

The radio crackled something in Spanish. Superman didn't have a clue. "Okay well, I didn't get that so I'm coming in, over and out."

Gear down, three green, a notch of flaps. He banked left to line up with the runway, feeling out the angle of descent, just as Mr. Pawley had taught him. He could feel Mr. Pawley's plump hand on his shoulder, props forward, ease back on the throttle, don't slip it, keep that airspeed up, steady on the throttle, thataboy....

He set down the mains with a solid thump. A fine landing.

The moment he congratulated himself, the nosewheel bounded back up into the air.

He wrestled it down. The smooth runway he'd seen from the air was in fact a collection of invisible chuckholes and ruts. Somehow Superman managed to scratch to a skiddering stop, ten feet before the pavement ran out.

He slumped back in the seat, blowing every last little bit of air from his chest.

A little brown man stood watching from the doorway of a tin shack.

Superman tossed off a salute to demonstrate that the landing had not freaked him out. He taxied around potholes toward a fuel pump in the weeds beyond the shack. He leaned the mixture, cut the engines.

Silence roared in his ears.

He popped the door and stepped out on the wing.

The brown man was missing two teeth from his smile. He let out a stream of words that didn't mean a thing in the world.

"Hey, good to see you!" Superman hopped down to shake hands. "You speak any English?"

The man laughed and nodded, and let out a long string of Spanish.

"Look, man, I'm Superman." He tapped his chest with both hands. "Me. Superman." Surely if they had electricity in Mexico, they had radios, and pop music.

"Superman," the man said, "hahahahaha."

"No, really. I am. Superman Willis. On the radio. You know radio? Ray-dee-oh." He made hand signals for a radio, for listening, for listening to the radio. He was never much good at charades.

"Superman," the man crowed, only he said it funny, like "Soo-peddemon," and held his arms out, like the comic-book Superman flying. Superman saw it was no use pursuing this line. All he needed was fuel, and to find out where he was. He'd flown off the bottom of his chart a while ago.

He pointed to the pump, then the plane. By some miracle, the man understood. While the gas was pumping, they stood by the wing grinning at each other.

"Where am I, anyway?"

The man nodded: yes, yes.

"Okay. We're here." He indicated the ground. "Us. Here." He shrugged and raised his hands, acting out puzzlement. "Where are we?"

The man grinned and pointed to a sign that said BIENVENIDOS.

"Bienvenidos? Never heard of it. I guess it doesn't matter . . . listen, man, I want to get back to America. You know, America? It's straight back that way, right?" He waved his hand. "To the north, right? El Northo?"

The man nodded and said a bunch of stuff, *yappida-yippida-yap.*

"Bad storm between here and New Mexico," Superman said, making noises of thunder and wind. The delighted man set about performing his own imitation of a thunderstorm.

Superman waved him off and waded into the weeds to take a breath of the Mexican air, and the nice leisurely piss he'd been dreaming about for the last two hours.

It might be good to come back down this way sometime. The people seemed friendly. You didn't really have to speak Spanish; you could make yourself understood. The night air was pleasantly cool, a sweet smell of something blooming in darkness.

He zipped up and went back. The little man was tucking the nozzle onto the pump. The dial on the pump said 242. Superman pulled three one-hundred-dollar bills from his wallet.

The man stuffed the bills in his pocket as if Superman might try to take them back.

"No that's fine, keep the change." He squatted to check out the landing gear. "Brother, I tell you, it was a mighty good thing to see your runway lights all the way down here, wherever the hell I am."

They shook hands again. He clapped the man on the shoulder, and climbed into the cockpit.

He needed to twist up a couple of joints for the return trip. He didn't know if it was cool with the man standing there watching, but decided to take a chance that it was, since the man was missing two teeth, and most weed comes from Mexico to begin with. He fished the tin box from his flight bag, took out his stash and Zig Zags.

The man's eyes widened. He cackled, and lit out running for the shack.

Superman had a paranoid flash—he's gone to call the Federales!—but in a moment the man came waving a joint and talking up a storm. From his gestures it was clear that he wanted to swap his brown joint for a white one from the tin box. In the spirit of potheads the world over, Superman agreed.

"Superman, marijuana," the man said, grinning.

Superman was amused to find the word for marijuana was the same in Spanish as in English. He traded joints with the man, shook hands for the fifth or sixth time. "Goodbye, goodbye, adios," he said, "gotta hit the road."

He latched the door, waved bye-bye, yes, goodbye now, stand back from that propeller, little brown smiling man, or you're gonna get sliced like a little brown tomato.

The engines whined and kicked over, a sputter that grew to a nice solid Continental roar. He stuck the joint in his teeth, released the brake, flashed thumbs-up to the windswept man huddling with his shirt blown up over his face. The plane trembled and jolted across the uneven pavement.

He opened up one engine, then the other: testing them, letting them yowl, feeling that particular vibration that told him everything was just swell. He was pleased to hear the engines sucking up that Mexican fuel without the first cough or sputter.

He sat at the end of the runway, smoking the doobie, running down the checklist in the dim cockpit light. It was good stuff in that joint. Real sweet.

He didn't know just how good until he opened the engines all the way, thundered jouncing down the strip, and lifted off just at the moment a great sizzling rush exploded in his brain.

He burst out coughing, stars whizzing past his eyes.

It was all he could do not to pull an aileron roll. Somehow he got the nose up and climbed and kept climbing until his body came back into the plane, his head came back down on his shoulders, his eyes rolled back into his head.

Holy Mother of God, that stuff was *strong*. He glanced over his shoulder and saw the blue lights of the airstrip receding, a smudge of white light from the shack, where the little man was probably firing up the joint from his tin box. If *this* was what that man was used to smoking, he was headed for a genuine disappointment.

Superman was so busy appreciating the head-rush that he forgot to make the banking turn to the north. When he remembered, and glanced at the compass, it turned out he had made the turn after all and forgotten he'd done it.

Man. He was too stoned to fly. He licked his fingers and pinched out the joint.

Soon he was leveled off at eight thousand feet, heading due north. He switched on the autopilot and sank back in the seat to enjoy the deep velvet sky full of stars. The thunderstorm must have swept past while he was making his visit to Bienvenidos. He pushed Jimi Hendrix into the eight-track, and relaxed into the howling guitar.

There was something so pure and clean about listening to Jimi while soaring between the stars and the dark, silent earth. Dim towns passed under his wings, and the black shining faces of lakes.

He flew and flew. He dozed off for one second, shook himself awake. Should not do that. He cranked the air vents wide open. Mr. Pawley: "The autopilot is not a substitute for the pilot."

He ate a Payday from his flight bag, smacking the gooey candy around his teeth. That one tasted so good he ate another, then fired up the joint again. Hendrix played on and on, winding the melody around himself, uncoiling, spinning around, shaking free.

Sometimes Superman got to thinking he was pretty damn good at this rock-star thing—easy to think when you've got thousands cheering you, four nights a week—but an hour or two in the company of Jimi Hendrix always restored his perspective. For Superman, making songs was work, hard and grinding lonely work. He sweated and scratched out verses, went back and put in what he'd cut, changed it all around and returned to his first idea, threw the whole thing out and started over. Whereas Hendrix just picked up his ax, plugged in, and let go. What came out was pure feeling, expressed as a musical line.

Superman was just thirty-four—too young to be stuck in the path of his life, greeting every new day as a series of obligations to be dreaded and got through. Maybe it took him too long to become an overnight success. By the time it finally happened, he'd been wanting it for so long that he didn't really enjoy it.

Already the thrill of adventure he'd felt flying south was beginning to fade. A quick stop for gas, and here he was flying due north again, back to a life that was boring him out of his mind. Why couldn't he be like Jimi Hendrix, wild and free? Where, inside himself, were the limits that prevented him from plugging into the great godhead amplifier and letting fly with such beauty and perfect pain?

Maybe Jimi felt this way too. Maybe he got up in the morning and scratched himself and made coffee, and felt just as irrelevant as anybody else. Maybe that's why he died in that slummy hotel with the needle sticking out of his arm.

Maybe, if Jimi'd had an airplane and had learned how to fly, he'd have gotten the hell out of there before that happened. Maybe he'd have flown off to someplace where he could have saved his own life.

Some of us are Jimi Hendrix, and some of us are not.

Superman dug down in his shirt to scratch an itch. He thought of the night he shook hands with John Lennon, backstage at a Badfinger concert, Madison Square Garden. John Lennon was the biggest star in the world, and the unhappiest-looking man in the world. All the life had been sucked out of him. Something very wrong with that picture. Superman began to question his own ambition. Why would anyone want to be a star, if *that* was the final result of the best-case scenario?

Then again, if Superman hadn't become a star, he would probably be dead or destitute by now. His ambition had pulled him out of some very dark holes on the way to the top.

Any minute he would be crossing the invisible border to America. The land of the free, and the unfree.

If he was a free man, he would turn this plane around and fly to Jamaica, mon, or to Africa, or back to Bienvenidos. Somewhere far. Take a break. Get a new life. Tell all those people waiting for him they would just have to wait.

It was shocking to think he could fly away from his life like that. Leave Alexa and feel not a twinge, not one inkling of regret. He had really loved her once upon a time, but he'd spent the last several years finding ways to get away from her. He did not think he would really miss her.

Ben Junior he would miss, or at least the idea of Ben Junior. They didn't know each other all that well. Ben Junior had the bad luck to be born about the time Superman's career took over his life, so they had skipped that whole father-son thing.

Other than that, there was nobody. His folks were dead, and Kirby Cook, his best friend from high school. Aunt Tolly, who used to sing him to sleep with "Were You There When That Great Ship Went Down?" The rest of them he could live without.

Hendrix started in on "The Star-Spangled Banner" for the eighty-third time. Superman ejected him and punched in the Everly Brothers—an unworthy substitute, to be sure, but the rest of the tapes had slid back out of reach.

The land below was lost under heavy clouds. The moon was hiding somewhere over his shoulder.

"Phoenix center, this is Baron four niner four Alpha Delta, come in."

He released the key. A low, steady hum.

He tried the 121.5 mhz emergency frequency. "Phoenix, El Paso, hello anybody, Baron four niner four Alpha Delta. Somebody talk to me."

He heard a faint static. Tried again. Nobody home.

As he worked down the frequencies, his gaze happened to fall upon the face of his watch.

He blinked, and looked again. The watch said 4:45.

That would mean he'd been flying for, oh, about eight hours since he left that Mexican airstrip.

The fuel gauge showed three-quarters full.

Whoo. He shut his eyes and gave thanks. His watch was screwed up.

He opened his eyes. The sweep-second hand kept sweeping around.

He tapped the crystal, pressed the watch to his ear. Like John Cameron Swayze's watch: still ticking.

How very strange.

"Dreeeeeeeam, dream dream dream," sang the Everly Brothers. Superman ejected them and swore out loud.

If his wristwatch was okay, then the fuel gauge was lying. After eight hours he would be down to—what, twenty gallons?

Less.

And he would be somewhere over the Upper Midwest. Minnesota, perhaps. Wisconsin.

He fought the swell of panic. He remembered that moment when he dozed off. He'd been certain it was just a moment.

Maybe it was longer. That was some really amazing dope in the joint from the Mexican man.

He was wide awake now. By instinct his hand started working the radio dial. Apparently every radio operator in the U.S. of A. had packed up his headphones and gone home for the night.

A piece of stray information tugged at his brain—something Mr. Pawley said. In the event of control panel malfunction. . . . A circuit breaker reset. A toggle switch. Which one?

Behind the instrument panel. Behind the hydraulics gauges, right there. He felt with his finger, and flicked it. The panel lights winked off.

For one long moment, flying in that overpowering darkness, Superman was completely alone in the universe. He didn't believe in God, but he saw a pretty clear outline of what God might look like, if you did believe.

He said a little prayer, and flipped the switch. The gauges flickered and glowed.

"Yes, sir," he said, "thank you sir." The fuel-gauge needle began climbing from zero . . . and stopped. Ten gallons, maybe.

He glared at the quaking needle, trying to will it higher—but his eyes were drawn irresistibly to the other gauges resetting themselves. The compass, for instance: the Haynes Magellan F-45 Electro-Gyro compass, the latest thing in aviation technology. That expensive red needle swung north, right past where it had been hovering all night, and kept on turning past due east, on around the dial until it was pointing due south.

And there it remained.

Superman began to comprehend the gravity of his situation. From a point somewhere in Mexico, he had been flying south for eight hours at an airspeed of one hundred eighty-five knots.

Which would put him somewhere over . . . the Caribbean? Central America? Assuming the compass was now telling the truth and he'd been flying due south, not southeast or southwest, which would put him somewhere over the ocean—Atlantic or Pacific, take your pick.

He smacked the window. The sting in his hand made him sit up and try to get hold of himself. Temper will get you nowhere, Ben Willis, said a hectoring voice. It's your own fault getting stoned woozing out with the stick of an airplane in your hand. A real airplane, you know, not a Disneyland ride. And you, Ben Willis, are not Superman after all. You can fall just as fast and as far as any other man.

But okay. Deep breath now. Nobody's falling. You are at altitude in a smooth-running plane, with time enough to find a place to land.

His first impulse was to duck under those clouds and see where the hell he was. When he gripped the yoke a picture loomed in his mind: green Central American mountains poking their heads up into the clouds, trying to get a look at him.

Better to wait for sunrise. He searched the horizon for the telltale softening of the void.

Maybe he should turn around and fly north. But he was so rattled he didn't know which of his instruments was lying to him.

If you are lost in the woods—he remembered Boy Scouts, the scoutmaster Mr. Jones, a tall sad-eyed man—if you are lost, you walk in a straight line until you cross a stream or a road, then follow that line back to civilization. But this knowledge was worthless at six thousand feet with a thick layer of clouds below.

He cut his airspeed to save fuel, and thumbed through the *Air Pilot's Manual*.

There was page after page of advice on how to keep from getting into a situation like this. But if you went past all their red lights, buddy, you were on your own.

He tossed the manual away. Any fool would know what to do—find someplace to land, find fuel, a telephone, a map. Then fly home.

He was nine hours overdue in Phoenix. How long before they would start looking for the wreckage? He wondered if they'd told Alexa yet. For about twenty minutes she would be useless, a puddle of tears. Then she'd collect herself and go straight to the lawyers to get her hands on the money.

He gazed out the port window into the starless night. In the space of an eyeblink, the blackness turned a deep shade of blue. The sun flashed its tiny mirror from the way farthest edge of the earth.

So he was flying south after all.

This must have been his secret desire. He had grown tired of his life. Somewhere deep inside he wanted to have an adventure. The plane's circuits had sensed his wish, and brought him to wherever the hell he was.

The dome of the sky lifted, fading. The sun glanced off his wing. A fluffy blanket of clouds stretched forever in all directions, obscuring the earth. It was like flying over the top of heaven. He wasn't even stoned anymore.

This would be a story to share with Ben Junior someday.

He didn't see the heads of any mountains, only a solid mattress of clouds turning pink in the sun. Time to find out what was underneath.

He lowered the gear to dirty up the aerodynamics, descending until his wings raced through the wispy froth just above the cloud layer. The plane sank into the feather pillow. Warm moist air washed through the vents.

The wings flexed. The plane started rocking and rolling, put the nose down, just so, blind in the white whirling air, then he flashed down from the clouds and realized, altogether too late, that the altimeter was the most badly mistaken of all the gauges in the Baron that day. He'd been flying at eight hundred feet, not eight thousand. That layer of clouds was a fogbank lying just over the surface of the sea.

Before he grasped this, before his arm had time to jerk back the stick, the plane kissed the face of a wave.

A crunching jolt rocked the fuselage—the impact of water at one hundred twenty-five knots snapped the landing gear like pieces from a model airplane. The plane groaned and staggered back into the air.

Superman fought to straighten the wings, get his head back up over the fog. A demented symphony shrieked in his ears: pure fear, and also relief thank you God for the ocean! If that had been solid earth he would be dead burnt-up pieces Right Now.

He flashed through a fog-ridden blur of gold light and out into dazzling clear air: the loveliest vision of his life. An island, dead ahead. Green jungle mountains marching down to the sea, a white skirt of sand beach. Craggy rock islets speckled the ocean offshore.

He hammered the throttle and climbed up to circle around for a look.

If a man had some wheels on his plane, he could land on that slender white beach. Sure as hell. If a man only had him some wheels.

Superman could fly, but he could not land.

The surf rolled in brilliant white lines. A matched pair of green mountains held their arms around a slender stretch of sand. The air sparkled with blue tropical sunlight.

He could keep flying. That was some sort of mainland across the channel, or a much larger island. Maybe he had enough fuel to find a town with an airstrip.

But what good is an airstrip to a man without wheels?

Not a soul on that beach. Oh wait—maybe, yes, were those people up under the trees?—were they waving?

No. That was driftwood or something, a shadow.

Without thinking it, Superman realized he would put his Baron down in the water, right here. He didn't know where he was, but this was a beautiful place. The water here was bound to be as soft as water anywhere. Maybe there were people up in the shade of those trees. Maybe if the plane tumbled end over end they would swim out and try to save him.

At the moment he realized he was going to die, his mind began clouding over with regrets.

He wished he hadn't thought such unkind things about Alexa.

He wished he hadn't smoked that joint from the Mexican Man.

He wished he'd had a record go all the way to Number One, but that grotesque Australian songbird Helen Reddy held the spot for ten consecutive weeks with "I Am Woman" and ruined his one decent chance.

He wished he'd gotten to know Ben Junior a little.

He wished for many things he did not have. A parachute. Life jacket. Wheels.

He circled the beach, imagining just how fine that hot sand would feel on his back, while the sun beat down on his eyelids.

He reached between his feet for the tape. Jimi, my man, we will go in together. "The Star-Spangled Banner," yes all right. He cranked it up loud. He put fire to that last inch of killer smash weed. Thank you Mexican Man, and congratulations. You have killed Superman with your kindness. You have given him the fatal dose of Kryptonite.

He wished he could have lived long enough to become a legend, like Jimi. He'd amused a few people, that's all—never changed anyone's life. Just the mere fact of dying does not turn you into a legend.

But it would be a big story, for a few days at least. They'd track him as far as the Mexican Man. Someone might even write a book about his disappearance, like all the books about Amelia Earhart. That idea gave him a peculiar satisfaction.

He put the plane into a steep banking circle, pointing his wingtip at the island. He needed to dump the remaining fuel before he went in, but no reason to hurry on that item. He could circle right here for a while. Maybe someone would come to the beach to watch him crash.

Wedging fingers into the crack of the seat, among dust-bunnies and sticky coins, he came up with a fine-point Magic Marker. His mind was rolling in clear, steady waves now, rhythmic and purposeful as the surf rolling onto the beach. No panic. No more regrets.

He needed something to write on, something to prove who he was.

He lifted the tail of his shirt and tried to tear off a strip. The sky-blue cotton was strong. Even after all these years this was the best shirt a man ever had.

He put the tail between his teeth; thought, Watch out don't break a tooth; then reflected with a bitter inward smile that a broken tooth is no big deal when you're dead. He managed to rip off a hand-sized piece of blue cotton, smoothed it on his knee, and wrote a hasty note. The ink blobbed in places, seeping through to his jeans.

In the pocket behind the copilot seat he found a Jack Daniel's bottle with an inch of whiskey still in it. He uncapped it, drained it off. The sweet hot explosion spread like pleasure through his veins.

He reached into his flight bag for the Polaroid Swinger he had loaded and ready for redheaded Becky in Phoenix. He pointed the viewfinder out the port window at the beach, pressed the button, grasped the brown-paper tab, and pulled out the film packet.

He held the camera at arm's length, aimed at himself. He worked up a smile, pressed the button with his thumb.

He circled the beach while the sweep-second hand traced a full sixty seconds. He peeled back the gooey chemical paper from the photographs.

Not bad. The shot of the island was very crisp. The one of Superman was blurry, but you could tell it was him. Nice smile.

No time to spread the lacquer with the sponge applicator. He would have to put his faith in Polaroid. He slid the rolled-up pictures and the scrap of blue shirt through the neck of the bottle, and twisted the cap on tight.

Grasping the T-grip emergency release, he gave a yank that nearly dislocated his shoulder. The hatch popped open and fell away.

Wind howled in, slamming him sideways in the seat. Dust and grit and bits of trash went whirling through the cockpit, sucked out in a rush. Hot wind filled his shirt, popping the buttons off *spk! spk! spk!* so the tails whipped at his flanks and flew up in his face. Jimi Hendrix was lost in the roar of the wind.

He grasped the bottle by the neck and sent it sailing over the great blue ocean. He imagined he could follow it with his eyes all the way to an infinitesimal splash near the beach.

He yanked the shirt over his head. The wind snatched it out of his hands and filled it with air. To his amazement the shirt stood up and began to dance.

For a long eerie moment it danced like a ghost in an eddy of air over the passenger seat—then dove across his lap and dashed out of the plane.

That was a sign, sure enough. Superman's got no powers without his shirt.

He tipped up the wing and drove in for a low pass over the bay, over the schools of rock islands, great whales with backs of jagged rock. Identical cone-shaped green mountains guarded both ends of the beach, joined to the island by delicate fingers of palm-shaded sand. The jungle marched down to the sea. Surf exploded on rocks at the base of the mountains.

All this time circling, and still not a soul had ventured out onto the sand. If Superman put down in the water and knocked himself out, he would drown. If he tried to jump out before he ditched, the impact would kill him.

Better to stay with the plane.

He unlocked the emergency fuel release. For some reason he thought of communion when he was a boy, a silver tray with forty thimble-glasses of Welch's grape juice, tiny glasses tinkling between an old lady's hands as she passed the tray down the pew. *This do in remembrance of me. . . .* Could this be his life preparing to flash before his eyes?

He flipped the switch. Gasoline hissed out, spraying the tops of the waves. The cockpit filled with fumes.

The smell took him back to a Sinclair service station, somewhere deep in south Alabama. A green dinosaur revolved on a pole. Gasoline fumes came sweetly up into his nose. His father smiled at him.

He turned the plane back out to sea. His idea was to come in low and slow, put her into a stall, belly down in the smooth water near the beach, without cartwheeling, flipping tail-over, smacking down sideways, dipping a wingtip, or slamming into a wave. He would have one chance only.

Of course this was all just an idea in his head. He didn't know if it would work. He wished Mr. Pawley were here. He had a few serious questions to ask.

Banking around the largest rock island, he swept in on a line for the beach, ten feet above the tops of the waves. The engines stuttered, gasping for fuel.

Without knowing he was going to do it, he began to howl like a dog. He unstrapped himself and got up on one knee howling.

All at once he was overcome with a terrible urge to get out of the plane, but too late—the ocean loomed in the windscreen and, beyond it, the beach and a perfect forest of coconut palms. He saw Ben Junior's bright smile. The last thing he thought before the plane hit the water was *God, what a beautiful place to die.*

2 / *Superman Junior*

I WAS ELEVEN YEARS OLD when my father died. He was a glamorous stranger who swooped in for birthdays and Christmas, and otherwise lived in the Admiral color console TV in Granny French's living room. My fondest dream was that he would take me with him the next time he came through town.

July 14 was the night of the Summer Piano Fiesta Celebration at the Opelousas Community Center. I was going to play "The Impossible Dream." I had chosen it myself and practiced it for weeks. Granny French said I stood a better chance of winning if I played and sang one of my father's hits, "When Time Stands Still" or "Superman's Revenge," but I wanted to make it on my own.

Looking back, I know the kids at Huey P. Long Elementary must have been impressed that I was Superman Willis's son, but in the way of all kids, they'd sooner have died than give me any indication of this. Nobody wanted to suck up to a kid because his father was famous. Instead they ignored me.

I was not used to being ignored. All my life I had lived fairly close to the center of the universe, and it shocked me to find myself just another planet circling in my lonely orbit.

Somehow I had convinced myself that if I won the Summer Piano Fiesta Celebration I would finally make some friends in this stupid town. People would see that I was someone to notice, a boy with intelligence and talent, not just this blurry thing standing there out of focus. I hated Opelousas, hated Louisiana, hated Granny French for taking me there and my mother and father for sending me. I wanted to go back to Encino and live in the big house with the swimming pool. There was a maid in Encino named Rita who gave me baths. She would wash me down there until my thing got hard and stood up. This made me feel good, and confused. There was no one like Rita in Louisiana. There was only Granny French, and a bunch of dumb kids who talked like banjos twanging, *twang twang.*

I practiced "The Impossible Dream" for hours every day. One afternoon Mrs. Delacroix came all the way across the street to ask Granny French if I please didn't know some other songs.

"The boy wants to do well at his recital, Louise," Granny said. "Practice makes perfect."

"It's driving me to distraction," Mrs. Delacroix said. "You know I would never come over here if it wasn't."

"Well, I'll ask him to shut the window," said Granny, "but I should point out that not once in all these years have I ever said a word about the condition of your azaleas."

Mrs. Delacroix puffed up and turned red, and said "Well!" and hurried back across the street to have a look at her azaleas.

"Go on and play your song, Benjamin," Granny said. "That woman has a tin ear."

After that I practiced my piece with the living-room windows down, sweltering in the heat of July for the sake of my art and my social standing. I envisioned myself center stage in a brilliant white light, astounding the crowd with the deep fervor of my left hand, the delicate phrasing of my right. "He's a born musician," they would say, nudging each other. "That's Superman Willis's son, you know."

To dream, the impossible dream. . . .

On the big afternoon I spent an hour in the bathroom, getting ready. It was the first time I remember being concerned with my own appearance. I soaked in the tub, scrubbed my toes, brushed my teeth four times. I tamed my cowlick with a squirt of Granny's hair spray, and splashed myself with the Old Spice aftershave my father had left in the medicine cabinet at Christmas.

I studied my face in the fogged-up mirror. Granny French said it was a good thing I took after my mother, since Mom was a Great Beauty and my father was Not Much to Look At. I had my mother's blond hair, my father's bright brown eyes. Certainly I was no Great Beauty. It seemed to me I was Not Much To Look At.

I didn't want to look like my mother. I was in the middle of hating her. I thought it was wrong for parents to send a kid away to live with an old lady in a smelly old house in a hot, stupid town. I thought it meant they didn't want me. (I was right.)

"You have a good soul, Benny, a very positive soul," Mom said, fixing me with a gaze so serious I had to squirm. "Your dad and I don't think it's a good idea for you to be hanging around the guys on the bus. You should be surrounded by positive energy."

"I want to go with you," I said. "Or I want to go back to Encino."

"I understand you're probably feeling some conflict right now. That's perfectly natural. I think you should talk it over with some of your friends and see if it's something you can work on, all right?" She peered at me, green eyes aglow.

"I don't have any friends," I said.

"Then you'll just have to get right out there and start making some, huh? It's a shame to be eleven years old and not have any friends."

"There's nobody in Louisiana but a bunch of idiots and rednecks," I said.

She gave me a dazzling smile. Mom was Miss Southwest Louisiana before she married my father and became a hippie. "Well, honey, you're right about that," she said, "but I survived it, and you can too."

The next Christmas, I begged my father to take me with him on tour. "Ask your mother," he said.

"I already did. She said to ask you."

"Well . . . ?" He shrugged. "What do you want me to do? It's my job, son, I've gotta hit the road. Your job is to go to school and learn stuff."

And that's how it was. They shrugged and sent me to live with Granny French. My happiness was entirely my own responsibility, and so I was miserable. It was no use wishing they would suddenly start caring about me. What I needed now was to play "The Impossible Dream" better than anyone had ever played it, and make a start on a life for myself.

To beat, the unbeatable foe. . . .

The air felt brisk after an hour in the bathroom steam. I put on a crisp white shirt, black trousers, black Sunday wing-tips, red-striped clip-on necktie. I took great pains not to disturb my hair, which was lying flat all over for the first time in weeks.

At last, when I looked as good as I was going to look until I got older and stopped looking like a kid, I went to the front parlor and seated myself on the piano bench. With my eyes closed I conjured a spotlight, a stage. I nodded to the breathless crowd in the dark. I turned to the keyboard, started the G and D rumbling in the lower register, and poised my right hand to strike the opening chord.

My pinky slipped off the F-sharp and came down on a sour F.

I stopped.

What if that happened tonight? I felt Miss Dalrymple's pointy-toed shoe, which delivered a sharp little kick to my shin every time I struck a wrong note at a lesson. She was more forgiving of the idea of mistakes at the recital. "If you mess up," she said, "take a deep breath and keep going. Whatever you do, don't stop."

I lifted my hands and started again. This time the opening chord sounded large, triumphal. In my mind I saw a vision of the sheet music, the notes I had memorized. My fingers followed the notes in my head.

I built a fire under the melody, slowly rising to the big pounding chords at the height of the chorus. I made the tricky key change between verses without missing a note. I sat in wonder at what my hands had learned to do. I sat back out of their way and watched them do it.

When it was over, my face flushed with pride. I bowed to the imaginary audience. Their cheers washed over me. A telephone rang.

I heard a strange noise from the kitchen.

I went to the door. I can still see Granny French sagging back against the china cabinet with the phone to her ear. Her face was gray, as if her life were being drained out through that twisted cord, into the wall.

"Oh dear God," she whispered.

My stomach felt cold.

Granny turned around, and noticed me there. Her eyes widened. She hissed at me, shooing me out.

I crept back behind the door to listen.

"Oh they'll find him, now Doris, of course they will," she said, "a person doesn't just vanish into thin air."

For a long time Granny didn't say anything. Then she said, "We're coming out there—of course we are. I'll get Harvey Loomis to drive us to New Orleans. We'll call you from the station. I love you, Dorisy," she said, her voice cracking. "You're gonna have to be strong now."

It got so quiet in there I thought she'd hung up. Surely now she would come in and tell me it was a mistake, or a joke, and everything was all right.

I poked my head around the door. Granny coughed—a brief, explosive sound. "I hardly think it's time to be thinking about lawyers yet, Doris. At least until we find out what's happened."

I wandered back to the piano. I didn't want to think about what might have happened. I decided to practice my piece one more time. I got my left hand to rumbling the G and the D. I'd just raised my right hand to strike the first chord when Granny barked from the kitchen: "Benjamin! For God's sake I'm trying to talk on the phone!"

I took my foot off the pedal, stifling the echo. "Sorry," I whispered.

This must be some very bad news. I'd never heard Granny French use any phrase that even vaguely resembled a curse. I knew that if I thought about what I'd heard in there, I would find I already knew what had happened. On the other hand, I didn't want to know.

Then she was standing in the doorway with a weird little half smile on her face. It scared me, that look. I think she was crying inside, and didn't want me to see.

"Good, you're all dressed," she said. "We've had a change of plan. We're going to California tonight."

"Tonight? After the recital?"

"No. We're going right now. The train leaves New Orleans at nine-thirty. Go get your things together, your clothes. Take those off so they don't get wrinkled. I'll go ask Mr. Loomis to drive us."

A wave of indignation rolled over me. "You mean we're not going to my recital?"

"No. Go and do as I say."

I leaped up from the piano bench. "But that's not fair! I practiced all summer! Didn't you hear me? I just played it the best I ever played!"

"Something has happened to your father," Granny said. "His plane has disappeared. He may be dead for all we know. Just once I wish you would think of something besides yourself."

I've spent my whole life trying to live down the shame of that moment.

If she'd known how it would hurt me—it still hurts to think about it—Granny French never would have said those words to me. I know how much she loved me, how the shock of the news and my brattish reply must have combined to bring those words from her lips. She probably forgot them as soon as she said them. But I did not forget. I did not touch a piano, or sing, or make music of any kind for many years. When I think of my father's death, the emotion that runs through me is that dark, burning shame.

I knew he was dead before she hung up the phone. I knew it when I sat down to practice my piece one more time. And all I could think, in those first senseless moments of knowing, was that this meant I would not be playing "The Impossible Dream" at the Summer Piano Fiesta Celebration that night. I would not win a prize. I would not be a star like my father. I would never have friends. My father who never loved me, never cared for me, left me to fend for myself—my father was dead, and I would not get to perform, and I hated him for it.

I did not cry. I spent the next days in a stupefied blur, hating him and myself in equal measure, shrunk down in the smallest corner of Mr. Loomis's Chrysler, then in the Pullman sleeper compartment I shared with Granny French all the way to Los Angeles. For a year I'd been praying that something would happen so I could go back to Encino, and now my prayer had been answered.

Those thirty-six hours on the train were the longest part of my life so far, yet I have no idea what was said, what we did, when we ate. I don't recall one vista that passed by our window. I remember a Negro man brought a telegram to our compartment; I wanted to see it because I'd never seen a real telegram before, but Granny read it and tucked it away in her purse.

When the train pulled into Union Station my mother was standing on the platform, crying. Granny French started crying the moment she saw her. The two of them came together at the foot of the steps. "Oh God, I don't have a husband," my mother wailed, sagging into Granny's arms.

It destroyed something good and innocent inside me to see my mother fall apart like that. She'd always been so beautiful. Now, in her grief, she was terrible to see.

She didn't notice me. I carried my suitcase to the end of the platform and stood looking down at the smashed chewing gum and cigarette butts. I wished I could get back on that train and keep going to the far other end of the earth.

A man walked to where I was standing. He had bushy red hair and a beard and the hairiest chest I'd ever seen. Hair spilled out over the neck of his T-shirt. I saw my face in his mirrored sunglasses. "Hey, little dude," he said, "I'm a friend of your dad's. You're Superman Junior, right?"

"Yeah."

"I'm Jimbo, listen—don't pay any attention to the ladies, they just gotta cry at a time like this, I don't know, man, it's hormones," he said. "Just between you and me, I don't think your old man's dead. He's just gone off somewhere. He'll turn up. Come on, we're going to your place, okay?"

I saw my mother leaning on Granny French, starting downstairs from the platform.

"Come on, man," said Jimbo, "I gotta go help your mom."

I followed numbly, trying to understand what he'd said. *He's just gone off somewhere.* Could it be true? But then why was my mother weeping? Granny French said my father's plane crashed and they hadn't found it. This man seemed to know something different. He had his arm around my mother. She was leaning against him. Who was this man?

When I woke up the next morning he was lounging on the sofa in the downstairs den, wearing my father's blue bathrobe with the smiley faces. "Mornin', little dude."

I was half asleep, yawning, rubbing my eyes. I don't like anybody until I am good and awake. "Where's my mother," I said.

"Asleep. She had a kinda rough night."

I didn't like this man wearing my father's bathrobe. "Where's Granny French?"

"Don't know; she's sleeping too, I guess," he said. "It's just us menfolk. And whoa, lovely Rita. Mm, *mm.*" He cut his eyes toward the kitchen and grinned. "Meet-ah maid," he said.

Suddenly the whole thing was too much for me. This man had comforted my mother, now he was wearing my father's robe and talking about Rita with that weasel grin on his face. "Why don't you get out of our house!" I cried.

His face crinkled in surprise. "Whoa, dude, hold on. What did I do?"

"This is *our* house," I said. "Who said you could stay here?"

"Your old lady," he said. "I guess she don't need your permission, huh, you little smartass."

"You get out or I'm telling my daddy when he comes home."

"He ain't coming home. He's deader'n hell."

"You're wrong!" I shouted. "He's alive, and when he comes back he's gonna—he's gonna *beat your butt!*" I ran up the stairs and hurled myself on my bed and cried until I ran out of tears.

Many things changed after that, but one fact remained: my father took off from the El Paso Regional Airport at 9:04 p.m. on Friday, July 14, 1972, and vanished from the face of the earth.

My mother and Granny French kept me away from most of the publicity. When he vanished, my father was an up-and-coming star with six hit singles, two gold albums, a Grammy, and a loyal college-audience following. By the time they stopped looking for him, Superman Willis was a legend. Church groups held prayer vigils. Radio DJs broadcast hourly reports. The Air National Guard conducted the largest search-and-rescue operation in its history. They couldn't have looked harder if the Lord Jesus Christ had crashed a plane within the borders of New Mexico.

At one point, when an airfield in Monterrey, Mexico, reported that a Beechcraft Baron had landed to refuel on the night of July 14, the governments of four nations were involved in the search for my father.

They didn't find him. After six weeks they gave up looking.

I asked my mother, "Does that mean he's dead?"

"I don't want you to ever give up hoping, Benny," she said. "His spirit will always be with us."

"But if they're gonna stop looking, they must think he's dead."

Mom's nerve pills made her a little glassy, dreamy-eyed. She didn't quite look at you when she was talking. "Let me tell you something, Benny. We're going to have kind of a service on Friday. A memorial thing for your dad. Would you like to come?"

"You mean a funeral?"

"No, a funeral is for when somebody dies. This is like a celebration. We just want to celebrate your dad, you know, send him off to wherever he's gone."

"Is Jimbo going?"

"Yes of course he is," she said, an edge in her voice. "Jimbo was Daddy's friend, too."

"I don't want to go," I said.

"When you grow up, you'll wish you had."

"No I won't."

"And also you'll wish you'd been a little nicer to your mother."

"I won't."

"Benny, don't act like this. Wouldn't you rather be nice? It would be so much easier on both of us. I was such a good child—ask your granny." Mom was rolling a joint while she said this. She always smoked joints after Granny had gone to bed, or to the grocery store. Then she went around giggling and spraying Lysol.

"I guess I could go," I said.

She bent to the candle with the joint between her lips, her hair shimmering in the soft light. She was very beautiful. She sucked in a breath and held it. "It's completely up to you," she said, blowing smoke through her nose.

She held out the joint to me, passing it out of habit, the way she and her friends did at parties. When she realized what she was doing, she burst out laughing and coughing.

"Sorry," she said. "Sometimes I forget you're a kid."

That moment summed up my life to that point. My parents treated me as if I was one of their friends, a small, needy friend who had dropped by and never gone home. They seemed to like me well enough, but they were always finding ways to get rid of me so they could get on with their lives. Mom no longer had the excuse of my father's concert tours to take off—

and Granny French had put the fear of God in her as well. "Don't you understand, that child has lost his father!" I heard her say one night, through the air-conditioning duct that served as my intercom to the first floor. "You should be home looking after him instead of running around with all your fast friends. What if something should happen to you, God forbid? That child would be an orphan."

"Oh Mother, don't be morbid. Benny's fine. He's handling it better than I am."

"It's disgraceful. You should be in mourning, not going to parties."

"I'm not Scarlett O'Hara, for God's sake. I'm not even a widow. They haven't declared him dead yet."

"You sound like you wish they'd get on with it," said Granny.

"Well, if you want to know the truth, I do, okay? What's wrong with that? This waiting is driving me crazy. It's so depressing! I mean, if he'd left me, that would be one thing. I could deal with that. Or if we knew for sure, we could have a funeral—but this is like—nothing! You don't know what I'm going through. This has not been easy for me."

"Oh, please. You didn't care a fig about Ben Willis," Granny said. "You were running around on him the night he died, and now you've got that— that *person* living here under your roof!"

I pressed my cheek to the vent. Cool air blew in my ear.

"I was not—*running—around.*" Mom's voice was scalding. "How dare you come to my house and sit here judging me!"

"Fine. I'll go home tomorrow. You raise the boy by yourself. Is that what you want?"

A long silence, then Mom said, "I wouldn't know how."

"That's exactly what I mean. I don't fault you, Doris. Some people are just not cut out to be mothers."

"My name is Alexa. I wish you could learn to call me by my legal, correct name."

"Your name is Doris, I named you myself."

"All right, Mama, stop it, you win. I'll stay home more, I promise. Please don't go. I need your help."

"You certainly do," Granny said.

We went to the memorial service in a long black limousine, me and Mom and Jimbo and nine of their friends. They put me up front with the driver. When Granny French saw the hookah in back, she got out and went to ride with Uncle Earl, who'd driven down from Fresno for the occasion.

A mirror-glass window sealed off the driver's seat from the passenger compartment, but the driver and I could hear sounds of the party back there. They were playing loud music—the Rolling Stones, I think—and shouting with laughter.

The driver, a thin elderly man, turned to me and said, "They're whooping it up, all right."

I wasn't sure how you were supposed to act on your way to a memorial service, but I guessed you weren't supposed to act like my mother and her friends. I tried to make up for them. I rode the whole way with a suitably grim expression, my gaze fixed straight ahead.

The sun was setting in the crown of a palm tree as we pulled into the Hollywood Bowl. Hundreds of people milled about in the parking lot near the entrance. Some had long hair and bell-bottoms and funny glasses and beads, but mostly they were regular people.

"Would you look at this mess?" said the driver. "I bet half of 'em hadn't had a bath in a month. They ought to go to Russia if they don't like it here."

I peered out the window. "Is this where we're going?"

"Where they told me." He steered toward a gate with a sign that said BACKSTAGE PASSES ONLY.

The guard waved us through. We drove into a section of the parking lot cordoned off with barrels and ropes, black limousines flocking around a big white canvas tent pitched on the pavement, as for a circus.

The driver went to open the door. A cloud of pungent smoke rolled out, followed by my mother, in her big floppy hat and wraparound sunglasses and the tiny black dress that made her legs look about nine feet long. She looked great, teetering on high heels with one hand on her hat to keep it from blowing away.

When she saw all the people pouring into the amphitheater, a big smile lit up her face. "Far out," she said, "look, Benny, look at all these people. This is all for your dad. Doesn't this make you feel proud?"

Proud was not how I felt—confused, amazed. I thought we were going to a quiet dark place with candles and church music.

An anxious woman hurried up with a clipboard and walkie-talkie. "Alexa, you're late," she said. "I've got VIPs tripping over each other in there."

"Cool," Mom said. "Who showed up?"

"Okay," the woman said, "walk with me while we do this, we've got Crosby, Stills, and Young, Nash isn't here yet, and Joan Baez—"

"Joan Baez?" My mother wrinkled her nose.

"I know, but she insisted." The lady read down a list as we walked. "Ike and Tina Turner—she's locked herself in a dressing room, she and Ike are fighting—and let's see, Joni Mitchell, Wavy Gravy, John Sebastian, the Four Tops—make that three of the Four—and Andy Warhol—"

Mom said, "Who?"

The woman peered over her clipboard. "Andy Warhol, you know. The painter. Campbell's Soup can?"

"Oh, right," Mom said. "Does he sing, or what?"

"No, this is the backstage list. There's another list of just the performers, do you want to see that?"

"That's okay," Mom said. "I'd rather let it just, you know, happen."

"Wavy Gravy," said Jimbo. "Far out."

Granny French and Uncle Earl caught up as we approached the open flap of the tent, the smell of sandalwood and cigars, sitar music, loud conversation. It resembled a lavish version of one of my parents' parties—swanky rugs, flowers everywhere, five kinds of curry on the buffet tables, waiters circulating with wine, a six-piece Indian orchestra zinging and zanging in the corner.

Jimbo said, "Lex, what are you drinking?"

Mom frowned. "Jimbo, you're going to have to give me some space today. I'm like the widow here, understand? I don't need you hanging around."

Jimbo's mouth pinched up. He went off to sulk at the bar. This made me happy.

It made Granny French downright triumphant. "Look at that one over there, Doris, can you fancy a man who would wear a yellow suit to a funeral?"

"It's not a funeral, Mother. It's a celebration of life."

"It's a freak show, is what it is. Look at that girl he's with—gracious, you can see her boobies right through that dress."

Mom touched my shoulder. "Come on, Benny, let's go say hello."

For the next hour Mom kept me close to her. The women hugged her and cried. The men looked solemn and shook my hand gravely. Neil Young showed me a neat trick involving a nickel and a wristwatch. Joan Baez gave me an authentic armband that symbolized something—she told me, but I forget. Everyone said I looked so much like my dad.

I noticed a strange man darting through the crowd, snapping pictures with one of those new Polaroid cameras that spat the picture into your hand. His skin was an unearthly white, like no human being I'd ever seen, his hair silver-yellow and wispy. When he brushed past me I breathed his peculiar smell, like a musty old house.

He stopped—as if he'd felt me sniffing him—and turned to peer at me through horn-rimmed glasses. "Wow, what a great expressive face! Can I take your picture?"

I was standing beside a mammoth silver platter of fudge brownies. I'd already eaten three and was into my fourth. "I got brownies in my mouth" is what I said, but it came out *bmmflgh glphl mmph.*

"What did you say?" He swung his camera up, studied me through the viewfinder.

I swallowed. "I got brownies in my mouth."

He smiled. His teeth were the same yellow as his hair. "What's your name?"

"Ben Willis Junior," I said.

"Really," he said, snapping the picture. The flashbulb went *puf!* and blinded me for an instant. The camera hummed and stuck out the picture, like a tongue. "Are you the actual issue of Superman's loins?"

I said yes, I thought so.

"My take on it is he pulled one of the great skedaddles of our time, did you ever consider that possibility?" Without warning he raised the camera and fired again. *Puf!* White stars streaked past the edges of my eyes. "To an athlete dying young? Stop while you're hot? Don't you admire the creativity of his vamoose?"

"I don't know," I said, blinking at stars in my eyes.

"Superman knows how to fly," he said, holding out the picture. "Here, want to see yourself?"

I looked like a dork.

He put the photo in his pocket. He scribbled something on the face of the second one, and gave it to me.

It said *Brownies N My Mouth,* with his name scrawled underneath.

He smiled and slipped away in the crowd.

Some years later, at the height of the Warhol craze, I sold *Brownies N My Mouth* at Sotheby's for forty-eight thousand dollars. I used the money to buy a fast red car. Apparently it was the only existing Warhol photograph of a child. The one he tucked in his pocket has never turned up.

The party in the tent went on until we heard the yowl of guitars cranking, amplified rock and roll. A massive cheer rolled like a thrill from the Hollywood Bowl.

My mother found me. "Come on, it's starting."

We moved with the partying throng across the parking lot, down a dark tunnel into the arena—a shock moving out of darkness into the glare of lights, the roar of the band, thousands of people on their feet, waving their hands in the air as Crosby, Stills, Nash, and Young sang my father's most famous song.

> *When he's up in the sky, do you know how he feels*
> *Not a bird, not a plane, just a man of ideals*
> *Watching people go bad in their usual way*
> *And he can't save 'em all, and he's had a bad day*
> *And his boss is a creep, and his girl is a tease*
> *And he feels like he's got antisocial disease*

I had never been to one of my father's concerts—never seen him perform, except on TV and once in the rehearsal hall in West Covina. I was astounded by the size of the crowd—ten thousand people, the newspapers said the next day. To me it looked like ten million.

The clipboard woman steered us through a narrow place between ropes, to the platform extending from stage left. All around us people chanted the words to the chorus:

> *You better run—it's time for*
> *Superman's revenge*
> *Superman's revenge*
> *Superman's revenge*

This was years before the video revolution. The only physical evidence of that night is a tinny four-track recording that has been so sweetened and digitized through the years you can barely hear the thunder of all those people singing along. But I felt it through the soles of my shoes. For the first time I understood how many people loved my father.

I felt awe, mixed in with my lingering shame, and an odd giddiness. I swayed along with the swaying crowd and the brilliant lights flashing and the guy onstage flailing away at his drums. The song ended in a vast cheer that prickled the hairs on the back of my neck.

My mother said something I couldn't hear. She grabbed my hand, pulled me to the side of the stage. People stood back to let us through. Too late it dawned on me what she intended—then we were out on the stage in that haze of hot light, and Graham Nash was introducing us to the crowd.

The roar died away.

At the time I didn't hear much of what she said—I was too busy staring in wonder at the ten million people staring back at me—but it's all there on the tape, every word. Many a night I have cringed and fast-forwarded past the four minutes and thirty-two seconds of my mother.

Even dazed as I was, I began to realize we'd been out there an awfully long time. ". . . And Ben always said, 'I think we ought to have peace, you know, I mean, like, why can't we have peace?' Vietnam is such a bummer. I mean, what did anybody in Vietnam ever do to us, right? And like, peace has a way of taking care of you, you know? If you let it. It gets down in your soul, and it gives you relief, and that's the kind of thing Ben stood for," and on and on and on and on and on.

The crowd stood in respectful silence, but I saw eyes glazing over as far back as the tenth row. I squeezed her hand: *Let's get out of here.*

"And so, anyway, it's just so—amazing. There's so many cool people here tonight to celebrate him, and I'll let you get on with it, but I'm not quite done yet." Even through the feedback and tape hiss, you can hear the crowd's disappointed sigh. "I just want to say you're the most wonderful, the most far-out people in the world to come here tonight and give him this send-off. Wherever he's gone. I don't know where he is. Do you? I haven't seen him in weeks." She stopped for a moment—nervous titters out there in the dark. "If anybody knows where he is, would you tell him to call me? I swear to God, it makes me want to scream! He's such an asshole. You don't know what he did to me. He did the worst thing to me anybody ever did to anybody, and he knows what it is, and I'll never tell, because I'm a better person than he is. I told him not to fly. I begged him, I did. But he never listened to me. He was *always* a self-centered son of a bitch."

At this point Jimbo came loping across the stage with a pained smile, waving to the crowd. He put his arms around my mother and me, shepherding us off to the wings. A roar of sympathy followed us off.

I squirmed out from under Jimbo's arm.

"Alexa, baby, what's the matter, are you all right?"

"Of course I'm all right, Jimbo, Jesus! That was embarrassing! Why did you come out there like that? I was almost through."

People stood around us staring as if Mom had removed her shoes and placed them on her ears.

Onstage, Helen Reddy was singing "When Time Stands Still."

Jimbo shifted uncomfortably on his feet. "Well you were kind of—I don't know, goin' on a little long, there, babe," he said. "I thought maybe you needed rescuing."

"*You* were gonna rescue me? That's a joke!" she flared suddenly. "You get away from me!"

"Aw come on, Alexa, cool down." He made a motion to soothe her, a kind of stroking of the shoulders. Mom turned and punched him so hard in the stomach that Jimbo went "Oof!" and his mirrored glasses fell off.

That struck me as just about the funniest thing that ever happened. I started laughing and couldn't stop. Jimbo grabbed me by the arm and snarled at me to shut up, which only made me laugh harder.

Granny French pushed her way through the backstage crowd. "Doris, are you all right?"

"Yes, Mother, why the hell does everyone keep asking me that?"

"Benjamin, be quiet," said Granny, "this is not funny."

That cracked me up. I laughed so hard my stomach hurt. I had to sit down on a speaker cabinet to wipe my eyes and try to catch my breath.

I looked up to find everyone staring at me.

"What's the matter with him?" Granny said. "Look at his eyes. Benjamin, are you sick?"

"Oh, no," said my mother. "Benny, did you eat any of those brownies on the silver tray?"

"Yup." I fought the giggle rising in my chest like an air bubble. "They were good."

"How many did you eat?"

"Four," I said. "Forty-nine. Four hundred forty-nine."

She snorted. "Don't worry, Mother, he's just stoned."

"He's *what?*"

"Those were hash brownies," she said. Granny French still didn't get it. "Hashish, Mother. He's stoned out of his gourd."

Granny drew herself up until she was taller than any of us. "Benjamin, come with me," she said, "we're going to the hospital."

"Would you please relax?" Mom said. "It'll wear off."

"Don't you tell me to relax, you—you—oh, I don't know what you are! Worthless! I can't believe I raised you. Feeding narcotics to a child! Earl, where are you? Earl? Benjamin, come on!"

All these years later, I can still feel Granny's iron pinch in the muscle of my shoulder. She marched me off through that crowd, past the roadies with the tags swinging from their necks, past the white tent, to Uncle Earl's Buick LeSabre.

For most of an hour we rode around Beverly Hills trying to find a hospital, but all the places that looked like hospitals turned out to be homes of the stars. I kept saying I was fine, I didn't need to have my stomach pumped—didn't know exactly what that entailed, but it sounded *bad*. Then I'd think of Jimbo going "Oof!" and another stream of giggles would come pouring out.

By the time we found Cedars-Sinai, Granny French was in such a state that the emergency-room nurse tried to put her on a stretcher. Granny explained that she was fine, thank you, I was the one who'd ingested the poisonous opium brownies. The nurse got a goofy grin on her face and called a couple of the other nurses over to have a look at me.

They thought it was funny, too. Granny let them stand around a minute laughing, then she lit into them like a dog into a flock of white chickens. When the feathers settled, a doctor hurried in to look me over. He said I'd be fine in an hour or two, and he offered to prescribe a tranquilizer for Granny French.

She hustled me out of there, raving about California and the drug-addled simpletons who lived here. "Even the doctors!" she exclaimed. "I'm taking you away from here, Benjamin. This is no place for a child. We're going home."

Uncle Earl drove us to Encino. Granny French packed our bags. I became a great deal less giddy at the sudden prospect of going back to Opelousas. Granny silenced my attempt at protest with one murderous glance. Rita waved goodbye from the porch.

We were on the train heading east before my mother got home from the Hollywood Bowl. I didn't know I would not see her again for eight years.

Mom's little speech on that stage was the first tremor of an earthquake that knocked her completely off her foundations. The collapse came in stages: a vibration here, the odd slippage there, a sudden lurch in an unexpected direction. Her reaction to our hasty departure was to drive to Las Vegas and marry Jimbo in one of those all-night wedding parlors. We learned this from the New Orleans *Times-Picayune* when we got off the train. The columnists had a great time making fun of her: in those days mental illness was still considered funny. The next weekend she and Jimbo drove back to Las Vegas and got a divorce.

She sent us a postcard from the Desert Inn:

DEAR MOTHER AND BEN,

WE ARE FINE HOPE YOU ARE TOO

L. VEGAS IS HOT. WILL CALL SOON

I HAVE BEEN EATING NOTHING BUT CANNED RAVIOLI

Wish you were here —Love, Alexa

"Your mother has gone off her nut," Granny French said.

In September, using a power of attorney signed by my mother, Jimbo cleaned out all the bank accounts and vanished with just over eight hundred thousand dollars in cash. Mom made a mess of slashing her wrists and ended up in a private hospital, Casa San Jacinto, in the mountains near Santa Barbara.

All this news came to us over the telephone. I stayed in my room, so it didn't bother me.

I made no friends in Opelousas. I went to school and came home and stayed in my room, building model airplanes. I sniffed a lot of glue trying to recapture the giddy feeling I'd felt at the Hollywood Bowl, but I never got anything better than a headache.

3 / The Afterworld

SUPERMAN OPENED HIS EYES to a world upside down. He lay sprawled on his back in the sand. Blood trickled into his mouth. The sun baked the side of his face. He knew he was dead, so it was surprising to taste the blood and feel the hot sunlight, the crushing weight of the fuselage on his pelvis and thighs.

Over the roar of the surf he heard a bird singing—a peculiar song, familiar somehow.

> *Whoo-hoo-hoo—*
> *Hoohoo?*

This must be the bird that welcomes you into heaven. Superman was surprised that he might have been allowed through the pearly gates without any objections from the management.

A woman walked across the sand toward him. She wore huge sunglasses, a white scarf on her sandy-brown hair—oh look at those saucy hips in the black swimsuit, look how round and how ripe, swinging across the beach in no particular hurry because Superman was already dead beneath the hissing wreckage of his plane. Even with his face mashed and blood dribbling onto his tongue, Superman felt the old friendly tug of nature. He was pleased beyond all counting to discover that he could still get a hard-on in heaven.

She bent over him. "Are you dead? Hello?"

He didn't see how she could expect him to answer, but he tried. He opened his mouth. No real words came out.

She lifted her sunglasses for a better look. "I told them you weren't dead."

Superman knew that voice from somewhere. Like the song of the bird in the coconut tree, it seemed sweet and familiar, lighter than air.

"Stay there," she said. "Don't bleed to death or anything, okay? I'll go get somebody."

Superman tried to move his hand, to implore her to stay with him, but she spun on her heel and went wiggling away, her fanny jouncing up and down. There came a heaving of blood throughout Superman's lower body, followed by a great rush of pain that roared up out of the sand and wrapped him in its arms.

The woman glanced back. Through the howling pain he heard her bell-like voice, distinctly: "You're kind of cute, too."

And that is when Superman knew he must surely be dead. He recognized that voice. There was no other voice on earth like that.

He had a moment to think, Christ what a stroke of luck, to crash-land in that exact part of heaven where *she* was, or at least to have this intoxicating hallucination before he went on and died the rest of the way.

Then the pain sank its claws into him, and dragged him under.

For days or weeks he was somewhere else. He spiraled through regions of darkness and heat, tortured dreams, vivid strobe flashes of light. He dreamed he was dying, in a land where the air was green and smelled of jasmine. Servants carried him in a sedan chair through gardens so beautiful that his eyes filled with tears. He watched everything as if through a filmy white curtain. When he reached out to part the curtain, he found that every silken layer opened onto another layer.

He found himself crouched inside a whiskey bottle, drifting along in a leisurely current, lodging in the knobby root of a mangrove tree, sprouting barnacles and a seaweed beard.

Then he saw his old grandma on the porch of the house in Blakelee, Alabama, with a .410 shotgun on her shoulder. She was taking careful aim at a rattlesnake coiled beside the stoop, preparing to blow it to bits.

A man floated through the woods singing "The hills are alive . . ."

Superman opened his eyes and found himself in a hot, airless room with walls of fat yellow bamboo, a ceiling of palm thatch. Sunlight punched through holes in the walls and fell in ragged hot patches on his shoulders. For some reason he could not move his arms or legs. His body seemed to weigh about ten thousand pounds, as if the weight of the airplane was still on him. A trickle of perspiration itched and tickled his sides. His mouth was desperately dry; his lips were cracked. He tried to cry out for water but the effort sent him into a swoon.

In the next dream an old woman rolled into his room in a squeaky wheelchair. She sat watching him while he sweated and slept.

This dream came back to him more than once. He could not turn his head to see her face, but he heard her: a tune hummed under her breath, the soft rustle of pages turning, the scratch of pencil on paper. Other times she was quiet, and only the occasional creak of the wheelchair told him she was there.

Superman floated, suspended in dark, humid heat.

The next time he awoke in the bamboo room, the throb pulsing through his body convinced him that he was alive: a thudding drumbeat of pain, as if midgets with rubber hammers were standing around him, whacking away at all his hurt places.

The pain filled him with joy. He was alive! Someone had saved him!

Every object in the room was intensely vivid, as if he were coming down off a long hallucinogenic trip. Beams of pure light streamed through gaps in the bamboo, illuminating dust specks in the air like tiny drifting jewels. Somewhere beyond the wall, the ocean pounded on rocks with a boom that trembled the floor and dissolved in a white sound, retreating.

Closing his eyes, gathering strength, Superman dragged in his arm, intending to scratch the itch beneath his lowest rib. His arm met his side with the *chink!* of stone against stone.

This is not a sound you expect to hear from two parts of your body.

He took a deep breath and got his head up, to see.

The top half of him was arranged on a narrow army cot. His arms were entombed in cocoons of cement. From his navel to his knees, his body was encased in a mushroom-shaped cement block, three feet square—a kind of oversized diaper and pedestal. His bare calves dangled out the other side. The surface of the block was plastered with handprints and petrified rags. Someone had built him into this thing, or had built it around him, to hold his bones in place.

He felt like a man in a magic act waiting to be sawed in half. The room had no windows or doors. The idea that he had crash-landed in paradise began to give way to the notion that he was in some sort of tropical prison.

The pain came swooping in, a strangling thirst. His groan came out a rattle.

A huge black dog leaped up from under the cot, barking. Superman jumped out of his skin but had nowhere to go. His concrete arm slid off the bed and fell *chunk!* to the floor. The hellish dog got up close to his face and barked louder, spraying his cheek with spittle, showing the luminous whites of its eyes.

It didn't seem possible that Superman had lived through the crash of his plane, only to be finished off by a dog.

He tried to summon the strength to raise his arm—if he could get it swinging with enough momentum, he could knock the dog's head through the wall. But he had been on this cot a long time. His upper arm was made of pitiful weakling jelly.

The dog barked louder at shouts from outside.

A portion of the wall slid away, flooding the room with light. *"Hai! Hai! Ha-lay ha-lay ha-lay!"* Brown-skinned children rushed into the room, flailing and shouting at the dog. *"Way poot-a! Way pooot-a, perro! Ha-lay!"* Two boys and a girl, scrawny kids with large eyes. Their faces scrunched up mock-ferocious as they drove the dog from the room.

They stopped in the doorway and turned to the spectacle of Superman in his concrete swaddling. *"Meee-da,"* said the girl, in a tone of wonder. The boys giggled and peered around her.

Superman dragged his hand along the floor. "Water," he said in a guttering voice.

"Doña! Doña!" They squealed and raced off as if a monster had spoken.

Superman fell back to the cot, exhausted.

Whoo-hoo-hoo—

Hoohoo?

The bird of paradise again. Jesus, what was that song? That was some actual song. A guitar line: C C C—F F . . . G G G—F F . . .

He strained to listen, heard instead the sound from his dreams, the squeak of a wheelchair. Rubber wheels thumping onto a ramp, rolling across hollow planks. The bamboo wall slid away.

In the dazzle of light, a wide straw hat cast its shadow over a face to remember: high, proud cheekbones, piercing hazel eyes, startling white eyelashes. A serene classical haughtiness that must have been left over from her youth, when she would have been handsome, not pretty. She was lanky and lean, all knobby elbows and knees. She wore a man's white shirt, baggy khakis, embroidered Japanese slippers with fire-breathing dragons on the toes. She seemed tense, from her tight little smile to the precise way she held herself in the chair. Her arms and chest were deeply sun darkened and freckled, but her face was pink, in the shade of the hat, the wrinkles so soft the touch of a finger would make them disappear. She might be sixty years old, or eighty.

The man behind the wheelchair was old, too—small and stooped, with powerful shoulders and strong-muscled arms. He was an Indian, his face impassively flat-featured and forbidding, like one of those Mayan statues in the *National Geographic.*

The lady murmured a few words.

The old Indian stepped into the room behind Superman and at once produced a sound of pouring water. All the freshness and lightness and hope in the world were contained in that sound.

The old man came to the cot. Superman tipped his head up and drank from a brimming coconut shell.

If you awoke every morning knowing water would taste that good, you would leap up out of bed with a shout of joy.

"Cuidado, no le des demasiado," said the woman. The coconut was withdrawn. "We don't want to drown you."

Superman croaked, "You speak English?"

"Of course, I'm American. Sorry Gyp startled you—she's a sweet dog, once you get to know her. She's been watching over you night and day."

"How long . . . have I been here?"

"More than a month now." She wheeled closer to the bed. "God-amighty, that was a terrible ditch. I've seen some humdingers, but that was just about the worst. What were you trying to do, put her down in the lee of a wave? Whoever taught you to land in the lee of a wave? Didn't you see you had a nice long beach right there to land on?"

"Water," he croaked.

She nodded. The old man stepped forward. Superman gulped as much as he could before it was withdrawn.

"I suppose it's not very kind of me to criticize," she went on, "but I happened to be watching and I just wondered who put that idea in your head."

Superman considered it a real achievement to have landed a plane without wheels and lived to discuss it, but he didn't feel like discussing it at the moment with this old lady. He knew there was something important he needed to ask her, but he couldn't quite get his woozy consciousness wrapped around what it might be, so he settled for the obvious question: "Where am I?"

Her smile was gentle. "Where were you trying to go?"

"Phoenix."

"You're a long way from there. Who was your navigator?"

Superman shook his head. "Just me. I had some—instrument problems. I guess I wandered off course."

"What's your occupation? Surely you're not an aviator?"

"I'm a singer."

"That's how you make your living?"

"Yeah."

"Fine, you must hurry up and get well so you can sing for us."

Superman peered down at the concrete encasement. "Who did this to me?"

"That would be Pito," she said, with a little flourish of her hand. The old Indian bowed. "He's a natural genius at these sorts of things. Of course plaster would have been better than cement, but we had to make do. Is it awfully uncomfortable?"

"My arm," he said. "Can you—get him to pick up my arm?"

She translated. Pito lifted the concrete arm to the cot.

"What's wrong with my face? It hurts when I talk."

"There wasn't much we could do about that," the lady said. "Couldn't put your whole head in cement. You broke a lot of bones all over. I don't know how you looked before, but you look different now. Your name is Benjamin?"

"Ben," he said.

"Everyone calls me Emily. I think we should be friends. We have things in common. Tell me, Ben, where were you the last time you radioed your position?"

"I don't know. I was lost."

"Where did you think you were?"

"Mexico . . . ?"

"Well, that's fine. Now you need to rest. Pito, *la tintura*—"

Pito put a glass vial to Superman's lips. A sweet, heady flavor of flowers: ylang-ylang, jasmine, and others he didn't recognize, borne on a base of pure alcohol. A lovely floral-scented moonshine. Superman swilled it.

Pito tucked the vial away.

"Listen, lady," Superman said, "I've got a problem here."

"What's that?"

"You got my rear end wrapped up in cement. What happens when I have to, you know, go?"

"That's what's so ingenious about Pito's design. Pito, *traiga la manguera, el caballero quiere bañarse.*"

Pito came with a garden hose, which he inserted into a hole atop the concrete block. He winked at Superman, and went out again.

"What is he doing? He's not gonna—" Outside, a faucet squealed. The hose wriggled on the floor. Water came blasting down into the block, flooding his nether regions with a wicked chill. He set up a shout that brought the black dog back into the house, barking.

Emily snapped her fingers. The dog dropped its head and lay down.

Water drained out through a pipe in the floor.

"I'll bet that feels lovely," she said. "It's awfully hot today, even for here."

Superman wondered if he had fallen into the hands of madmen. "Lady, I want you to tell me where the hell I am."

"I can't, Ben. If I tell you, you won't be permitted to leave." She delivered this news without the first hint of a smile.

"What did you say?"

"This is a private island. Uninvited guests are invited to leave. As soon as you're in shape to travel, we'll get you out of here and back to the other world. Just don't ask a lot of questions and you'll be fine." She patted the concrete block. "At least you won't be wandering around poking your nose into things."

"Which . . . which ocean are we in? Atlantic or Pacific?"

"My, we were lost, weren't we? I'm serious, Ben. No questions. If you want to leave, you have to trust me to help you. Your ignorance will help me do that. Of course maybe you'll like it here and want to stay. It has been known to happen. It'd be nice to have a singer. Do you know 'Moonlight in Vermont'?"

"What happened to my plane?"

She shook her head. "Too bad about that. The natives are wonderful people, but if you leave something lying about, they think you must not want it. They were carting the pieces away before Pito got you out from under. He managed to save most of your things. . . . I was studying that electronical compass of yours. That's a beautiful piece of equipment."

"Yeah, it works great," said Superman. "I thought I was going to Phoenix." The taste of flowers lingered on his tongue, and now his mind was sidestroking pleasantly through the sultry air. "What was that stuff you gave me?"

"A sleeping potion. Nectars and bark infusions. Pito's recipe."

"Listen, you can't just . . . you gotta . . ." He blinked, and smiled. "Wow, it's pretty trippy, huh?" The air in the room shimmered and rippled.

Emily placed her hand on his arm. "Sleep," she commanded.

Superman closed his eyes and fell back into that dreamland where he had been keeping himself.

The bird sang while he slept. The rest of the song filled itself in. He awoke when the sun was very late, or very early. He recognized the song, and laughed out loud.

> *Whoo hoo hoo*
> *Hoo hoo?*
> *Whoo hoo hoo*
> *Hoo hoo!*
> *Uh, Louie Louie, oh, no,*
> *sayin' we gotta go.*
> *Yeah, yeah, yeah, yeah, yeah.*

In a place where an old lady and her Indian medicine man wrap your ass in a loaf of concrete, and sedate you with nectar of flowers, it should not come as a surprise that a bird might be singing the first four bars of "Louie Louie." The lead guitar line.

Superman had not made it to paradise, not yet. But neither did this seem like quite the same old earth.

Suddenly he remembered what he had forgotten to ask. His delight melted into anger. His yell roused the dog to furious barking just past the bamboo wall. He called it a goddamn sonofabitch dog and told it to shut the hell up.

The bamboo wall slid back. Superman roared, "Go get her and bring her to me!" The old Indian gulped and beat a retreat. Apparently he understood English if you spoke it loud enough.

In two minutes the wheelchair came squealing up the path. Superman tried to pull up on his elbows to face her, but couldn't find the strength.

Her hair all askew. An embroidered kimono over rumpled red-striped pajamas. "What on earth is the matter with you?"

"What did you do with the money?" Superman demanded. "I had a lot of money in that plane. Where is it?"

"Why, you ungrateful—how dare you! Do you realize it's five o'clock in the morning? For God's sake, it's in the safe at my house."

That was not the answer he expected. He felt like an instant fool. "Oh . . . well, hell, why didn't you tell me?"

"I suppose I was more concerned with saving your life. You don't seem very appreciative. You seem to think we're *all* thieves." She sent Pito off with three words. "I knew this was trouble, bringing you here. But I really didn't have a choice, did I? I couldn't leave you to die. And this is the thanks I get."

"Lady, what did you expect me to think? You said they took my plane apart. You didn't say anything about my money."

"If you'd just *listen* instead of leaping to conclusions—I told you Pito saved some of your things, papers and some of the instruments, a guitar, that sack with all the cash. The guitar is broken. He's been trying to fix it for you."

"Look, I'm sorry, just—you haven't told me where I am, or who you are, or . . ."

"Those are not things you need to know."

"I gotta get out of here," he said. "I've got a kid, and, and a wife, and a career . . . I've got friends. They'll be looking for me."

"You'd be amazed how quickly they forget."

"You can't just keep me here. I'm famous, okay?" He hadn't wanted to play that card, but there it was, on the table.

She stared at him coolly. "I've never heard of you."

He puffed up a bit. "My name's Ben Willis. They call me Superman. I've got six gold records, okay? They're not gonna stop looking for me."

"In time they will."

He mulled the certainty with which she said that.

"But you should be up and out of here before then," she said, an after-thought.

Pito appeared with a tray, steaming saucepans of coffee and milk, two coconut shells. The dog followed him in.

"On the beach, when I crashed," Superman said. "I saw Marilyn Monroe."

Emily tasted her coffee. A smile crinkled the corners of her eyes. "Really?"

"She asked if I was dead. And she said I was kind of cute."

Pito proffered a shell filled with coffee and milk. Superman craned over to the paper straw and took a sip: hot and dark, with a flavor like burnt chocolate.

"That's quite a dream," said Emily.

"It wasn't a dream," Superman said. "She was real."

"Her name is Daisy. I've never seen any of the Marilyn Monroe movies, but everyone says the resemblance is uncanny."

He thought about that for a moment. He turned it over in his mind. "It wasn't a resemblance. It's her. She's not a blonde anymore. I heard her voice. I had a real good look at her."

She laughed, lightly. "You're not the first person to think so."

She was a bad liar, he thought—especially this early in the morning, with the crease of the pillow still in her face.

"That's what you don't want me to see," he said softly. "That *is* her. She's not dead. She's here."

"Oh, Ben, that's silly." Her smile seemed frozen. "You took a pretty good bump on the head."

"How did she do it, how'd she get here? I mean, she's dead. They had a funeral and everything."

"Obviously it's impossible." She clasped the kimono to her throat. "You should really try to eat something today. You've lost too much weight."

"I know what I saw," he insisted.

She raised two fingers. The old man moved behind her chair. "We'll mash up some fruit for you, I think you can tolerate that," she said, gliding out. "If it doesn't rain, we'll open the house up later on and give you some air."

Superman sank back in wonder. He had fallen in love with Marilyn Monroe as she sashayed up the aisle of the train in *Some Like It Hot*. The day she died, he was driving from Birmingham to Gadsden to sing in a bar called the Cattle Drive. The news came over the radio. They played "Diamonds Are a Girl's Best Friend" then went back to their regular rotation. Ben pulled in at a roadhouse, got drunk, felt sad the whole day, missed the gig. She was a suicide, in a bungalow. The housekeeper found her lying naked across the bed. The coroner said sleeping pills. What a waste! Superman imagined that every American man spent that day grieving over the death of his secret dream—the dream that he, Mr. Joe Hot Blood Average Guy, would one day have his chance to make love to Marilyn Monroe.

And now she was here, in this place. One hundred percent alive. He knew it was true because the old lady kept her eyes down while she lied.

He smiled to himself. He had picked an interesting place to crash.

4 / *Me No Understando*

Every night it rained harder than it has ever rained.

On the fine mornings, Pito slid back the bamboo wall to bring in the jungle air. Large oaklike trees were blooming and shedding their blooms, a soft rain of red trumpet flowers drifting down through the air. Hummingbirds raced to dip their snouts in the blossoms before they touched the ground.

A high pink stucco wall surrounded Miss Emily's estate. Jungle lapped over the top of the wall like a green river spilling over a dam. Inside the wall, the vegetation was tamed and shaped into luxuriant gardens, huge stands of heliconia and bougainvillea and birds-of-paradise. Superman lay in one of several bamboo shacks scattered across the plunging hillside. At night he could hear Pito and the brown people in their shacks, cooking and laughing. Ramps and footbridges connected all the buildings, crisscrossing a pair of tumbling streams.

On a promontory below, hidden by lush palms and gigantic elephant-ears, was a structure Superman had come to think of as the Big House, though he hadn't been down there to see it. From the prison of his concrete toadstool he caught glimpses of a red-tiled roof through gaps in the jungle. It was obvious from its placement on the knoll that the Big House must have a fine view of the sea.

Emily must be a wealthy old bird. Once Superman's jaw had healed, splendid meals began to arrive on Noritake china, flanked by gleaming silver and crisp linen napkins. Every dinner was a revelation: fat sweet scallops on a bed of black beans and fried pineapple, spiny lobster grilled over coffee wood, plantains and saffron rice, tamales baked in banana leaves, split open and steaming. He had never eaten such food in his life. He savored each forkful as it was fed to him.

Maids, gardeners, handymen busied around the grounds all day. The kids raked the lawns, swept the paths, shooed the peacocks into their wire enclosures. No telling what it must have cost to carve this place out of the jungle, to shape those streambeds into pools and waterfalls, to plant lemon trees and brilliant arching sprays of bougainvillea and hibiscus and the nine varieties of palms Superman counted from where he lay. He hadn't seen the swimming pool yet, but he had heard the splash.

The old lady stopped coming to sit with him. He must have truly pissed her off with that 5 a.m. wake-up call. She came once, to show him his sack of money. She gave him a brass bell and abandoned him to the people who didn't speak English.

Old Pito the Indian took the morning shift, his blunt-faced daughter Catalina the evenings. They spoke to each other in a language that sounded like birdcalls. One ring of Superman's bell always brought someone running. They brought herb teas, fruit juices, flowery potions. They replenished his ice bucket ten times a day, and massaged his aching shoulders and feet as often as he worked up the nerve to ask.

Catalina stayed around after supper. She sat outside the house in a cane-backed chair, listening to mournful *música romántica* on her transistor radio (an old man wailing in Spanish, a plinking guitar). With the other servants Superman pointed to what he wanted and said *gracias,* but with Catalina he could carry on philosophical conversations for hours through the open door. He spoke in English. She listened in Spanish. Neither understood a word the other said, but they became friends.

Later, when he'd learned a little *pachuco* Spanish, he was stunned to realize that Catalina had been insulting him vividly, sweetly, night after night for those weeks. At the time, though, he was happy carrying on this dual-lingual cross-cultural mind-meld conversation. When you knew the other person couldn't understand you, you were free to say whatever came into your head.

"I wonder what they're doing right now." He scratched the scuzz on his chin. "Do you think anybody really misses me? Or is it like, well, he's gone, too bad, next?"

Catalina's soft voice rose above the radio. *"No sé porque tú me dices estas cosas,"* she said. *"No me importa, entiendes?"* (I don't know why you tell me these things. I don't care, understand?)

"Before I came here I was just so full of it, man. I had the kind of life most people would dream of. But I was just—bored, you know? Trapped. I kept thinking how cool it would be just to walk away from it all. That was my fantasy, can you imagine? I got everything I ever wanted, and it *bored* me. It takes something like this to make you see that what you had was pretty damn good. I had things, Catalina, a lot of good things. I was too caught up in my own head trip to know which ones were important."

"*No me importa nada lo que digas.*" (I don't give a damn about anything you say.)

"I admit it, I've been a pretty lousy father, but I can change that. I don't have to spend the rest of my life on the road. Haven't I got enough money? Jesus. I don't even have time to spend what I make."

"*Tienes cara de mono.*" (You have the face of a monkey.)

"The night I came here," he said, "was the very first time I ever thought about leaving my wife. I just *thought* about it, man, and the next thing you know my instruments are screwed up and I'm down on the goddamn Equator. I don't know if it was an accident or, like, maybe I meant do to it—self-fulfilling prophecy, you know, careful what you wish for . . ."

The man on the radio roused himself to a trembling high note, then settled back with a sigh, like the end of a night.

"They all think I'm dead," he said. "I can't wait to see the look on their faces when I walk through that door."

"*Naturalmente si tu madre era una puta, su hijo sería un hijo de puta*" came the answer. (Naturally if your mother was a bitch, her son would be a son of a bitch.)

He told Catalina about growing up all over Alabama and Mississippi in the back of his daddy's Ford pickup, always on the move to the next place. Everybody in America made money off World War II except John Ray Willis. He had flat feet, bad eyes, zero ambition. He cut timber, painted houses, dug sewer lines, swept floors, drove a bread truck, fed hogs, picked up garbage. He was always going off drunk, forgetting to show up for work—then it was time to pack up the truck and move on.

There wasn't room for Ben in the cab with Mama and Daddy and his two sisters. He rode in back with the mattresses and the whistling wind. Usually he liked how the wind snatched the words from his lips as he spoke them. It was nice to watch the stars drifting by overhead. But sometimes it rained, and once it got so cold the rain turned to lumps of ice in his hair. He banged on the roof of the cab. His father wouldn't even slow down.

His father was not a bad man, just shiftless. His mother was all right, but she would never stand up to his father. She was satisfied just to ride along listening to him tell how much better the next town would be.

"That's why I worked so hard all my life I don't even know my own kid," Superman told Catalina. "I was bound and determined that what-ever happened, I was gonna turn out a thousand times better than my old man."

He told her how surprised he'd been to discover his voice, at sixteen. He'd dropped out of school and was living in a trailer park in Bay Minette with a homely girl called Myra Ratcliff. He was beginning to worry that he might turn out like his father—he didn't seem to have any special talent, and he thought a person needs some kind of talent to get through the rough patches. He worked days at an auto-parts warehouse. Nights he rode on a Pabst Blue Ribbon delivery truck with a fat boy named Smiley Wooster. No matter how high or low you went on the Mobile nightlife scene, you were likely to run into Smiley and Ben—in the classy places, the Holiday Inn and Wintzell's Oyster House, in the bowling alley across from the Second Baptist Church, and in the causeway joints like the Midnite Lounge and the Slap-N-Go Bar, where a good Baptist would never take his wife.

One night they were on the Florida line at a honky-tonk called the Flor-A-Bama. Smiley was chatting up the bar gal, as usual, while Ben rolled cases of longnecks down a ramp into a cooler. On a low stage at the end of the room were four middle-aged hillbilly boys whangin'-and-a-twangin,' making an awful mess of Hank Williams's "Lovesick Blues."

Now, Ben had always loved Hank Williams. He placed Hank in the same category as Marilyn Monroe, a superior being not quite of this earth. Especially he loved "Lovesick Blues," with its beautiful yodeling melody. To hear these boys murdering that song was more than he could stand. They played as if they couldn't care less whether anyone was listening.

There were plenty of folks in the bar, some even trying to dance to that mess. Ben had heard worse music in other joints, but this band's perfor-mance got on his nerves in a new and provocative way. Somehow, he just knew he could do better than that. He set down his dolly with a clang, and walked closer to the stage to have a look.

His face must have carried some of what he was thinking. The players stopped playing and looked at him. The prissy redheaded singer cleared his throat. "Something we can do for you?"

"There's a better way to sing that song," Ben said.

"Oh, yeah?" said the singer. "Who the hell are you?"

"Ben Willis."

"You think you can sing it better than me?"

"I might."

The man's face turned a darker red than his hair. "Well why don't you get on up here, then, and try." He leaned to the microphone. "Folks, we got a young fella here says he can sing. Y'all want to hear him?"

No one was paying attention. People were talking louder to fill up the space where the band's noise had been. The dancing couples were draped over each other in the dark corners.

Ben felt Smiley's eyes on him. He'd never sung anywhere but in the shower, and now he was about to make a fool of himself, but that's what it's like at sixteen—you find yourself suddenly big after a whole lifetime of being small, and you stretch out to all the possibilities of your new size. Ben huddled a moment with the band, counted them off, and sang "Lovesick Blues."

He just stood up in his Pabst shirt and sang the song. The people stopped talking and lined up all along the bar to hear him. It was like an Elvis movie.

> Oh, I love to hear it when she calls me sweet Da-ha-haddy
> Such a beautiful dream

At the end they burst into applause, whistling, shouting "Yeah, boy! Get it!"

At that moment Ben knew what he would do with his life.

He turned to thank the singer, who stood clapping with everyone else. The man's face was so red he looked as if he might pop. He stepped onto the stage. "That was a fine rendition," he said, squeezing Ben's hand a bit harder than necessary.

Ben saw the flash of humiliation in the man's eyes. He drew back with a sudden jolt of shame for what he had done.

This guy hadn't been hurting anybody with his singing. He'd been keeping 'em entertained enough here at the Flor-A-Bama; he was up there earning his pay, however indifferently. But from now on, every time he stood up to sing, these people would remember the kid from the beer truck who got up and blew him off the stage.

You can't undo a hurt you have done to someone. All you can do is get out of there quick, and get ready to regret it for the rest of your life.

Ben thanked the musicians, stepped around the ruined man, and pushed through the throng to the back of the bar. People reached out to pat his shoulder.

Smiley said "Goddamn, boy!" about sixty-five times on the way back to Mobile.

Ben had spent the years since then looking over his shoulder, waiting for that moment to catch up with him. So far it hadn't. His life was charmed. Good fortune descended upon him exactly when needed, as if his career were being mapped out and managed from some well-organized secret headquarters. He started singing in honky-tonks like the Flor-A-Bama, moved on to roadhouses and the better town bars, crossed a state line or two, and began climbing the ladder one rung at a time, bar singer to opening act to headliner. All without too much fuss—just year after year of hard steady work, hundreds of thousands of miles on the tires of the bus.

Then came Monterey. Before he knew what hit him he was a Top 40 sensation, a hitmaker, a star. The image thing grew large, and the fame thing got away from him completely. People started angling in from every direction. Every one of them wanted something. He found himself running sideways to keep from flying.

Then he became Superman, and learned how to fly.

"And look where it got me," he said to Catalina. "If this ain't the end of the world, by God you can see it from here."

"*Tal vez te mueres mientras estés durmiendo,*" she said. (Maybe you will die in your sleep.)

He was sorry when she switched off the radio and came to tuck the mosquito net around his cot. She turned down the flame of the lamp and moved it to where he could reach it. "Awkay, *buena' noches,*" she said, and Superman said, "*Buena' noches.*"

Gyp slipped into the room, clicking toenails on the floor. Superman snapped fingers. The dog came to lick his hand. Gyp had fleas something awful, but the *thump-thump* of her hind leg on the floor was not an unwelcome sound in the night, when the jungle was bristling with animal sounds.

The Louie-Louie bird sang in the heat of the day, leaving the night to the spookier birds, bats, and bugs and creatures that rattled the bushes and flapped against the ceiling in the dark. Some of the monkeys sounded big as dogs, crashing through the treetops, snapping off limbs. Others came in skittery troops of twenty or thirty, chattering, squabbling, moving like rain through the trees. Unidentified animals made weird little cries, like wounded children, and there were foxlike things that barked and laughed.

Deep in the night he was startled awake by the sound of a woman just outside the hut, weeping her heart out—good God, the most heartrending sobs, loud at first, then trailing off in a decrescendo of pain.

A moment's silence, as if she were drawing a breath, then she started sobbing desperately.

Superman rang his bell so hard the little clapper flew off and went bouncing across the floor.

The woman wept as if her heart would surely break. She had cried herself hoarse, as if her lover had abandoned her.

For one awful moment he imagined it was Alexa, weeping for him.

He fired the bell at the wall *bam!* He strained to raise his concrete arm, got it up swinging, sent the ice pitcher off the table with a crash that roused Gyp to barking.

The bamboo panel slid back and there was Pito with his lantern, looking no sleepier than at any other time. *"Señor?"*

"Come on, man, there's a woman in trouble out there! Somebody's hurting her! Aren't you gonna do something?"

Pito furrowed his brick-colored brow. He nodded, and backed from the room. In a moment he came back with the garden hose.

"No, get that thing away from me! It's not me, it's her! Don't you hear it?"

Pito shrugged and started out again.

Through the door came a peal of unbearable misery.

"There!"

Superman's cry halted the old Indian in his tracks. He cocked one ear to the door: that sound?

"Yeah! That! Are you gonna let her keep crying like that?"

The planes of Pito's face smoothed out into a smile. *"Madretriste,"* he said.

"Madre . . . I don't get it. Me no understando."

Pito stepped to the door. He held out his hands, palms upturned as in supplication. He whistled a note that started high and soared downward.

The woman answered with a burst of weeping.

Pito whistled again.

A sudden flutter of wings—a jewel-green bird flapped out of the night and settled on the old man's wrist.

"Wow." Superman blinked.

The eyes were bright black. The bill was like a black claw, shot through with a brilliant red stripe. The feathers of the body were luridly green, iridescent. A fan of red feathers trailed behind, the same vivid red as the stripe on the bill. The bird was so gorgeous it looked almost ridiculous— like a cartoon bird, or a fabulous hat. It sat poking at its shoulder feathers.

The old man said something in the language he spoke with Catalina, an odd mix of twitters and chirps. The bird opened its beak and sang the song of the weeping woman.

Even when you watched it sing, that was not like an animal sound. It was human, and surpassingly weird.

"Ah-vay," the old man said. *"Se llama madretriste."*

"Bring it here." Superman beckoned. "I want to see."

Pito came in with the bird on his hand.

"Jesus, bird, what's your problem? No reason to sit out there boo-hooing, huh? You are one sad-sounding bird." It cocked its head and studied Superman with its glassy eye, then shivered, ruffling its wings. "I don't think it likes me," he said.

The old man went to the door, lifted his hand. The bird made an unpretty squawk and glided up into the night.

Pito stooped for the end of the hose.

"Nope, huh-uh, thanks," said Superman, "I'm okay."

Pito bowed and slid the door shut.

The bird took up its song again, weeping softly in a tree just outside. Superman wondered how it had ever learned to make such a sound. It just wasn't natural for a bird to sound so damn human, and sad.

He wished Pito would bring some magic flower-potion so he could float off to sleep. He'd thrown his bell away.

It was always too damn hot in this place. The heat started early in the morning and grew up till noon and blasted down all day, hour after hour, and did not let up even long after sunset. There was nothing to do but lie there listening to the teasing of faraway thunder, praying the storm to come this way.

A mosquito whined in his ear.

Superman blew a sharp stream of air across his face. The mosquito bobbled backward then circled around, dancing up and down on an invisible elastic string. Superman huffed and puffed. The mosquito fell back, and came bouncing in again for the kill.

From the mosquito's point of view, Superman was a vast expanse of naked white flesh, exposed and fragrantly inviting. The mosquito veered into position as the great sweaty thing heaved and twisted and sent out fierce blasts of air to drive it away.

Normally, one swat could have settled the question. But the odds were a bit more even than normal: Superman had these unwieldy forty-pound arms, and the mosquito had only his blood on its tiny mind.

Dodging out of range, it touched down on his belly and plunged its needle into his skin.

It filled him with rage for the thing to feed off him *while he was watching it.*

When it was finished, the mosquito licked its chops and took off.

Reaching down deep for super-strength, Superman swung forward like a gymnast on parallel bars. He brought both arms up and smashed them together at the precise point in the universe that contained the mosquito.

He smiled at the smear of blood on cement. His own blood. It was self-defense, of course, but it felt like murder, and he enjoyed it.

Next morning he found himself riddled with mosquito bites, his casts shot through with fine cracks. He'd lost a sizable chunk of concrete near the right elbow. He showed this to Pito when he brought in the hose for the daily humiliation.

"I killed the hell out of a mosquito," he explained.

Pito pressed his hands on the fleshy part of Superman's arm, above the cast. He held tight for eight or ten seconds, then repeated the procedure on the other arm. He tucked the end of the hose into the hole in the cast, and went out again.

Superman braced himself. Lately he had tried to quit fighting the chill of the water, but the squeal of the faucet sent an automatic shudder down his length.

"Ow ow ow ow ooo shit!" He couldn't help yelling. His gonads shrank up to pebbles. Why did his crotch have to be the one chilly location in this whole steaming jungle?

Usually Pito ran the water just until Superman stopped screaming, then he'd shut it off and come to sponge-bathe the rest of him. Today he let the water run on and on. After some minutes the shock wore off and the water came to seem rather pleasantly cool. These weeks in the cast had given Superman the kind of itches you simply can't discuss with anyone. His private zones were on fire all the time; he'd been locked up in this concrete diaper so long that even flat-faced Catalina was starting to look good.

The water seemed to be soothing the worst of that itch. Maybe Pito should leave the hose on all the time.

He wiggled to let the water into the tight spots. He'd give anything to get out of this cast and run down to that ocean that was torturing him night and day with its sound. He would throw himself in, float and splash and swim until every inch of him was drawn and puckered, then stretch flat on his back on the sand and let the sun bake out the wrinkles.

Then he'd find her. He knew she was somewhere beyond the pink wall. He had to see her again, to be sure. Sometimes he thought he could smell lavender on the breeze.

After that he would find his way home.

A crunch on the gravel path, rubber wheels rolling on the ramp. "Morning, morning," called Emily. For the first time he noticed a faint New York accent.

He turned his head. "I thought you'd run off and forgot me."

"Would that I could." She looked crisp in a blue-striped shirt and khakis.

"You still haven't told me where I am."

"Oh gosh, still feeling mistreated?"

"Not really," he admitted. "It's a great place you've got here. The lobster last night was incredible. But I'm just about ready to start getting on home."

The faucet squealed. Water dribbled away through the floor.

"Pito said you had some kind of mishap with your casts."

"Me against a mosquito," he said. "It was close, but I won."

"We'll have to take them off. I hope it's not too soon." Grasping the rim of the wheel, she spun her wheelchair through the door. Pito slipped in with a chisel and a square-headed mallet.

"Hold on." Superman tried to sit up. "I got bones here. He's not gonna just start pounding away with that thing."

"Maybe you'd rather we leave the casts on," said Emily. "Or you could bash them off yourself, and reduce the mosquito population. What do you think? You decide."

Superman frowned. "Tell him to go easy."

She told him, in Spanish. Pito stacked a pair of cinder blocks by the cot, placed Superman's right arm squarely on top, and took up his mallet and chisel. *Pink! Pink! Pink!* He struck a few tentative blows.

Superman tensed, but didn't feel anything.

"What was all the excitement last night?" said Emily.

"God, there's this bird, have you heard it? Well, sure, you must've. That's like no kind of bird I ever heard in my life. I could have sworn it was a woman crying."

"That's a *madretriste*. It means 'sad mother.' "

"It's one sad mother, all right. It gave me the willies. How did he teach it to make that sound?"

"He didn't. It's a wild bird. That's the way it sings."

"No, this bird was tame. He called it. It came down and lit on his hand."

Pito stuck the blade of his chisel in a crack, and tapped with the hammer, *pink! pink!*

"*Madretristes* don't live in captivity." Emily toyed with her silver elephant-foot bracelet. "It came to Pito because it trusted him. He's from a very old tribe. He knows things."

"Like . . ."

"Like how to talk to the birds."

He just looked at her.

"It took me a while to believe it myself. I thought it was some kind of trick, but he talks to them. To all the creatures."

Superman couldn't help smiling. "What do they talk about?"

"The sun, the weather. Things they have in common."

"You mean they talk back to him?"

"It's not conversation the way we think of it," she said. "Not an exchange of information so much as . . . emotions. Sometimes they let him know when a bad storm is coming."

"Lady, that's all very interesting, but I believe he is pulling your leg." Superman kept his eye on the chisel tip chewing through concrete toward his arm.

"There's a lot you can learn here, Ben," she said. "At first I was like you. We're Americans, we're trained from birth to avoid anything the least bit supernatural—except Halloween and Santa Claus, of course, not to mention the whole Jesus business. Which, when you think about it, is at least as unlikely as the idea that we could learn to understand birds. If we could keep quiet long enough to hear what they're saying."

"How long have you been here?" said Superman.

"Twenty-seven years."

The mallet slipped. A sliver of concrete shot out and glanced off Superman's chin. The old man murmured an apology. He had opened a

V-shaped channel from elbow to wrist, exposing the cotton batting around the bare flesh. He placed the chisel in a crack, gave a knock with his mallet. The cast split like a chunk of kindling, crashing in pieces to the floor.

Superman's arm floated up from the cinder block, defying gravity. His hand rose into the air and kept rising until it was floating over his head.

Gently Pito lowered the arm to the cot. When he turned to reach for the scissors, the arm floated up again.

"I'm not doing it. It's like it's weightless."

"Your muscles are used to the weight of the cast," she said.

His arm felt lighter than a child's balloon. If it hadn't been attached to the rest of him, it would have floated to the ceiling.

Pito held it down with his knee and began snipping at the gauze. Superman stared in horror as the flesh was revealed—dried, crusted, leathery as lizard skin. "Aw God," he cried, "it looks dead!"

"Just the skin," Emily said. "You'll shed that pretty fast. Can you move it?"

"I don't know . . . I could try." The sight of his arm unnerved him. It no longer resembled any part of him. What about the parts farther down, entombed in cement?

Pito let go. The arm floated up in midair.

Superman stared at his hand, willing it to move down and touch his head.

The elbow was a bit creaky, the wrist had a new lump on the outside, but the arm was in working order. He grasped the back of his neck to keep the hand from floating away.

"When I woke up and saw what you'd done to me," he said, "I thought you people were crazy. But you did a hell of a job, considering."

"I didn't do anything," she said. "It was all Pito."

"Pito. Great work, man. Mucho greato."

The old man nodded and moved the cinder blocks to the other side of the cot. He knelt to begin chipping at the left arm.

Emily said the wrist fractures hadn't seemed too serious—"you must have held your hands out on impact, and the bones just snapped"—but his pelvis had been causing her a great deal of concern.

"Me too," he said. "Definitely you want the ol' pelvis to do what it's supposed to."

She pursed her lips.

"I mean, you know, walking," he tried. "I'd hate to wind up in a wheelch—" He stopped. "The reason I've got such a big mouth is so I can get my whole foot in at once."

"No, I know what you mean." Her eyes twinkled. "I'm not too old to remember that the pelvis is a pretty significant bone." When she laughed, he glimpsed a much younger woman inside.

He decided Emily was a good sort, despite her coolness and distance. Kind of sexy, too, for a woman her age. He wished he'd known her when she was young, and both their pelvises were in working order.

Pito broke the cast into four pieces, and took his scissors to the gauze. Superman's left arm floated up. It looked as scaly as the right arm. Also it felt just as light, and worked just as well.

He waved his hands like an orchestra conductor, savoring the motion, the sudden onset of freedom.

"Pito's been working on your guitar," said Emily. "We can't wait to hear you sing."

Superman patted the body cast. "Let's get on with the main event."

"Ben, let's not press our luck. We should leave that on a few more days, to be sure."

"No. Now. I'm ready now."

"If we take it off too soon, we'll just have to do it over. Can't you be patient for one more week?"

"Listen, lady. You saved me, I'll never be able to thank you enough. But I'm tired of being patient. I want out of this thing. Today. I've got to go home."

Emily frowned, said a few words in Spanish.

The old man pressed cool hands to Superman's belly, slid his fingertips under the lip of the cast, to the hipbones. He poked at Superman's knees, the backs of his calves.

At last he delivered his verdict. Emily translated: "Your body still has too many parts."

Superman floated his hand down, closed his fingers around the handle of the hammer. "Better stand out of the way."

He meant to take one good swing at the cast, make a noise and raise a little dust—at which point they'd see he was serious, and Pito would step in to finish the job. The problem arose when he tried to lift the hammer.

It didn't look heavy, but when he tried to pick it up with his rubbery arm, he discovered that it weighed about three tons.

He grunted and strained. To their credit, neither Pito nor Emily laughed at his pitiful effort. They watched as he struggled, sweating, the cords standing out in his neck.

He scooched around to get his other hand on the handle, *surely with both hands . . .* but no. That hammer stayed where it was.

He slumped back, spent. He couldn't believe it. Last night he'd swung both casts at once, he had truly *abolished* that mosquito—and now he couldn't lift a five-pound hammer!

Emily retrieved it with one hand, plopped it on his chest. "Pito didn't want you to hurt yourself. Go ahead. Pick it up."

He grasped the handle, lifted it, waved it about in the air. "But—what did he—"

"Ben, it's probably not in your nature to respect anybody," she said. "But I think you will learn to respect Pito. He says we should wait."

"What, he made the hammer heavy and now it's not heavy? What kind of a trick is that? 'Scuse me, lady, you've been out in the jungle too long. You're starting to imagine things."

"I've been imagining things since the day I arrived," she said. "You're the one who's just starting."

He brandished the hammer. "Are you gonna get me out of this thing, or am I gonna have to do it myself?"

Without warning the hammer became uncountably heavy, pure distilled gravity, like the densest portion of a collapsed star. It plummeted from his hand, broke a hole through the floor, and thudded to the earth below.

Pito gazed at the hole in the floor.

Superman whistled. "How does he do that?"

"I'll be damned if I know." The old lady smiled sweetly. "Just a week or two more."

He groaned. "One week. You promised."

"Good boy." She touched his hair. "I knew you'd come around."

5 / *The Cock-Eyed Optimist*

OH IT WAS VERY SEDUCTIVE, this tropical thing. Papaya juice in the morning, a chatter of birds, a warm breeze, the changeless rhythm of blue skies and surf pounding, sunsets, nights sprinkled with moonlight. A man could get lost in all this, he thought: a man would need a strong will to keep from melting away under the sheer pleasant strangeness of it all.

The obligations of his former life huddled in his mind, dim scarecrows watching from a fencerow in the distance. He missed Alexa more than he'd imagined, and, missing her, thought he was falling in love with her again—decided, in fact, that he had never really fallen out of love with her. Just the noise and distraction of his success put all that strain on their marriage. The squabbles and long silences, the late-night hotel-room arguments faded away until only the nice memories remained, burnished and golden.

He missed his old life the way you miss a friend who has died: sadly, but with a little smile. He missed the good nights on the road, when the crowd came pumped up and the band caught their energy and magnified it into something hot enough to set the air on fire. He missed the funky glamorous Hollywood parties with naked girls in hot tubs and Ravi Shankar playing, the kind of party he used to sail through with a generous smile, knowing he was a star and his wife was the best-looking girl in the place. Sometimes after such a night they would wake Ben Junior from his sound rumpled sleep and bring him to their room, where they'd sit up in bed eating spaghetti, watching a late movie. These were the times that hurt most to remember, the times when they were just like a real family, together and happy, dripping carbonara on the sheets.

He tried to think of what Ben and Alexa must be doing now, but all he got were these hazy snapshots, a day at Malibu, a car trip through Yellowstone, the Grand Canyon, Disneyland: postcards he'd bought, places he'd barely seen. He couldn't imagine Ben Junior a single day older than the last time he saw him.

He hated the fact that he'd disappeared at a time when he was so totally caught up in his own story, so oblivious to the needs of his family that he'd actually entertained the notion of leaving them without a glance back. He had gotten so high and so mighty that he thought he didn't need them. He'd fantasized running away from his problems, and now, looking back, he saw that his only real problem was himself—and he'd brought that one along with him.

He suffered for this. Somehow he had brought this adventure down upon himself. When he got back to the real world he would have one hell of a mess to straighten out. But he could face that. He had figured out a few things. The jungle was an excellent place to think, since there was absolutely nothing else to do.

He passed the days picking scraps of dead skin from his arms and collecting them on a corner of his bedside table. The skin underneath was fresh pink, hairless and tender. He rolled the scraps of dead skin into a ball the size of a walnut. He bobbled it in his hand, reluctant to part with it—but what could you do with such a thing? In the end he pitched it out the door.

That night he dreamed that the skin ball assembled itself into a hideous scaly brown arm, and began clawing back up the hill toward him. Someone screamed—

He awoke in a tremble. His own scream? Christ, he had to get out of this place. His own dead arm dragging itself up a hill, trying to get at him. He felt dizzy and spinheaded, off-center, as if his brain had been knocked out of alignment.

Gyp planted her paws in his rib cage and stuck her nose in his face.

"Phew! Quit! Giddown!" He shoved her off. She nudged him, whining. He made his hand into a blade and ran it along her spine. Gyp sank to the floor, crooning.

Outside, he heard singing.

Not a bird. It was a man, a tipsy and boisterous man, crashing through the bushes toward Superman's shack, bellowing a song.

A show tune. Rodgers and Hammerstein . . . ?

Footsteps lurched onto the porch. The bamboo panel shot open. A man in a frilly yellow bathrobe sank to his knees with his arms spread wide, selling the song in a rich tenor voice:

I could say life is just a bowl of Jell-O
And appear more intelligent and smart

His platinum-blond wig made quite a contrast to his prim gray mustache. The bathrobe was a satiny Technicolor-yellow number like the one Doris Day wore in *Pillow Talk*. Underneath he wore a white nightdress and black rubber boots.

> *But I'm stuck like a dope with a thing called hope*
> *And I can't get it out of my heart . . .*

He stopped in midsong with his arms out. "Stop me if you've heard this one."

Superman laughed. "Who the hell are you?"

"I'm Frank." His grip was as manly as his voice. He would have made a distinguished-looking old guy, but as a woman he was unconvincing. His resemblance to the actor Douglas Fairbanks Jr. was canceled out by the bathrobe and blond wig and blood-red lipstick. "I heard you were getting cabin fever up here, and I said, 'All that poor boy needs is a cocktail and some live entertainment.' I hope to God you have ice."

"In the bucket," said Superman. "You live here?"

"If you can call it living." From the lining of his robe he fished out a sleek chrome-plated cocktail shaker, streamlined like the fuselage of a Boeing Flying Boat. "I'm not interrupting anything, am I? Of course not. What could I be interrupting? That savage has imprisoned you in cement."

"Whatcha got in the shaker?"

"Martinis," Frank said, "more or less. You have to use your imagination."

"Bring 'em on." Superman propped up on one elbow. "Where has she been hiding you?"

Frank did a little cha-cha with the shaker, ambling over to fetch a pair of coconut shells. "Nobody wants Frank to meet the new people, because Frank is just so very *unusual*. Do you think I'm unusual?"

"I would say so, yeah."

"Well then, bully for me," Frank said. "Welcome to paradise."

"Cheers." Superman lifted the shell to his nose. One whiff sent icy vapors way up in his head. The liquid was frigid and scalding hot—a straight blast of hooch, like the clear stuff you use to spike the punch at a prom. "Man, that's got a kick. What is it?"

"Trust me, it's better not to know." Frank settled on Catalina's cane-backed chair, propped his foot up to tug off his boot. "What I wouldn't give for a Tanqueray straight up with double olives."

"You're a friend of Emily's?"

Frank waved the boot in a gesture of dismissal. "She is my friend, and she is my Emily," he said. "After forty years the lines begin to blur. Let's say we endure each other. Although I think she's terribly uncivilized to keep you locked away up here by yourself, as if you're some sort of diseased creature." He tossed the boot in a corner, and pried the other one off with his toe. "You know what I think? They're afraid of you."

"Why would anyone be afraid of me?"

"You're very powerful. We don't get a lot of unexpected company. You come from *beyond*."

"Beyond where, Frank? Where the hell are we?"

"Oh no, Mr. Benjamin Willis, don't try to trick me." He waved a finger. "You know the rules. My lips are sealed. They'd kill me if I told you."

"But why?"

"If I answered the why, I would have to tell you the what," he said, "and that I cannot do."

Superman took a swing in the dark. "She's afraid I'll go back and tell people I saw Marilyn Monroe."

"You *saw* her?"

"On the beach, when I crashed. She told me I was cute."

"Well whatever you do, don't call her that name. She despises it. Her name is Daisy." He patted his platinum wig. "This was hers, you know. She wore this the day she married Arthur Miller."

"You know her?" said Superman.

"No, I snatched it off her head when she wasn't looking—of course I know her! She gave me this for my birthday. She's a sweetie, that one."

"I don't get it, Frank. Marilyn Monroe died, right? She OD'd on Seconal. They buried her in L.A."

"That's what I heard."

"Then what the hell is she doing here?"

"Taking some time off, I suppose. She really enjoys her life here."

"Aren't you a little bit curious? I mean, the woman is famously dead. Joe DiMaggio sends a dozen roses to her grave every day, and she's not even in it!"

"Suppose you decide to change lives," Frank said. "Step out of one life and into another. You can do it, you know. It's not easy. You have to be willing to give up everything."

"She faked her own death?" Superman remembered entertaining exactly that fantasy, the last time he flew his plane.

"If you spend any time here, Mr. Willis, you'll find that it doesn't pay to be too curious. This is a very small place. Why are *you* here?"

"It was an accident," Superman said. "I got lost."

"And now you're found," said Frank.

"What about you, Frank?"

Frank regarded him for a long moment. Then he snapped his fingers.

I gotta be meeee
I gotta be—meeeeee!

Superman had to laugh. Frank applauded with such enthusiasm that he spilled his martini down the front of his nightdress. "Oh, look what I've done..."

"Shut up and pour yourself another," said Superman. "And don't leave me out." He'd almost forgotten how much fun it was to get drunk. He held out his coconut shell.

Frank poured.

"That's a great-looking shaker. The Flying Boat, right? Do you mind?"

Frank handed it over. "You know your airplanes. I'm impressed."

"Where'd you get this?"

"On the Pan American Clipper," Frank said. "Aeons ago."

"You swiped it?"

"Actually, I worked for Pan Am."

"You were..."

"Not a stewardess, thank you. I was a navigator."

Superman doubled the pillow under his head. "For real? A navigator? Where did you fly?"

"The Pacific, mostly. San Francisco to Manila was five days back then—you had to do it in hops, Honolulu to Midway, Wake Island, and Guam. And we did a lot of scouting flights. The company was opening up all these new islands."

It was Superman's turn to be impressed. The famously intrepid crews of the Pan Am Pacific Clippers took up a whole chapter in *The History of*

American Aviation. He tried to imagine Frank, minus the wig, in the uniform of a Pan Am officer. "Man, you guys were the real pioneers. That must've been exciting."

"Sometimes a little too exciting. The ocean was big and those islands were terribly small." He took a long swallow. "At the time I didn't realize those were the good old days, but I suppose they were."

"When was that, the thirties? You didn't even have instruments, did you?"

"We had RDF, but the receivers were piss-poor. Mostly we did it the old way—stuck our heads out the hatch and took sun shots." He leaned back, absently tucking a stray curl behind his ear. "It wasn't till the war that they brought out the long-range direction finders, and I was out of it by then."

"You were this hotshot navigator, and you just chucked it all and came here?"

"Something like that."

"But why here?"

"It wasn't entirely my decision."

"Emily?"

"Señorita Emilia," he said.

Something clicked in Superman's head.

"Let's not talk about those days," Frank said. "I get nostalgic and then my mascara starts to run. . . ." He trailed off for a moment, but the sight of his cocktail perked him up. "It is nice to have someone new to talk to. The way some people act around here you'd think I was an old shriveled geranium."

"Nah, Frank, you're a cool guy. And you make a mean martini. Any more in there?"

Frank upended the shaker. Three drops. He sang softly: *The party's ooooover . . .*

"She's not going to let me go, is she, Frank."

Frank sighed. "It's not really her decision."

"Whose is it?"

"Ah-ah-ah," he said, wagging his finger.

"Because of what I saw," said Superman. "She wants to keep me here."

"You haven't really seen the place yet," Frank said. "You might like it and want to stay."

"That's what she said, but I'm leaving. And you'll help me, won't you, Frank?"

Frank bent to retrieve his boots. "I've got to go."

"Just tell me one thing."

Frank straightened. "Please—"

"Give me a straight answer. Don't lie. I'll know if you lie."

Frank lifted the wig, ran his fingers through his sweaty crew cut. "One thing."

"What *is* this place?"

"I told you, Mr. Willis. This is paradise. Heaven on Earth. Shangri-La. You've found it. You're here. You can be one of the chosen."

"Chosen for what?"

"Think of a very exclusive club. Invitation only. If you're invited, you get a nice place to live, all expenses paid, and you get to disappear completely."

"How do you get invited?"

"That's a bit of a mystery."

"Are they all famous, like . . . Daisy?"

"Nobody's famous like Daisy. Some of us are a bit notorious . . . however you want to put it. People who needed a place to get away."

"Who else is here?"

"No, I really must be going. I can't believe I've allowed you to ply me for information with my own moonshine. I may never forgive you." He stuffed the hem of his nightdress into his boots.

"Tomorrow night, same time?" Superman said. "I'll see if I can get hold of some olives."

Frank shrugged. "I might have another engagement."

"Well, you know I'm not going anywhere."

Frank put his finger to his lips—as if he hadn't made all the noise of a Broadway chorus on his way up here—and hastened off into the night.

Superman lay awake, adding two plus two as many times as it took to see that the only possible answer was four.

6 / *Your Secret Is Safe with Me*

EMILY CAME UP from the Big House for the unveiling. Pito decreed that Superman's body now had the correct number of parts. He squatted with hammer and chisel to begin chipping at the block.

"I had a visitor last night," Superman said.

Emily didn't blink. "I thought I heard Frank rambling around. I hope he didn't bore you with all his nonsense. He's quite mad, you know. Even when he's sober, which is hardly ever these days."

"Seemed fairly sane to me," said Superman. "Other than his outfit."

"Was he wearing the pink bathrobe?"

"It was yellow."

"The pink suits him better," she said firmly. "Did he tell you about the club of the famously disappeared, all that business?"

"Matter of fact, he did."

"He loves to try that one on new people. If he'd ever lay off the sauce, I think Frank could be a successful writer of fairy tales. As it is, he's just an old bore in a wig."

"Yeah, he told me where he got the wig."

Pito struck confident blows with his hammer, detaching the saddle of concrete from the pedestal. Every swing sent a tremor through Superman's bones.

Emily said, "I wish we were as interesting as Frank makes us sound. This is a kind of retirement community. People who like to be left alone. That's all."

"Lady, why don't you trust me?"

Her white lashes flickered. "Who says I don't?"

"You've been lying to me since I woke up."

"I'm trying to help you," she said. "I'm trying to get you well and out of here. That may be risky, and I don't want to mess it up. This is not like other places. You can't just drop in and drop out."

"Why not?"

"There's a powerful force on this island. If word gets out that you survived that crash, you won't leave. It's that simple."

"What the hell are you talking about?"

"We're guests here. We're given everything we need. We're asked for nothing in return, except that we stay here and keep our secrets. The only way to guarantee total privacy is to make sure no one leaves. Do you understand?"

"No."

"Now be honest with me. If that *was* someone famous you saw on the beach, wouldn't you go home and tell the world about it?"

"Sure. And they'd think I was out of my mind."

She smiled. "But you're famous yourself. We're not totally isolated, you know; we get the occasional newspaper. I've managed to read up on you. You're quite the celebrity. Don't you think people would listen to you?"

"Maybe," he said. "Maybe I wouldn't tell."

She sat up in the chair. "What would it take for that to happen? For you to go home and keep it to yourself, what you've seen here?"

"Wait a minute. First you try to make me think I'm seeing things. Now you want to pay me off to keep my mouth shut?"

"It's too late for that," she said. "You know too much and I'm afraid you're not reliable."

Pito struck the blow that cleaved the saddle. The pedestal collapsed, dumping Superman on the floor. Pain shrilled up his spine like a wild trumpet solo. Fireflies danced in his eyes.

He gulped air until the darkness retreated. "Yow." Pito dug through the debris. Superman batted him away. "Ooh ow—careful, man—wait, let me do it."

"*Espérate!*" Emily commanded. "Oh no, did we break you again?"

Superman shifted his weight off a chunk that was poking him in a very personal way. "No, I—whoo there, that's better."

"I knew it was too soon." She turned her wheelchair away.

Superman saw distress in the old Indian's eyes. "Hey, Pito, it's okay. Really. I'm fine. Get me back on the bed." Bracing his feet on the floor, he slowly straightened his body, lifting his hips from the mound of rubble.

His middle third was brown, shriveled, peeling, but he was intact: hipbones, pubic hair grizzled as an old Brillo pad, his private parts a glossy, embarrassed red-purple. He blew out a sigh of relief. He wouldn't win any naked-man beauty contest, but he was all there.

Pito eased him up to the cot. Superman wriggled back, dragging his hind end across that scratchy canvas, and that was just about the finest sensation he had ever felt. There's something to be said for an injury that puts you down on your back, he thought. Like listening to Jimi Hendrix, it forces you to take a new perspective. Not long ago he was standing in front of thousands of cheering people, and it didn't do a thing for him. Today, just wiggling his butt on the canvas made him entirely happy.

He pulled on the shorts Pito brought. Emily edged her chair into the doorway. "How'd we do?"

"Man, it hurt like a motherf—it hurt bad for a minute. Not so bad now. I guess I can try to stand up."

"Just sit first. Pito, *levántalo*."

Pito took hold of his wrists, and raised him to the edge of the cot.

His body felt different where it had been broken. His pelvis had fused into one piece, but now he sat in the saddle at a slightly different angle.

"How are your legs, Ben? Do you think you could operate rudder pedals, that kind of thing?"

"Let's see." He gripped the table with both hands. "Tell him to pick me up."

She translated. Pito latched on with strong hands, and stood him on his feet.

Superman tottered and weaved, grabbed the old man's shoulders for balance. He shuffled his legs apart, rocking in place, struggling to stay upright. "All right," he cheered, "looking good . . ."

Bobbing sideways, he caught himself on the side of the cot, slowly straightened until he was standing on his own. His legs felt like stilts on the rolling deck of a boat.

"Careful," Emily warned.

He waved Pito away. It should be the easiest thing in the world just to put that old left foot out there and walk. He considered it. He stuck his thumb between his teeth. With a great rush of emotion he felt like a little boy again: a wobbly unbalanced thing in danger of diving face first to the floor.

He slid his foot out a few inches, shifted his weight, and swung his other foot forward. The balance was off. His left leg folded up like an ironing board. He toppled back to the cot. For a long minute, no one spoke.

"I have another wheelchair," said Emily.

"No. Thanks. I can do it." He shook his head. "Maybe if I had a cane or something to get started." He sank back on his pillow, fighting a wave of disappointment. "Guess I won't be running down to the beach this afternoon."

She rolled to the door. "Give it time. There's a hot spring below the house. I'll bet a nice long soak would do you good."

Pito summoned four of the younger yardmen. Shirtless, brown, giggling, they lifted Superman's cot and bore him out into the blinding sunlight. They wound down zigzagging paths, through flowering vines, to a grassy clearing. Emily's chair squeaked along behind.

Smooth black rocks surrounded an aperture in the earth, a pool of bubbling water as clear and dark as the pupil of an eye. Tendrils of steam trailed up from the surface. The water simmered and stirred. Huge ferns nodded among the rocks, and spiky blue flowers stuck out their tongues. Up in the canopy the Louie-Louie bird sang its four bars. This place felt enchanted.

The boys placed the cot beside the spring, and disappeared.

Emily kicked off her dragon slippers, grasped her trouser cuffs, placed her feet in the water.

Superman slid in with a groan of pure pleasure. God is great, God is good, let us thank him for this hot water. It was almost worth all that time in the cast to feel this splendid upwelling of heat and relief. He settled on a shelf of polished rock, waving his knees to bring the current into every tight place. "Frank said this was paradise. I see what he meant."

"Lovely, hmm?" She rested her fingers on her eyelids.

He stirred the bubbles with his hands. "You haven't aged very much from your pictures."

She opened her eyes. "Sorry?"

"We don't have to play these games anymore," he said. "I know who you are. I have figured you out."

"Oh, Lord." Her smile was unreadable. "What did Frank tell you?"

"He didn't tell me. You gave yourself away. Only a pilot would criticize another pilot's crash landing."

She held on to the smile. A red flush spread up from her throat. "I did a good bit of flying when I was younger."

"I know." He kept his voice even. "You told me. You learned not to land in the lee of a wave."

"That was not a very nice thing to say. I apologize."

"No, ma'am. If I'd realized who you were, I'd have paid more attention. You had some fairly famous crack-ups yourself."

"What are you getting at?"

He raised his toes to the surface. "I'm on to you. Amelia."

Her look of puzzlement was very realistic. "Amelia?"

"Señorita Emilia. The last time anybody heard from you, you were flying, where? To Howland Island, I think. Only you never got there."

For a long moment the only sound was the hiss of bubbles breaking the surface.

Superman said, "I would sure love to know how you got *here.*"

"Did Frank tell you this?" she said. "Because Frank suffers from delusions."

"He doesn't look at all like his pictures," said Superman. "He's aged more than you, hasn't he? Frank Napier. He was famous, too. A famous drunk, right? There must have been a lot of jokes about him. The navigator who couldn't fly straight."

"I've read a lot about the last Earhart flight," she said. "I knew Amelia. We flew against each other in the very first Powder Puff derby, Reno to Chicago, 1929. There were eleven of us in that race. We all crashed at least once. In those days you cracked up all the time. I came in sixth. Amelia cheated and came in third. She was a very ambitious young lady. I don't think that Howland flight was Frank Napier's fault. I think he probably had her on course and she ignored him and got herself lost."

This was all very smooth and elaborate, but Superman was not fooled. He'd been putting this puzzle together since Frank laid the last pieces into his lap. The truth had grown larger and more incredible the longer he pondered.

In retrospect, the resemblance was unmistakable. And her unrattled response was just what you would expect from an old publicity maven like Amelia Earhart.

"Do you have any books about her?" he said. "It's been a while since I read anything."

"I'll look around. For now I have wrinkled my feet. I'll let you stay and soak." She called Pito.

"Don't worry," said Superman. "Your secret is safe with me."

She reached down for her slippers. "I wonder," she said, as the old man wheeled her away.

7 / *Electra*

FRANK CAME UP to the shack with a jug of red wine. No martinis tonight, no show tunes. He wore white pajamas and a pink satin bathrobe with fluffy trim. Amelia was right; the pink suited him better.

"Nice surprise, Frank. I thought you had another engagement."

"I managed to get out of it." Frank held up the jug. "Cojones de Toro. Straight from the balls of the bull."

"Is it good?"

"It will take paint off a car," he said. "Wine makers to the world, don't you know, the Guatemalans. It's awful. You want some?"

"You bet." Superman held out his coconut shell. He was thrilled to be sitting upright in a chair. He'd pushed back the wall to let in the night sounds. Catalina had brought brown cotton shorts and a clean white T-shirt; he'd dressed himself and was sitting like any other man in a chair.

With the help of the knob-headed stick Pito gave him, he was learning to walk again. His gait was peculiar, a kind of sidesaddle leg-slinging maneuver like some old galoot in a Western, but the walking stick balanced things nicely. He barely noticed the pain in his hip. In a few days he would toss away the stick and stroll out of here on his own.

The wine was not all that bad. Superman raised his shell. "Hey, cheers, thanks for sharing."

"Here's to your liberation from the evil toadstool," Frank said.

"I never knew sitting up could be so much fun. I got to scratch my butt today and it was incredible."

Frank smiled. "It's the simple pleasures that make life worthwhile."

Superman said, "Did you talk to Amelia?"

Frank got a rabbit-in-the-headlights look. You could see his eyes darting around in search of the right answer.

"It's okay, Frank, we're all out in the open now. I know who she is, and I know who you are. I figured it out. I'm surprised she didn't tell you."

"She's not speaking to me today." Frank sipped his wine. "She's furious, and now I know why. I suppose I spilled the frijoles."

"It's not your fault. I think I knew it already."

"Of course it's my fault," Frank said. "Everything in the last forty years has been my fault."

"I wanted to ask you about that. How you came here. I figured she wouldn't tell me, but you will, won't you, Frank ol' buddy ol' pal."

"Oh, you won't hear the truth from me," Frank said. "There's only one official version of the truth, and that's hers."

Superman glanced at the jug. As long as there was wine, he thought he could keep Frank talking. Frank wasn't a stumbling, obnoxious kind of drunk; he was the long-as-you're-pouring-I'm-drinking kind, who keeps just enough wits about him to get himself home. You could read all about it in the map of blood vessels on his face.

"Let me guess," Superman said. "You were trying to get to Howland Island, and you got lost."

"We were never more than ten miles off course," Frank said. "When we reached the position line, I told her to turn south. She turned north. She said I was a good-for-nothing drunk and I'd gotten us lost. Understand, Mr. Willis—New Guinea to Howland was nineteen hours nonstop, and I had the worst hangover in recorded history. But my course was accurate. She ignored my advice."

"I believe you, Frank." Far be it from Superman to criticize anyone for flying in an altered condition. "What happened?"

"We flew on fumes for a while. She spotted a coral atoll with the sweetest little shallow lagoon in the middle. Oh, we got excited. You could hear the engines coughing, you know, the last *hint* of fuel. She lined it up and— Mr. Willis, there were people who said Amelia was not such a good pilot, but you never saw such a beautiful landing. She parked it in six inches of water. Barely got our feet wet getting out."

Superman realized afresh that he had cracked up his plane in front of the most famous aviatrix in history. He winced: *Whoever taught you to land in the lee of a wave?*

"We sat there a couple days. Finally late afternoon of the second day, we saw a boat and sent up a flare. It was on top of us before we realized it was full of Japanese. This atoll was part of their outer defense for some secret submarine base."

"They weren't happy to see you."

"They thought we were spies. They found a radio transmitter on the island and claimed it was ours."

"Yeah, that was one of the theories, didn't I read that? You were on some kind of spy mission and got captured."

"Amelia chooses to read those books. I don't. She loves them, and why not? She's always the heroine, the poor doomed pilot, and I'm the navigator who got her lost. It's just too depressing."

Superman topped off the wine in Frank's cup. "I got nothing but admiration for you, Frank. It took big guts to fly over all that water in those days."

"What it took was a kind of stupidity people don't have anymore," said Frank. "Except those poor boys they keep sending to the moon. Now tell me, why would anyone want to go to the moon? You can see it from here. Does that look like a nice place to you?"

Superman raised his eyes. The moon looked cold, blue, and very far away. "I guess for the same reason you were trying to fly around the world. To say that you did."

"I did it for the money, myself," Frank said. "And besides, we were going to end up in Oakland. In those days Oakland was lots nicer than the moon."

"But you never got there."

"They took us to Saipan. We had a nice little house. The guards stayed outside. We lived there a year—we gained weight there, they brought us books. . . . Then our colonel got shipped out to Okinawa, and they took us to Tokyo. They asked us a lot of questions."

"Like what?"

Frank stared at his polished nails. "They said they were starting air service into some of the islands. They needed details about approaches and such."

"And you knew that stuff?"

"Oh, sure. I'd seen a lot, you know, flying for Pan Am. I did what they told me. I didn't want to get hurt."

"I don't think that's a crime, Frank. You were a prisoner."

"Oh, you bet it's a crime—aiding and abetting the enemy in wartime? That's high treason, Mr. Willis. They execute people for that."

"But how did you help them?"

"I corrected their charts. The approaches to Lae and Guam and Wake Island, and . . . Honolulu. Pearl Harbor. Later I taught English to officers who interrogated American prisoners. I taught them how to torture our boys." His voice was hollow, and old. "I was a good teacher, too. My students liked me. I had my own room at the Ginsha Hotel. I took a trolley to work."

You had to admire the man's honesty, but this story was making Superman queasy. He took a swallow of wine. "Amelia worked for them too?"

"As far as I know they left her alone. She really didn't know anything that could help them. She read books and stayed in her room."

"Frank, if the Japanese had hold of somebody that famous, why wouldn't they tell the whole world about it?"

"They would've had to admit they captured us. In peacetime, in direct violation of the Geneva Convention. For years they'd been denying it. They couldn't lose face by admitting the lie."

"Wow."

"When the bombing got bad they moved us out of Tokyo, to this place in the mountains. Beautiful place, all these lovely fragrant pine trees. . . . We thought they'd taken us there to kill us. But they gave us back the plane and let us go."

Out in the jungle, a bird cried *doop! doop!* Superman shivered: a chill. "Just like that," he said. "Thanks and goodbye."

"Just like that," said Frank. "You said you wanted to hear this."

"Sure, I—"

"You weren't there. You don't know what it was like. Pour me some more."

Superman obeyed. For what possible reason would you tell such a story on yourself if it wasn't true? On the other hand, if it *was* true, if you *were* a traitor who'd gotten away with treason, why tell a stranger about it? Why not carry that story straight on with you to the grave?

Frank seemed to read his mind. "I don't expect you to *approve*, Mr. Willis. But I thought you might try to *understand*. If we hadn't cooperated, they'd have killed us. They wouldn't put us with other Americans—we were too famous, they couldn't take the chance. They let us go because it was too much trouble to keep us, and they knew we would never tell, after what we'd done for them." Frank clutched his knees. "I should go. I drink too much when I talk."

"Wait, Frank. Tell me the rest."

"That's all. We did our bit for the Emperor. They gave us back our plane. We couldn't go home—at home we were dead people. We'd been dead for eight years." He spread his hands. "Somehow she found out about this place. We ended up here. And here is where we still are."

"Why can't she walk?"

"It was one morning, maybe a year after we came . . . she just couldn't get out of bed. I don't know, I think they'd hurt her some way. We never really discussed it."

"That's a hell of a story." Superman shook his head. "The thing is, I don't know whether to believe a word of it."

Frank seemed to mull that as he pulled on his boots. "Can you walk?"

"Sure, but—"

"Not far. Follow me." He cinched his robe and set off down the ramp.

Superman struggled to his feet, grabbed his walking stick. Frank was halfway down to the spring by the time he reached the porch. "Frank, wait up. I'm not all that quick on my feet."

Frank waited at a fork in the path, playing the beam of his flashlight on a little hill. "Just through here."

Superman snagged his stick in a tree root, stumbled, caught himself. A night hike in the jungle? Why not? Swell idea. The light beam skittered away. He followed Frank through a wooden gate in the wall, shambling, swinging his leg.

Frank flashed the light down a path tunneled into a hibiscus hedge. At the end of the tunnel was a door, painted black.

The hinges groaned as if they hadn't swung open in a thousand years.

Frank's boots echoed off the floor. Superman followed him in.

The lights came on.

This was a cave, enlarged into a large subterranean room. Human hands had scooped out the earth, poured a concrete floor, hung industrial lights and a steel roll-up door on the opposite wall. There was no question why they had gone to all this trouble: the cave was exactly big enough to hold the shining silvery streamlined twin-engine Lockheed Electra that sat glowing under the lights.

The plane had lines and curves like a song, like a woman, like the most beautiful locomotive that ever flew down a track. A glossy stainless-steel nose projected forward. The engines were great bulbous breasts with propellers, tapering back to slender points behind the wings. The sleek line of the fuselage was broken by a small rectangular window on the flank and a lollipop antenna mounted just above the cockpit. The plane leaned forward, as if longing to race down a runway and fly.

Superman's walking stick clacked on the floor. He inspected the Lockheed star-and-wing logo on the twin tail fins, the block letters NR16020.

He placed his hand flat against the fuselage, midway down the cool flank. He ran his fingers over the wing's trailing edge, peering up into the cockpit at the old-fashioned instruments gleaming like a museum display. Mounted above the panel was a squarish black box that looked familiar.

He moved closer. That was his very own Haynes Magellan F-45 Electronic-Gyroscopic Compass, the latest thing in aviation technology.

They were getting this plane ready to fly.

8 / Welcome to the Boat of the Music

FRANK LOCKED THE DOOR. "I'm dry. Should we go for a drink?"

"Sure. Where?" He followed the bouncing flashlight beam.

"There's only one place."

"I can't walk very far."

"We're not going to walk." Frank climbed into a battered army-green jeep beside the roll-up door.

Superman paused a moment to wonder why anyone would build a hangar into the side of a mountain. You could roll that Electra out the door, but once you got it out on this flat patch, what could you do with it? You couldn't take off. The jungle loomed all around. The mountain fell away sharply toward the sea.

Come to think of it, how the hell would you haul a plane up here in the first place?

Frank started the jeep with a sputter that grew to an unmuffled roar. Superman boosted himself up to the passenger seat. Frank rummaged on the floorboard for a clear plastic bag, into which he tucked his wig. "Watch out for low-hanging branches," he said, running one hand through his silvery crew cut. "It's not really much of a road."

"Sure you're okay to drive, Frank? We drank that whole jug of wine."

"Relax, I'm one of the world's great drunk drivers." The headlights showed a solid wall of jungle ahead. Frank put the jeep in gear and drove straight for the green wall, slammed into it and through it, lurching bumping plunging down the mountainside.

Superman grabbed the roll bar and hung on.

Somehow Frank missed all the trees big enough to stop a jeep. The smaller ones he mowed down and kept going. He never shifted out of second. The road existed purely in his imagination. They jounced through a creek bed through a tangle of vines down a ditch over a fallen log, and across the face of a cliff.

Frank began to sing "I Whistle a Happy Tune."

Superman ducked branches and braced himself for the sound of an axle breaking. He glimpsed the fleeting shadow of a road—then it was gone, and they plunged down again, crashing through thick underbrush. Terrified birds darted in front of the headlights.

A vine snaked around Superman's neck, half dragging him from the jeep. "Jesus, Frank! Slow down!"

Frank just kept singing, and driving. They went down and down, fish-tailing sideways, bounding out onto a road—not much of a road, to be sure, nothing more than a widened-out track, but at least there were no trees in it. Frank shifted up and took off. The road doubled around and switched back and wound down in dizzying S-curves and loops.

Superman shouted into the rush of air: "How did you ever get the plane up that hill?"

"I had nothing to do with it," Frank said. "Hang on!"

The road split abruptly. The jeep slung off to the right, spraying rocks, roaring down off the mountain to a low place where the jungle spread out. The lights of little houses winked through the trees.

Superman picked a bug from his teeth. It felt good to be out of the cast, out of the shack and going somewhere.

The dirt road spread out and turned to sand. Frank downshifted. Suddenly they were out on a wide beach under a shiny moon.

The great ocean glistened and shifted, spreading the moonlight for miles. The beach sloped a quarter mile from the dark mass of the jungle to the sea. If the tide had been this low when Superman flew over this beach, he could have landed on it, even without wheels.

He sat back to take in the vast curve of sand, the luminous lines of surf. At the far end of the beach, a sprinkling of lights in the trees: civilization.

The jeep sent up a great roostertail of spray. Anyone out for a stroll on the beach would have been drenched or run over.

Superman's hair whipped at his skull. All at once there were people popping up in the headlights, leaping out of the way. Frank swerved up from the water, heading straight for a grove of coconut palms that looked plenty strong enough to stop a jeep.

Somehow he slipped between two of them, slid to a halt, popped the clutch. The tires went *herk!*

Frank reached under the seat for his wig. "Lafayette, we are here!"

Superman brushed leaves from his hair. "Man, you oughta sell tickets for that."

From beyond the coconut grove came the thump of loud music, a bumptious salsa rhythm, with trumpets.

> *Da duddleeda BUM—ba BUM—ba BUM*
> *Da duddleeda BUM—ba BUM—ba BUM*

Frank tugged on the wig, regarding himself in the rearview mirror. "Now how do you suppose it got windblown inside a plastic bag?"

"Frank, what is this place?"

"La Restaurante Discoteca Amor Y Mar Y Sol Y Blues," he said, "which means 'Love and Sea and Sun and Blues,' in that order." He applied a smear of lipstick to his lower lip, smooched his lips together. "How do I look?"

"Words don't exist to describe you," said Superman.

"Why, thank you. I do feel rather pretty tonight."

Superman clambered out with his walking stick. The ride had left him feeling wobbly, but the sounds of a party washed over him, reviving him. Ahead he saw twinkly lights strung through the trees, people sitting at tables, dancing, milling around.

La Restaurante Discoteca Amor Y Mar Y Sol Y Blues was a collection of flat-roofed shanties sprawled at the top of the beach: a walk-up bar, plywood booths, soda tables scattered under trees, a dance floor with a mirror-ball twirling, and salsa music blaring from four cabinet speakers:

> *Da duddleeda BUM—ba BUM—ba BUM*
> *Da duddleeda BUM—ba BUM—ba BUM*

Superman had imagined that he was alone on the island with Amelia and Frank, Marilyn Monroe, Pito and Catalina, a handful of servants. He'd never dreamed of all these people living here, dancing, laughing, drinking beer, eating barbecued chicken, lounging in corners, strolling out to the beach. Among the copper-colored faces was a scattering of gringos with permanent tans, a table full of them near the barbecue pit: an ancient lady in a long white dress, a hoody-looking man in black Ray Bans, a tweedy Ivy League sort, and two guys, obviously brothers, whose faces looked vaguely familiar.

All the dancers were sweating, and so were the people drinking, and the bottles of beer in their hands. Children scampered among the tables, chasing ugly little dogs. Nailed to a tree was a hand-painted sign:

WELCOME TO THE BOAT OF THE MUSIC
(WAS HAPPY AND DIVERSION)

"Which will it be," Frank said, "happy or diversion?"

"Look at all these people!" said Superman.

"Huddled masses yearning to breathe free," said Frank. "The natives are friendly. Just wade in if you'd like, or I can introduce you around."

"Will *she* come here?"

"Daisy? I doubt it, she's not very social," said Frank, "but you never know who you'll meet here. I am perishing. What will you have?"

"They have rum and Coke? Let me get it."

"Tell them '*la cuenta de* Frank.' I'll have a *cerveza*. Can you manage?"

Superman headed for the bar. He knew Frank and Amelia were toying with him, feeding him just enough information to intrigue him into staying, for whatever reason. He would not resist in an obvious way. His plan was to find a way to get around them, and home. Maybe one of these people could help.

"Step up, step up brother, come and be saved!" cried a man with a luminous green feather stuck crosswise in his ponytail. "All who enter here shall be saved!"

"Amen, brother," said Superman.

"And amen to you, too," the man said. "I can smell the sin rising off you like a cheap aftershave. What is your name, son?"

"Ben Willis. Who're you?"

"They all call me Rabbit. Whatcha drinking, Ben Willis?"

"Nothing yet. I'm on my way to—"

"Not so fast there! Don't try and slide past old Rabbit when he's in the process of making your acquaintance! Does it make you uncomfortable when I speak of the Lord, son, is that it? Maybe you'd like to tell me why." He was a big man, red-faced, with a glowing golden beard and a ham-sized hand that he laid across Superman's shoulder to steer him away from the bar. "What did you do, beat your wife? Kick the dog? Steal the cash from the till? Whatever it is, the Lord can make it right. All you have to do is believe!"

"I believe I will get me a drink," Superman said.

Rabbit wore Big Smith overalls with no shirt, the better to show off the curly gold fur on his chest. He hemmed Superman against a table, downwind of the barbecue pit. "Don't look to Satan to do the Lord's work," he boomed. "Don't sail east when you want to go west. You're new in these parts, friend—have you appointed anyone as your personal spiritual adviser?"

"No . . ."

"Well, allow me to appoint myself, then. Do you mind? A man might find himself in need of spiritual advice."

Superman had a feeling this conversation was not really about the Lord. "I'm always open to advice," he said.

"In that case," said Rabbit, "I advise you to close your eyes, and open your hand."

Superman did as he was told. He felt fingertips grazing his palm.

"Now, open . . ."

A shiny white pill, with a red dot on one side and the number 9 on the other.

"What is it?"

"It's the way to go west. It's five hundred thirty-five micrograins of sheer happiness, suspended in an inert sugar base. Red Dot Number Nine. Are you game?"

Superman smiled. "I don't know. . . ."

"Aw come on, son—be good to me here. Don't tell me you're the one rock star in the history of the world who doesn't engage in chemical recreation."

"You know who I am?"

"Everybody knows Superman Willis. You're famous, my friend, even here. Go ahead, take it," he said, with a nod at the pill. "It's good for you."

"I'll save it for later." Superman tucked it in the pocket of his T-shirt. "I had my heart set on a rum and Coke. Can I get you something?"

"I have everything I need," said Rabbit, "and so do you. March on, if you must. When you're ready, just step through the door. I will meet you on the other side."

Superman smiled, edging around him. The last time someone handed him something and said, "Go ahead, take it," he'd ended up in his bed clinging to the wall for nineteen hours, because the wall was the only thing he knew for sure was real.

At the bar six native men were dispensing drinks through the windows, racing each other to the coolers, calling orders to the burly mustachioed woman at the cash register. Pushing in beside a tall guy in a long-sleeved tropical shirt, Superman raised a finger. Bartenders whizzed past. He drummed fingers on the sticky bar and inspected the gallery behind the cash register: framed portraits of Albert Einstein, Mao Tse-tung, and an old stiff-necked hombre who was probably the granddaddy of the man who owned this place. Built into the ceiling was a realistic full-scale mock-up of an airplane, painted Pepto-Bismol pink, spilling plastic oranges and pineapples from its cockpit. Hand-lettered signs dangled from the propeller, including one in English: WE'LL BE WITH YOU IN A FEW SHORT HOURS.

Superman was tipsy already, and wondering how to go about getting all the way drunk. It felt great to be up on his feet in the world. He glanced down the bar to see what the guy next to him was drinking, and saw the hand.

Not hand. Claw. Shriveled, finger-shaped nubs curled around a beer bottle.

The guy turned toward him.

Superman couldn't help flinching.

He had seen burn victims but never one this bad. No telling how old the guy was, or what he had looked like before his face was burned. Whatever fiery situation he had managed to get himself into, he had not gotten out in time. He was a monster in a red-and-white stocking cap. His eyes were pink and hairless, the size and shape of almonds. His nose was a nub with two holes. He had no lips.

"Heff-ay!" he called in a strong, youthful voice, pounding his bottle on the bar. He caught Superman staring. "Bet you never saw anything as scary as me, huh."

Jesus, it speaks! And in English! "Sure," he said, "plenty of times."

"Where? Tell me where. *The Blob* doesn't count; it's a movie."

Superman stammered for an answer.

The corners of the mouth bent upward: a smile. "It's okay, I'm not gonna bite."

Superman put out his hand. "Hi, I'm Ben."

The skinless hand closed around his. There was strength in that grip. "Spike. You're new in town, right? Wait, are you—Ben? You're not the guy who crashed the plane?"

"That's me. I guess I'm famous around here."

"Not just here, man—you're Superman Willis!"

Ben nodded.

"Unbelievably far fucking out!" Spike showed a row of perfect white teeth. "I'm a huge fan, man, I've got three of your albums! I heard them all talking about you, and I said, 'Hey you guys, don't you know who that is? That's only Superman *Willis!*'"

"Good to meet you, Spike."

"Jeez, I'm glad I said hello," said Spike. "You don't look at all like your album covers. Maybe it's the beard."

Superman stroked his stubble. It must have turned into a beard while he wasn't looking. "I'll take that as a compliment."

"Oh sure, man, you're the greatest. 'Superman's Revenge' is one of the truly great songs. When are you gonna play for us?"

"Let me buy you a beer," Superman said, "if you can get their attention."

Spike lifted his finger. Three barmen sprinted over. "I'm kinda bloated on beer," he said. "Let's have cucarachas. Put some life in this party."

The only cucaracha Superman knew was the cockroach in the song, but he was up for anything that might help him past this awkward moment. The sight of the kid's face spooked him in a serious way—so cheerful, so amiable. Not at all the way Superman would feel if that were *his* face.

Spike placed his order in rapid Spanish. Superman chimed in to get a beer for Frank.

"Cucaracha," the barkeep said, waggling his eyebrows like Groucho Marx.

Spike waggled the place where his eyebrows had been. "Cucaracha, *pura vida!*"

A cucaracha, as it turned out, was a dark black liquid that looked like motor oil. Superman took a whiff. "What is it?"

"Tequila, vodka, Café Rica, and a splash of gasoline, I think. The pre-ferred after-dinner drink of burn victims worldwide."

The bartender struck two matches at once and held the flames under the bowls of the glasses, rotating the snifters with his fingers to warm the liquid.

"Get ready," said Spike, "you gotta suck it all down before your straw catches fire."

The man handed them each a paper straw, and dipped a match in each snifter. A wondrous blue flame leaped up, deep blue, hypnotically licking the surface of the liquor.

Spike cried "Go!," stuck his straw in the flame, and bent over the glass, sucking up the burning fluid. Fire glowed in his eyes.

Superman followed suit. A jolt of heat sprayed his throat—the flame raced up the straw and flickered around in his mouth. He slurked the straw around the bottom of the glass. The flame danced in the bowl, and died. The liquor went *poof!* in his head.

"Yowsuh!" Spike slammed his hand on the bar.

The bartender said something.

Spike translated: "He wants two-fifty."

"Oh. Right. Put it on Frank's *culo.*"

The barman smirked.

"You told him to put it on Frank's ass," Spike said. "I think you mean his tab. *La cuenta de Frank.*"

The barman nodded and went away.

"Unbelievable," Spike said.

"What, my Spanish?" The fire in his mouth had left Superman breathless. He tossed cold beer in there to put it out.

"No, man—me, sittin' here drinking with goddamn Superman! What are you doing here?"

"Kind of an accidental vacation." He braced his hip against the bar. "I sure wish you'd tell me where we are, Spike. I haven't got a clue."

"Naw, you know we're not supposed to do that. We gotta keep you pure, so you can split if you want."

Superman shrugged. "That old lady does get around."

"You're lucky. She's trying to get you out of here. Some people would give anything to get out."

"What do you mean? Everybody keeps telling me this place is paradise."

"That's fine until you're ready to leave," Spike said. "Don't ask too many questions. Maybe he'll let you." His eyes shone, unblinking.

"What do you mean, 'he'?"

"Nobody sees him. Nobody knows who he is. Being invisible gives him power."

"He won't let you leave?"

"It's a life sentence. We knew that when we came here."

"But how does he keep you here? Why not just leave, if you want?"

"He moves in mysterious ways." Spike dropped his voice. "Does Emily know you're down here? I thought you were supposed to be this big secret. She told everybody you died."

"Frank brought me."

"Watch out for Frank. Come to think of it, watch out for *everybody*."

"How old are you, Spike?"

"Free, white, and twenty-two. When I had hair, it was red."

"You mind talking about it?"

"What, my hair? Nothing to tell. It burned up."

"Yeah, but—"

"My mom tried to barbecue me when I was asleep. She poured lighter fluid on my mattress. Put the can down and struck a match. It blew up. Killed her, but it didn't kill me." The corners of his mouth went up.

"Jesus. Why—why'd she do it?"

"She didn't say." Spike's eyes glittered. "Mom was pretty weird."

"How old were you?"

"Twelve."

Superman shook his head. "How long you been here?"

"I did two years in the hospital and four in rehab. Then I got the invite from the Magician . . . I guess it's been more than three years ago now."

"The Magician?"

"Letter showed up at the rehab. 'You don't know me, but I know you.' He'd read about me in the papers. Offered me an all-expense-paid vacation to a warm place with a nice beach."

"And you just . . . came?"

"Hell yes, wouldn't you? One-way ticket, first-class? I was ready to go anywhere I could be a stranger. All the people I knew from before—man, after I got toasted, they changed. They couldn't look at me without making these sad old cow faces, like you did a minute ago."

"Sorry . . ."

"Don't worry, I'm kind of outspoken. They're used to me here. Everybody's so weird anyway, I blend right in. I'm not one of the famous ones, you know—he brings in an oddball from time to time, just to keep things interesting. I guess Frank's told you about the rest of 'em. Did you meet the Princess?" He nodded toward the gringo table, the antique figurine in the flowing white dress. She hadn't moved since Superman spotted her. She sat watching the dancers with her head cocked to one side, a little smile on her face, silver hair swirling up into her hat. "Princess Annie," said Spike. "Anastasia. Her old man was the last king of Russia. You've got to admit that is pretty far out."

"Oh come on, Spike, she can't—a lot of people claimed to be Anastasia.

They shot that whole family in a basement; I read a book about it. They threw the bodies down a well."

"Go ask her, she'll tell you. She got the hell out of there. Some Gypsies hid her and kept her alive. She's been on the run her whole life. The guy next to her is Danny Cooper. In the Ray Bans. Ever hear of D. B. Cooper?"

"The name rings a bell. . . ."

"Hijacked a jet, got two hundred thousand in ransom, and parachuted out of the plane."

"Yeah, now I remember. He got away clean, didn't he?"

"Not exactly. The money was marked, and he broke his back in the jump. He and the Princess play backgammon, she beats him two out of three. The guy in the glasses is Mike Rockefeller. He freaked out on jungle hallucinogens and ran away from a fortune, can you imagine?"

Another cucaracha went by while Spike pointed out the former King of Siam, a deposed president of Uruguay, the elderly mistress of Nikita Khrushchev, and the two men Superman had half recognized—the Sherman Brothers, American stand-up comics of the sixties whose career famously crashed and burned when one of them uttered an unforgivable obscenity on live TV.

"You hungry?" said Spike. "You gotta meet the guy that cooks the chicken."

The fragrant blue curtain of smoke at the barbecue pit parted to reveal a squat, barrel-chested man wielding tongs. Flames leaped among the sizzling chickens. He was sweating and turning the birds, sloshing liquid from a metal pan when the fire jumped too high. He had a red, veiny nose and a face that had been punched a few times. "Hey hey, Spike!" he bellowed. "Where the hella you been? I had three bottles of great vino from Santiago, man, we drank it all widoutcha."

"Hey, Jimmy, how's the chicken tonight?"

"You want it any fresher, gotta pluck it yourself." A nod for Superman. "How you doin', pal."

"Good," he said. "Chicken smells good."

"Come on over here, Spike, let me finish cookin' ya," Jimmy said. "I don't think they let you get done on both sides."

"Yeah yeah, ha ha—Jimmy, this is Superman Willis. He's a big star back home. I've got three of his records."

"Oh yeah? A singa?" A brawny rough-knuckled hand came over the counter. Superman shook it. "Good ta meetcha there, whatcha Superman, yeah, that's a new one. Lissen, I got an idea for a little supper club here, you know, with a nice ambience. Live music. That's what I was thinking. You know, some music, some chicken, some wine . . . not too classy, but classy. You ever done any singing in a place like that?"

"Sounds great," said Superman. "Let me know."

"He claims he's just passing through, Jimmy. He hasn't tasted your chicken."

"You guys want a half, or you wanna go a bird each?"

"Half for me," Spike said.

"Um, I already ate." As soon as he said it Superman knew this was not the right answer.

"You gotta at least try it," said Spike.

"If the man don't like chicken," said Jimmy, glowering, "don't force it on him."

"Half," said Superman. "It smells really good."

Jimmy took a long sideways look at him and split a whole chicken with one stroke of his cleaver.

Superman juggled his plate and two beers to a table. "I know I've seen him before."

"Jimmy Hoffa. The Teamsters, remember?"

"That's Jimmy—aw for Christ's sake, Spike! Jimmy Hoffa's cooking barbecued chicken in Central America?"

"He says it beats his old job," said Spike. "His chicken is great."

Superman took a bite. Ginger, soy sauce, lemon, odd Chinese spices . . . delicious.

The music bopped along in syncopation. On the dance floor, twirly girls in skirts danced with boys in white shirts. The mirror-balls sprinkled dots of light on their hair.

Anastasia. D. B. Cooper. Michael Rockefeller. Stu and Lou Sherman. Amelia Earhart. Frank Napier. Marilyn Monroe. The King of Siam. The multitalented Jimmy Hoffa at the grill.

The famously disappeared, and assorted odd nuts. Someone had built quite a collection. Someone—what did Spike call him? The Magician.

It was all just too strange, and Superman wasn't drunk enough to make sense of it yet.

He went for more drinks. At the bar he sucked up another cucaracha, to keep things moving. On his way back he found Frank engaged in conversation with a muscly Indian boy, all planes and lean lines, a hawklike face, like an Aztec warrior. The kid tried to act nonchalant, but was visibly enthralled by Frank's whitish-blond curls.

"Hey Frank, here's your beer. I got distracted."

"Not to worry." He handed it to his young friend, who tipped it up and drank half in one gulp. "Thirsty boy," Frank murmured. "Mr. Willis, are you making new friends?"

"I met Spike," he reported. "And Jimmy Hoffa."

"Did you taste the chicken?"

"Yeah, great."

Frank beamed. "I knew you'd like this place." The Indian boy fingered the feathery trim on his bathrobe.

> *Da duddleeda BUM—ba BUM—ba BUM*
> *Da duddleeda BUM—ba BUM—ba BUM*

That was still the same song playing as when they arrived—or had it changed? Not much. Superman marveled at the endless energy of the dancers. The heat seemed enough to melt the clothes right off their bodies. Maybe it was all the drinks he'd had, but suddenly he felt an overwhelming desire to get out of this humid crush and find some air.

"Have fun, Frank." He grabbed his beer, pushed off on his cane, wobbled through a group of boys standing with their arms folded, pretending not to watch the girls. He stepped under the lights, out of the music and heat, onto the beach.

A velvet breeze traveled up from the water. The sand was cool underfoot. He sank to the base of a coconut tree and stretched his legs, relieving the strain of being upright. Ohh, yes. That felt fine. That breeze coming across the sand felt like a second wind.

From a distance, La Restaurante Discoteca Amor Y Mar Y Sol Y Blues was a small village glowing with happiness and inebriation.

Superman knew it was coming time to go home, but just now, for this moment, the urge had faded. After months as a dead celebrity, he knew, his reappearance would shoot his career into a whole new orbit—but just thinking the word "career" left a sour streak in his mind. Somehow it didn't seem important on this beach, at this end of the world. Looking back, he couldn't believe how much energy he'd spent getting famous. He could have lavished all that time and attention on something useful, like raising a son.

His life had been a restless journey. He had never lingered long in one place. Sitting on the sand, hearing the wash of the waves, the salsa beat endlessly beating as the mirror-ball flung glitter on the breakers, Superman had the most peculiar sensation that he didn't need to go home. This was it. He was already there.

Possibly he was drunk. (Possibly!) Tomorrow he might wake up with another idea. But for tonight, anyway, he was famously disappeared, and this felt like the place to be. He had no appointments, no obligations, no history. These people had escaped their celebrity. They lived as they pleased, away from the lights and the cameras and the need to put on an act for the public. They were living a new kind of life—or maybe it was an old life they had come here to find, a time when music and thunder were the loudest sounds in the world.

His first night on the town, and already he was feeling sentimental about the place.

He would like to go back for Alexa and Ben Junior. Bring them here. Raise his son on this beach. The boy would like this beach. He didn't know much about the boy, but what boy wouldn't like this beach? It was perfect. Every wave just gave way to another wave. The moon settled down at the end of a glittering highway.

He pulled himself up, brushed sand off his shorts, and remembered the pill in his pocket.

He turned it over in his hand.

He was drunk and somehow that wasn't enough, now he wanted to be stoned, and that's just how things were. He'd been cooped up too long. He wanted to get just as free as a person can get.

He put the pill on his tongue and washed it down with the last inch of beer. Set me free, why don't you babe.

"*Now* you have done it!" Rabbit stepped from the bushes.

Superman jumped. "Jesus!"

"*Now* you have opened the door and walked through! Let the angels sing and the trumpets resound! Hallelujah, Superman, you've passed the first test!"

"Where did you get that pill?"

"I made it myself. Not to worry, son, I'm a trained pharmaceutical chemist."

"Am I going to be sorry I did that?"

Rabbit glanced at his watch. "In about thirty seconds you're going to be the happiest man in the world."

"What does it do?"

Rabbit showed a row of fine white teeth. "Mostly a mood thing. With some interesting size variations. You'll remain fully functional at all times."

"Oh God," Superman said, "what have I done."

"Careful, son, it acts as a mood *enlarger.* So you want to get in a good mood real quick, and stay there."

Superman said, "I'll do my best."

Suddenly someone scooped his brain out of his skull, dipped it in a freezing-cold solution, wrung it out like a sponge, and put it back in.

At once everything became sweet and clear. The music sparkled and tingled and rang. Superman swelled up and up like a Macy's Thanksgiving balloon until he was enormous, looming and bobbing over the tiny people in the bar, lighter than air, unbelievably happy.

He glanced down.

Rabbit was a wee thing about five inches tall, way down by his ankle.

"Twenty-two seconds," Rabbit squeaked. "A new world's record. Has anybody ever tested your gastric acid?"

Superman smiled. "Man, you're so small!"

Spike spoke up from his other ankle. "What's the matter with him? What'd you do to him, Rabbit?"

"He did it to himself."

Spike said, "Here's Daisy. Stand up straight." One nudge of his elbow brought Superman zooming down to normal size.

She wore a white dress with a gold rope knotted at the waist. The dress was cut low in front, and there they were, the most perfect, touchable breasts in the human kingdom, straining against that diaphanous material like a pair of fabulous airplanes lifting off. A brilliant red scarf covered her hair. The same oversized Jackie Kennedy sunglasses she'd worn on the beach, only now it was night and she opened a path through the dancers to the bar where Superman stood.

"Hello, Rabbit." That whisper, that whisper.

"Oh, my beautiful Daisy. Please take off that dress, it only gets in the way."

"Keep dreaming," she said lightly. "Hi, you must be Ben. We haven't actually met."

She put out her hand. Superman took it and tried to speak. No sound came out. He wanted to thank her for saving his life. He wanted to tell her he loved her forever, he was so grateful to be alive and standing here holding her hand. He opened and closed his mouth a few times.

Daisy seemed accustomed to this reaction. She squeezed his hand. "I'm glad you're not dead," she breathed. "Come by my house for lunch sometime. We'll get to know each other."

Superman swallowed, and nodded.

"But first shave off that awful beard." She patted his cheek and walked away, trailing an air of lavender.

She was real. Not a dream. The lights flickered when she left the bar.

Superman's joy expanded, inflating him upward until his hair brushed the ceiling.

Get to know each other.

Oh honey, let us do that. I want to know you and know you, until we know each other so well we can't walk.

He sniffed his hand: lavender.

Spike sighed. "Hell, she never invited *me* to lunch."

"She saved my life," Superman said.

"She could surely save mine," said Rabbit. "How you feeling, son?"

Just the question was enough to shrink Superman to a height of eighteen inches. The top of his head barely reached Rabbit's knee. He peered up. "Kinda small."

Rabbit aimed his grin toward an astoundingly tall pair of identical girls coming past them from the beach, headed for the dance floor. Superman rubbed his eyes—yes, there were two. One wore a red miniskirt and white top, the other a red top and white skirt. They were identical down to the waves in their wavy blond hair. Their little pug noses kept them from being classically beautiful, but from this angle, at least, they looked like a whole lot of fun.

"There are two of them, right?" Superman said.

"The Twins," said Spike. "Sandy and Linda. My roommates, and I still can't tell them apart."

"Why even try?" Rabbit said. "They're exactly the same."

"We always call the one on the left Sandy," said Spike. "It's the easiest way."

Superman felt himself beginning to grow. It had been so long since he'd seen side-by-side sets of perky young breasts that he felt old Jolly Roger threatening to stand right up and wave hello. He felt about fifteen years old. He wished for schoolbooks to hold in front of himself. "What's the story, Spike? Are they famous?"

"Only locally," Spike said.

"They work as a team?"

"I think that is a possibility."

Superman shot him a look. "You get a lot of girls, Spike?"

"You'd be surprised. They all think they're doing me a big favor, you know, the Sister of Mercy charity thing, but really they wonder how it would be to make it with a guy who looks like me. It's a fantasy, you know—beauty and the beast. I just sit back and reap the rewards." Sandy and Linda moved out under the disco lights, Rabbit lumbering along in pursuit.

Spike snapped his fingers. Tequila arrived with stunning speed. Superman licked salt from his hand, bit into a lemon, and tossed back the shot. It went off in the middle of his chest like a nice soft artillery shell.

The salsa gave way to a slow dance, a tremulous ballad. The dancers wilted against each other, barely moving. Superman spotted Frank leaned against a trash barrel, the Aztec boy murmuring into his ear. Or was he nibbling his ear? Hard to tell. It was dark back there.

Pito stood Buddha-like with his hands folded on his stomach, watching Catalina chattering with a table of homely and fat girls. One of the Sherman Brothers leaned down to whisper in Anastasia's ear. The President of Uruguay played backgammon with Michael Rockefeller.

Superman noticed a large black Land Cruiser with dark-tinted windows, idling in the shadows opposite the dance floor. He pointed. "Hey Spike, who's that?"

"Don't." Spike grabbed his arm and turned him away. "Don't look at them. Look at me."

"Who is it, the cops?"

"They're not cops. Turn facing me. I can't believe Frank brought you down here. Now they've seen you."

"Spike," Superman said, with the air of superiority that came from being four feet taller, "if they aren't cops, what the hell is the problem?"

Spike laughed, but not as if it were funny. "She's hardly told you anything."

Rabbit popped up just then. "That's as it should be. You, on the other hand, seem to want to tell him everything."

"He's got a right, you know. He's not one of us. He came here by accident."

"Yeah," said Superman.

"And now he'll never leave. Frank made sure of that."

"And now I'll—the hell I won't! Who's gonna stop me?"

"Not me," said Spike. "Rabbit, what did you give him?"

"Red Dot Number Nine. One hit. He's fine."

Superman tottered, grabbing a column for support.

All four doors of the Land Cruiser swung open.

Suddenly the blond Twins loomed into view, all smiles and hellos and pug noses and flashing white teeth. "Girls, this is Superman," Spike said. "He needs to go for a walk on the beach *right now*."

"Hello, Superman," said the girl on his left. "We're Sandy and Linda."

"Come with us," said the girl on the right.

They each took an arm. They moved him through the throng, away from the dance floor to the top of the beach. Superman shrank down and down, until he was limping along trying to keep up with them.

"Why do they call you Superman?" said the one in the red skirt.

"Are you really the Man of Steel?" said the other.

They looked at each other and burst out in a peal of identical laughter.

"You girls sure are large," he said.

That made them laugh more. "Why are you looking at us that way?"

"Like he's seen a Martian."

"What did Rabbit give you?"

Superman said, "Do I look kinda small to you?"

"No," they chimed together. The red-skirted girl reached down to touch his elbow.

Superman grew four feet in three seconds. "Hi. I'm Ben."

"We're Sandy and Linda," one of them said.

"Do you always do that—I mean, which one is which? How can anyone tell you apart?"

"They can't."

"That's the neat thing about it."

"We're exactly the same."

"If we told you, you'd get it mixed up anyway."

"Okay. Okay. Which one is Sandy?"

"I am," said the girl on the left.

"No she's not, she's Linda," said the other. Their laughter had a light, tinkly sound, like wind chimes.

"One of you go stand over there," said Superman.

"Nobody can ever tell us apart. What's the use? We have fun."

"Do you like to have fun, Superman?"

What could he say? "Sure I do."

"What kind of fun do you like?"

He scuffed his toes in the sand. "How old are you girls?"

"How old do you want us to be?"

"Are you trying to seduce me?" he said.

Hands began running up and down his T-shirt, four hands at once. "Does that bother you, Superman?"

"Don't you want to be seduced?"

"I'm not sure," he said, thinking, *What, have you lost your mind? Of course you do! Twins! Blond twins on the beach!*

Without even trying, Superman found himself headed for glory land. He felt the heat permeating his body, three months in a body cast and the wild mix of liquor and drugs in his blood. His good long look at Daisy had given him the kind of full-body hard-on that could take weeks to subside. His brain had moved down to the part of his body that had no concept of future or past—only the right here, right now—and as far as that part was concerned, Sandy and Linda were perfect.

Five steps into the shadows and they were all over him, climbing him like a tree. He dropped his walking stick. One girl wrapped his head in her hands and kissed him, hard. The other embraced him from behind and began lapping at his ear.

He groped and squeezed with what he hoped would register as equal passion, but that was impossible. It was two against one, and these girls were on fire. He knew the symptoms: rapid breathing, clutching and grappling, whites of the eyes. They wanted it even worse than he did, and he had every intention of giving it to them. But first he had to get them horizontal. It looked as if they might like to go the whole way standing up, and his hip was threatening to collapse.

He tore his lips away. "Wait—wait—here, let's—ow—let's find someplace to—"

"No, do it here, now, overpower us!" Sandy cried.

"Throw us down and take us!"

"Me first!"

"You always go first!"

"Bad leg," he gasped. "I need to—here, over here." He grabbed their hands, pulled them across the sand. He thought he might have ruined the mood, but the moment he passed out of the moonlight they were on him again, moaning, running fingers over his chest, down the seat of his pants. They toppled together to the sand.

Superman felt his body dwindling down until he was a tiny thing sandwiched between them. If either of them rolled over, he would be crushed. His voice came out an eensy little squeak: "Sandy?"

"Linda," she whispered. "You okay?" She touched his arm. Just that soft pressure threatened to bury him in the sand.

"Don't move," he said. Slowly he grew, until he was about two-thirds normal size. The tequila sang a song in his head quite apart from the sound of waves crashing. Sandy kissed his ear. Linda kissed the flat of his shoulder.

They moved as different parts of the same girl. They chuckled and whispered to each other, kissing a trail across his chest to his nipples. Where before they'd been all thrashing and bumping, now they tickled and teased and nipped at him. He lay back and let them kiss wherever they had a mind to. He cupped one left breast in each hand.

Fingers fumbled for the button of his shorts—couldn't find it—slid on down inside and around his hard part.

Superman began to expand. In a short time his whole body grew very large. The tops of the coconut trees tickled his shoulders. The waves washed the tips of his toes. Beneath him in shadow were these poor normal-sized twin sisters who had no idea that they were about to be ravished by a giant.

He popped the button off his shorts, yanked down the zipper. Oh God that thing was too big, it would kill them. They were smiling at it saying oh my, look at that. Sandy took it in her hand and pointed it up at the moon—and then she was growing, too, she was a gigantic girl swinging her leg over him, coming down on top of him, engulfing him.

And then Linda grew large and her nipple swam into his mouth and they were three giants making the beach shudder with their thrusts, thundering harder than waves on the shore. They knocked over trees, they crushed houses and bridges as they rolled around in the sand.

They hissed yess yess and he grunted ohLinda, ohSandy, and other stuff that made sense at the time. He ground down in the sand and bounded up. Linda began to tremble and whimper and she did it faster, clutching her knees together, slamming down at the very moment Superman was slamming up.

He felt something pop.

Oh. Fuck.

It was too late to stop. They started an earthquake that rocked the beach, shook coconuts from the trees, got every dog barking and every frog in the jungle to hopping straight up in the air. The tremor traveled all the way around the world and came back, reflected in waves.

Linda settled on him. "Oooooooooooo," she purred.

"I think—I broke—my pelvis," he groaned.

Sandy squeezed his sides with her knees.

"Oh no! Stop! Oh! Get off!" He pushed. He didn't mean to be rough but they were hurting him. The girls fell over onto the sand.

"Bastard." Sandy snatched up a handful of sand and threw it at him.

"No, I'm—oh, Christ—I'm serious." He spat sand from his mouth. "I think I hurt myself."

She got up on hands and knees, feeling around for her clothes. "Come on, Linda, let's go."

"Wham bam thank you ma'am," Linda said.

"No, you don't understand! I've been in a—ow, shit—in a body cast for three months. I think I just—broke myself again."

Linda peered down. "You're not serious."

"Here, put your hand . . . does that—? Can you feel it? Does it feel broken?"

"No, I don't—oh, Sandy, we've hurt him!"

"Oh, God!"

"Go get Frank," he groaned. "Tell him to bring the jeep."

Sandy made a desperate noise and took off running.

"Oh God," Linda whimpered, "are you in pain?"

He'd had about ninety-six drinks, and a pill that kept changing his dimensions in unexpected ways—but yes, underneath all that, with her breasts in his face and his first orgasm in months still sending down shimmers of sparks—there was a sharp lively sensation that felt exactly like pain.

"Yeah," he said, "could you just—wait, don't *touch* me!"

"I know first aid," she said, wriggling into her miniskirt.

He tried to raise up on his elbows. "Just don't touch me, okay?"

She backed off.

He had the presence of mind to grope around for his shorts, but he couldn't roll onto his side to get his feet in them.

He sank back, defeated. Oh yes, he'd done it this time. His first night out, and he'd messed himself up all over again.

He heard the hiss in the instant before the wave crashed over him.

He flailed, gulping salt water. The wave dragged him halfway down the beach. Somehow he managed to dig his hands into the sand and get his head up, to keep from being swept out to sea.

The wave retreated, leaving him spluttering.

Another wave loomed and hissed and broke over him, but this time he was ready. He planted his hands in the sand and held tight until it drained away.

The moon loomed in his eyes. The roar of the sea filled his head until he thought he might drown but it was the roar of the jeep, voices shouting, people running across the sand.

Rabbit seized his ankles. Spike took his arms. They lifted him like a sack of rice, lugged him up the beach.

"You okay, man?" Spike shone a flashlight in his eyes.

People spilled out of La Discoteca, running toward the commotion. By the time he convinced Spike to switch off the flashlight, Superman was surrounded by a crowd. He lay on the sand coughing water from his lungs, his weenie flopping in the breeze. Sandy was there, and Linda. Pito and Catalina and her friends. Rabbit. Jimmy Hoffa. Several bartenders. Frank and the Aztec boy.

Frank clutched the front of his robe in one hand. "My word, Mr. Willis! Have you lost your pants?"

"That's Superman Willis, you guys." Spike turned the light into his face so everyone could see. "He's a big star back home."

And then the world faded to black.

9 / *The Hell of It*

SUNLIGHT POURED THROUGH the open wall, the dead middle of a hot bright morning. Superman's tongue was a piece of dry toast lying on the dirty floor of his mouth. The jungle was atwitter with birds. He hated them. Goddamn sonofabitch birds. If he had a gun he would kill them all.

Gyp put her head up and nudged him with her moist nose.

He belched a cloud of tequila. Blood thumped in his temples:

Da duddleeda BUM—ba BUM—ba BUM

Wild night. No idea how he got home. The last thing he remembered was Spike the burn victim shining a light in his eyes.

Before that, though, there was a drink on fire in his mouth, a Land Cruiser with dark-tinted windows, the Twins riding him joyfully, yipping like cheerleaders at a naked rodeo. That memory brought a little smile to his face.

Gyp whined. Superman rolled over to give her a pat. A muscle in his lower back twanged like a busted guitar string. Sweat dripped off his nose.

Last night he'd been certain he'd broken himself again, but now, feeling around, he found his pelvis still in one piece. Maybe he'd pulled a muscle. Maybe that (and an ocean of booze, and the drugs, and the Twins) had been enough to lay him out flat on the beach.

Drums thundered in the hollow cave of his head. His body was crusty with sand in places you would not expect to find sand.

On the table was a tray of orange juice, ice water, *aspirina*. He shook five of them onto his tongue, washed them down with juice, and started in on the water. It felt good streaming from the corners of his mouth. He glugged half the pitcher and dumped the rest over his head.

That helped.

With a lot of slow bending and reaching he got his cutoffs up and zipped. A hand-mirror stood on the dresser beside the basin, a razor and shaving soap. The first mirror he'd seen since the crash. He went closer.

He cringed, forced himself to look again. His nose had a leftward crook, his cheekbone was visibly flatter—but he was recognizable, under the beard. What was it Alexa's mother called him? Not Much To Look At.

He lathered his face and began scraping. Scraggly hairs floated in unsightly clumps in the basin.

The birds chirped and sang.

"Shut *up!*"

Gyp looked up, thumping the floor with her tail.

"Not you." He shuffled onto the porch, glaring at all the bright light. Every step brought a greeting from the muscle in his back.

A hot soak in the spring would sweat it out of him.

Gyp led the way down the path, wagging and smiling. It was sad to feel this lousy when the world was chirping and whistling and wagging its tail at you. No one had forced all those drinks down his throat, nor that Alice-in-Wonderland pill. No one made him take the near-fatal moonlight stroll with the Twins. He'd done those things of his own free will. He'd been happy to do them. Given a chance, he would probably do them again—though maybe not all at once. . . .

From beyond the pink wall came a *clackety-clack* like a roller coaster, then a thunderous *bang!* that chased birds from the trees. Gyp left off sniffing bushes and trotted toward the gate.

Down the shady tunnel, the black door stood open. Sunshine streamed through the open wall. The big sound he'd heard was the steel door rolling up. The Electra was gone.

He tapped his walking stick to the middle of the floor. The only sign of the plane was a grease spot shaped like Florida.

Gyp bounded out to the grassy clearing. Superman followed.

The old Indian sat on the hood of the jeep, looking up at the sky. He took no notice of Gyp's whining. A wheelchair sat to one side.

Superman looked up.

The Electra hovered in midair, silently flying in place, thirty feet above the clearing.

He started and took a step back. This was some kind of optical illusion. He rubbed his eyes, blinked, looked again.

The plane made no sound at all, which made it so much like a dream, a daylight walking-around hallucination that could not possibly be real—

but there it was. The sun glinted off the fuselage. The starboard wing dipped as the plane rolled into a steep-banked turn, a flash of silver-white hair. The wing lifted, leveling off.

Gyp settled at the feet of the old Indian, who gazed up without expression. Superman shrank into the shadows, holding his breath, afraid the slightest noise might interrupt whatever karma or voodoo or hypnotic spell was holding tons of solid airplane in midair.

He tried to reconcile what his eyes were seeing with what his brain knew to be possible.

The plane cast a shadow on the grass. It soared and dipped, swooping gracefully, silently, going nowhere.

The force of Pito's gaze seemed to be holding it in the air. But that was impossible. There was major juju around this old man; he was very clever with tricks involving weeping birds and superheavy hammers—but for God's sake you cannot fly an airplane with your *eyes*.

The nose tilted down. The flaps slid back. The landing gear unfolded and chunked into place. The distant roar of surf was the only other sound. Gently, almost imperceptibly, the plane began to settle toward the clearing.

Gyp jumped up and ran in a circle, waggling her whole hind end.

The Electra revolved as it descended, its nose swinging away from the hangar. The wheels touched down.

Pito walked the plane and the wheelchair into the hangar as if they were of equal weight. He was reaching to open the hatch when he saw Superman. *"Buenos días."*

Superman nodded good morning.

Pito clambered into the plane. Gyp jumped in behind him and was shooed out again. Voices carried through the hatch.

In a moment the old man emerged with Amelia in his arms. He settled her in the chair and went to roll down the door.

"Grief, Ben, I didn't expect to see you up for hours. I heard you and Frank coming in while I was having my coffee."

He shrugged. "A night on the town."

"I shudder to think. Have you had breakfast?"

"No, I . . . I got distracted watching you fly."

She propelled the chair to the back of the hangar. "Hope you don't mind I borrowed that compass of yours—it's simply ingenious. The artificial horizon, too. If the world ever needs a new religion I suppose we can worship the electrical engineers."

The door came down, *clacketa-clacketa Boom!*

Pito tilted her chair over the threshold.

"What were you doing up there?" Superman said.

"Check flight. Got to get my hours in."

Pito moved the wheelchair through the tunnel of hibiscus.

Superman said, "You know what I mean."

"You mean, how does it fly without engines?" She glanced up. "You have to learn to think in terms of possibilities, Ben. You're absolutely impaled on what you already know."

"What I know is I just saw something impossible."

"How could it be impossible? If you saw it, I mean."

She had a point there. He didn't know how.

Pito braked the chair and went to shut the gate.

"I can't really fly with these old bad legs of mine—can't work the rudder pedals. We've experimented with hand controls, but takeoffs and landings are too much for two hands."

The Big House was tucked into its gardens so that even when you were beside it, you saw it in parts: a wall, a window, a patch of terra-cotta tile between lush palms. The shadows gave way to a courtyard paved with black stone, inlaid with a turquoise oval swimming pool on the edge of a cliff.

The view started here and went on forever, a vast sweep of blue ocean, green jungle mountains, white beach. To stand on this terrace was to fly without leaving the ground. The ocean stretched from here to the horizon, which might be fifty miles off, or five hundred. Fleecy clouds drifted through the sky, towing islands of shadow across the sea. The massive sweep of currents made the line of breakers at the beach seem a piddling thing.

The view filled Superman's eyes and spilled out his ears and set his heart pounding, a view like God must have had when he was designing the world: Let's put a mountain here, a matching one over there, spread a white beach in between, paint the land ninety-five shades of green, and speckle the ocean with gigantic rocks.

The Big House sat near the summit of the north mountain. Tucked behind the beach at the foot of the south mountain, the glint of a tin roof under coconut palms: La Discoteca.

To the east, a broad channel separated the island from a mainland covered with misty green mountains. At the narrowest part of the channel was some sort of village, a collection of shanties on a sandy peninsula pointing like a finger toward the island.

Amelia, behind him: "What do you think?"

"Hell of a view." The table was laden with platters of scrambled eggs and fried bananas, papaya and mango and pineapple, a basket of tiny yeast rolls. Gyp sat down at his elbow to get a good view of his plate. "All this for us? Where's Frank?"

"He doesn't arise before three, sometimes four, depending on what sort of disaster he got into the night before."

"You two don't get along."

"Oh, I love Frank, but he doesn't love me." She sipped coffee. "He blames me for everything bad that ever happened to him."

"That's what he says about you."

"He does? How interesting. I guess we've known each other too long. We ran out of conversation about twenty years ago. Here, the juice is good."

"Where did Pito learn the birdcalls and the tricks, levitating the plane and all that?"

Amelia buttered a roll. "You make it sound like some kind of circus act."

"If that's not what it is, what is it?"

"I don't pretend to know. Pito has it the strongest. But it isn't in the people. It's this place. It has its own power. Anyone can drink from the well."

"So Pito taps into this . . . power, whatever, to fly you around in your plane."

"I don't really go anywhere," she said. "I'm just staying in practice."

"For what?"

"I need your help, Ben. Just help me with this one thing. When we're done, I'll give you that plane and you can fly yourself home. If that's still what you want."

"What do you need me for?"

"If I was young and healthy, I wouldn't." She tucked a strand of hair under her hat. "But I'm old now. I'm running out of time. I'd like to keep waiting for a real pilot, but it looks like you're the best I can do."

That ruffled him, as she intended. "Hell's that supposed to mean?"

"Ben, I need a copilot." She folded her napkin. "For years I have watched and waited and listened for someone. Every time a plane flew within two hundred miles of here, I felt it. I knew one day someone would come—and then it turned out to be you. The guitar player who lands in the lee of a wave. Well, that's my luck, and I'll just have to live with it. I can't wait any longer."

"What do you need with a copilot? Where are you going?"

In a heartbeat the years melted away. Her eyes came up, burning with excitement. "I'm going to fly around the world."

The transformation was uncanny. Here before him was the handsome young flier from the photographs—that uncanny resemblance to Lindbergh!—eyes flashing, chin raised in prideful anticipation.

"You're serious," he said.

"Damn right I am."

"Didn't you already try that?"

"And I mean to finish it. I've come close a couple of times, but something always stopped me, the weather, or an engine, or—something. I'd just about given up when you came along. I've gone over my plans. I'll be ready in April. And I'll have you to help me." She reached for his hand. "Come with me, Ben. It'll be the biggest adventure of your life. When we've done it, you can go back to the States and be famous again, whatever you want. By April I'll have a thousand gallons, that'll take us across the South Atlantic. We can do the whole world in forty days, give or take. We'll hop to the Azores and fly the spring tradewinds across Africa. Have you ever flown Africa?"

"No."

"Spectacular. Not to be missed. You navigate by elephant graveyards and banyan trees."

Superman had to admit the idea of flying around the world with Amelia Earhart had a certain ring to it: the ring of massive publicity. Their arrival would be the biggest headline since the moon landing. He thought of Barney, his publicity man at A&M Records. Barney would get a hard-on, have a stroke, and die of happiness, simultaneously.

"Why wait for April?" he said. "What's wrong with now? I need to go now."

"We don't have enough fuel."

"But—you don't have to go all the way around the world! You'd make just as big a splash flying from here to L.A."

"Why do anything, Ben? For the hell of it! If I just showed up and said 'Hello America, I'm back,' do you think they'd believe it was me? There's been a string of Amelias through the years. But if I went on and did it, really did it, in my plane, at my age—now, that would be something. They'd have to believe. It'll start as a rumor. It'll build at every stop, all the way around the world. By the time we get to the States they will never forget us."

"But they *haven't* forgotten. You're still famous."

"Only because I disappeared, don't you see? Not because of who I was, or what I did. I can't stand the whole world thinking I got lost and just fell into the sea. I want them to know what happened. One press conference, that's it. I'll tell the whole truth, and then—I'll disappear."

"Why don't you tell me?" he said. "The truth, I mean."

And she did.

She was the most famous woman in the world except for Eleanor Roosevelt, who had taken a liking to her. Eleanor was a dear homely old thing, always liked having handsome young women around. Amelia enjoyed having the First Lady make a fuss over her, and of course George Putnam was thrilled. George Putnam was her husband. He called her AE and insisted she call him GP. They made a good team. He was a bigger hustler even than Amelia. For weeks he'd been trying to scrounge government help for the world flight. A note from FDR would open all doors.

On her third visit to the White House, Amelia came down from the family quarters to find two freshly barbered young men in dark-blue suits waiting for her. They said the President had a favor to ask. She followed them to the Cabinet Room. Under a fierce portrait of Andrew Jackson they explained what the President wanted her to do.

Her country needed her, they said. A patriotic duty. Andrew Jackson glared down from the wall, daring her to say no. She said yes.

They led her to the Oval Office. The President flashed a grin around his cigarette holder. "My dear!" A shifting cloud of blue smoke hung over his desk. "Bravo! I knew you would help. I'll put you up for the Medal of Honor the minute you're back. Can you keep the secret?"

"I think so."

"Good girl. Take care of yourself, and don't get *too* lost—" He waved one hand and returned to his newspaper. The men ushered her out.

Pennsylvania Avenue was full of headlights and honking horns. Amelia felt glamorous and important, walking out the front gate into purplish dusk. The world felt less innocent than it had been an hour ago, and infinitely more exciting.

The plan was simple. Amelia was to get herself famously lost in the South Pacific. She would pretend to run out of gas near Howland Island, but in fact she would land seven hundred miles northwest, at Mili Atoll. There she would find a stash of food, fresh water, a transmitter to broadcast a homing signal.

The navy would mount an exhaustive search for the second most famous woman in the world, which would provide cover for a sea-and-air reconnaissance of Japanese-controlled islands in the southwest Pacific. Once the navy had a good look around the forbidden zones, they would happen across Amelia and Frank on their atoll.

The navy would get valuable intelligence, and Amelia would have a thrilling tale of survival to boost the sale of her memoirs.

All at once the doors of official Washington swung open to her. Charts, classified weather reports, letters of permission flowed freely from all departments. Barrels of aviation fuel headed off on navy ships to stopping points along her flight plan. Behind every act of bureaucratic generosity, Amelia saw the shadows of the young men in blue suits. They were always there, just out of sight, watching to see if she would keep her end of the bargain.

The hardest part was keeping the secret—from GP, who was involved in every detail of the flight, from Frank Napier, from the investors and her mother and sister and all the reporters who kept asking *What's the most dangerous part? Are you afraid?* She couldn't tell them, but yes, she was very afraid.

All the way around the world she resisted the growing conviction that the plan was bound to fail. Every night she fabricated cheerful reports of her day's thoughts and experiences, and cabled them off to GP for distribution to the newspapers.

By the time she reached New Guinea, she had decided to forget the whole thing, fly to Howland as planned, and home. If the President asked, she would tell him the truth: she lost her nerve.

The night before takeoff, Frank stumbled down the steps of the Papua Bay Hotel and headed off on another debauch. Amelia sat in the hotel bar, fuming over why she always seemed to be putting her life in the hands of unreliable men.

The man at the next table said, "It's a good thing we didn't tell Frank. I'm not sure we can count on him."

Amelia gasped. "What are you doing here?"

The man looked as crisp in gray slacks and a white shirt as he had in his navy-blue suit. "Do we need to talk?" he said.

"You bet we do."

They walked down a muddy backstreet. Second thoughts? he said. Plenty. She poured out her heart to that man. He listened in silence, then said an astonishing thing: "You can call it off now, no hard feelings. We wanted to give you that chance."

"Give me one good reason I should go through with it."

"You know the reasons," he said. "The weather looks good. It's entirely up to you."

She thought: This is a test. From the other side of the world, the President is testing me. He doesn't think I have the guts.

"Okay," she said. "I'll do it. Get out of here before I change my mind."

The young man hastened off.

She went to her room, willed herself to sleep. At three they woke her with a wire from GP. Weather delays had spoiled his elaborate Fourth of July welcome-home gala, and he'd been nagging her with ill-tempered telegrams ever since. This one said ANY CHANCE ARRIVE OAKLAND BEFORE MONDAY PLEASE REPLY PRONTO VIA ITASCA GP. Go to hell, George, she whispered. I'm flying as fast as I can. You can damn well celebrate me when I get there.

A mechanic named Skip drove her to the airfield. In the silence before dawn she heard the breakers crashing at the end of the runway.

Frank dragged in two hours late. His eyes were vacant black holes. He worked up a preliminary bearing, put his head down, and passed out.

The dawn came windless, groggy, and gray. Amelia made the final walk-around with the hangar crew. They smoked cigarettes and spoke in the toneless mutter of early morning. She heard nothing until Skip's words as he closed the hatch: "Okay then, fly safe."

The overloaded Electra used every inch of the runway, falling away from the end, sinking so close to the sea that the propellers threw spray from the waves. Amelia prayed that ship into the air. It took ninety minutes to climb eight thousand feet.

Four hours out of Lae, Frank bestirred himself to send up the first course correction. Amelia unpinned the scrap of paper from the pulley wire, noted the bearing, and set her course one point three five degrees north of the line: a dead-reckoning course for Mili Atoll.

All night Frank sent up careful plottings and adjustments. All night Amelia crumpled them, dropped them on the floor.

Toward morning, the Howland radiomen began to sound anxious. They could hear her, they said, but her signals were breaking up and she wasn't transmitting long enough for them to get a fix.

She sent fragments of messages. By sunrise the radiomen were skittering all over the frequencies, demanding a position report.

"We must be on you but cannot see you," she called, holding and releasing the key, "can't hear you," and "circling now but our gas is running low—half an hour or less." She let a bit of real fear into her voice, for authenticity.

Frank sent up a note that said "1911 GMT arrive line 157–337. Turn S 90 deg."

Amelia snapped the fuse out of the radio and tucked it in her pocket. She wrote a reply: "Wrong, Frank. We are S of Howland. Turning N."

That brought him clambering over the catwalk. He ranted and called her a silly overambitious female who couldn't navigate her way out of a burning barn. She said that was better than being the lousy hopeless good-for-nothing drunk who had gotten them lost. They screamed at each other awhile, and oh, it felt good, all her pent-up anxiety rushing out, clearing her head for what she knew would come next.

"The radio's dead, Frank."

His anger collapsed in a rush of fear.

Just as the port engine began to sputter, Amelia saw the ragged white ring of an atoll at the top of her windscreen. Frank hollered and praised the Lord and cheered her to a flawless landing in the lagoon.

He splashed through the water, fell to his knees, kissed the coral. For the first time, Amelia let herself imagine that everything might turn out all right.

She scanned the reef for a clump of palm trees. The men in blue suits had shown her a photo of a broken-backed white reef with wax-crayon arrows pointing to a clump of trees. There were no trees here. Maybe a typhoon had blown them away. Maybe this was the wrong atoll.

All day Frank stayed near the Electra, firing flares at seagulls he mistook for rescue planes. Amelia trudged across the dazzling coral, pretending to search for fresh water while really looking for a transmitter, a stash of supplies.

That night they took turns watching and trying to sleep. Amelia lay on the floor of the aft cabin, staring at the stars through the optical-glass window. She prayed: Oh God, what have I done? Please send help.

The next morning she put the fuse back in the radio, but the battery was dead.

Then came the answer to her prayer: a launch full of Japanese soldiers. They made Amelia and Frank stand for hours in the sun while they searched every centimeter of the atoll. At last three of them came running with a crate they'd pulled from a coral mound. C rations. Canned goods. A transmitter.

After that it was bad. Saipan, Tokyo. Frank was there for a while, then not there.

She never told him what they did to her in the white room at the end of the hall. They tied her to a table and slapped her with lengths of garden hose: on her toes, fingertips, the backs of her knees, the small of her back. Her hands and feet lost all sensation. She came close to losing her mind. The administration of pain was so subtle, so carefully planned, the evil opposite of an exquisite massage.

It was only after they damaged the nerves in her spine that she told them what they wanted to hear, the whole story. Frank doesn't know, she said. Don't hurt him.

After that it was easier. She wished she'd told them sooner.

They lived through the war, the firebombing of Tokyo. A man came to Amelia's cell, a red-faced old American in a tan suit and straw boater. Friend of a friend, he said. A ransom had been paid. The Electra was waiting at Yokohama. "You can't go back to the States," he said. "It wouldn't do to have your story booted about while there's still a war on. You'll have to stay disappeared for a while, anyway."

He gave her a map. A tiny island, circled in blue ink.

Amelia pushed back her wheelchair. "That was a long time ago. We're still here."

"You never told Frank why you landed on that atoll? Doesn't he deserve to know?"

"It seemed better to let him think the whole thing was my fault, which it was—and for nothing." She shook her head. "Ah hell, I got greedy. I got what I deserved."

"Greedy?"

"It wasn't enough to be the first woman to fly around the world. I thought I could save the world, too. Of course they used me. I was dying to be used. I adored being famous. I knew it would make a great story for my book. Of *course* they abandoned us when the Japanese captured us—that was always the fallback plan, and I was too blind to see it. I volunteered, for God's sake. I didn't know I was volunteering the rest of my life."

"I'm sorry," Superman said.

"They put us on this island and forgot us. The war ended, but it was easier for them to leave us here."

"Why here?"

"Because *he* was here. This was his island. There aren't too many people who own a whole island. And he paid the Japanese a great deal of money for me. He saved my life. At the time I was grateful."

"The Magician?"

That brought a faint smile. "That's what the islanders call him. The name comes from an old story, a giant who sleeps in the mountain—El Mago, the Magician. He's almost always invisible, but every thousand years he wakes up to work a new trick."

"You know who he is?"

"Of course. I knew him from the old days. I was the first one he brought to this place. He was a good man, a brilliant man. . . . I watched that man disappear." She straightened in her chair. "He's become something of a monster. He wants to change this place forever. The islanders have lived very happily for thousands of years with things as they are—but he doesn't care. No one ever stands up to him. I have to try."

"I'd really like to help you, but I can't sit around here till April."

Amelia frowned. "It's the only way you'll ever get out of here."

"What does that mean?"

"He knows you're alive. That was a secret until Frank took you out on the town. I warned you, but you wouldn't listen. Frank exposed you on purpose, to keep you here. You'll live a nice life, but they won't let you leave. These people are bored, Ben, they're like prisoners here, they're just dying for someone new to play with. I'd hoped to slip you out quietly, but now that's impossible. We'll just have to chance it and go."

"You sound like you're afraid."

"Strange things happen to people who try to leave," she said. "I've thought about it a lot, and I don't think he'll dare try to stop me. We made a deal when I came. He let me keep my plane, even built me a hangar. I promised to stay, as long as he treated the islanders well and left the island alone. He's breaking the deal. He'll have to let me go."

"Well then, what do you need me for? Let Pito fly you with his brain waves. You'll save on gas."

"Don't make fun of me, Ben. I've told you the truth. I can't fly the plane by myself."

It was a pure tragedy, this great old woman held prisoner not by some invisible Magician on a tropical island, but by this obsession with the one great misadventure of her life. At an age when she should be telling her story to biographers and grandkids, she had seized on the idea of flying that last flight again—as if by reliving her biggest mistake she could somehow make the rest of her life come out right.

Superman creaked up from his chair. "You are one amazing woman," he said, "and I'm proud to know you. But I think you're just gonna have to wait for a real pilot."

"Oh please, I was only needling you—"

"Lady, this is your trip, not mine. If you want to go now, I'll go with you. Otherwise I have a life to get back to."

She regarded him calmly. "Get back to it, then. Don't expect me to help you. If you turn me down, you're on your own."

"I'll ask Frank."

Her eyes turned to ice. "Fine. Ask Frank. See how far you get."

"Forget it, then. I don't need help. I can get myself off this island."

"Don't you see I'm offering you a chance at something incredible? Don't you want to try something you've never done? Do you know how that feels?"

"Oh, yes," he said. Once, at the Flor-A-Bama Lounge, he got up on a stage and gave his whole soul to the singing of a Hank Williams song. Everything in his life since then had been coasting, in one form or another.

"Where's your sense of adventure?" she was saying. "You're a young man. When I was your age, I wanted to do everything."

"I'm not so young now. I just want to go home."

"I can't honestly believe you'd refuse me," she said, "after all I've done for you."

"Ah, come on, lady, that's not worthy of you. I'm going back to planet Earth. Maybe you and Frank should come with me. You've been out here too long."

"We need your help, Ben. We're in trouble. Don't just walk away from us."

"It's not my fight," he said.

"You only fight for yourself?" she flared. "I should have known better. If that's honestly the way you think, you can go straight to hell."

Superman tottered three steps and pitched headfirst into the pool. He blew air from his lungs. He waved his arms and settled to the bottom and floated there until he thought his chest would burst, then pushed off the bottom and came shooting up out of the water.

Amelia was gone. A hummingbird hovered over the breakfast table, trying to drink from a red napkin.

10 / *The Road of Trials*

PLAINLY AMELIA WAS NOT in the mood for discussion or negotiation. By the time Superman got up to the shack, Pito had his forty thousand dollars packed into a rice sack with clothes, odds and ends from the plane, and the old battered Gibson, its neck glued and wired in place.

Superman enjoyed holding the guitar in his arms, but felt not the slightest desire to play it. Strange to think this instrument had once been the center of his life. "She's throwing me out?"

The old man shrugged.

"I know, what can you do. Any chance I can talk to Frank, get a ride down the mountain?"

Pito shrugged again.

"Come on, old man, you understand more English than you let on."

Pito hesitated. "Is true," he said. "I unnerstand more."

Superman felt himself grinning. "You sly bastard."

"La Doña wants you fly," said Pito. "*Por qué* you no fly?"

"Look . . . your whole setup here is a kick to the noggin. Really. But I got a life back home, you know, things going on. I need to go check it out. I been lazin' around here too long."

"Chickit out," said Pito. "What means 'chickit out'?"

"You know, get a handle on things. Get the drift." The old man still looked mystified. "I gotta go see about my boy."

"You need stay fly," Pito said. "Is better you stay."

"I'd like to come back sometime, but if she's throwing me out I guess I wouldn't be welcome, huh?" He slung his guitar over one shoulder, stuck out his hand. "Pito. Thanks, man. You saved my life. I'll never forget it. If you ever get to America, be sure and look me up." He reached into the sack for a bundle of bills. "Here. Half is for her, for my room and board. The rest is for you. For all your good help."

Pito stared at the money as if it were some nasty disease-ridden thing. Superman let it dangle there a minute, then tossed it at Pito's feet.

The old man reached out to clasp his hand in both hands. "You need stay fly."

"You'll be all right." Superman smiled. "You're a pretty smooth flier yourself."

They stood looking at each other a moment.

"Well . . ."

Pito shrugged.

Superman stepped through the gate, bumping and clanking. Pito shut the gate, and shot the bolt.

Just like that. Adios. Locked out. Superman hadn't exactly expected a committee to come hang a wreath around his neck and beg him to stay, but in view of all the time he had spent here, this farewell seemed rather abrupt.

He heard Gyp snuffling along the gate, whining for him.

He wobbled through the woods to the hangar and stood awhile in the grassy clearing, getting madder by the moment.

Amelia had been so hospitable right up to the moment she realized he wasn't going to be of use to her. Then she tossed him out without a second thought, and locked the gate behind him. He bluffed, and she called his bluff.

All her talk of a mysterious Magician was the purest kind of nonsense. She was nothing more than a formerly famous woman who longed to be famous again, a seeker after publicity, just as she had been in the thirties— look how her eyes lit up when she imagined the headlines that would announce their return! She couldn't simply admit this, of course. She had to cook up these tales of a mysterious Magician, strange forces holding her here against her will.

Well, this was a mighty fine prison to be in—the most beautiful place he'd ever seen, the kind of life he'd always dreamed for himself—but its beauty and her stories weren't enough to keep Superman here. This had felt like home, but that was an illusion. His real home was with his family. He had duties, responsibilities, a life to get on with.

The deed was done. He was outside the wall. He could stand here stewing all day, but that did not address the very real problem of how he was going to get the hell out of here.

He could wait for Frank to get thirsty and come out to his jeep, but Frank wasn't even due to wake up for hours. He could hot-wire the jeep and leave it down on the beach, but stealing cars wasn't really his style. Hadn't he bragged that he could get off this island without anyone's help? Speaking too soon had always been one of his character flaws.

He walked to the spot where Frank had crashed into the jungle. The trail of broken greenery plummeted straight down.

That was definitely some kind of a town on the far side of that channel. Where there was a town, there had to be a way out of town.

Hiking the rice sack on his shoulder, Superman began his descent.

The sun beat down from an altitude of fifty feet. He brandished the walking stick like a machete, thwacking out a path through the undergrowth. Sweat sprang from every pore. Within seconds it was stinging his eyes, dripping into his mouth, streaming down his flanks in ticklish rivulets.

From a distance, the jungle looked soft and green and inviting, like a fat million-green pillow you could sink yourself into. But once you were in it, you found an impenetrable tangle of vines, bushes, sharp sticks, weeds with claws, gooey mud slick as axle grease, branches that flew up and slapped your face, biting bugs and gnats that flew in your ears and eyes, up your nose. Superman slipped and grabbed on to vines to stay up. Thorns bit into his hands. He swore, fumed, regretted his actions, and goaded himself into keeping on.

After toiling downward for most of an hour, he risked a glance over his shoulder. The shiny roof of the hangar was still visible above, through the trees. He'd come all of two hundred yards down the hill.

He sank to his haunches, blowing out a sigh. If he had his old legs, he'd be halfway to the beach by now, but his rickety hip kept collapsing and landing him *thud!* on his butt.

He began to give serious consideration to how his pride would taste when he swallowed it.

He got to his feet and set off again. He'd always been proud of his determination in the face of obstacles. That was how he became a star: he never gave up. No amount of sweat or discomfort could make him surrender.

After a while he got to thinking he was making better progress, learning to plant his feet sideways on the slope so they didn't skate out from under him—then *whoops!* he was on his back again, sliding into the trunk of a tree.

At last he came to a little streambed. He fell to his knees and put his face in the water, glugging it in. The water revived him and gave him hope, which faded when he glanced back and saw the tin roof of the hangar still gleaming above. It had taken him ninety minutes to travel a distance that Frank's jeep had covered in fifteen seconds.

A high-pitched peeping arose in the trees. The limbs overhead began waving, as if invisible hands were grabbing and shaking them. A glimpse of red fur: monkeys!

Superman sank his feet, shoes and all, in the blessed cool water, and sat back to watch them go by.

There was joy and giddy freedom in their wild trajectories from one tree to the next. They flew heedlessly, grabbing on at the last instant with a hand or a crook of the tail. A mother monkey ran along a branch with a baby clamped on her back. She launched out through space, landed nimbly, and hurried off after the others.

They were there and gone in thirty seconds. Clearly the way to travel through this jungle was through the treetops. Superman was the only creature trying to slog it out on the ground.

Or so he thought until he felt a weird caress on his leg and looked down to find a snake as thick as a tree trunk slithering over his ankle.

The snake was so long he couldn't see the head or tail—just the long, bright-green body stretching out of one bush, through the clearing, over his leg, and on into another bush. He felt a faint rippling tickle on his skin, not the slightest sensation of weight.

He faded to white. All the blood drained out of the upper portions of his body and pooled at the backs of his legs.

He was pinned to this spot forever. He did not breathe. He did not do anything or even think about doing anything. He waited.

He waited, and the snake kept coming, like a freight train you know has to end sometime, but it just keeps coming.

A fire ant got down inside his shoe and stung him three times and there was nothing on earth he could do about it.

He had to breathe sometime or he would pass out, and the snake would turn on him and swallow him up, and that would be the last anyone ever heard of Superman. Maybe someone would notice a plump snake around town. Maybe not.

White dots whizzed past his eyes. Slowly, so slowly that his chest ached from the exertion, he released the air in his lungs and took a breath.

The white dots faded.

The snake began to taper down, growing gradually slimmer. The tip of the tail came out of the bush on his right, slunk over his ankle, and vanished into the bush on his left.

Superman staggered to his feet and threw up in the crystalline stream.

He started to his knees to wash his face, then realized the snake might have heard him retching. He wiped his mouth on his arm, and kept moving.

Now that he knew what kind of jungle this was, he began to make better time. He didn't worry about slipping and falling; he traveled faster down the steep parts on his rear end. Every log in his path was a snake. Every rustle was a snake in the bushes.

He sang "In-A-Gadda-Da-Vida" and generally tried to make enough noise to alert all future snakes to his presence. He kept telling himself that snakes were more afraid of humans than the other way around, another long-lost bit of wisdom from Scoutmaster Jones. It hardly seemed possible that it was true, yet it comforted him somehow.

A thing plopped on his neck. He screamed and batted it off. It scuttled off through the leaves before he could see it—lizard? spider? tiny snake? The guitar whanged into a tree.

Superman heard someone breathing, a high-pitched, hysterical sound, and realized it was himself.

Hold on, now. Get ahold of yourself. There was only one snake, and it did not hurt you. Do not get in a hurry and fall and bust your pelvis. That would be some real trouble, to be out in this jungle all busted up.

A few clouds had drifted in, blocking the sun, stirring a breeze through the underbrush. He pondered whether to risk another glance over his shoulder. What if he could still see the hangar? Would he give up and go back?

Only one way to know. He turned, and looked up.

The hangar was nowhere in sight. He was a long way down the mountain. The pounding of surf was distinctly louder than it had been a few minutes before.

He was making progress.

He started off again. No more snakes, not a snake in the world. Any minute now this deep green tangle would give forth onto the road to the beach.

He was careful not to gloat, but he was glad to have hung in there long enough to taste his impending success. A breeze stirred, blissfully cool, moving through the jungle with a wash of white sound. Beyond that, the ocean lunged against the shore. And beyond that sound, rising now, a sibilant hissing: a sound like distant applause, a thousand sheets of paper ripped in two, a million snakes rising up on their tails.

A sudden splatter of fat, cold bloblets—then the downpour was upon him utterly, sharp-stinging bullet-drops fired from the sky.

In the time it took to raise his hand, he was drenched.

Water fell in buckets, barrels, sheets. Superman's groan was drowned by the thunderous sound of its falling. He moved under a tree. The rain bent the tree over sideways. Instantly every ditch and depression in the mountainside became a river, a torrent of brown foamy water joining with other torrents, pouring around him down the slope.

He wished he could march up that hill and pound on that gate until Pito opened up and led him to his cozy shack and brought him towels and hot coffee. But he'd come too far down to ever think of climbing back up.

A slender gray snake swam by like quicksilver through the downracing stream.

Superman's heart sank. He wanted out of the jungle.

He plunged through nets of clawing vines, feeling for the bottoms of streambeds with his walking stick, hurrying across patches of volcanic rock. The rain beat so hard that he'd lost even the primitive track of Frank's jeep. The downpour roared in his ears. He scrambled down a steeper slope, lost his footing, and slid on his back twenty feet down the mountain, crashing sideways into a fallen log.

Thank you God for that log, the one thing that kept him from plummeting over the bank into a fast-rushing white-water river. A real river, this one, not a rain-swollen ditch.

It was raining harder than it had ever rained before, and every second it rained even harder.

A big log swept past in the current, bobbing along light and easy as a toothpick. That log would be down on the beach before Superman made it another ten feet.

Somehow that didn't seem fair.

Somehow, it began to seem like an idea.

The river knows the fastest way to the sea. Why not take the fastest way? Wouldn't it be better than staggering along through this sopping tangle until it was dark and the snakes came to swallow what was left of him?

There are times in a man's life when he has a choice to make. One choice is smart and the other is stupid, and sometimes a man is drawn irresistibly toward the stupid choice because he's too distracted to see the difference.

Superman saw a palm frond floating by, and thought: I'm already as wet as I can get. And by God if a log or a palm frond can float, so can I.

He tied the rice sack around his neck, slipped the walking stick through the knot, bound the Gibson to his chest with the shoulder strap. His plan was to make like a log, hold himself very still and straight, and let the current just take him.

There was the problem of how to enter the water. He would prefer to wade in from the bank, but the gorge was fifteen feet deep on both sides.

The roaring rain and the thought of more snakes and more *thump-thud-bump-oof!* down the mountain was too much to endure.

He took a deep breath, backed up three steps for the head start, and went vaulting out over the river.

He entered feetfirst. A shocking chill. He struggled to get his head up but the current tumbled him over, banging him into rocks. Make like a log, he told himself. Straight. Narrow. Buoyant.

He got his face out of the water, gasped for air, tried to straighten himself out with his head facing upstream. At the heart of the torrent there was no upstream or down, no sense of where he was in relation to the air. He was just as powerless as any log or palm frond ever swept down a river.

So this was what pride tastes like: drowning. Someone (Mr. Jones?) once told him that drowning was the pleasantest way to die, but now he wondered how the hell anyone could claim to know a thing like that.

One thing he had failed to consider: when water takes the fastest course down a hill to the sea, that means *straight down,* over waterfalls and tumbling rock chutes. A log doesn't necessarily reach the bottom of a river without getting bashed to splinters. Superman took so many hits off boulders that he gave up trying to be a log and made like a fetus instead, arms wrapped around his head, knees drawn to his chest. Only the great rushing current kept the rocks from smashing his brains out.

He flailed to the surface. A whirlpool sucked him under. He bumped his head.

Time went away from him then; it just floated up out of his body and hung there before him, a clock with no hands. He lost his place in the universe. The stars reached down and swept him up in their twinkling net. They carried him up through the rain to the place where the darkness began.

SOMEONE DRAGGED HIM by his ankles, facedown, across gritty sand. Someone placed a foot in the small of his back, and stepped up on his rib cage.

He coughed and belched water. "Get off," he wheezed.

"Don't you love the beach in the rain?" A musical whisper. She stepped off.

He rolled over. Rain streamed from her yellow rain slicker onto his face. "You . . ."

"I keep finding you like this," she said. "If you're trying to kill yourself, you know, there are easier ways."

Superman took a census of his body. Every part reported in battered but alive. The rain dripped from her face onto his belly, and he was so amazed to be here, to have her standing over him dripping rain on him.

"I got lost in the jungle. I saw this—Jesus, this snake was like a hundred feet long."

She smiled. "What color?"

"Green."

"Just a boa. They won't hurt you. You're too big. Now if you were a poodle . . ."

Superman untied the rice sack from his neck. His walking stick was gone, and his guitar.

He had lost his blue shirt, his airplane, and now his old friend the Gibson. The three material possessions that truly mattered to him.

What is Superman without his shirt, his plane, his guitar?

Just a man, sitting on the sand in the rain, talking to Marilyn Monroe. Which, when you thought about it, was not so bad.

Maybe he would go home tomorrow.

He tied the rice sack around his neck, slipped the walking stick through the knot, bound the Gibson to his chest with the shoulder strap. His plan was to make like a log, hold himself very still and straight, and let the current just take him.

There was the problem of how to enter the water. He would prefer to wade in from the bank, but the gorge was fifteen feet deep on both sides.

The roaring rain and the thought of more snakes and more *thumpthud-bump-oof!* down the mountain was too much to endure.

He took a deep breath, backed up three steps for the head start, and went vaulting out over the river.

He entered feetfirst. A shocking chill. He struggled to get his head up but the current tumbled him over, banging him into rocks. Make like a log, he told himself. Straight. Narrow. Buoyant.

He got his face out of the water, gasped for air, tried to straighten himself out with his head facing upstream. At the heart of the torrent there was no upstream or down, no sense of where he was in relation to the air. He was just as powerless as any log or palm frond ever swept down a river.

So this was what pride tastes like: drowning. Someone (Mr. Jones?) once told him that drowning was the pleasantest way to die, but now he wondered how the hell anyone could claim to know a thing like that.

One thing he had failed to consider: when water takes the fastest course down a hill to the sea, that means *straight down,* over waterfalls and tumbling rock chutes. A log doesn't necessarily reach the bottom of a river without getting bashed to splinters. Superman took so many hits off boulders that he gave up trying to be a log and made like a fetus instead, arms wrapped around his head, knees drawn to his chest. Only the great rushing current kept the rocks from smashing his brains out.

He flailed to the surface. A whirlpool sucked him under. He bumped his head.

Time went away from him then; it just floated up out of his body and hung there before him, a clock with no hands. He lost his place in the universe. The stars reached down and swept him up in their twinkling net. They carried him up through the rain to the place where the darkness began.

SOMEONE DRAGGED HIM by his ankles, facedown, across gritty sand. Someone placed a foot in the small of his back, and stepped up on his rib cage.

He coughed and belched water. "Get off," he wheezed.

"Don't you love the beach in the rain?" A musical whisper. She stepped off.

He rolled over. Rain streamed from her yellow rain slicker onto his face. "You . . ."

"I keep finding you like this," she said. "If you're trying to kill yourself, you know, there are easier ways."

Superman took a census of his body. Every part reported in battered but alive. The rain dripped from her face onto his belly, and he was so amazed to be here, to have her standing over him dripping rain on him.

"I got lost in the jungle. I saw this—Jesus, this snake was like a hundred feet long."

She smiled. "What color?"

"Green."

"Just a boa. They won't hurt you. You're too big. Now if you were a poodle . . ."

Superman untied the rice sack from his neck. His walking stick was gone, and his guitar.

He had lost his blue shirt, his airplane, and now his old friend the Gibson. The three material possessions that truly mattered to him.

What is Superman without his shirt, his plane, his guitar?

Just a man, sitting on the sand in the rain, talking to Marilyn Monroe. Which, when you thought about it, was not so bad.

Maybe he would go home tomorrow.

11 / A Bottle

I WAS SINGING ALONG with "Superman's Revenge" when Granny French knocked. "Benjamin?"

"What!"

"Can I come in?"

"Yeah."

She flinched when she opened the door. My room was one of those caves that only a lonely adolescent can build for himself, full of dangling airplane models and wadded-up Fritos bags, strewn clothes, the smell of hormones, black-light posters on the wall.

I was gluing the tail joint assembly on a Messerschmitt ME-101. "Whatcha need, Granny? I'm kind of busy."

She stayed where she was in the doorway. "There's a package came for you. I opened it while you were at school."

I turned down the music. In her hands was a cardboard box, trailing the torn ends of brown paper and shipping twine. "What is it?"

"It came to the house in Encino," she said. "Those Jewish people that bought the house were nice enough to forward it on." She went to put it on the worktable where my delicate landing gear was drying. I grabbed it just in time.

A sea smell rose up from the box. Wedged down among newspapers was an old whiskey bottle, encrusted with barnacles and dried ocean muck.

Granny said, "Look in the box."

A scrap of blue cloth, faded letters bled through to the other side. Tiny shaky letters.

7/14/72 Pls send to Benj.
Willis Jr 4587 Lind a
Vista Encino Calif.

> Dear Ben One thing to
> know I love y ou ALWAYS
> Love Dad PS you should
> see this place

Two curled-up Polaroid pictures, faded and bleached as old bones. In the first, you could make out the wing of a plane, and, in the distance, an island: two misty cone-shaped hills and a blank white curve that might be a beach.

From the second photo, my father's face grinned out at me.

"It's him, isn't it," Granny said. "It looks just like him."

My head reeled. "Where did this come from?"

"There's a note from the people that found it," she said. "They were sailing a boat through the Panama Canal this summer. They spotted it in the water. It's like something out of Robinson Crusoe."

"Do you think—"

"That's a piece of his shirt," said Granny. "I would know that blue shirt anywhere. I tried to get him to change that shirt for ten years."

"Does this mean . . . he's alive?"

"Now Benjamin, look at the date. That's the day he disappeared. He must have written it before he crashed. If he was alive we'd have heard from him by now."

"But we've got to tell somebody." I waved the picture. "This must be where he went. Maybe he can't call us. But he tried to show us. We've got to find him."

Granny spent most of the day on the phone with the Air National Guard and the office of Senator Russell Long in Washington, D.C. The FBI sent a man to our house. He put the whiskey bottle and the scrap of blue shirt and the Polaroids in a cardboard box and took them away.

Months passed before a UPS man brought the items back to us in the same box, without comment. "I reckon that's the end of it," Granny said. But she knew how much it meant to me to know that my father loved me and was thinking about me at the end. She had the Polaroids framed with the scrap of blue shirt, and gave it to me for Christmas. I hung it on the wall above my bed.

PS you should see this place.

12 / The River Knows the Way to the Sea

1973

IN THE MIDDLE of that afternoon, in the midst of falling raining swooning making love and more love to that beautiful woman, Superman had an idea about the evolution of skin. Suddenly he knew why our ancestors' tough hairy hide has evolved into our soft, sensitive, increasingly hairless skin, why our natural armor has smoothed into great exposed stretches of nerve endings, the opposite of armor. Skin renders us helpless, defenseless, and quivering, gasping for more. It shudders at the slightest breath, flinches at the graze of a fingertip. We are constantly evolving to improve the sensation of one smooth skin rubbing against another. This means our children's skin will be more sensitive than ours, and their children's after them, and so on through time, until our great-great-great-grandchildren will be so exquisitely tender that we cannot imagine how it will be for them to make love. If we could feel what they will feel at a simple caress, our poor primitive brains might explode, our neurons burst in a rupture of ecstasy.

So we shoulder along at the job of improving the species. We surrender to this animal feeling, this stroking, this rubbing, this delicious friction and lack of friction—bodies tingling, hungering for the next touch. In a world that grows harder every day, we are becoming softer, more vulnerable. The ancient feelings overwhelm our modern minds, and lead us to lie down in green pastures.

Think of it: in the future, sex will get *better*. How will they ever have time to think about anything else? At this moment, all over the world, people are doing it the old way, working out a million improvements and variations on the old familiar theme. Someday we will be perfectly sexy creatures having perfect sex, all the time. Only a superior being could think up such a system. Maybe it was this unconscious connection that led Superman to cry out, as he gripped the headboard and thrust firmly inside her: "Oh God! Oh God!"

She was an athlete, a goddess, a tyrant, a girl, all things at once and in turn. She materialized above, behind, below him, so changeable and beautifully attuned that she had to be some newer finer version of the species. The curve of her hair flowed down to her shoulder, leading to her breast, her waist, each curve softly sculpted. . . . He blasted another salvo of pure lust. He forgot who she was. The only thing in his mind was this rabid desire to touch taste lick and impose himself upon every inch of her.

It was there in the air between them from the moment she stepped off his back on the beach. He followed her down the wet sand in the rain, limping along behind the bright glow of her yellow slicker. They climbed a trail into the jungle.

He did not notice her house. It was a house with a door, which she kindly unlocked. Then they were inside and everything unsaid was discarded. He seized her and kissed her, wrapped his wet body around her. They sank to their knees in the kitchen, their mouths melting together.

He saw the earth through a gap in the floor. His tongue found her ear. She twisted out from under him, slinking around and over him. She clamped him in the softness of her thighs and held fast.

"Mmm," she purred, "I oughta save your life more often."

He grinned. "You're good at it."

She stretched her arms, and those great pale mountains stood up, demanding attention. He buried his face in the fragrant warm valley between them, applying his tongue along the length of her breastbone, tracing it out. He came around the underside, flicking and nipping up the long curve of her breast to the glorious summit, the sweet knobby nipple. He worshiped it with his whole body, making soft ecstatic cries that vibrated her flesh and provoked cries of her own. His hands roamed her skin. The rain slicker squeaked on the floor. He lay locked to her, mouth to breast, suckling to mother, sinner to God, making noises of pure supplication.

Suddenly there it was before him, beautiful, glistening like a bed of moist ferns. He slid up under her, from the side, and in.

And then what else to do but bring himself back out, and in.

And back in.

This is when the higher brain switched off and Superman's mind went traveling out over the jungle to roam over Darwin, the smoothness of flesh, woman as goddess virgin mother and whore, and a pelican he'd seen on the beach, making a perfect hit on a fish at the top of a wave. He breathed the smells of this woman: baby powder, sweat, lavender. Mushrooms. The sea. He thrust up and up, took her in his arms and fucked her across the room to the bed, threw her down and kept on without missing a beat.

From a cupboard behind the bed Sinatra was singing

That sudden explosion when two tingles intermingle

—the smug trumpets swaying, crooning along. Superman did not break stride shoving her up to the headboard, dear God could it rain any harder? The room had no walls, only screens. The rain blew in, soaking the bed. The springs squealed.

He got his head up, gasping air full of rain. "Oh, God!"

"Ooh yes, hm hm hm hm—"

"Jesus! Oh!"

"Come on—"

And when he came, the beauty and force of this woman passed through him like delicate electricity. A flash of lightning froze the world for an instant. Superman exploded, sailing out across the darkness of space in five million glittering bits of satisfaction.

The thunderclap left them breathless. They burst out laughing and rolled over on the damp sheets, clinging together. The rain pounded harder. She licked her lips and kissed him.

Oh God, he thought, thank you God. Thank you Darwin.

They lay quiet for a while, breathing. Rain spattered through the screen. She laid a hand on his thigh. That was all it took to bring him up, and then they were at it again, devouring each other. This time she wound up on top, knees pressed together, playing rockey-horse with her eyes closed. She was not rambunctious, like Sandy and Linda, not a bundle of quivering needs like Alexa—this Daisy was weightless as a flower, floating above him. Her second coming was quieter than the first, but she trembled and jumped and made happy little shouts.

When it was over, she slid down beside him, twining her legs around his.

After a while she whispered, "I'm wet."

"What, again?"

"No, the rain. Let's go in." She drew the sheet around her and climbed off the bed. He grabbed his shorts and went after.

His head reeled. How many women in his life, how many times had he done the thing?—hundreds, thousands—but never had he done it like this, with that furious passion pouring out of him, like a river of molten silver. He folded her into his arms. "Jesus, Daisy. That was incredible." His voice sounded two notes lower on the scale.

She put her head back to let his lips graze at her throat. "I'm glad you enjoyed it."

"What about you?"

"Hmm?" She reached for a packet with a squat bird on the side: Emu filters.

He hated to ask, but he was dying to know: "Was that—was it nice? Did you like it?"

She lit the cigarette, inhaled sharply. "On a scale of one to ten?"

"Well, I don't necessarily—"

"A six. And I mean that in the nicest possible way."

"Six?" He frowned.

"Maybe six and a half. You are sweet." She batted her eyes. "Well, you asked."

"I hope you'll give me a chance to raise that score."

She pulled away. "What are you grinning at?"

"I'm happy," he said. "You're incredible. You make me grin."

"That's nice. Keep talking that way, I may give you a seven."

"Do you always rate men on a scale of one to ten?"

"If they ask that stupid question. 'Was it good for you?' " She touched a match to the burner under the kettle. "You want a cup of tea?"

"No, thanks."

"The British always have tea after sex, you know. It's an ancient tradition."

"You're not British."

"No, but I've had sex with some of them." She rattled in the silverware drawer. "They tend to be kind of inhibited. I like the tea, though."

"Do men always fall in love with you after you . . ." He waved at the bed.

"Not always," she said thoughtfully, as if admitting some minor personal failing. "You're not falling in love, are you?"

"I don't know. I probably could."

"Well, don't. I'm not looking for love. Love can kill you."

"Sometimes it sneaks up on you when you're not looking."

"Oh"—that breathy giggle—"a ro*man*tic." Watching the blue flame lick the bottom of the kettle, she was profoundly unglamorous, and all the more beautiful: hazel-brown hair rumpled and tangled; wide violet eyes untouched by makeup. She was not a movie star, not some stylized Technicolor vision, but a real woman in a state of superb disarray, clutching a sheet to her bosom.

Already Superman was having trouble believing what he had been permitted to do. Naked, this woman comprised one of the great landscapes on earth. Through some miracle he had been granted access to every one of her most exotic locales. For a moment he turned his whole body into a camera, and inscribed a photograph in his mind.

"What we need is cookies," she said, bending to search a low cabinet. "Do you like macaroons?" Her heart-shaped bottom loomed before him.

He stretched out his arms and knee-walked across the floor. She peered down with a mixture of sympathy and amusement.

He said, "God, you're beautiful," and buried his face in the sheet.

She picked an ant off a cookie. "Ben, you need to get hold of yourself."

"Let me stay with you. I can make you happy." He blurted these words without thinking.

"I barely know you," she said.

"I'm a good guy, I swear. I'll do anything you want."

"Anything?"

"Yes."

"All right then, stand up. Come on—up, up. Thataboy."

He got to his feet. It took all his willpower not to toss her back on the bed.

"I have bats," she said.

"I beg your pardon?"

She nodded gravely. "I know they're supposed to be good and they eat mosquitoes, but they give me the creeps. You said 'anything.' "

He glanced around the room. "Where are they?"

"Up there." She eyed a trapdoor in the ceiling. "They're sleeping now. They sleep in the daytime, you know."

"Yeah, I'd heard that. How'd they get in?"

"Well how would I know," she said, her voice rising, "what do you think, I went up there and interviewed them?"

"I thought you weren't afraid of stuff like this," he said.

"What gave you that idea?"

"You seemed pretty calm when I told you about that snake."

"Snakes are one thing. Bats are a whole different category."

When she unwrapped the sheet to rewind it about her body, Superman caught a glimpse of that lickable navel. He had to lean against a chair for support.

She draped the sheet over her shoulder. "What's the matter?"

"If I get rid of the bats, will you promise to fall in love with me?"

"Let's keep our minds on the job," she said, scraping a chair across the floor. "This is not going to be high enough. There's a ladder on the porch."

The kettle shrieked. Superman fetched the ladder while she made tea.

He pushed up on the trapdoor. Moldy air flowed through the hatch, a light flutter of wings. He climbed up a step. The attic was alive with bats, several dozen of them flitting about, dried-up brown things hanging like used tea bags from the tin ceiling, chuckling softly in the light from a pair of vent windows.

Superman reminded himself that he was a grown man, and unafraid of bats. "That's your problem right there," he called, "screen's torn out of these windows. Looks like the Bat Hilton up here."

"Oh God, are they still there, do you see them?"

"Oh yeah. Got some window screen? A staple gun?"

"I think so."

"Whyn't you find 'em while I try and chase these guys out."

"You are so brave," she said.

Of course Superman would have gladly tamed all those bats and taught them to sing "Amazing Grace" in four-part harmony, if that's what it took to get her back into bed.

He shut the hatch. First he tried swatting with a towel, but that only provoked a lot of desultory flapping around. He wanted not to kill them, but to make this place inhospitable to them.

What do bats hate? Bright lights. Loud noises.

Noises.

He cupped his hands and clapped. Loud.

The brown pods exploded in a rush of wings. He clapped again. With every report of his hands, the bats staggered in midair as if they'd been shot. They whirled around in a cyclone, trying to get out.

Superman clapped louder, ringing the air. Wings brushed his face as they streamed for the exits. He crouched low and kept clapping, trying not to think about rabies, which drives you so frothing mad they have to chain you up outside somewhere until you die.

A knock on the hatch—"What on earth are you doing?"

He opened it. "Bats hate loud noises. A little-known fact."

She handed up a staple gun and a bundle of screen wire. "This is really great of you."

"Glad to be of service." He chased out the remaining stragglers with an emphatic flamenco flourish, *clap-clappidy-clap! clap! clap!* The last bat made three frantic tours of the attic before it found the opening and dived through.

He balanced on the shit-slippery beam to the end of the house, stripped off the torn screen, and began tacking a new piece in place. He worked fast, knowing Daisy was down there wrapped in a sheet. He finished one window and tromped to the other.

It surprised him to see another house out there, a simple cabin like this one, maybe twenty feet away, partly hidden by a huge stand of heliconia. If the neighbors were home, they'd have heard everything.

Sinatra's lazy voice floated up through the trapdoor: *If you are among the very young . . . at heart. . . .*

At the moment, Superman felt young indeed. He finished the window, dusted his hands, and went to the trapdoor. One look at Daisy made him forget the neighbors. She had pulled on a pink sweater and white clam-diggers, which meant he would get to undress her all over again.

"Are you sure they're all gone?"

"Absolutely. Just had to show 'em who's boss." He lowered himself through the hole.

He went down a step. Her hand slid up his leg.

"Keep going," he said. "You might find something you like."

She pinched his thigh, and spun away giggling.

He hopped off the ladder, pulled her to him. Usually kissing a woman was something you did with your lips, while your mind was working on how to get her clothes off, what to do first, whether to save that or jump on it now, what to savor, what to treat roughly so that you can come back later and be especially gentle with it. But now Superman's mind, mouth, and body all joined in together to kiss this woman down to her cherry-red toe-nails.

He moved in, pressing flat against her belly, nothing tentative now that he knew she liked being mauled by an animal, liked the tongue in her ear and his expanding hardness and his hands skimming up her back, tugging the sweater. She fell back laughing, pretending to fend him off. He backed her to the sleeping porch and launched them both onto the bed.

"Don't—no, please—wait," she said, laughing, but she didn't want him to wait.

He yanked down her clamdiggers and flung them away. He fumbled with his zipper, brought himself out down and glory hallelujah there he was, right there deep inside heaven. Yes indeed, yes indeed. His belly rubbed against her fuzzy sweater. His cutoffs worked down his shins. The rain started again.

She smiled and stuck out her tongue.

He worked changes in that smile, throwing in a slow curve, a long sideways slide, rotating the rhythm. She scratched down his back with her nails, soft with an edge.

This is the work we do, the work we do, the chant ran through his head, the hard sweaty work we must do to improve the species. He buried his face in her neck and swarmed over her, nudging her, pushing and covering her, bringing himself to the edge of a vast dark canyon. If he left this bed he would fall into that darkness and disappear forever.

Daisy began to glow the warm colors of sunset. Superman held on for dear life, he said *I love you* and rode the sensation all the way out to where the colors burst and faded.

Oh what a beautiful thing. Especially the moment just after, when they lay sprawled across each other, sharing the pounding in their veins.

I love you. Don't hurt me.

The voice sprang up inside him.

He knew he had been trying to go somewhere. Something important about Ben Junior. But just now that whole side of his life seemed blurry, indistinct.

He was on his way home. He got lost and jumped in a river. The river dumped him out on the beach. Daisy found him, saved him, brought him to her house, and showed him a whole new way to make love. The stupid choice had worked out exceedingly well. That was the lesson for today: when you see a river, jump in. The river knows the way to the sea.

Every time he thought he knew what he wanted, this place worked another change on his perspective.

"You okay?" she said. "You look serious."

He lifted his chin to her shoulder. "Yeah."

"What are you thinking?"

"You're wonderful," he said.

"That wasn't it." She mashed his nose with her finger. "I am, but that wasn't it."

He grasped her finger, and kissed it. He kissed the knuckle, and all the knuckles in the row.

"The judges have reached their decision," she said. "Do you want to hear?"

"I don't know. Do I?"

She squeezed his hand. "Eight point five. Very impressive advancement in the second round."

"I'd like to thank all the little people who made it possible." Superman kissed her wrist, up the inside of her arm. He was drunk on her, dying of thirst for her. "And now I'd like to try for a perfect ten."

"Whoa, whoa—" She pushed him away. "The judges are exhausted."

He rested his mouth on her shoulder, breathing her smell. Sleepiness settled over them like an invisible net. The rain slowed to a patter. Bugs zinged through the trees. The world began to stir and come out from under its shelter.

Superman sank back on the damp pillow. "I'd like to stay here forever." His fingers stole across her belly.

"Hey!" She stopped his hand. "You've had enough."

"Never," he whispered. "I will never get enough of you." He knew it was true. He had fallen into something bigger than a river. He yawned, closed his eyes. The ability to move drained out through the tips of his fingers and toes.

This felt too good to be true. How had it happened that she was there waiting when he washed onto the beach? Maybe the whole thing was some kind of fever-dream—maybe he *had* killed himself in that river, and she was an angel, and this was heaven at last.

But her taste on his lips was real, and the silky heat of her skin. He couldn't imagine an angel doing the things she had done to him all afternoon. That would be too fine, even for heaven. Word would get out. The pearly gates would be mobbed.

He let out a sigh, and drifted away.

The house was dark when he awoke. He lay tangled in a sheet at the foot of the bed. Leftover rain dripped from the trees. A bird laughed, as if it had found the only dry spot in the jungle.

He felt around with his hand. "Daisy?"

. . .

He got up. His foot skidded on the wet floor. He took small steps. "Daisy?" He padded through the dark house. He felt strangely out of place in his body, as if something had changed forever while he was asleep.

Get out of here now, an urgent voice said.

No, stay, wait for her, sleep with her, make love to her. No one on earth ever made you feel that way.

Get your pants on and get out. Now, while she's gone. She is the siren and you must lash yourself to the mast. Turn your head away. Do not listen to the song.

Stay . . .

They want to keep you here. She is part of their plan. If you don't go now, you may never escape.

That was love sure enough welling up through the cracks in the floor, or something as awful and all-consuming as love, and right now Superman didn't need anything like that.

Get out while you can. Go home.

—but did you see when she rolled on her side with her hand just touching her face? Dear God. I could die twenty times. A naked woman is a pure blessing.

You can't know a woman from one afternoon in bed, but you can learn enough to know she would swallow you up, you would vanish inside her, never to be seen again. Every breath every waking moment would be given to adoring her, inhaling, imbibing her. She would become your addiction, the thing that you did with your life.

Superman imagined making love to this woman every day, morning and night, for the rest of his life. Would he ever grow bored, or unhappy?

Maybe not. But Ben Junior would always be there, in his mind, waiting for him to come home.

He put on damp shorts. He looked around for some way to leave a note, but the desk drawer was empty and anyway what could he say? *Love, fun, goodbye.*

He gathered his belongings and went out. A light shone in the window of the other house. He stepped around a puddle to the side of the porch, hidden behind a dense, sweet-blooming hedge.

"You have to eat something," she said.

"Wanna play." A cracked voice. A man's voice, but the words were a child's, and strange in a way that made Superman uncomfortable. A man pretending to be a child? . . .

"Look how good it is. Look, it has raisins, and I put lots of sugar, just the way you like."

"Play!"

"No, eat first, then play."

Superman crept down the side of the house.

Daisy stood by the window—if she turned, she would see him standing there. He held his breath and stepped back.

A spoon, poised above a bowl of steaming oatmeal. A skinny old man in a wheelchair, baggy white pajamas, a shawl around his shoulders. A Boston Red Sox cap threw his face into shadow. His toes were clenched so tight that Superman's toes curled in sympathy.

The man pounded his fist on a plastic tray-table. Checkers jumped up off a checkerboard. "Play!"

"Come on," she said. "Just one bite. For me."

Abruptly the man swung his hand. The bowl sailed through the air and smashed against the wall, splattering a wide arc of oatmeal.

"Oh, hell!"

"Don't *want!*"

"Jack, you are really pissing me off," she said. Just then she turned to see Superman.

He looked past her to the man slowly turning, the light stealing up his shoulder onto his face. The scar reached almost to his eyebrow, an occlusion that distorted the famous profile into a weird caricature of itself.

"Play *now!*" he bellowed.

One glimpse was enough to know who that was.

Superman stumbled back from the window, moving as fast as his bad leg would carry him. Daisy called his name. He ran and never looked back.

13 / Cliff-Diving

SUPERMAN STARED INTO the darkness beyond the ghostly breakers. The tide lapped at his toes. He could not let himself believe what his eyes had seen. He could not even bring himself to speak that man's name aloud on the beach, where no one could hear.

The whole world knew that man was dead.

But no, he was here, in a cabin in the jungle, and Daisy feeding him with a spoon. It made an awful kind of sense—and no sense at all.

Happy birth-day, Mr. President . . .

The light in the cabin was dim. Superman had only a glimpse of the face. It had to be some mistake, or illusion—a trick of the mind.

That man's death was an established fact, a piece of history. Superman was beginning to see that history is not a puzzle made of neatly interlocking pieces. History says JFK lies beneath an eternal flame at Arlington. Marilyn Monroe died facedown on a bed in her Holmby Hills bungalow. Amelia Earhart died in a crash somewhere near Howland Island in 1937. Anastasia and her family were riddled with bullets and dumped down a well. Michael Rockefeller disappeared while studying Stone Age tribes in New Guinea. D. B. Cooper parachuted from the rear hatch of a 727 and perished in the remote blackness of Washington State. Jimmy Hoffa drove away from lunch at the Red Fox restaurant and wound up under the end zone of Giants Stadium.

The things we think we know are just stories we have been told. They are not necessarily true.

The moon spread a cool blue light upon the ocean, illuminating great floating pillows of cloud in the sky. Superman wandered farther out on the sand, fuzzy-headed and confused and more than a little desperate. He stepped around the big rock and was surprised to see a very old man waiting there, with a boat.

He looked too old to have dragged that boat to the waterline. He wore a felt derby, white shirt, baggy trousers. He was thin as a bone. He stood ramrod-straight with the line in his hand, as if he'd been waiting.

"Good evening," Superman said.

The man nodded.

"My name's Ben."

"Harry."

"Nice boat." In fact it was a ridiculous boat: a squat, deep-keeled craft, maybe ten feet long, pumpkin orange with green trim, bright and silly-looking as a circus wagon. But it was a real boat with a ten-horse putt-putt motor, and it seemed to float okay. "How much you want for that thing?"

"Not for sale," Harry said, his gums working.

"Can I rent it?"

"Nope."

"Borrow it?"

"Do I look like a fool?"

"Okay. I'll give you five hundred bucks."

The man made some *phew-fluh-pfft* sounds of dismissal.

"Look, how much do you want?"

"It's not for sale," Harry said, "but I got another just like it."

"Another . . . ?" Superman turned. Indeed there were now two ropes in the old man's hand, two identical boats bobbing in the surf.

"You can have that other one," the man said.

Superman had to smile. "How'd you do that?"

"Indirection. Hocus-pocus. Sleight of hand."

"What are you, a magician?"

"I was," said Harry. "I'm retired now."

Superman stared. "You're not by any chance the guy that owns this place?"

"Nope."

"There's a lot of magicians around here," Superman said.

"It's in the water," said Harry. "Superior magic. Which one you want?"

"Either one would be fine."

"Hold this." He put a wet rope into Superman's hand. "Shut your eyes and count backwards from three. No cheating."

Superman did as he was told. When he opened his eyes, the old man was gone, and both boats. The rope in his hand was a piece of seaweed.

He flung it down, turned all the way around. The beach was deserted.

The nearest patch of jungle was a hundred yards off. "Where'd you go?" he said to thin air.

He walked back around the looming lava rock, big as a sailing ship, catching waves on its prow. He stared hard at the seaward end. That looked like a human being on the point where the boulders divided the surf—on the last pinnacle, a figurehead leaning out into the spray.

The man lifted his arms and hurled himself off the rock.

Superman jumped up with a shout, stumbling cursing barking his knees on ragged blades of lava. Rounding the point he saw a burly figure scuttling up the face of the rock, nude, streaming water, advancing with his hand out. "All hail mighty Neptune, ruler of the deep!" came the booming voice. "Divest yourself of those vestments, my son! The breakers await!"

"Are you out of your mind? There's all kind of rocks down there!" Superman glanced fearfully over the edge. "You trying to break your damn neck?"

Rabbit pushed sopping hair out of his face. "He who breaks his neck in the pursuit of joy is a lucky man! It's the straightest path to Nirvana! You don't go when the wave's down; you wait for a big one and jump into it. Observe while I demonstrate." He hastened off, all aglow.

Climbing to the last rock, he spread his arms as if he were some great Greek god figure, instead of a brawny hairy guy with his big white butt showing. He greeted an oncoming swell with a shout and launched himself into it, barely missing a rock.

He bobbed up again in a spume of foam, howling for joy.

In a minute he came huffing up the face of the cliff. "Face your fears, Superman! Confront your destiny! Hurl yourself into the void!"

"There ain't enough money in the world," Superman said.

Rabbit shook his head like a dog shedding water. "That, my friend, is what's known as a natural high."

"Listen, there was this old guy, I thought you were him—I mean, he was just *right there*—" He knew he was not making sense. "Rabbit, you gotta help me. I need a boat."

Rabbit fastened his overall straps. "What kind of boat?"

"Whatever will take me to a town with a phone. I gotta get out of here. This place is doing weird things to my head." They picked their way across rocks to the beach. Superman found the sack of money where he'd left it.

"Paradise burnout, son. I've seen it a million times. I've got something up at the house that I think might just do the trick. Red Dot Number Ten, new and improved. I've been working on the color bounce, and—"

"Tell you, Rabbit, I've never been one to turn down a chance to have fun, but what I really need more than that right now is a boat. With a motor, you know, not a rowboat. A nice American Evinrude."

"Acute progressive burnout, late stages," said Rabbit. "The overwhelming desire for familiar American things. The irrational belief that all your problems will be solved if only you can get out of here and get home. Dissociated anxiety mixed with classic homesickness and unresolved guilt over the actions that led to your presence here—'There's no place like home.' Does that describe it?"

No, Superman said quietly, that wasn't really it, more a question of needing to get across the channel to whatever mainland that was. The best way to do that, he assumed, would be in a real boat with an outboard motor, if such a thing could be found.

"Son, you're not as much fun as I remember," said Rabbit. "You've got this grim look on your face. Tell you what—come with me. I'll get you a boat."

"Now you're talking," said Superman. "I'll pay good money."

Rabbit led the way around a brackish lagoon. "Forgive me for asking, I do hate to pry, but—anyone might think you'd been mistreated here, you're so all-fired anxious to leave. What happened, did Frank take a peek at you in the shower?"

"No."

"The old lady get mad and throw you out?"

"How did you know?"

"It was only a matter of time," Rabbit said. "Miss Emily's getting cranky in her old age, the mood swings, the irrational behavior. It's hard to control even with medication, which she refuses. So now you'll be needing suitable lodgings."

"You don't understand. I'm not staying another night in this place. I am getting the hell out of here."

"You want to talk about it?"

As it turned out, Superman did want to talk. He told about getting lost in the jungle, the boa constrictor, the deluge, the river, the ancient magician, and Daisy—not everything about her, but enough so that Rabbit's eyebrows went up.

"Did you . . . ?"

Superman nodded. "I know, I could hardly believe it myself, but see, then I woke up and she was gone and . . . I looked into this cabin next door. I saw who lives there. I can't . . . it's impossible, but I know what I saw."

Rabbit patted his shoulder. "Not to worry, you've got your spiritual adviser on the case. You did the right thing coming to me."

The jungle gave into a clearing, a rambling lopsided ramshackle pile of a house that appeared to have been built by some scrap-metal dealers having a drunken party.

"Where's the boat?"

Rabbit opened the door. "It's not mine. I'll have to make a call."

"You have a phone?"

"Walkie-talkie. Come in, you're letting the air out."

If a house can be said to give a glance inside the mind of its inhabitant, Rabbit's brain was an unholy mess. The front room was strewn with books, papers, trash, not just piled here and there but wildly disarranged, as if someone had gone around kicking and flinging things.

"Welcome to my nightmare." Rabbit waded through a wash of papers, flinging open a door which led into the other half of his mind: spotless white tile on walls, floors, and countertops; a window unit chugging cool air; tidy shelves of jars, beakers, Bunsen burners, instrument trays, centrifuges, scales, mortars and pestles, all gleaming and dust-free. One corner was arranged as a sitting room, with a stereo, coffee table, La-Z-Boy recliners.

"Beseat yourself, son, and have a look through the music. Let me dry off and see who I can raise on the horn." He disappeared through a third door.

Superman caught a glimpse of a bed, a tiled bathroom. He heard a crackle of static. He squatted to flip through the albums: Rachmaninoff, African Pygmy chants, Mahalia Jackson, Doris Day, the Everlasting Holiness Gospel Choir—and ho, what have we here? A battered copy of *Ben Willis: Songs and Things,* the first album, with that bushy-haired sensitive Poet on the cover, cradling the Gibson in one hand and a cartoon Dove of Peace in the other.

Superman flipped it over to read the dedication he'd sweated out through his pen: "This album is for Alexa, prettiest flower ever to grow in a man's garden. For Ben the Tiny, with the magic shine in his eyes. Also for Hank Williams, who saw the light and paid the price." The schoolboy pretension made him slightly queasy, but "Ben the Tiny" brought a smile to his face.

The disc bore the scratches and scuffs of well-loved vinyl. The stereo was an old Telefunken with side-hinged speakers. Superman cocked the spring on the tone arm. His voice jumped from the speakers, so young and hopped-up intense that it sat him back in his chair.

Tell me, baby, did you do the twist
Did you twist did you twist did you twist it like this?
Tell me, baby, did you do the thing
Did you rock did you swing like the rockin' bird swings?
Wo Lolita
I'm a bona fide fool—
Dance me, baby, like you dance it in school!

At the time he'd been trying for irony, but now "Statutory Romance" sounded like a straight three-chord rockabilly throwdown. He found his foot tapping, rocking along. He'd forgotten that raw edge he once had in his voice.

Rabbit emerged in fresh overalls, hair slicked back in a ponytail. Something about him brought to mind those old daguerreotypes of Confederate generals: something fierce and immovable, with a glint of the fanatic about the eyes. "Strolling down Memory Lane?"

"My first album. I was always hoping to meet the guy who bought it."

"That would be Spike. He let me borrow it. I found it quite lively."

Superman reached for the tone arm—*brzzp!* and off.

"Wait, that was a compliment."

"It was starting to get on my nerves," Superman said. "What about the boat?"

"It'll be at the beach in an hour. Meantime I have some excellent spiritual advice." He reached for a rosewood box and brought out a slender hand-rolled cigarette.

"No, thanks, listen—I've got a long trip to make. The last time I smoked any of that stuff, I got really lost."

"There you go again, shattering my illusions. Don't you know that the Lord loves an expanded mind? Did I lead you astray at La Discoteca?"

"You sure did." He glanced around the laboratory. "All this equipment is just for making drugs?"

"The hallucinogens are for my entertainment." Rabbit lit the joint and began puffing. "My main concentration is in synthesizing oxidization inhibitors for carbon-based organisms. I've done lots of work with psychoactives, hypnotics, psychotropics. Also I'm a Ph.D. in psychology, and I like to play with viruses."

"A real brain, huh? You just work all alone out here?"

Rabbit smiled. "I have friends."

"But why here? Are you famous and I just don't recognize you?"

"I'm here because my work is here. How about you, Superman, did you really just happen to stumble upon us, or did somebody send you?"

"I got lost. I had to put the plane down."

"That's what you remember? You came here in a plane?"

"I crashed on the beach."

"Hmm." Rabbit folded his arms. "Interesting. Go on."

"That's all. Now I need to get home."

"Why?"

"Because—I've got a career, you know," he said, waving the album cover, "a lot of people depending on me. I've got a family . . . people I care about."

"Like who?"

"Well, my wife, and my kid. Look, it's none of your damn business, okay?"

"Whoa, whoa—" Rabbit held up his hands. "I'm sensing a lot of anger here, son. Can you tell me where that's coming from?"

All in all, Superman preferred Rabbit in his messenger-of-the-Lord mode. "Are you gonna get me a boat? Because if you're not—"

"I told you, it's on the way. You know, son, you're so suspicious you're borderline paranoid, yet you're also completely gullible. Do you realize you swallowed that pill I gave you at La Disco without even knowing what it was?"

"Well, yeah—I mean, you seemed like a good guy, and Frank said . . ."

"Frank. What do you know about Frank? Or any of us, for that matter? You know what we've told you. You don't know anything."

"What's that supposed to mean?"

"I'm trying to straighten you out," Rabbit said. "I think you've probably been misinformed on a few issues. What else have you noticed? Any side effects, blackouts, hallucinations? Come on, you can tell me, I'm an M.D."

Superman remembered the shiny Electra hovering over the clearing, the weirdly terrifying glimpse of Daisy and Jack, the little old man who was there, then not there. "No, nothing," he said. "I'm fine."

"Are you sure? Tell me this, Superman—do you know whose house you've been staying in? Emily? Do you know who she is?"

"She's Amelia Earhart. I know the whole story."

"Exactly," he said. "The story is what you know. You don't know anything. Her name is Emily Lakenfield, upstate New York manufacturing family. She was an original member of the Ninety Nines, flew in air races with Amelia. Crashed her plane in Wyoming in 1942 and was paralyzed.

Never got over it. She developed this Earhart fixation and she's been here for thirty years, acting out. She never was able to stomach the fact that Amelia got all the publicity."

"Look, Rabbit, I saw the plane. She's got a goddamn Lockheed Electra up on that mountain. What are you trying to do to me?"

"You saw a plane. Anybody can paint registration numbers on a plane. Have you seen this plane fly?"

"Sort of, I mean, yes," said Superman. "Pito . . . makes it fly with his eyes."

"I think you'll be having these flashbacks for the next month or so," Rabbit said. "The formula still needs some adjusting."

Superman felt his panic growing, as if his body had been invaded by a slender and ravenous worm, gnawing at him from the inside. Rabbit gave him the worm. Rabbit was crazy, or evil, or else Superman had some serious panicking to do. His inverted sense of reality was threatening to turn inside out again.

Sometimes a man has to choose between the smart and the stupid choice, and realizes too late which choice he has already made. "What was in that pill, Rabbit? What was that you gave me?"

"I've been thinking of calling it Sunbeam. Kind of a can opener for the mind. I needed to open your mind up a little, get a look inside. You're sealed up tighter'n a can of beans. There's something eating at you in there, I know—something you ran away from. Something you're really ashamed of. Why don't you try to let it out?"

"I think you're getting a little wacky on me. You're trying to tell me Frank is—"

"Frank Collins. From Oklahoma, the Collins Oil people. Frank was chairman of the board for twenty years before he cracked up. Wore a muumuu to a board meeting. Got busted a couple times in public toilets, like that. The family shipped him here. He and Emily hit it off, she was looking for someone to act the part of Frank, and even the name was the same. They are happily deluded together. The technical term is folie à deux." Rabbit shrugged. "Who else?"

Superman did not want to hear it. He knew it was coming and he didn't want—

"Daisy. As far as I know that's her real name. The resemblance is striking, anyone would have to admit. When she got here and saw how much fun it was for Emily and Frank, she took it from there. But you've seen her—I mean, you've *seen* her. What do you think?"

Superman blew out a breath. "It's her, I'm telling you. And the man in the yellow house, she called him Jack. He looks exactly like—"

"Jack Rutherford. A vice-president of Hartford Insurance. Fell off a Harley and cracked his brainpan. All the king's horses could never quite work that one out. Daisy is sweet to look after him. You didn't think he was—oh now, Superman, you know that's not possible. Your imagination needs a vacation."

"I know what I saw," he said grimly.

"Our local legends," said Rabbit. "They really had you going, huh? Listen, Daisy's a beautiful woman. You got to spend some time with her. What difference does it make who she pretends to be?"

"But Spike said—"

"Poor Spike. Did he tell you about his accident?"

"Yeah, his mother. Horrible story."

"And completely untrue," Rabbit said. "Spike was a janitor in a propane plant that blew up by accident. Forty-two people died. He was lucky to survive. It's no surprise he came out of it with emotional problems."

"If all this is true, then why are they here? What the hell *is* this place?"

"Think of a refuge for the richly disturbed. We're a long way from civilization, son. Every one of these patients has somebody paying big money to make sure Cousin Jack is never heard from again."

"Wait. Just a minute."

"And they love it when somebody new stumbles in, they can diddle around with your brain. They're functional cases, that's how they get their jollies." He smiled. "So do I, I suppose. But I'm too busy running the place to play games."

"Aw come on. You don't run this place."

"I'm a psychiatrist, son. These people are my patients. Maybe at first glance you might say I'm not doing such a great job. But trust me, every one of these people was a basket case, individually. They're much better off here, much more functional than they were in the other world, with what I can do for them in the way of mood control and behavior modification."

"You haven't been here thirty years treating Emily, whoever she is."

"I took over when David Washofsky retired in '66."

"Then who's this . . . Magician? Amelia—Emily says he runs everything."

"That's their nickname for me. *El Mago.* Simple transference. The patient projects his fantasies of authority onto the therapist." He smiled. "I'm certainly no magician, but I have made some good strides with them.

And I'm doing some very exciting work on the side. What about you, Superman? Have you ever had any therapy?"

"Nuh-uh, not me."

"Why not?"

"I've never been crazy."

"What about now? You seem confused."

"Well I am, for God's sake."

"Why don't you tell me about it," said Rabbit. "This confusion. Any ideas on the source?"

"I don't—listen, put on another record or something. I'm tired of this game."

"It's really not a game," said Rabbit. "It's your life we're talking about."

"My life?"

"Your family sent you here, son. You cracked up. Okay? You started crying one night at the supper table and you couldn't stop. Perfectly understandable, all the pressure you were under. So they've sent you here to me, and I think it's about time we get to work on getting you well. I think you stand an excellent chance of recovery."

Superman rose from the chair. "Thanks for the mind-fuck, Rabbit. I gotta go."

"Hold on, son, what's your hurry?"

"Somewhere on this island there's a boat."

Rabbit gazed up with a patient smile. The overhead lamp turned his glasses into disks of hard light. "You can't leave, understand? It's not allowed."

"Watch me." He thrashed through the paper maelstrom, out of the house, into the moist, heavy air.

"Hey, son, come back! I was just having fun!"

Superman flailed along the path. He did not slow down until he was out on the beach.

The sky showed the first pale fading of dawn.

For one moment in that chilly white room, Superman thought Rabbit must be the devil—unless he was telling the truth, and Superman had somehow lost his mind without realizing it. How logical it seemed when Rabbit described it: a tropical madhouse, populated by crazy people who like to pretend they are famous.

He forced himself to take deep breaths. His wits gathered around him in a worried little circle.

Rabbit wasn't the devil, he was something more dangerous: a scientist, a freelancer. Superman shuddered at the thought of the homemade hallu-cinogen still lurking in his bloodstream. He didn't know whether to trust any of his swirling emotions—every thought in his head might be the result of a chemical reaction.

He limped past the big rock where the waves smashed down on Rab-bit's jumping-off point. He was lost, turned around, rattled. He couldn't find where the river came out. He couldn't find the road up the hill to the Big House.

In desperation he turned toward the faint lights of La Discoteca, and that's when he saw the little orange-and-green boat, tied up and waiting for him.

14 / His Idea of Nature

THE BOAT BOBBED and wallowed in the surf. Superman grabbed up the paddle to move past the breakers. He remembered Amelia's warning: *These people are bored, Ben, they're like prisoners here, they're just dying for someone new to play with.* How close he'd come to falling under any number of spells: her subtle persuasions, Frank's plotting, the old Indian's tricks, Rabbit's wild fabrications that made Superman doubt his own sanity. . . . Paddling out from the beach, he realized he could still be sucked back into it all, if he let himself think about Daisy. She was the one force on this island strong enough to get him to stay. He would not let himself think about her.

He paddled with a strength of purpose that reminded him of his old self, before the crash. One day he would have to come back, to find out which parts of this dream were real. He unstuck the choke valve and yanked the starter cord. The motor started up *yut-tut-tut,* a cloud of blue smoke in his face.

Steering off through the swells along the beach, he looked up to the north mountain, where Pito would be raking the lawn and talking to birds, Catalina spreading damp sheets on the hedges, Gyp barking, Amelia wheeling out to the gazebo for breakfast. Maybe she would look down and see him making his escape. He sent off a salute, just in case. Thanks for everything, lady. Hope you get to make your flight.

Now leaving the enchanted zone. Please fasten your seatbelts.

On the beach, the coconut palms nodded their heads *yes, yes, go.* The sky was the softest pink imaginable, like a rose petal just before it drops from the stem. The water reflected the sky, and even the sand was pink—everything rosy and early and warm.

He wished he had kissed Daisy one last time, really kissed her, to make her remember.

He set a course around the south mountain. His toes squished in his shoes. Away from the beach, the rolling sound of the surf dwindled to the *putt-putting* motor and the liquid *glonk!* of waves on the hull. The sea was a shifting plain of swells rising, falling.

Collect call to Encino, California. Hello, Ben Junior, this is your dad. I'm alive, how are you? Have I got a story to tell you when I get home. . . . Is your mom there?

The seaward end of the point ended abruptly at a sheared-off cliff, plunging straight down to a graveyard of boulders. Superman set his course around them. He'd been wondering where on earth he might be, exactly, and had decided that since the sun rose over the mainland, the island must be somewhere on the Pacific coast. That mountainous land across the channel would be Central or South America, possibly Mexico; he had no idea how far south he was. Maybe that wasn't a mainland at all, but only a larger island, in which case he was totally lost—but if his theory was correct, he could drive this boat north along the coastline and eventually reach the good old U.S. of A.

He hoped to find a faster way.

He skimmed around the point. Yellow sunlight came dancing over the water. Eight pelicans flew over in a diagonal line. The air smelled like fresh fish.

His spirits began to rise. He felt happy to be out on the water in this little boat, heading home. Before he came here he never would have enjoyed such a thing. In his old life, his idea of nature was sitting in the back of a limo, watching a National Geographic special.

He remembered the mosquito that sucked blood from his stomach while he lay immobilized in concrete. He remembered how good it felt to bring his arms up and kill that little fuck. He hadn't felt so completely alive in a long time. The overwhelming abundance of life in this place had awakened him to all that was missing in his own life, the wonders of a world to which he'd always turned a blind eye.

Now he saw that he needed this time on the island for learning these things. If he hadn't crashed and been forced to hold still awhile, he would never have witnessed a hummingbird trying to drink from a red napkin. He would never have had time to study the dances of butterflies. He would not have met Amelia, or the old Indian, or any of the island's other exotic creatures. He would have lived his whole life without ever hearing the song of the Louie-Louie bird, without once making love to an actual goddess.

It would be hard to keep these lessons alive in the other world. Superman could only imagine the chaos of reentry: cameras flashing, shouted questions. Somehow he would have to hold on to the memory of this morning on the face of the water, skimming along as the sun poured light on his head.

He couldn't imagine going back to his life the way it was before, hotel to limo to airport to coliseum—a dark, filtered, airless existence, for all its glittery charms. He was a different man now. He would have to find a new way to live. He would go home to his family, and spend the rest of his life wondering how he ever imagined he could live without them.

The island turned a rocky, forbidding face to the mainland. From the channel it looked uninhabited—no place to land or launch a boat, no hint of the gorgeous white beach on the other side. A perfect place to disappear.

The channel was wider than it seemed from the top of the mountain. Superman squinted through the haze to the village on the sandy peninsula. Tied-up skiffs bobbed like waterbirds in the shallows.

The unshapely boat plowed through the swell. Superman leaned into the throttle. It was stuck. He leaned a bit harder. The throttle snapped off in his hand with a *ping!*

He stared at the little metal stump.

Now how could that be? He hadn't leaned hard enough to break it. Cheap-ass boat, even if it was conjured out of nowhere by a hundred-year-old magician.

Something struck the side of the boat, a dull thump. A slender golden stream arched up from the fuel tank.

Good God. Someone shooting at him.

Gasoline spewed on his chest, his arm, the smoky-hot motor.

In a moment of clarity, a voice spoke: Get out of the boat.

He scrambled to the bow, scraping his leg on the oarlock, and launched himself into the water.

He struggled to the surface, gulped a lungful of air. The boat turned and bore down on him, *yut-tut-tut-tut*.

He reached down inside for his super-strength, kicked his feet. He felt the propeller whiz by, a jet of water on his legs.

He bobbed up in its wake. The boat circled around to make another run at him. He was trying to decide whether to dive or try to outswim it when the motor blew up: a muffled *crump! crump!* a white flash, then the fire reached the tank and five gallons of gasoline exploded *ka-WHOOOM.*

A fat gassy ball of orange fire flowered and filled the boat, a rising seething stalk of orange-black combustion. The explosion lifted the boat from the water and broke it in two pieces, which fell back in the water and sank.

The fireball dissolved in a puff of black smoke. A blast of hot air blew past Superman's face. Twenty-dollar bills fluttered down like confetti.

He treaded water.

He brought his leg up to examine the bloody scrape. He swashed the water around with his hand. He couldn't remember ever hearing about sharks in these waters. . . .

He scanned the mountainside for whoever was shooting at him. He heard a chorus of voices: You'll never be able to leave. It's not allowed. He won't let you.

"Okay, you son of a bitch," he screamed, "show yourself, you damn coward! Here I am! Go on and shoot me in the damn water!"

He thought he heard a bullet smack behind him, but maybe it was just a wave. He was a long way from the mainland—he set his sights on the island, put his head down, and set off in a serious crawl, kicking and churning along. He felt an itchy patch on his back between his shoulder blades, where the bullet would slam in.

He glanced up. He didn't seem to be making much progress. He put his face down and kept swimming. He swam hard for fifteen minutes. He couldn't see the tidal current dragging him swiftly out of the channel, toward the open sea. By the time he understood what was happening, he was half a mile beyond the island, headed out.

They weren't bothering to shoot at him, now that they saw he was going to drown.

He flopped over on his back to catch his breath. Something nudged his side, just below the rib cage.

He raised out of the water and traveled three feet on his back like a water bug before gravity took over and pulled him back under.

Oh God please do not let me die in the mouth of a shark, I do not want to die. He flailed wildly, looking for the fin.

Something nudged his back.

"Oh! Shit!" Swimming was not fast enough, he needed to rise from the water and sprint across it, and he truly tried, he leaped forward with all the energy that comes to a man in a time of extremity, but it was not enough. He collided with something large. Something thudded into his back. Something scraped up the side of his thigh. He started shivering crying "oh please" his eyes shut he did not want to see don't make me look go on kill me but don't make me look.

After a long, long moment during which he did not die, he opened his eyes to find himself gazing into a large yellow eye.

Large, yellow-gold, and so old that its stare froze the scream in his throat.

The head was a pale shapeless knob with those weird golden eyes, a primitive claw-mouth. A massive oblong shell, dark spinachy green. Four flippers outspread like wings, waving in the current.

There were others: the water was full of them, hovering, watching him.

He reached out his hand and touched the flipper. It felt cool as seawater, nervelessly cool and slick for something that looked so alive, and so wise.

Superman laid both arms across its back. The turtle lowered its head and moved off, towing him sidesaddle. The others followed, swimming without effort, lazily batting their wings.

Superman knew he was the object of a miracle. He clung to that shell, and gave thanks, silent and fervent, the kind of thanks a barnacle would give.

A wave knocked him off. The turtle waited while he climbed aboard again, then swam on.

The beach shimmered in the distance. A man stood there, waiting.

The turtle stroked steadily through rolling water without tiring or slowing. As if on a signal, the others dropped back. Superman's turtle shouldered into the shallows.

Superman slipped off. He patted the shell. "Best goddamn turtle I ever saw."

A wave crashed on his head. When he got to his feet, the turtle was gone.

He put his head down and rode the wave in. He staggered out of the surf, fell to his knees on the sand. Pito came up with his guitar and the knob-headed walking stick. "You come back," he said.

Superman rolled over. The sunlight was hot and terribly beautiful. "Yeah," he said, "I come back."

Pito patted his shoulder. "Soon you fly."

15 / *There's No Place Like Home*

AMELIA LOOKED UP from a book of old maps. "I knew you'd come back."

"I didn't have a choice." Superman flung himself into a chair. "Someone blew me out of the water."

"Now you see what I was trying to tell you." She closed the book. "It's a good thing you're still alive. We can fly this thing, Ben, I just know it. I've done some new calculations, we can leave sooner than I thought. You have dollars, we'll buy fuel in Caracas—"

"Ah no, just you hang on a minute, lady, you and me need to have a little talk."

She folded her hands. "A talk?"

"In the first place, my dollars went down with the boat. Now I got no money, no plane, no boat, no way out of here. I guess it's my own fault for landing in the Twilight Zone, but today it nearly got me killed. I want some straight answers from you. No more of your lies."

She assumed an expression of weary equanimity. "I did lie at first, Ben. I told you what you needed to know, nothing more. Maybe that was wrong, but I was trying to protect you. I'm not the one who tried to kill you."

"Where is he, then? Where does he live? Come on, take me to him. He and I need to talk."

"When he's not off on business, he's a total recluse. You'd never get past the guards. That's his place at the top of the mountain. See there, the white roof?"

Superman followed her finger to a glint of reflected light near the summit of the south mountain, high above La Discoteca. "What does he do up there by himself?"

"We hear rumors. Supposedly he has big plans for this island. They say he wants to cut trees and take the top off that mountain and build something, I don't know what. Probably some kind of monument to his ego. Lord knows, he can do what he wants. He's got a couple dozen men with guns, to keep everyone in line."

Superman remembered the hulking men in the Land Cruiser at La Discoteca. "Big dumb-looking guys in camouflage?"

She nodded.

"He's got his own army? That's crazy."

"The whole idea is an abomination. Sometimes I think he's just waiting for me to die so he can start cutting down trees. All these years he's kept our bargain—he had some leftover respect for the island, and for me. But that's gone now. He's changed. Trees and monkeys mean nothing to him. To him this is a piece of real estate, but he doesn't own it any more than you do. It belongs to the people who've lived here for hundreds of years. It's a holy place for them. The rest of us are just visitors."

"Then why don't they fight back? Join together! Put everybody together, you'd outnumber his guys ten to one."

"Four years ago there was a *huelga*, a strike. The natives threatened to leave unless he gave them a week off the island at Christmas. Three of them washed up on the beach, shot through the head. That put an end to the *huelga*. Someday maybe they'll stop being afraid, and get angry again."

"What are they, his slaves?"

"Yes." She stared hard at him. "That's precisely what they are."

"And you?"

"Oh, for years now," she said. "Bought and paid for."

"This guy Rabbit makes a pretty convincing argument that you're all just a bunch of head cases." Superman studied her face for anything that might give her away. "He says he's a shrink and you're his patients. Your name is Emily Lakenfield, and all the Earhart stuff is just a delusion."

Amelia smiled faintly, as if hearing an old joke for the tenth time. "That's a very clever rabbit the Magician keeps in his hat. They're trying to throw you off guard. They're worried about you, Ben. You've upset the natural order of things. Pito sensed it right away—you have your own power."

"Why shouldn't I believe Rabbit? What he says makes more sense than anything you've told me."

"Believe what you like," she said. "I've asked you to help me. I'm not going to beg. If you think you stand a better chance with Rabbit, go." She waved him away. "I just want to make the flight and tell my story. I want the world to know what this man is trying to do. I'm not doing it for me, Ben—

I've had my share of fame and all that. I'm just trying to stop him. If we can't stop him, more people are going to disappear, and one day this island will die."

He raised his eyes. "Then let's go."

"You'll help?" Her face lit up.

"No waiting," he said. "No flying around the world. We're getting out of this place. We go now, soon as we can get that plane ready. We go straight to America. They'll believe you, I'll make them believe you. You have to trust me on that."

"Fine," she said. "We have work to do."

HE DID NOT think about Daisy.

He moved into his shack on the hill. In the mornings Catalina brought his breakfast and cursed him politely. In the afternoons he sat in the cockpit of the Electra, practicing takeoffs and landings. He did not allow himself to set foot outside the pink wall. He lashed himself to the mast. He absolutely did not think about Daisy.

He stood with Pito in the clearing beside the hangar, watching a forty-foot swath of jungle swiftly fall to the long knives of the men. The line of machete men snaked across the perilous slope he had once spent a whole afternoon falling down.

A troop of titi monkeys popped up in the trees, squabbling, screeching. The men laughed and tossed rocks at them, and kept chopping.

Pito hooked his fingers in his mouth and whistled. The monkeys melted away.

The clearing advanced down the mountain, exactly as wide as the wingspan of a Lockheed Electra. Insects flittered about in a dance of praise to the unexpected sunlight. A pungent chlorophyll scent filled the air, the smell of plants split open and trampled.

Superman had no idea how Pito intended to get this plane down that slope, but ordinary difficulties like gravity and a forty-degree incline posed no problem for Pito. He used his magic casually, like taking a handkerchief from his pocket. Superman had spent hours floating in the Electra above the clearing, powered only by the old man's steadfast gaze. Flocks of parakeets hung out in the trees near where Pito was working. Iguanas watched from the shadows. Tools sailed up from the toolbox into his waiting hand.

Superman and Frank spent three days and nights cleaning and reassembling the starboard engine, and then it wouldn't turn over. They fiddled with it for hours. Pito climbed the ladder and spat once into the air intake, nodded for them to try it again. The engine coughed once and roared to life.

Night before last, Superman heard a noise outside his shack and parted the bamboo panel an inch. On the stoop sat the old man, surrounded by a circle of squatting white-faced monkeys—lanky fierce-looking black-and-white monkeys, three times larger than the titi, and not at all cute. Occasionally Pito grunted or made a face, a lip snarl or a nose rub. The monkeys watched him, scratching at fleas, looking vaguely bored. This went on for most of ten minutes.

Finally the monkeys ran up to touch Pito, one at a time, shyly—just a glancing tap on his shoe and they were off rocketing up a tree.

The old man turned. *"Buena' noches."*

"What were you telling 'em, Pito?"

"I no tell. *Monos* tell."

"What did they say?"

"Soon is coming big storm. Then you fly."

"They're watching out for us, huh?"

Pito laid a hand on Superman's shoulder. *"Tú eres muy importante aquí, entiendes?* You is impartant."

"Gracias, Pito. You're important, too. You've been a good friend."

"No, is not *friend.* You is *impartant.* After the fly," he said, "you come back more?"

"Maybe. We'll see."

"You come back more. *Los monos dicen que será una guerra aquí. Necesitamos tu fuerza. Tienes una fuerza especial."*

"Right on," Superman said. He had learned that when people spoke Spanish, all you had to do was agree with them. It was amazing how well this seemed to work.

THE MONKEYS' PROPHECY had not come to pass. Today was the day of departure, and there had been nothing but blue skies and high, drifting clouds. The *macheteros* passed out of sight at the bottom of the hill. The whing of their blades carried up through the trees.

A clang of tools from the hangar as Frank climbed down from the starboard cowling. Lately he had forgone his wigs and nightwear ensembles for a sensible pair of mechanic's zip-front overalls. At first he refused even to consider the idea of the flight—he was too old to go back to the world, he said, he'd gotten used to things as they were—but then he changed his mind and said he would go.

Most days he lit up the hillside with choruses of "Fly Me to the Moon," but today he was too busy to sing. Since sunup he'd been in the hangar, checking, adjusting, making last-minute lists. "Mr. Willis, the Very pistol and the flares?"

"In the box under the raft."

"You checked them again?"

"Three times, Frank. Why don't you try to relax?"

"I keep feeling we've forgotten something."

"I don't see how, with all your lists."

Frank wiped his hands on his overalls. "In that case, I suppose it's time to get dressed."

"What, dressed? You look fine."

"Oh, please. You don't think I'm going like this?" Frank had spent the morning sprawled on the hangar floor with his charts, calculating fuel consumption. Superman pointed out that the charts were forty years old, but Frank just said "best we can do" and went on drawing plumb lines between landing fields that had probably ceased to exist.

The whole enterprise carried this faint air of picturesque unreality. At Amelia's insistence they'd spent a night rewiring the antique Bendix radio direction finder, though Superman tried to tell her that the five-hundred-kilohertz band hadn't been used for aviation since World War II. She clung stubbornly to "kilocycles," and said well, fix it anyway.

Amelia and Frank seemed to think they were flying back into the same world they'd left in 1937. They'd never even seen a freeway. Superman couldn't wait to see their faces when they flew into L.A.

Frank snapped the toolbox shut. "I guess that's it, then. As the poet said, 'We got nothin' to hit but the heights.' See you at the beach."

"How'm I supposed to get there?"

"You and Gerónimo are taking the plane down. We'll come in the jeep." Pito nodded.

Superman said, "Nobody tells me nothin' around here."

Pito placed one hand on the wing and walked the Electra out of the hangar. That was seven tons of airplane and fuel he pushed into the clearing like a baby buggy.

"You fly," he said.

Superman stepped up into Frank's cubbyhole behind the reserve tank: charts in an overhead rack, a glass circle in the chart table above the master aperiodic compass, three chronometers clamped to the optical-glass window beside a sort of telescope called a pelorus, the use of which Frank had explained in excruciating detail. Compasses, protractors, and rulers were held fast to the table with large rubber bands.

Crawling along the catwalk above the reserve tank, Superman tried not to think what a hell of a bomb he was riding. Five hundred gallons of fuel would make the explosion in his boat look like a popgun. He swung through the hatch into the copilot's seat, and looked out.

Pito lifted his hand from the wing. The plane bobbed up from the ground like a balloon, yawing, floating in place.

Pito stepped over the brow of the hill. The plane's nose dropped abruptly; the cockpit canted down; they fell off the edge of the earth. The old man came back into view, tramping through the new-fallen jungle just ahead of the wing. The Electra fell in behind him like a huge and obedient animal. The slosh of fuel in the tank sent big echoes booming through the fuselage.

Superman rested his hands on the yoke and braced his feet behind the rudder pedals to stay in the seat. He wasn't sure how his presence was supposed to be aiding this maneuver, but it made for an amazing ride. The Electra floated above the carpet of wilting greenery, keeping pace with Pito's downward march.

Superman had lain awake nights worrying that the beach was not long enough to lift off this plane with its huge load of fuel. Once they started those engines, Amelia said, the old man's magic would cease to apply—but she wasn't concerned. She'd lifted off with a heavier load than this on a nine-hundred-yard strip in Bangkok, with room to spare. Superman asked if the airstrip in Bangkok also featured a mountain at each end.

She patted his hand. "Don't worry, Ben. I'll be right there beside you."

Once they were airborne, she would share in the flying, but takeoffs and landings were a job for Superman. He was not all that keen on his ability to fly this large, ungainly craft. The Electra lacked the automatic devices that made flying the Beech Baron almost like driving a car. The Lockheed panel was frighteningly simple: fourteen analog gauges and one Haynes Magellan Electronic-Gyroscopic compass. Superman didn't know why Amelia put such faith in the very gauge that had led him so badly astray. He would be glad to have Frank aboard with his magnetic compasses and outdated charts.

Ahead down the slope, families stepped out of the trees to marvel at the great new highway the *macheteros* had carved through the jungle.

When the kids saw the floating Electra they began to yelp and jump. An impromptu procession sprang up, fathers running for their machetes, mothers holding up toddlers to see, little boys in a frenzy of delight.

Superman rested one hand on the yoke, as if this somehow helped keep the plane in the air. He felt vaguely foolish grinning and waving like that, but if he'd seen a man come floating through the jungle in an airplane, he would definitely want that man to wave.

The undergrowth thinned out near the beach. The *macheteros* yipped and hollered and capered ahead to attack the last line of trees.

The Electra glided out into the sunshine, settled on the sand. The crowd swarmed around, and more people came from both ends of the beach. Pito hustled about trying to keep little boys off the wings.

Superman opened the door to a burst of applause. He recognized faces in the crowd: a yardman from the Big House, a bartender from La Discoteca, Catalina, Jimmy Hoffa, the Sherman Brothers, the ancient magician who gave him the boat. . . .

The green jeep roared out of the jungle. Amelia clung to the roll bar with both hands. It took a moment to recognize the dashing figure at the wheel as Frank, in the full-dress uniform of a Pan American Pacific Clipper crewman, bristling with epaulets, braid, and gold wings. The jeep skidded to a stop. Frank stood and saluted. The crowd cheered.

Superman shouldered through.

Amelia beamed at him. "Would you look at this!"

"Your farewell committee," said Superman.

"I've never seen such a crowd for a takeoff!" She was dressed for adventure: battered leather flight jacket, checked shirt, crisp khakis, her fire-breathing Japanese slippers.

Frank hoisted a suitcase from the back of the jeep. The gold buttons on his jacket were under some strain, but otherwise he was the image of a spit-and-polish military man from an old newsreel. The effect was simultaneously startling and impressive, like seeing your favorite old auntie dressed as General Patton.

People surged around him, chattering, pumping his hand. Superman spotted the Aztec-faced boy, Frank's young friend from La Discoteca, and the ever-cheerful Spike striding through the ranks, probably smiling. "Miss Em-o-lee!" He knelt to embrace her. "Your big day at last!"

"Oh, Spike, I can hardly believe it," she said, clasping his tiny fingers. "I wish we could take you with us."

"You're coming back, right?"

"Of course, dear. A month or two. I'm counting on you to look after the place while I'm gone."

"I'll be here. Where would I go? Hey Superman, don't forget you promised us a concert."

"You got it, Spike. Soon as I'm back. Take good care of yourself."

Everyone on the island had come down to the beach except the one person Superman secretly hoped to see. It was too much to think she might be somewhere back in the shadows, watching him, wishing him well. He smiled and said *hasta luego* to everyone. He tried not to think of the possibilities he was leaving behind.

Rabbit skulked up from the edge of the crowd. "Emily, you're not going today? What about your going-away party!"

"This is it," she said coolly. "We've got low tide and good weather, and we're going. I think you know Ben."

"Oh sure, of course," Rabbit said. "Ben's been pissed at me since I had him up to my place for the ol' newcomer reality shakedown. He didn't crack, though. Strong mind." He put out his hand with a smile. "Friends?"

Superman looked at the hand, but didn't shake it.

"Aw come on, Superman, don't go away mad. I was only having a little fun with you. You can shake my hand."

Superman relented. He was vacating this place for good; why leave an enemy behind? Rabbit pressed something into his palm, the secret handshake performed by drug dealers the world over.

"What's this?"

"Red Dot Fifteen. New and improved. So you'll remember us when you get home."

"Oh no, no thanks," he said, trying to hand it back, but Rabbit edged out of reach and the chesty blond Twins crowded in, all hugs and entreaties.

"You can't leave, Superman!" said Sandy.

"We barely even got to know you!" said Linda.

"Am I glad to see you girls." He dropped the pill in his pocket.

"Will you bring us presents when you come back?"

"Ooh yeah, bring perfume. Bring Chanel."

"And chocolate-covered cherries."

"Peanut M&M's."

That delirious night on the beach, he'd have sworn these girls were teenagers—but in full sun he'd have to say late twenties, at least. There was something lacking in their chatter—as if the two of them together didn't quite make up one person. Superman thanked them for keeping him out of the hands of the camouflage guys at La Disco.

"Our pleasure," said Sandy.

"Hope we didn't hurt you," said Linda.

"Sometimes we get carried away."

He grinned. "Anytime, ladies. Anytime."

All the famously disappeared people came to see them off. Jimmy Hoffa brought three sacks of barbecued chicken—"bad business to fly on an empty stomach," he said. Her Imperial Highness Anastasia was wheeled out to the jeep, where she presented Amelia with a rhinestone bracelet once worn by her father, the Czar. (Why the Czar would wear a woman's bracelet was a question Superman did not pursue.) Michael Rockefeller kicked at the sand and kept his hands in his pockets. D. B. Cooper hung back in his Ray Bans, smoking, glancing nervously over his shoulder.

Superman followed his glance. Ten men in camouflage stood in the shade at the top of the beach, making sure everyone got a good look at the guns slung over their shoulders.

Pito lifted Amelia and carried her to the plane. Superman saw a look pass between them, an unmistakable flicker of electricity.

He knew that look between people. For a moment, they ceased to be old.

"No, no, *corazón*." Amelia brushed Pito's cheek with her fingers.

The old man buried his face in her shoulder.

Superman turned away, blinking in the light of new knowledge. Of course: it was personal between them. He saw in one glance how they must have been when they were younger, a handsome and helpless woman, a young man with mysterious powers.

Suddenly Frank was at his elbow, smiling an odd smile.

"Quite a send-off, eh Frank?"

"Mr. Willis, there's no easy way to say this. I'm not going with you. I'm sorry. I've decided to stay."

"*What?*"

Frank nodded. Sweat trickled down his pendulous earlobes. The Aztec boy stood watching. "I guess I'm just not ready to go back," Frank said. "Oh, I know, I complain about the place, but this has been my home for too long. I wouldn't know how to live anywhere else. You don't need me, anyway."

"The hell we don't! Who's gonna navigate?"

"Just fly north," Frank said. "You can read a compass, can't you? You'll be fine."

Superman inclined his head toward the boy. "He'll wait for you, Frank."

"I wouldn't count on it. I'm getting old. I think I'd better stay here and try to be happy. I haven't got that much time."

Superman saw Pito hovering over Amelia in the cockpit, settling her into her seat. She waved: Get Frank and let's go.

"Have you told her?"

Frank shook his head.

"You're not planning to?"

"I thought I'd let you. I know just what she'll say—'good riddance.'"

"But you got all dressed up. . . ."

"Best of luck to you, Mr. Willis. Fly safe." He tossed a salute and walked away.

This was not in the plan. Superman had cleaved to the plan as his only way out of here, and now suddenly it was changing. "Frank, wait!"

Frank put his arm around the boy and merged into the crowd.

Superman reached the cabin just as Pito came over the catwalk, the knob-headed walking stick in his hand. "You forget."

"No, I didn't forget it—just you got me walking so good I don't really need it anymore. Do you know that Frank says—"

Pito placed the stick in his hands. "You need."

"What for?"

Pito turned to the cockpit: *"Cómo se dice 'buena suerte'?"*

"Good luck," Amelia called.

"For goodlock," said Pito.

"All right, then, I thank you. Watch out for yourself, hear? And tell all those people to get the hell out of our way. When we go, we're going fast."

Pito reached out to shake hands. "You fly goodlock."

"Don't worry, man. I'll take good care of her."

The old man bowed, and stepped out.

Superman scuttled across the tank, grasped the hatch in both hands, and arched his back over the sill, landing *thud* in the seat. "Guess what? Frank's not going."

"Oh, really? I can't say I'm surprised."

"He says this is home, and we don't need him anyway."

"I knew he would pull something like this," said Amelia.

"But we had it all worked out! What's he doing changing his mind at the last minute?"

"He think I might not come back. He's always dreamed of having me out of the picture. He thinks—ah well, good riddance. Between you and me we ought to be able to find North America."

Superman tucked the walking stick beside his leg. "I keep trying to get rid of this. Pito keeps bringing it back to me."

"Maybe he thinks you should hold on to it." Amelia's eyes were shining. "Surely by now you have learned to listen to him."

"He's a good man. I didn't realize you two were so close."

"That was a long time ago. I don't know why . . . he's known all along I would have to do this someday."

"He doesn't want you to go?"

"He doesn't think I'll come back, either." She cleared her throat, and flipped a toggle switch. Needles quivered on dials. "Panel, check."

Superman fished up the clipboard on its string. "Check."

"Fuel analyzer, check."

"Check."

They ran down the list. The drone of hydraulics started low and rose higher and higher, filling the cockpit with a tense, insistent whine.

Superman poised his finger on the starboard starter. The giant Wasp engine went *chung, chung, chung* and coughed to life, a stutter that became a big supercharged roar, five hundred horses thundering. He punched the port starter *chung, chung, chung* and five hundred more came roaring off the other wing, vibrating the fuselage down its every inch, rattling the fillings in Superman's teeth.

"Loud," he shouted, goosing first one then the other, opening the throttles all the way to blow gunk from the valves. The Wasps threw blue smoke and one hell of a noise. Through the side window Superman saw people scrambling out of the hurricane backwash. That's good, go on and run now, all you nice little island people, and you camouflage men in back, you stay the hell out of our way. We are leaving this place.

Amelia craned out the side window, studying the treetops. "Looks like ten knots," she yelled. "South-southwest. This is our lucky day."

Superman glanced out at Pito. He flashed a thumb, eased off the brake.

The old man stepped back. The Electra trundled to the north end of the beach. Superman juiced the engines, left, then right. The plane wobbled just as it was supposed to. The propellers kicked up a sandstorm. He tested the rudder pedals, leaning forward to check the motion in the mirror.

At the end of the beach he turned and taxied to align his nose with the strip of sand packed smooth by the retreating tide. He allowed himself one mental snapshot of Daisy in her kitchen, wrapped in a sheet, smiling at him.

He shook it off and turned to the problem before him: a high-speed run on a steeply banked runway with a pronounced curve to the right. To bring it off would take every ounce of his strength, and more pilot savvy than Mr. Pawley had ever imparted. He said a tiny prayer, then: "Ready?"

Amelia grasped his arm, leaned in. He felt dusty lips on his cheek. "Ben, thank you for this."

"Thank me when we get to L.A." He leaned into the throttles. The engines howled. The Electra shuddered and jolted ahead, bumpety-bumping at first, smoothing out as it gathered momentum.

The plane rolled faster, sand flying under, bright glitter off the water, flashing past the big rock down the white beach toward the people jumping and waving, running out of the trees—and then flash! they were gone, a distinct smell of gasoline, the Electra gobbling a half mile of sand—Superman struggled hard against the pull—engines singing a full-on combustion chorus, the south mountain growing larger and larger, the plane racing along ever lighter and faster until just when it seemed they would run out of beach Amelia cried "Pull up! Pull up!" and the starboard engine exploded.

The thrust of the port engine spun the plane lazily to the right. By instinct Superman's left foot jammed the rudder pedal into the floor. Three hard jolts as the frame crumpled and gave way, then the world blurred to one long smear of light, a lurch of the gut. The plane ground-looped, whirling, burning, disintegrating, caroming into the trees.

He tried to reach the fuel cutoff valves, but the g-force pinned his arm to his side. Everything happened too fast. He raced toward a green wall then spun away like the Scrambler at the fair, spinning around again then he went through the window with a blinding crash and everything was quiet except for the crackle of burning, and—people screaming?

Birds.

He was out on his back in the jungle, still strapped in his seat, gazing up at the sky. The walking stick clenched between his knees. A flock of toucans darted among the trees, shrieking *whick-IT! whick-IT!*

The front half of the Electra lay on its side, a hole blasted through one eye, one wing ripped away, the other wing engulfed in flames that licked at the fuselage, where the reserve tank—at an angle—

Superman wrestled free of the harness. Blood streamed into his eye. The plane let out a terrible groan.

He ran to the hole his body had punched in the cockpit. Amelia slumped in her harness. He dashed around back. The rear half of the plane was sheared off clean. One corner of the reserve tank had plowed a trench in the earth, rapidly filling with—

Water, he told himself, only water, splashing through it ankle-deep, jumping to the crazy-tilted catwalk, skiddling up and over. He thrust himself into the cockpit, groping for the catches that held Amelia in her seat. He felt heat on the side of his face—don't stop to *think!*—sprang the last catch, seized her arms, dragged her out. They tumbled down the tank to the ground. He lifted her. She weighed nothing. He splashed through the gasoline, running for his life.

Something was chasing him—his gas-soaked footprints bursting into flame, the fire jumping from one footprint to the next. His toes squished in his fuel-soaked shoes. He watched in helpless fascination as the fire gained on him.

At that moment someone took a brilliant flash picture of the jungle. The shock wave knocked him down. The earth rocked and rolled.

He huddled over Amelia. All five hundred gallons went off in one heart-stopping boom. A firecloud rose up through the trees and sent pieces of the Electra screaming and whistling through the air.

Superman kept his head down amid the banging crashing like refrigerators falling to earth—then a weird fluttery sound. He looked up. A bird on fire, a toucan with feathers burning as it thrashed and fluttered through the air, batting into trees, staggering out of sight.

That was something he never expected to see, no matter how long he lived.

He rose up on all fours. Amelia was not hurt anywhere. She stared past him at something in the sky. He closed her eyes with his fingers.

People came running in, shouting. One of them was Frank. He looked shocked to find Superman kneeling there. "My God, Mr. Willis! You're alive!"

"Oh come on, you son of a bitch, what did you do to the plane?"

"What?"

"You were the last one under that cowling. What'd you do, punch a hole in the fuel line?"

"You must have hurt yourself. You're talking nonsense." Then he saw Amelia. "Dear God, is she . . .?"

"Dead. Isn't that what you wanted?"

"Not at all. This is terrible. I never thought—"

Superman seized his lapels and threw him back against a tree. "God-damn it, Frank—you killed her!"

Frank straightened his uniform jacket. "I did nothing of the kind. This is all her fault. She insisted on trying to leave. I told her it would never happen."

"You got out of the plane. You knew what was coming."

"Just don't try to leave," Frank said. "In case you haven't noticed, *nobody* is allowed to leave."

And then Pito was there, weeping, falling to his knees in the sand.

PART TWO

PART TWO

16 / The Worst Thing

THEY BURIED AMELIA in a circle of giant bamboo just down from the bubbling spring. The coffin was so light it seemed hardly possible she was in there. Superman lifted from the right side, nursing the sprain in his shoulder. People came from all over the island to toss in a handful of dirt. Pito said a prayer in the language of the birds.

Gyp barked and whined, trotted over and lay down with her head on Superman's feet.

Frank wept quietly through the service. Everyone hugged and comforted him. His grief seemed authentic.

Only Superman saw irony in that. Only he remembered Frank's unsettling calm in the face of disaster.

She is my friend, and she is my Emily.

I love Frank, but he doesn't love me. He blames me for everything bad that ever happened to him.

Just don't try to leave.

The mourners followed Frank to the Big House. Superman stayed with Pito and Spike to watch the men fill the grave. "I don't think she could've felt any pain. It happened too fast."

"Tonight she is sleeping," said Pito.

"I had a bad feeling about it," Spike said. "Damn it, I wish I'd tried to stop her. She was so sure he wouldn't touch her." He shook his head. "I'm just glad you made it."

"Thanks, Spike. So am I." Superman knew his survival was a matter of the purest luck, the luck of a knob-headed walking stick clutched between his knees. That stick had brought him through some very close calls.

Pito's eyes came up from the black earth. "*Cómo se dice venganza?*"

"Revenge," Spike said.

"That's a good word to know." Superman tamped the dirt with his foot.

Spike said, "That's not your way, Pito."

The black eyes flashed. "Is good word to know."

"Spike, you were her friend. Doesn't this kind of thing start to get to you after a while?"

"She knew the risk," Spike said. "She was a fighter. She died trying to get out of here, to stop him. There's hardly anybody left who's not on his side. What about you? Will you stay and fight with us?"

Superman shook his head. "I have to get home. That's all I've been trying to do since I got here, and something keeps dragging me back. I've made up my mind for the last time. This is not my fight."

"Wrong. You didn't volunteer, but you're in it now as much as any of us."

"You stay," said Pito. "You stay fly."

"I already tried that, old man. It didn't exactly work out."

Spike grimaced, or maybe that was a smile.

"Is coming big storm," Pito said. "Then you fly."

"No. I have to go. My wife and kid are probably ready to give me up for dead, if they haven't already."

Spike's eyes crinkled, an expression verging on sympathy. "There's something you need to see," he said. "Come on up to my house?"

"Well—why not, I can't stand watching Frank do his grief routine."

They left Pito on his knees, poking flowers into the dirt. That picture carried them in silence over the mountain, through a stand of royal palms to a shady knob overlooking the sea, a simple thatched shack with a porch. This was the house Spike shared with Sandy and Linda, who'd headed off to the beach to get drunk in honor of Amelia.

"*Venganza*," Spike said. "I've never heard Pito talk like that."

"He loved that old lady," Superman said.

"We all did. You know this changes everything. If the Magician will kill her, there's nothing he won't do." Spike brought out a bottle of *guaro,* the local sugarcane moonshine.

"I've thought about it, Spike. We ran that engine for two hours at the hangar, and it was fine. Frank must have done something."

"More likely he just looked the other way. The Magician never dirties his hands. He pays people for that."

"You think Frank did it for money?"

"He did what he was told," Spike said. "They all do. Ol' Mago owns everyone on this island, except me, and you, maybe a couple others. The gringos talk against him, but they all take his money and spy on each other for him. The island people hate him, but they're afraid of him." He tossed another shot of *guaro*.

Superman took a sip—

"No, don't taste it. Throw it down."

Superman obeyed. It burned like gasoline all the way down.

"Did you see how many people came today?" Spike said. "They loved Emily. She stuck up for them. The doctor comes from Gato Negro once a month now—that's because of her. And the school, and every good thing they've ever had. I guess we thought she'd always be around, she'd outlast the Magician or . . . I don't know. Somehow she always seemed strong enough to keep it from getting worse."

"Some of those people looked at me like it was my fault," Superman said.

"They looked at you because you're damn lucky," said Spike, refilling his glass. "Have another."

"No thanks, it's too early for me."

"You sure?" Spike leaned back in his chair and lifted a manila folder from the windowsill. "You might want to take a look at this."

A yellowing section of the *Los Angeles Times*, September 21, 1972, unfolded to the "Lively Arts" page. Beneath a photo of Crosby, Stills, Nash, and Young at the Hollywood Bowl, an old publicity photo of Superman, and a shot of Alexa arm in arm with Jimbo. Both of them stoned, grinning like idiots.

SUPER-MEMORIAL MARRED BY SCANDAL AS MRS. "SUPERMAN" WILLIS REMARRIES

FROM STAFF AND WIRE REPORTS

LOS ANGELES—A star-studded rock-and-roll "Be-In" to commemorate the presumed death of folk-rock star Ben "Superman" Willis was overshadowed this weekend by the haste with which his wife, Alexa, took a new husband.

Two days after appearing before 10,000 fans at a Hollywood Bowl memorial concert in honor of the missing musician, Alexa French Willis, 31, married Harvey James Thurlock, Jr., 28, of

Rattlesnake Springs, Colo., at the Chimes of Love Wedding Chapel in Las Vegas, Nev.

"Of course I'm sad that Ben's gone, but I have to move on with my life," the blonde former Miss Southwest Louisiana told the *Las Vegas Sun*. "I hope Jimbo and I will be very happy."

Midway through her speech at Friday's memorial service, Mrs. Willis was escorted from the stage by Thurlock after she made disparaging remarks about her missing husband. "He did the worst thing to me anybody ever did to anybody, and he knows what it is," she said. "I'll never tell, because I'm a better person than he is."

The singer's twin-engine Beechcraft Baron disappeared July 14 en route from El Paso to Phoenix, where he was scheduled to appear at a concert to benefit the Zuni Indian tribe. Search parties in six states and several Latin American nations found no trace of the plane despite exhaustive search efforts.

Willis, an amateur pilot with about 500 hours of flying time in the Baron, was a Grammy-winning songwriter and performer of such hits as "Superman's Revenge," "When Time Stands Still," and "So Nice to Be Home."

A spokesman for A&M Records said Thurlock worked as a personal assistant to the singer. He said the newlyweds planned to spend their honeymoon in a suite at the Desert Inn.

"It's shocking," said James Perry, 19, a fan of the missing entertainer. "Nobody knows if he's even dead, and she goes and marries this guy. I think it shows no respect at all for his fans." Perry was one of dozens of Willis enthusiasts gathered today at a Sunset Boulevard record store to celebrate the release of the singer's greatest-hits album, "Superman's Final Revenge."

The mystery of Willis's disappearance has fueled a boom in sales of his recordings. Last week's Billboard "Hot 100" listed six Willis songs among the top 20. "The entire catalog has not been off press since his disappearance," said an A&M Records official. "We only wish he'd had this kind of success when he was here to enjoy it."

Nevada officials said they would review the legality of Mrs. Willis's Las Vegas marriage, since Willis is still officially considered a missing person. The Federal Aviation Administration regards his disappearance as an active case, pending further investigation.

The couple's 11-year-old son, Benjamin Willis, Jr., lives with Mrs. Willis's family in Louisiana.

Superman smacked the wall. *"Jimbo?* Jesus Christ, he's—he's a leech, he's, like, this bloodsucking *thing*. She's lost it—totally, completely lost it. I knew she would freak out, but damn!"

This eruption of jealousy surprised him as much as the story. Since his first weeks on the island, when absence made his heart grow fonder and he thought he was falling in love with Alexa all over again, he'd thought of her only occasionally—and then only as part of that vague glowing memory, "home." Now here he was ablaze with indignation and wounded pride. Remarried? To a trashy no-good piece of work like Jimbo? Superman didn't believe it.

He was a dead man. There it was in black-and-white. His death had given his career the jump-start it needed. Six hits in the Top 20. Crosby, Stills, Nash, and Young harmonizing in his memory. His wife getting on-stage to make "disparaging remarks," then rushing off to marry their dope dealer, wishing herself every happiness along the way.

What could have possessed her to bad-mouth Superman at his own funeral? He hoped Ben Junior had not witnessed that.

He scanned the list of celebrities who'd come to celebrate his demise. He'd never even met half of them. When he read that Helen Reddy had been invited to sing "When Time Stands Still," something rocklike inside him crumbled and gave way.

That was maybe his best song. Alexa knew that. Alexa had done that to him, one last jab at him beyond the grave—for what? For getting her out of Louisiana, away from the detested rednecks of Opelousas? For installing her in a fancy house in Encino, listening to all her sensitive neospiritual jabber, squiring her around in a limousine, paying the most preposterous credit-card bills without a word? Where had he failed her? What the devil had he ever done to deserve this?

The worst thing anybody ever did to anybody, and he knows what it is.

He flung the paper off the porch. The breeze caught it up and took it—like his famous blue shirt, the newspaper actually stood up and danced away from him, floating over the clearing, spreading its pages like wings.

Not every man has the opportunity to read what his wife has done to him after his death. From Superman it brought a surge of rare desire: havoc, murder, revenge.

"Sorry, man." Spike poured more *guaro*. "Emily showed me that months ago. I thought she'd shown you. If it was me, I'd want to know."

"Sure," Superman said. "Goddamn it."

"Don't be too hard on your wife. You're the one who didn't come home."

"Oh hell, Spike, what do you know about it? I mean, Helen fucking *Reddy*. Do you know what that means?" Superman felt his eyes burning. He had really loved Alexa once upon a time, and the thought of Jimbo's hands on her. . . . Way to go, Jimbo. Smooth move. The lady is loaded, good-looking, and easily led. The hairy bastard must have gotten her high and talked her into it. Probably at this moment they were zooming around in Superman's red Spitfire, having a wonderful time.

How could she do this to him? What were his crimes? Sure, he'd thought about leaving her—once, in twelve years!—and it was true that he'd cheated a little. Okay, a lot. He let her ride on the bus (with Jimbo) while he flew between concerts to get away from her. When she came up to him after the encore, all dewy-eyed and lovey, draping herself over him—sometimes he pushed her away.

But he never dumped her for some other woman. Never yelled, like some husbands, never asked her to cook a meal or stay home with the kid. She got to live the fast life. Riding the bus was her choice. (With Jimbo!) Superman made good love to her. He had sex with other women, but they didn't mean anything. He didn't make love to them. He didn't *marry* them, for God's sake.

The worst thing anybody ever did to anybody.

He knew what it was.

It was so awful that he rarely let himself think about it.

It was after Monterey, when the crowds first got big and Superman was surfing a hundred-foot tidal wave of attention. Alexa got bored watching from the wings and decided she wanted some of that for herself, she wanted to get onstage with him, play keyboards, sing backup harmony. She had this thing about Sonny and Cher, she thought it was cool the two of them holding their little daughter up to wave nighty-night to the TV audience. "I can sing at least as well as Sonny Bono," she said, "and I'm better-looking than Cher."

Superman had to concede both points. He promised to think about it.

He kept hoping it would slip her mind, but he'd come home afternoons to find her in the living room with a mike and electric piano, playing and singing along with his hits. She'd yank off the headphones—"Oh, Ben, this is great! I can see why you love this so much! It's fun!"

But you see, darling, he would snarl in his most bloodcurdling interior voice, it's not supposed to be *fun*. This is my *work*. This is what I *do*. I tear my heart out to do this. This is not about you and your silly desire to get up onstage and share my applause. It's mine. I've earned it. And I don't want to share it with *you*.

He said something like "Soundin' good there, hon," and went on to the fridge.

The truth was, she sang worse than Sonny Bono. Her sugar-honey speaking voice turned into a dreary nasal whine when she tried to sing. She had a white Southern Baptist sense of rhythm, which is to say no rhythm at all.

For a while he was able to put her off, but she started talking up the idea with the guys in the band, first as a joke, and then not as a joke. The guys said it was a great idea—what else could they say? Superman saw how they rolled their eyes when she wasn't looking. They knew he saw it, too. They were all in on the joke. This was typical wife-of-the-star behavior, and they would all just have to put up with it until she got over it.

Then she called Barney at A&M Records, who thought it was actually a very good idea, what with Sonny and Cher and Paul and Linda and John and Yoko etc. Might create a kind of press wave, he said, sympathetic feature-page stuff. "Let her give it a try, Ben," he said, "what can it hurt? Get her some really short skirts, she'll look great."

"Barney, she can't sing."

"Who cares? You think Yoko can sing? I'll tell you what, we'll mix her mike through to her monitor, but we don't have to put it through the PA. Get it? She'll hear herself, but nobody else will hear her."

"Hm. That sounds too easy."

"See, Ben, what am I here for? To solve all your problems. What else you got?"

Superman hoped Alexa would do a show or two and go back to Opelousas where she belonged, or at least back to the speaker tower. But she was so thrilled when he told her. She squealed and hugged and kissed and thanked him. He felt slightly guilty, knowing the truth.

"Don't I even need an audition?" she said.

"Nope, it's unanimous. You're in."

"I don't even get to rehearse?"

"When have you ever missed a show, Alexa? You know the songs better than we do."

"Oh, Ben, you're too wonderful!" She whirled past him to the closet. "God, what can I wear?"

She bought eight thousand dollars' worth of sparkly short dresses to show off her legs. Three nights later she walked onstage to a roar from the fans at the Peoria Coliseum. She looked great in her little red dress, swaying her hair to the beat. She took her place behind a rack of keyboards. She played and sang her heart out. The crowd loved her. In the up-tempo racket of the second set, they didn't realize they weren't hearing her.

Superman was impressed with her poise: she knew how to toss that hair and get a reaction. He glanced back during the fast break to "Low Down and Dirty" and saw her shimmying with a tambourine, bringing the cheap-seat crowd to its feet. He didn't like that. Those were *his* fans, *his* cheap seats. He prided himself on controlling the mood of a show: he liked to get them dancing in the aisles, ease them back down to ballad-land, hold them rapt with two or three soft ones, then bust loose with a sudden wild rocker that would blow off their heads. He didn't need his wife behind him acting sexy in a dress that was way too short.

When she bounded up in the dressing room, he forced a smile and told her she was great.

"Oh come on, Ben, be honest with me, did you really think so?"

"You're a natural. They loved you."

"No, but what did *you* think," she persisted, "you're the only one that counts."

"Honestly?"

Her face fell.

"Tell Gordon to turn up your mike," he said. "I could hardly hear you."

She lit up. "Really? Through the monitor it sounded like I was too loud!"

He smiled at her. "Not at all. What I heard sounded great." He crossed a line with that smile. That was an act of intentional cruelty.

On the phone the next day Barney said, "How'd it go last night?"

"Oh, Barney, I don't know."

"A.G. said they loved her."

"They did! That's the problem. They loved her, she loved them, she wants to keep doing it."

"What's wrong with that?"

"It's not fair, that's what! She's making a fool of herself, and I'm helping her do it! You got me into this, Barney. Somebody has to tell her the truth."

Barney fell silent. "Not me."

"I guess not. Although . . ."

"No. Ben. Now listen. Relax. She'll have fun for a while and then she'll get over it."

"You don't know her like I do. This woman was runner-up for Miss Southwest Louisiana three times before she won. She does not get over things."

"I'll think of something," said Barney.

He didn't. The next night Alexa wore a salacious blue-spangled number that looked as if it might slide off any second, the way she was shaking it. Superman heard wolf whistles mixed with the cheers. His show, his own complex and evolving creation, the carefully designed sequence of songs by which he transmitted the contents of his heart to ten thousand people, was now to serve as a backdrop for his wife's ambitions as a hootchy-kootchy dancer.

Gordon reported Alexa's request to turn up her volume.

Superman smiled. "Thanks, Gordo. Tell her you've done it."

Gordo winked and went back to the soundboard.

Alexa began to act like a member of the band, chiming in with suggestions for stage business and set sequences. She got fan mail (fan mail!) and made sure to answer each letter. The feature-page articles duly appeared, with kind words for her miniskirts and stage presence; she clipped them and saved them in a scrapbook. She was delighted when the Memphis newspaper mentioned her "graceful keyboard work, which gives a potent new shimmer to the patented 'Superman' sound."

She didn't realize that Barney had quietly commissioned a professional keyboard track, synchronized through the main PA, to complete the illusion that Alexa was making music out there. She had not caught on, that's how bad her ear was: she actually thought her flailing at the keys was producing those lush, pretty sounds.

Superman just smiled and told her she was great.

One day he drove to Pasadena to lay some vocal tracks on the bridge and third verse of the new single "Last Bus to Armageddon." He arrived early, stepped into the cool darkness of Eagle Rock studio, and heard the howling all the way down the hall—spasmodic, choking, uproarious laughter.

He sneaked up to the door, flung it open. The guys coughed and spluttered and turned away. Superman grinned—"Okay, you assholes, what are you . . ."

The only sound came from the monitors, a live dub of "Take Me Anywhere but Heaven." The band and Superman's vocals were muffled, but Alexa's voice came clearly out into the room.

She wasn't off by that much, but every note was just flat, or just sharp, or wandering flat to sharp, just enough to be wrong. You could hear the effort she was putting into it—the unsteady attack, the quailing attempts at vibrato, the way her voice dropped to a teensy whisper on the high notes. When the band got loud at the chorus she cut loose, singing out. The louder she sang, the more badly out of key she fell, and then she slipped completely off the rhythm, meandering all over the place like a child humming nonsense.

"Awright," she congratulated herself, sotto voce under the sound of applause, "awright, pretty good!"

Superman listened, mortified: then he couldn't help it, he saw the guys eyeing him, fighting to keep their faces under control, and that cracked him up.

They went wild with relief when he laughed. They howled, slapping their legs, bent over, whooping for air.

"Gordon, you son of a bitch!" Superman cried.

"Wait wait, that's not—Gordo, play the next one! Listen to this!"

A distant drum kickoff, the lead-in to "Giving It All Up for You." Alexa cleared her throat, *Rrrra-hm, rrrra-hm,* like an opera singer preparing to shatter glass. The boys stood around glancing up at the speakers with this glad expectant look, as if the really great part was coming up next.

Then she was crooning "oooooohhhhh, bay-beh." She was not even in the same county with the rest of the band. The note had a weird Oriental harmonic effect that sent them all into convulsions.

"Ooooooohhhhhh, bay-beh!" crowed Lenny the drummer. They laughed and guffawed and then they all stopped laughing except Superman, chuckling, wiping his eyes. He turned to see what everyone was looking at, and of course it was Alexa.

She wore an unsteady smile. "Hey guys, what's so funny?"

Two of them lunged to shut it off, too late. She heard herself loud and clear: "Ooooooohhhhhhh, bay-beh!"

It took her a moment to factor it all together: the deception that went into making the tape, the phony compliments they'd been laying on her since her first stage appearance, the unspeakable malice of a man who would encourage his wife to do something, then gather with his buddies to laugh at it.

She took two steps into the room. "Gordon, give me the tape."

He already had it in the box and rubber-banded. He handed it over.

"Are there any copies?"

"No ma'am."

"I guess you won't be needing me at the session," she said with a little hurt smile that went like a needle through Superman's eye, straight into his brain.

He dropped his face into his hands.

Her heels clicked up the hall, the *squeal-bang!* of the door.

"Listen—boss—tell her it was all my idea—"

He looked up at their stricken faces. The hell with them—he ran after her. He slammed out the door just in time to see her Mustang streak through a red light.

It was the kind of thing you never even try to live down. Alexa went off to Louisiana for two weeks. When she returned, she went back to her place by the speaker tower and never said a word about what he had done. But it changed the air between them.

Sometimes he almost forgot it. Sometimes he told himself it was the result of a string of unhappy accidents, with no evil intent on his part. Sometimes he recalled how embarrassed he'd been, that first instant of hearing the tape, before he started to laugh.

But now he could not lie about it. He had done it to her on purpose. He couldn't stand sharing the applause. He could have called it off anytime—it was his band, after all—but he wanted to watch her fail, wanted to see it with his own eyes. He never said, "Honey, I love you, you can't sing a note." Never tried to signal his real opinion, give her a chance to avoid the humiliation he knew was coming. He let it come. He encouraged her, deceived her, told her how good she was. He let the joke go on and on until she made a laughingstock of herself, then he *joined in laughing*.

His life wasn't over yet, but so far that was the worst thing he'd ever done to anyone. And he did it to the woman who loved him, the woman he had loved more than any other. She would never forgive him, and who could blame her?

Superman liked to think of himself as a good man, but way deep inside lived another man, who was cruel. He liked to think of himself as the reluctant object of Alexa's undying adoration. He liked to believe she would go on adoring him no matter what he did to her.

Now he realized that she hated him, and with good reason. Probably she'd made sure that his son hated him, too. He didn't deserve her, or any of the good things that had come to him in his life. And so fate had taken him away from them.

The cozy family picture, the image to which he'd been so anxious to return, was just a fantasy he'd invented to ease his conscience. He could no longer flatter himself—no one was pining for him. They had forgotten him and gone on with their lives. Time had not stopped when he crashed on the beach. The fact of his disappearance had not erased the man he had been. All the mean, low moments of his life had finally caught up with him, all the lies, pretenses, artificial emotions, ambitions, obsessions, all the ruthless urges that go into making a star, the slick bits of business he'd picked up on his way to the top.

He tried to remember one instance in his life when he felt something true, and actually said what he felt. One moment when he was good to someone, not to get his own way or to improve his situation, but just to be good, without asking, What's in it for me? He could not think of a single time.

That first night, leaning against a palm tree at La Discoteca, he had sensed the truth, but he'd been too drunk to face it. He *couldn't* go home. He was already here. This was it. This was the life he had earned for himself. If he hadn't been in such a hurry to fly off to redheaded Becky in Phoenix, he would never have ended up in this place. If he'd treasured and cared for the people he loved, he would be with them now. There was no one to blame for his life; he'd lived it exactly as he wanted to; he had started from nothing and turned himself into a rich, famous, selfish bastard who knew only how to hurt people. He could shake his fist at God, but why should God pay attention to him? He never paid any attention to God.

This was his payback, his sentence: to stay here forever, brooding over his crimes.

He was better off dead—better off living here, in this dangerous maddening seductive place, than trying to go back to a life that no longer existed. The world was better off without him. He was a bigger hit dead than alive. A&M Records was happy. Alexa was happy. Ben Junior would grow up in a decent home, and there would be money enough for them all. Superman was too far away to ever be able to hurt them again.

As for his own happiness, he would have to try to find that on his own. He would have to become the kind of man who deserves to be happy.

Sitting on Spike's porch, watching the newspaper pages float into the jungle, Superman learned the hardest lesson of his life: in the great scheme of things, his existence was not important to anyone but himself.

"Let me have another taste of that, Spike." He reached for the bottle. "I might be staying awhile."

17 / Go Ahead, Send It In

GRANNY FRENCH LOVED entering sweepstakes contests the way some people love sex, or God. She approached her obsession with the high hopes and deadly intensity of the true fanatic. "One day, Benjamin," she would say as she licked the stamp, "one day, our ship will come in."

When I was younger this conjured up an image of a great white ocean liner steaming up the river to New Orleans, where Granny and I would step aboard our brand-new lives.

Much later I realized what a hopeless dreamer she was. Her name was on every mailing list in the world, and she filled out every sweepstakes entry form they sent her: *Good Housekeeping,* American Family Home, $50,000 a Year for Life, Win a Home, Win a Fine Kentucky Thoroughbred Horse, Win a Winnebago, Win a Hawaii Vacation Every Summer Forever. Every Saturday night she would watch *The Carol Burnett Show* while she filled out a new batch of entries. "Look at her, Benjamin, with her eyes slung over in her head that way," she'd say, squawking with laughter. At a commercial she'd wipe her bifocals and peer down at the paper in front of her. "All right, help me with this one. How many Kleenex would you say our household consumes on a weekly basis?"

She didn't notice how that particular question made me blush.

On Monday she would toddle off to the post office with another stack of envelopes. She never won anything—not so much as a magazine subscription—but this run of bad luck only served to intensify her faith. With every year that passed, she believed, the odds were building inevitably in her favor.

Two weeks before my sixteenth birthday, we gathered around the old Admiral set for the seventh year in a row to watch Ed McMahon bestow the Publishers' Clearing House grand prize on someone other than us. Publishers' Clearing House was the big-daddy life-changing bonanza of them all: five million dollars, paid out in installments over twenty years. This year, as every year, Granny French was certain she was going to win.

On the day after New Year's, she'd gone up and down Forrest Street begging entry forms off those neighbors who weren't going to bother filling them out. She spent hours peeling off the mailing labels, filling in her name, checking all the little boxes.

I was aware, of course, that if Granny had actually won the sweepstakes, we would know it already. The camera crew comes to your house days before the show to tape you receiving the surprise of your life, then you're flown to New York to answer live questions from Ed McMahon. (I guess they don't want the winners suffering heart attacks on live TV.) But Granny insisted on the reality of what was before her—if she could see it happening right now, well sir, now must be when it was happening. She had never accepted the concept of tape-delayed television, any more than she had accepted the moon landing, rock-and-roll music, or frozen chicken pot-pies. When I tried to explain it, she told me to hush up and go check the popcorn.

I headed for the kitchen.

"I can feel it," she called. "Tonight's the night. Our ship is definitely going to come in."

"About time," I said.

Instead of a white ocean liner steaming up the Mississippi, I discovered a popcorn popper that had blown its top and sprayed the kitchen with white kernels. I put another batch in the pan, taking care to fasten the catches on the side of the thing, and fetched the broom to begin sweeping up.

"Oh come on come on, Benjamin, it's starting! Just unplug it and come on!"

"In a minute. . . ."

"He's giving the third prize right now, hurry!" Like all true zealots, Granny French assumed that everyone around her shared her obsession. In truth I was humoring her. I had my own set of obsessions these days, chiefly the Sex Pistols' *Never Mind the Bollocks*, Elvis Costello's *My Aim Is True*, and the solitary sport I practiced in my room with a box of Kleenex.

I didn't really understand the connection, but about the time I gave myself over to these pursuits, I stopped hating Granny for bringing me to Opelousas. I realized that the stern little tyrant who'd raised me had been replaced by a frail old lady who forgot things and seemed tired all the time. She was my whole family now. My father was gone, and my mother, too—three years since the last Christmas card from Casa San Jacinto. We got a monthly check from the lawyers handling my father's estate, but that was it.

Once I understood that I was alone in the world, I began helping out around the house without being asked. This alarmed Granny at first, though she adjusted. I made it a point to come out of my room, to spend part of each evening watching TV with her.

Now she appeared in the doorway, begging me to hurry. In her excitement she didn't notice popcorn all over the floor. I let her drag me to the living room.

Ed McMahon beamed at the winners of the million-dollar second prize, a farm couple from somewhere cold: Minnesota, Wisconsin. Their faces were pale, and I thought they looked oddly unthrilled, considering. "Tell us," Ed boomed, "the one question on everybody's mind—what are you gonna do with the money?"

"Well, we're giving some to charity," said the wife.

"And ten percent goes to the church," said the husband.

"And we want to get my mother a better car."

"Ho ho ho," said Ed, "those are all wonderful things, but aren't you going to just blow a little of it—just spend it on yourselves?"

The couple glanced at each other, as if they'd vowed not to discuss this in public. A grin broke through the man's face. "I'm gonna buy me a new tractor," he said. "The seat on my old one is all rusted through."

Granny French hooted. "A tractor! The man just won a million dollars and he's gonna buy a tractor?"

"And I always wanted a London Fog raincoat," said the wife.

I groaned. "They don't deserve to win."

Granny laughed. "Maybe she'll put on her raincoat and they'll go for a spin on their new tractor."

I propped my feet on the ottoman. "What are you gonna buy if you win, Granny?"

"A house in Hawaii and a trip to Paree," she said, "and I'll buy you a car. What kind you want, a Cadillac?"

"A Zee."

"A what?"

"A Datsun 280-Z. Or a Porsche 914."

"I don't even know what that is," she said. "Hush, here comes the grand prize."

"All right, ladies and gentlemen, the moment we've all been waiting for." Kettledrums rolled. The live studio shot of Ed switched to a handheld camera moving unsteadily through a tree-shaded neighborhood. I smelled faint smoke in the air: burning leaves?

"We're in Opelousas, Louisiana," said Ed, in a conspiratorial voice, "and we're just about to make an unannounced visit to the home of our grand-prize winner."

I heard a little peep—the first half of a hiccup. I turned to find Granny burning holes with her eyes in the television screen.

That was Forrest Street on TV. Ed McMahon and a camera crew walking past Annie Laurie Darling's house, headed toward our end of the block. Mrs. Darling's house looked small and rather shabby on television.

I blurted "Jesus!" then "Sorry."

Granny hadn't noticed. She made no sound at all. She sat unmoving, unblinking.

I ran to yank back the curtain. It was dark outside—as it usually was, at night. Lights shone in Mrs. Darling's windows, and the Smithsons', and Mrs. Delacroix's.

I glanced back at the TV. A sunny morning on Forrest Street. Ed strode ahead of the camera crew, up the sidewalk toward a small white frame house. . . .

Our house. That was our house. A border of hot-pink azaleas, a black mailbox beside the door.

I felt a rip in the fabric of time—I was watching it happen. But it had already happened. Before. But not to us. But that was our house! It was happening now!

Ed aimed his finger at the doorbell, and pushed.

I jumped.

The *ding-dong* came from the TV.

Ed turned with a wink for the audience. "Somebody's coming," he said.

The door opened. Louise Delacroix peered out, a picture of cheerful, well-dressed obesity. When she saw who was ringing the bell, her eyes widened. "Oh my stars, aren't you—aren't you—"

"Ed McMahon, ma'am, from Publishers' Clearing House. Are you Louise Delacroix?"

"Why—why yes!" She pressed a hand to her bosom, just so. Now I saw the house number at her elbow: 457. We were 458, across the street. Until that moment, I had never noticed the two houses were identical except for the numbers.

"Mrs. Delacroix, you've just won *five million dollars!*"

"Ohhhhhhhh," she wailed, waving both hands at her face to keep from fainting. "Oh my Gaaaaaad, I don't be-leeeeeeeeeve it!"

You would have to know Mrs. Delacroix to notice that beyond that wide-eyed amazement, she was holding up her head so her double chin didn't show. Her surprise was an act. She'd known the camera crew was coming. She'd had time to get dressed up and put on makeup.

I felt a tremor right then. Whether it was a real earthquake, the result of all the people in Opelousas jumping to their feet at once, or something shifting inside our own house, I do not know. I swear the china rattled in the china cabinet.

The image of Mrs. Delacroix froze in midsurprise. At a burst of applause from a live audience, the frozen picture zoomed up to a screen above a stage where Ed McMahon and Mrs. Delacroix stood watching themselves.

Mrs. Delacroix was enormous, and that expensive jewel-blue pantsuit made her look even bigger. That was one large, happy woman watching herself on the overhead screen, turning to Ed with a radiant smile, accepting the audience's cheers for her magnificent luck.

I heard a little scratching sound. Granny's hands on her knees. She was scratching the skin with her fingernails—*scritch! scritch!* I doubt she even knew she was doing it.

"Granny," I said.

She looked at me then. Her face was slack, as if the person inside it had died. Her eyes glowed, strange and green. She didn't seem to recognize me.

"Granny, it's okay, listen—it's okay. It's some kind of a joke or something. Somebody's playing a joke on us."

A lame effort, I know, but my own astonishment was met by a vacancy in her eyes. Our ship had come in, all right—it had steamed right into Opelousas and tied up across the street at Mrs. Delacroix's house. Can you imagine how it feels to sit there watching your neighbor—the one who's spent her life turning her nose up at you—bringing home the big one, the whopper, the big-daddy life-changing thank-you-ma'am sweepstakes prize of all time?

And to know that you are the one who entered her in the contest?

The best I can figure, Granny must have been paying a bit too much attention to Carol Burnett one night. She must have neglected to remove Mrs. Delacroix's mailing label and write in her own name.

That little mistake cost her five million dollars, paid out over twenty years.

It might have been my fault. Maybe I said something that distracted her just at the moment she was tending to Mrs. Delacroix's entry. I tried to convince her of this—but that was later, after the weird glow had faded from her eyes.

She blinked. "Well," she said softly. "Isn't that nice for Louise."

"Granny—"

"Benjamin." Even softer. "I have a little headache. I'm going to bed."

She stood up from her chair, and floated down the hall to her room.

I went to the window to look out at the warm lights of Mrs. Delacroix's house. Some of the neighbors were out on her lawn, shouting, laughing, ringing the same doorbell that Ed McMahon had rung. They staggered as if they were drunk. Of course she was not home. She was in New York, on live television with Ed McMahon.

At the time, I thought this was the saddest night of my life.

A smell of burning—I ran to the kitchen. A cloud of greasy smoke billowed out. Coughing, bent over, I waved my way to the back door and flung it open.

The plastic dome of the popcorn popper had melted, oozing down the cabinet, searing a yellow pool into the linoleum.

Later I learned that Ed McMahon had come to Forrest Street the previous Thursday, while I was at school and Granny French was stitching a quilt with her Fellowship Circle. Incredibly, no one else in the neighborhood had witnessed the Prize Patrol vans pulling up to the corner of Forrest and Maple to disgorge Ed and his camera crew.

Mrs. Delacroix had phoned Granny that very evening. After a little chitchat, she said that her sister-in-law in New York was ill, something with the pancreas, Mrs. Delacroix was flying up there to see about her, would Granny mind watering the azaleas while she was gone?

"Of course not, Louise," Granny said, knowing full well (as she confessed to me) that she would not put the first drop of water on those azaleas—in fact, she would have gone across the street with a hair dryer and blown hot air on them if she thought that would make them die any quicker.

She hung up the phone and thought nothing more of it.

Until she saw Louise Delacroix on TV with Ed McMahon. And then she remembered.

The FOR SALE sign went up across the street the next day. Mrs. Delacroix flew straight from New York to her new home in Los Angeles, and sent Mayflower to pack and move her things. Apparently she regarded her millions as a fast ticket out of Opelousas. She never came back to lord it over her neighbors.

Around town this was seen as the ultimate proof of her insufferability. The town had gotten itself all braced to throw a parade for her, to smile and be good sports about her amazing good fortune, and she didn't even have the grace to come home and pack her own underwear.

I have no idea what happened to Mrs. Delacroix after that. Her azaleas withered and died before the new owners moved in. I hope she enjoyed her five million. I hope she lived to spend every last little dime.

Granny French never admitted she'd swiped the entry form from Mrs. Delacroix's mailbox, and certainly the winner of a five-million-dollar grand prize would have no reason to reveal the fact that she had not actually entered the contest. That was something I figured out only years later. But the strangest thing was that Granny French was a good Christian woman who'd spent her life feeling sorry for sinners, those who were so weak that sin reached up and grabbed them without the least struggle. And then she died of envy, the deadliest sin of all. She lived her last months in a livid green cloud of it. The woman who pitied the sinners became a sinner herself, and it ate her up even faster than the cancer.

GRANNY'S COUSIN KATY came up from St. Martinville to stay with us. Katy had been a nurse before she married. She gave the sponge baths, changed the sheets, got up in the night to dispense the pain pills. She was a small woman, pretty as a porcelain doll, with a turned-up nose and a breathy childlike voice. Whenever Granny started moaning or fussing, Katy would sing songs her grandfather taught her. Those last months, for me, will always resound with her high, tiny voice singing "Molly Malone." It was a song about a girl who died, and maybe you wouldn't think it appropriate for a dying woman, but it soothed Granny French's nerves, and mine.

> *She died of a fever*
> *And no one could save her*
> *And that was the end of poor Molly Malone*

I lay on the floor in the living room, watching *The Love Boat*.

"I think she's asleep now," Katy said. "It's getting so it's hard to tell."

"She was up a lot last night. She's probably just tired."

"Benny, she's not tired. She's dying. You know that, don't you?"

I traced a circle on the floor with my finger. "Of course."

"I don't think it'll be all that long. Dr. Eustace came today, while you were at school. He wants to admit her over to the County General."

"Granny hates the hospital."

"I know. She says hospitals are for hypochondriacs, and if she has to die, she'd rather do it right here. But Dr. Eustace is concerned because she's so . . . down. He's afraid she might try something."

"Like what?"

"Like try to, you know, take her own life or something."

Until that instant I had never conceived of a dying person committing suicide. At first the idea seemed absurd. Why go to all that trouble when all you had to do was wait?

But I knew why. Granny was hurting. Her life was no good now. When she wasn't ranting at the long-gone Mrs. Delacroix, she was groaning, raging, sobbing. Sometimes I'd wake up in the middle of the night and hear her calling "Mama" like a little lost girl.

Katy perched on the sofa and placed a hand on my shoulder. "I know this is hard on you, child."

I felt heat in my eyes, but I was too old to cry. "What difference would it make?" My voice sounded strange, half choked. "She's gonna die anyway."

"That's not the way it's supposed to happen in God's plan," said Katy. "Evvy is a good Christian. It would just be so bad if she went that way. It's bad enough as it is."

"But she wouldn't be hurting."

"She needs to go to the hospital. I'm not a doctor, and Dr. Eustace can't keep coming by here all the time."

"Well, so send her to the hospital, then. What are you asking me for?"

Katy smiled. "She told the doctor you were the only one in the family with any sense, so she'd leave it up to you."

I raised my eyes. "She did?" At that moment I loved Granny French more than I ever loved anyone. I knew what she wanted from me. "Would you be mad, Katy? If we kept her here. Would you stay and help me take care of her?"

"Well sure, sweetheart, I'm here till the bitter end. But they have things in the hospital to make her more comfortable."

"Like what?"

Her face turned grim. "Well, morphine."

"Can't you give it to her here?"

"It's the law, you have to give it in a hospital. I've tried calling your mama three times. They won't let her come to the phone in that place. I told them it was an emergency. They said she was on some kinda retreat and they'd have to give her a message. They seemed rather rude, if you ask me."

I smeared *X*s on the floor. "I don't care about her."

"Aw, now don't say that, of course you do."

"No."

"She's your mother!"

"You don't know a damn thing about it!" The anger in my voice startled both of us.

Katy reached out to try and hug me. I pulled away. I had not been hugged in years. Granny French loved me, but she was not the hugging type.

I went to the door of her room. The illness had dwindled her down until she had no more substance than the wadded-up sheet. It seemed she might simply sink into the mattress and disappear before it came her time to die. The room smelled of Vick's VapoRub and some other sickly sweet odor that was hard to identify.

"How much longer does he think?" I said over my shoulder.

"There's no telling."

"A week? A month?"

Katy sighed. "No one can answer that, Benny. It's in the Lord's hands. Maybe we should pray about it. Would you like to do that?"

I shook my head. "No. I don't need to. I think we should keep her at home, Katy."

The moment I said it, I knew it was the right thing. I did not know it would change my life forever.

Or maybe I did.

Seven nights later, I awoke to the sound of Granny French calling my name. I pulled on my bathrobe and stole down the hall.

Lamplight washed her walls the color of a candle flame. Katy slept on a chaise at the foot of Granny's bed, hands tucked under her chin, one toe sticking out from under the covers. Granny was sleeping just as soundly. But how could that be? I'd heard her calling.

A dream? It sounded so real. "Benjamin?" and then a little cough, and "Benjamin?"

She looked as if she'd been asleep for years. A jewel strand of spittle stretched from her mouth to the pillow. Her lungs made a wheezing sound, like a dog toy.

It was too awful. I could not look away.

I eased down to the edge of the bed. Granny stirred, and licked her lips. Her eyes swam open. She saw me.

"Well, hello," she said.

Lately she hadn't known who I was. The doctor said the cancer had spread from her spine to her brain. "Hey, Granny," I whispered, "it's Benjamin."

"I know who you are. What are you doing up at this hour? Don't you have school tomorrow?"

"Tomorrow's Sunday." I was startled by the strength in her voice—as if someone had pumped a shot of pure life into her veins. "I thought I heard you calling."

"I was sleeping. Like you should be. Have you got a clean shirt for Sunday school?"

I hadn't been to church in years, but I said, "Yes, ma'am."

"Benjamin, what's going to happen to you?"

"What do you mean?"

"Who's going to cook your breakfast?"

"You are. Soon as you get better."

A wave of pain crashed over her. I swear I heard it, a wave crashing onto the rocks. Granny shuddered, and swallowed. Her eyes loomed out of her face, staring at nothing.

I closed my eyes until it passed. Something soft nudged my arm.

Granny held up one of the lacy yellow square pillows that decorated her bed. "Take it."

"What for?"

"Just take it."

The pillow smelled of VapoRub. I held it on my lap.

"It's time, Benjamin. It hurts too much. If I hadn't been worried for you, I'd be gone by now."

"I really need you to get better, Granny." The water in my eyes was not warm enough for tears.

"I shouldn't worry. You're almost—grown-up, you're almost—" A splash of pain cut her off.

"I'm sorry it hurts." I squeezed the pillow.

"You've got to help me."

"What can I do?"

"Help me." Her gaze drifted over to Katy, snoozing.

"How? Tell me what you want me to do."

"It's taking too long. It's not supposed to take this long. Help me go, Benjamin."

A sick feeling started up from my stomach.

"Please, I shouldn't ask you but I can't—do it myself. I don't have the strength." Her breath came in gasps. Her skin was translucent. Only her eyes blazed with life. "The pillow. Hold it on my face. It'll be over quick."

I fought the urge to throw up. "Granny. You know I can't do that. You just feel bad now. You'll feel better tomorrow."

"No. It's time. You're here with me. Help me go."

"I can't do that!"

"Do as I say."

"No!" I wanted to throw it down and run, but I did not do that either. I did not leave her.

"Go on, hold it up." She reached out bony fingers, pulling my arm and the pillow toward her. "That Louise Delacroix is a monster," she murmured. "She bears direct responsibility for this."

I pulled out of her grasp.

Her hand fell to her side. Her face lost its bitterness, and she smiled at me with the wisest kind of love in her eyes, just gazing me through. I wanted to tell her how much I loved her, how sorry I was for all the trouble I'd caused her. Then I realized she was not looking at me. Her eyes were open, but she was gone. Her head sagged to the side.

"Oh my God," cried Katy, behind me, "Benny, what have you *done!*"

The pillow still in my hands.

Katy rushed over. I saw fear in her eyes.

I flung down the pillow. "I didn't do it!"

"Oh my God," Katy wailed, "oh my God. . . ."

AT THE FUNERAL everyone stared at me. Katy swore she'd told no one, but they knew, the whole town knew. I heard the whispers in the ceiling fans, the screen doors slapping shut. I had not done it but Granny had asked me to, I held the pillow in my hands and actually considered doing it. I was caught in the act of not doing it, but it felt as if I had.

We stood on a patch of fake grass beside a rectangular hole, downwind of a mound of chrysanthemums. The drone of the preacher blended with the cicada buzz and the roar of the cars on the highway. Granny's casket was gray and shiny as a new Cadillac.

I stared at the hole in the ground, tasting dust in the air. Katy wept softly. An electric motor whirred as the casket sank into the hole.

We walked up the slope through the dazzling afternoon. A large woman in white came floating down toward us from the line of cars.

At first I thought it must be Mrs. Delacroix in a blond wig—those huge sunglasses hid half her face. But then she threw out her arms and cried "Benny!" and lumbered toward me and I saw, oh dear Jesus, that was my mother.

Whatever else they'd done at Casa San Jacinto, they had fed her well. She'd put on at least a hundred pounds. Her beautiful Miss Southwest Louisiana face was the center of a wide, fleshy moon. In that flowing white pantsuit she looked like an inflated balloon version of herself.

I felt myself drawn in like a satellite to a planet. "Mom?"

"Oh my God, I'm too late," she cried, wrapping me in her arms. "I don't have a mother. . . ."

I was smothered in the big soft warm cushion of her: unmistakably that was her smell, a sweet tang of patchouli, a lovely mustiness that belonged just to her.

"Doris French, is that you?" Katy said. "Girl, you look so good I didn't recognize you."

"I'm big as a house," my mother wailed, clutching me tighter.

"You came." I breathed into her shoulder. "You came."

"Well of course I came! I'd have been here sooner but I just heard." She held me at arm's length. "Jesus, Benny, look at you. You're a big grown-up man. Oh, it's all just too much." She grabbed me and squeezed me again.

A little crowd gathered. Mixed with the comforting murmur was a hum of surprise as people recognized my mother and registered the change. I didn't care how fat she was—she was my mother, and she was here. I was not alone in the world. All my anger seemed to dissolve in that moment when she held me. Is there any child of any mother on earth who wouldn't feel that?

People took turns hugging her, welcoming her home.

She and Katy went to look at the grave. I couldn't stand any more crying. I wandered off to stand by the car.

The sympathetic looks of the mourners glanced off me like bullets. I was invulnerable. I kept my hands in my pockets and stared at a clump of pine trees across the way.

We went back to Granny's, where a great spread of food had been laid. The kitchen bustled with ladies rattling aluminum foil. The neighbors loaded their plates with fried chicken, green-bean casserole, Jell-O, potato salad, three kinds of cake. They spilled onto the porch, the front yard, eating and talking in low voices. Whenever I approached, the conversation seemed to pause, then pick up again in a different tone.

Harvey Loomis, the neighbor, squatted beside me on the front stoop. "How you holdin' up there, young man?"

"Okay." I stared at the grass.

"Anything you want to talk about?"

"Nosir."

"It can be hard on a fella," he said. "I know Evvy raised you like you were her own."

"Yessir." I wished he would go away.

"Son, don't you mind the gossip," he said. "That's all folks have to do in this town is just talk about each other."

I glanced up in surprise. Mr. Loomis had never said more than five consecutive words to me.

"God f'bid they should ever say anything nice," he went on. "I know whatever you done was best for poor Evvy."

"I didn't do anything," I told him.

"I know you didn't. You just take care of yourself, all right? Let me know what I can do." He clapped my shoulder, and went in.

I knew he was trying to make me feel better, but suddenly I had an overwhelming urge to get up and walk out of the yard, down to the bus station, get the hell out of this town. There was nothing to keep me here now.

The door slapped open. My mother was there. "Here you are! What are you doing out here by yourself?"

"Nothing."

"Come join the party. Uncle Henry's telling stories about the olden days."

That was my mother, all right. Her own mother in the grave less than an hour, and here she was telling me to come join the party.

"I'll stay here."

"You mind if I sit with you?"

"Go ahead."

She eased into the porch swing. The chains let out a dangerous groan. "You ever miss me at all, Benny?"

"What do you think?"

"I wouldn't be surprised if you didn't. If you hated me. That's really what I expected."

I shook my head. "I don't hate you."

"You know, I haven't exactly been on vacation all this time. I was really sick. I got in a lot of trouble after your Dad died—you know, drugs and things, and Jimbo. . . ."

"I know."

"And don't think I'm not aware of how I look. I don't like it, but you've got to understand that inside I'm much better now. I'm a million times better."

"That's great," I said. My heart was a small, cold, radioactive lump.

"Talk to me, sweetie. Tell me what's on your mind."

"They think I killed her."

"Who?"

"Everybody. Katy. They think I killed Granny."

"What are you talking about? She had cancer."

I told her what happened. I poured it all out. By the end, I was squeezing my eyes with my thumbs to keep the tears in.

"You poor thing. It's good that you're able to talk about it. Do you need a hug?"

"No!" I snarled. "I don't need a *hug*."

"I think you've got some guilt about this," she said. "Obviously you feel responsible for her death."

"Look—forget it, okay? I'm sorry I brought it up." She had not changed a bit.

"Don't, Benny. I think it's wonderful we can pick up and have a heart-to-heart talk after all this time. Like we'd been seeing each other every day. If we're going to be together, that's important."

"You're not going back to that place?"

"I'm not sure. I'm pretty pissed off with them, I'll tell you. We were off on an isolation retreat, of course you're supposed to be isolated—but you'd think they could've told me my damn *mother* died."

"You're gonna stay here?"

"For a while." She glanced around the yard. "I thought I would hate coming back, but it's not so bad. It feels like home."

It was easy to forget that she'd grown up in this house, before me. She'd put so much distance between herself and Opelousas that I had never imagined her coming back.

"You must be ready to start thinking about going to college, right? Have you given any thought to that?"

"I'm gonna go out to Long." Russell B. Long Junior College was the only show in Opelousas; I'd wanted to stay close to Granny French.

"You're way too smart for that. I bet you're Ivy League material, if you want to be."

I didn't dignify that.

"Well, there's still time to decide. Don't you have another year of high school?"

I'd graduated third in my class, in May. I was set to start at Long in August. My mother had been off on an isolation retreat for the last eight years. She didn't even know how old I was.

"Look, *Mother*," I snarled, "just give it up, okay? You're not very good at this. Just forget about me. I can take care of myself. I've been doing it for a long time."

"Whoa, whoa." She held up her hands. "What did I say?"

"Just go back to the crazy house, okay? Don't worry about me. I'll be fine. We all got along just fine without you." I started for the screen door.

She seized my arm. "Wait—Benny. Don't be mean to me, please, not today."

I shook her off. "Don't touch me."

"I know you resent me. It's natural, I resented my mother at times. It's all part of growing up."

"I don't resent you," I said in the coldest voice I could find. "I don't feel anything at all about you."

That stung. Her eyes clouded over. "You don't mean that."

"When did you ever care about me? Not once. Take your hands off me."

She hung on. "Of course I cared. Do you think I wanted to be in that place? I was sick—I was taking all these drugs, and I tried to—I don't know, Benny, I missed your father too much. It just destroyed me when he died. Without him, I didn't know who I was. I couldn't take care of you. That's why I sent you to Granny. Don't you know I did it for you?"

"You didn't send me here. She brought me after you got me stoned at his funeral."

"I don't know what you're talking about."

"The memorial, remember? When I ate those brownies? Or were you too stoned to remember?"

A flicker of recognition passed over her face. "I suppose I deserve that. I was kind of a mess at the time."

"Yeah, well, that's fine." I jerked out of her grip. Her tears didn't move me at all. "You're my mother, and you forgot about me. Like I'm gonna forget about you."

Katy came through the door just then. From the look on her face you'd think I was whacking my mother with a stick. "Benny! Good heavens! Don't talk to her that way!"

"You stay the hell out of it!"

Katy drew back.

Mom said, "Benny, wait!" I shoved past them and stormed inside.

Everyone glanced up from their plates as I thundered by. I wanted to scream at them all to get out, get out and leave me alone with my hurt and my guilt and my thoughts of Granny French. I charged down the hall to my room and slammed the door.

The airplane models jumped on their strings. For some reason this made me angrier. I swung my fists, bashing the models to pieces against the walls, *wham, wham,* smashing to bits my stupid wasted years in this room. The black-light peace-sign poster made a sucking sound when I tore it from the wall. I seized the lava lamp—still plugged in, glowing unearthly orange—and heaved it against the headboard.

The glass shattered. Lava oozed down the pillow. The water made a dark stain on the bedspread.

Breathing hard now, I scanned for something else to destroy. My gaze fell on the picture frame over the bed—two Polaroid shots, a note scrawled on a scrap of blue shirt.

I snatched the frame from its nail, raised it high, and brought it down *smash!* on the back of my desk chair. Glass flew out in a shower.

Worried muttering beyond the door. I reached down to retrieve the photo and the scrap of cloth. I fished my stash from its hiding place behind the bookshelf—three hundred forty-five dollars, many miles of green grass under the wheels of my Lawn Boy. I stuffed my backpack with T-shirts and socks. The anger cleaned out my mind. I felt clear and strong, almost happy. I knew exactly what I had to do.

I opened the window and kicked out the screen. My old life was over. There was a great big world out there, a world that the people of Opelousas only glimpsed in their nightmares and on TV. Somewhere out in that world was a pair of twin mountains, connected by a wide curve of sand. Somewhere out there was my father, the last human being on earth who might possibly love me.

Someone rattled the doorknob. I propped a chair against it. My mother said, "Benny? Come on, open up, please? Honey?"

I swung my leg over the windowsill, soundlessly dropped to the grass. I imagine I was halfway to the bus station before they broke down that door.

18 / The Church of the Fiddler Crab

He had tried asking Frank: why?

"Mr. Willis. Please stop torturing yourself. She's gone. It was an accident, a terrible, horrible accident. It was nobody's fault. Nobody made it happen. You were flying the plane, were you not? You don't hear me blaming you."

"Come clean, Frank. Tell me what you did to that engine."

A strained little smile. "If you can't get over this ridiculous delusion," Frank said, "maybe you should find some other place to live."

And Superman found himself once more outside the pink wall.

That night he drank a whole bottle of *guaro* and stumbled along the ridge trail to the summit of the south mountain, intending to find this mysterious Magician and set him straight on a thing or two. At the end of the trail he caught a glimpse of chain-link fence and, beyond that, an expanse of polished white tile, a covered dance floor, big as the floor of a basketball gym.

He approached the fence, stuck his toe in a link. Rough hands seized him, dragged him back, threw him down on his stomach in the dirt. Someone stuck a boot in his ribs. *Click-click!* said the guns at his head.

"Whoa whoa hold on," cried Superman. "*Tranquilo!*"

The men shouted at him, or maybe at each other. There were five of them, and more running from a guardhouse at the end of the fence.

"*Qué quieres?*" a rough voice demanded. "*Qué quieres aquí?*"

"Just walking along mindin' my own damn business," he said. A cold metal finger prodded the base of his neck. He was too drunk to fight one of them, let alone all of them. "*Yo soy amigo de Pito*," he tried, "*tranquilo*, guys, okay? I'm lost, I—I had a little too much—*borracho*, you know?"

They waited until there were about fifteen of them playing their flashlights on him. Then they picked him up and gave him a shove down the hill and chased after him a few yards to make sure he went. He could hear their mild laughter as he stumbled down the trail in the dark.

THE NEXT DAY he found himself on a knoll down the mountain from Spike's house, with Pito and five *macheteros*. In two days, all sweating together, they hacked out a clearing, chopped a stand of bamboo into poles, and raised a one-room shack with a thatched roof and a little side porch.

The next evening Pito came back with his Gibson guitar, intact and shining, a new coat of varnish, only slightly out of tune. A miracle! Superman had assumed it had been bashed to splinters in his descent of the river.

He sat on his little porch for months, strumming the guitar, watching the jungle, sifting through the mysteries of this place and the mistakes of his life, the wrong turns that had brought him to this dead end. No one saw how he tortured himself, endlessly replaying his worst moments, as if by reliving them he could somehow make the rest of his life come out right. The terrible afternoon at Eagle Rock studio. The night at the Flor-A-Bama Lounge when he humiliated the singer. The time he spanked Ben Junior and sent him to bed for spilling grape juice on the stupid white carpet. The day he fired Billy Broward, his first manager, for daring to contradict him in front of the guys in his band. The hazy morning in New Orleans when he woke up at the Hotel Monteleone in a room with three hookers and a stevedore.

In his old life he never dwelled on these things; they were momentary lapses to be learned from and gotten over. But now he could think of nothing else. He felt himself spiraling downward, on fire and out of control, plunging toward the jungle with nothing to stop him but thin air. The daytime was not as bad as the nights, when the thudding of blood through his veins brought on wild storms of self-torment that left him wrecked, exhausted, bashed to splinters on the rocks in his head.

If he was religious he would think he was losing his soul. Can you lose your soul even if there's no God? How can you save yourself if you don't believe?

He wished he could believe. He remembered the way his mother's perfume filled the cab of the pickup on the way to church. It had always seemed to him that God would smell like that: sweet, dense, overpowering.

He found the Red Dot he had tucked in his pocket that day on the beach, and swallowed it. For the next four days and nights he sat on his porch without moving. He watched the sun rise and fall, the jungle bristling with life.

At the end of that time he had a new feeling about God. God is everywhere, he had learned. God is the frog, the spider, the firefly with twin headlamps, the moth with the photo-realistic owl's eye in its wing. God is the genius of ants, whose sentries can locate the tiniest crumb, swiftly marshal an army of workers to carry it off, and leave the field in an orderly file. The brain of an ant is a very small thing; how could ants have worked out this system on their own? God created the system. God is every ant. God is every fiddler crab dancing in and out of a hole on the beach. When the fiddler crabs come out, they trace sand figures around their holes in the shape of hibiscus blossoms. God showed the crabs how to draw flowers on the beach. Why would crabs draw flowers, if not to please God?

If God is in a fiddler crab, then God is in us, too. If God is in us, we must have souls, or else what is the point? If a man has a soul, maybe that soul can be saved. If a man spends enough time regretting his sins, if he dedicates himself to living a life that is pure and empty and clean, maybe one day he will find a way to save himself.

Superman learned to recognize the seven iguanas that lived in his yard, each standing guard on its own sunny branch. He littered the clearing with fruit peels for the coatimundis that loped through every day around noon.

Whenever he heard monkeys rattling through the trees, he whistled the same three-note greeting, C-A-F! He hoped they would send him a message, or at least come to be less fearful, but they always peeped at him from behind the branches, sometimes twenty baleful, distrustful stares at once.

Good old Pito gave back the money Superman had once tried to leave as a tip, so he was able to buy supplies at the *pulpería*. He slept on a cot. He made coffee on a camp stove. He ate mangoes, papayas, canned tuna, saltines. He bathed in the ocean. Large red ants set up housekeeping in his shoes.

Gyp showed up wagging one day, and just stayed on, as if she knew how lonely he was.

He borrowed Spike's transistor radio and sat for hours strumming along with *música romántica*, the mournful songs Catalina used to love: old men wailing their longing, husky-voiced women crooning a hopeless passion. He even tried writing a couple of songs, but his brain was even rustier than his fingers on the strings. The lyrics came out sentimental, like the radio songs, or else the kind of nonsense he used to clown around on between takes in the studio. He hung the guitar on a nail by his bed.

At night he saw a vapor ring around the moon, with the North Star set in its edge like a diamond. For some reason it made him think of Ben Junior. Hoping he was looking up at that moment.

After that it became his nightly ritual to bounce a good wish off the North Star to that other fixed point in the universe. Just in case.

After months of reflection, he decided that all this silence and soul-searching were not making him any better. Just lonelier.

He walked to the beach. The fiddler crabs ducked his shadow. He found the trail and followed it up into cool green shade.

He found her watering the garden between the two houses. It appeared she'd been painting, from her color-smeared shirt and the red polka-dot kerchief in her hair. She was so lovely, so perfectly mussed, that he wanted to wrap himself around her then and there. She was a bit softer, a bit rounder than he had remembered. She actually smiled when she saw him. Her eyes traveled lazily over him. "This is a surprise," she said.

"Hello, Daisy."

"Who is that—God, is that Gyp? Oh hey, Gyp, hey tweety, long time no see!" She knelt to nuzzle the dog. "What's she doing down here?"

"She's with me," Superman said. "She's mine now."

Daisy stroked Gyp's neck, and was rewarded with a moist nose in the ear. "She looks good. You're taking good care of her."

Daisy's garden was lushly in bloom, torrents of flowers spilling through ferns and philodendrons big enough to swallow a tree. One of the cabins was painted a bright tropical pink, the other a pale, chalky yellow. A fountain splashed in a grassy vale between the cabins, a kind of outdoor sitting room with wrought-iron chairs and a chaise longue.

"Hey, this is nice." He offered himself a chair. "Really. You've got a green thumb."

"I love gardening in the jungle. You get such fast results." She perched on the edge of the chaise. "Did you come to see my flowers?"

"Well, no . . . I came to see you. I was beginning to wonder if I'd ever see you again."

She spread her hands. "Here I am. Easy to see."

"You look beautiful."

"Oh, you men. You're all alike."

"How's your bat situation?"

She looked puzzled, then the memory brought a faint smile. "Oh, right. I had those windows glassed in. No more problems."

So far this was not going quite as he'd hoped. She was polite, but just that. "You're still mad at me," he said, "because of the way I ran off that night."

"Oh please, Ben, that water went under the bridge a long time ago." She curled her legs under.

"I wanted to tell you . . . I wasn't spying on you." He glanced toward the yellow house. "When I saw you with Jack. I didn't mean to see that. It was an accident."

"That was a hard time for me," she said, tilting her head. God, what a face. You could read every word of her story in those violet eyes.

"It was a fine thing, what you did, taking care of him."

"I wasn't Florence Nightingale," she said. "I had no choice."

"Spike told me he died. I wish I could have met him."

"You could have," she said, "but you ran off and never came back."

"I'm sorry for that, too."

Her eyes threw off sparks. "I've waited a long time to hear you say that. You may have to say it some more. Nobody *ever* ran away from me like that."

He took a deep breath. "Well, it scared the hell out of me," he said, "the whole thing. It was just . . . you were so perfect. We had such a wonderful time, nobody ever made me feel that way. And then—you didn't warn me or anything. I saw him, I freaked out, I admit it, it just turned everything upside down in my head. I had to get out of here. Suddenly everything I knew was wrong. He was alive, he was here. For God's sake, Daisy, how did it happen?"

"Why didn't you ask me then? Instead of just running away?"

"I didn't have the guts," he said.

"So all of a sudden you've got the guts. I'm not impressed."

"I'm not trying to impress you. I just wanted to see you."

A breeze came over her shoulder, bringing a scent of lavender. "Even the parts I know don't make sense. They tried to kill him. They screwed up. He was strong, it took him a long time to die. They couldn't let people see him like that. When they saw he was not going to get better, they brought him here."

"But who? Who did it? Who were they?"

"I don't know."

"But how did they—"

"Don't ask me, Ben. It's better not to know."

"Were you in love with him?"

"On a scale of one to ten?"

Superman couldn't stop the flicker of a smile.

"Jack was a ten." She rubbed absently at a mosquito bite. "But the end part was awful. You saw him."

He nodded. "I felt sorry for you, I wanted to tell you—but I didn't. I stayed away. I was afraid. It seems stupid now. I mean it, I really am sorry."

"All right, you've said it enough."

"What do you think would happen," he said, "if the world found out?"

"About Jack?" Her eyes clouded over. "He's dead. It wouldn't change anything."

"But everything they told us is a lie!"

"Welcome to the real world, Ben. Where've you been keeping yourself? People don't want the truth. They just want confirmation of the lies they've already heard." She reached for her packet of Emus.

"How did you come here?"

She flicked a lighter, blew a cloud of smoke. "Invited, like everyone else."

"The Magician—he's a friend of yours? You knew him?"

"I . . . suppose he's a friend, although I've never met him. Tell you this, though, I respect him. I'm not like some of these people, I'm not dying to get away from here. I knew what I was getting when I came. What I gave up seems very minor by comparison. He did me a big favor. He arranged the whole thing. I never lifted a finger. My life was hell, and he got me out of it. You have to understand, I'd been trying to kill myself for years. This place saved me."

"You know he's killed people. Not just Amelia. He almost killed me."

"I saw it," she said. "I was there."

He raised his eyes. "You were?"

"On the rock at the end of the beach."

This admission flooded him with pleasure. "You came to watch us take off?"

"Well, yes."

"I didn't think you cared."

She shrugged. "Amelia was my friend. I barely knew you. I still don't."

"If you ever decide you want to . . ."

She thought for a moment. "I think we should leave it alone, Ben. It's a nice memory."

"Nicest one I've got," he said. "Anybody living in that other house?"

"Do you mean am I seeing anyone?"

"Yes."

"That's none of your business, but no. No one since you. Why do you think my life was a mess? I kept falling in love with the wrong man. That takes too much acting, and I gave up acting a long time ago. I was never very good at it."

"What do you mean? You were the biggest star in the world!"

"That had nothing to do with my acting."

He didn't know whether to argue. He thought of *Niagara,* a perfectly ordinary melodrama—until *she* walked onto the screen, in a red super-saturated Technicolor dress. Was it strapless? He couldn't remember; it seemed beyond the realm of gravity. She radiated pure sex. It was weird, the aura of unreality she gave off, like a glowing alien creature. The other actors looked impoverished, gray, drained of life, standing beside her. Maybe that wasn't acting, but it was something greater: the breathy whisper, the halo of sex in the air.

It was a long way from that siren in the dress to this beautiful forty-eight-year-old woman in the paint-stained shirt. "You were great," Superman said. "I loved your movies."

"Thank you," she said, eyeing him. "What's happened to you, Ben? You seem different."

"Different how?"

"Not as cocky. You seem . . . I don't know, sadder? Something."

"I've been thinking a lot," said Superman. "When I met you I had one thing on my mind—getting out of here, getting my career back on track. That's why I stayed away from you. You don't know how many times I wanted to . . . I was afraid if I really got to know you, I'd never want to leave. But then I found out I didn't really have anything to go back to. So I stayed."

"I'd like to hear about it sometime," she said, "but I need to get back to work."

He followed her gaze to the yellow cabin. "What kind of work?"

She smiled. "Oh, it's silly. Just something I do. Would you like to see?"

He followed her up the steps, through the screen door. On the floor in the empty front room was a heap of rounded beach rocks. She snapped on a light. "This is my studio now. I don't know if I'm getting any better, but it's good for me."

He stared at the pile of rocks thinking: Must be one of those conceptual sculptures. Smile and say something. "Very nice."

"Those are just rocks. In here."

He stepped into the larger room and was stunned by the sight of dozens and dozens of faces, painted stone faces arrayed in floor-to-ceiling rows, a crowd of faces smiling, yawning, singing, rolling their eyes, sticking out their tongues.

Each face was different, and intricately detailed: blue curly hair and green lips, black skin with thin silvery eyes, zebra-striped hair with red eyes. The shape of each rock defined the personality she had painted on it, from plump gap-toothed baby to skinny old crone.

Superman stepped around a table heaped with paints and rags, jars of turpentine. He felt Daisy watching to see which faces caught his eye, which ones made him smile. He felt oddly reluctant to turn from one wall to the next—as if the faces might start laughing at him the minute he turned his back.

This was the room where Jack lived. Superman didn't know which was spookier: the memory of peering through that window, or the uneasy sensation he felt right now, at the center of this painted crowd. He didn't know whether to be delighted or appalled. How many hours had it taken her to gather these stones, lug them home, paint each one with its own identity?

"Jesus, Daisy, I don't know what to say. Who are all these people?"

"My fans." She lowered herself to a castered chair. "I like to have them around me. Go stand in the middle—doesn't it feel like a premiere? God, that was my favorite thing, all those faces, and the cameras flashing . . . do you remember the sound of those old-fashioned flashbulbs? Like champagne corks. What a wonderful sound."

"You did all these yourself?"

"I started when they brought Jack to me. It was something to do. Look at this one." She reached into the pail beside her chair, and brought out an unpainted stone, a smooth gray oval with a prominent bulge at one end. "See, there's a man in there, an executive type, he's got this Dr. Evil Genius forehead, and kind of slanty eyes, really a nasty expression. Like Darryl F. Zanuck." The joy in her smile made the whole thing seem harmless: the star puttering with her paints, the audience gazing down from the walls. She took up a brush and dipped it in a pot of red.

"I hope you don't mind," said Superman, "but I think you need to get out of the house more often."

She turned an eye on him. "Oh, do you."

"These are great, don't get me wrong, but—you need to go dancing or something. I know what this island can do to you. It's not good to spend too much time alone."

"I'm happy when I'm alone," she said. "I have finally found something that makes me happy."

"If I asked you out, would you go?"

"You mean on a date?"

"Yeah."

"No," she said.

"If I brought Gyp along as chaperon?"

She smiled faintly. "I don't think so, thanks. I really need to stay here and work."

He peered into the third room, where a new audience was taking shape along the tops of the walls. "How many are you planning to do?"

"I've got this pile here, and all those in the front room," she said, "and there's more washing up on the beach every day. I can barely keep up." She put on a pair of gawky magnifier eyeglasses, switched on a lamp, and bent over the rock. "It was nice to see you, Ben. Don't be such a stranger."

"Thanks, I won't." Superman let himself out. He walked down the steps and all the way out of her garden before he stopped.

What? Are you crazy?

He ran to the cabin—bounded the steps in one leap, threw open the door, hurdled the rock pile. Daisy peered up, paintbrush poised in midair. "What'd you forget?"

He stood over her, breathing hard, his wild expression reflected in her glasses.

"Ben, what is it?"

"You," he said, shaking. "I'm onto you."

"What on earth . . . ?"

"You don't want me to go. You're *acting*." He snatched the paintbrush from her hand and flung it to the floor, grabbed her wrists, and brought her up from the chair. "You want me to kiss you."

She tried to pull away. "You let go of me *now* or I'll scream."

"You can't scream while I'm kissing you." He pulled her in, bringing to her mouth the whole fire of his longing, the whole wet long tongue of his lust. He kissed her, and kissed her, and if there was a part of him that always held something back when he was kissing a woman, he opened up and let it on through. He had one kiss to convince her. If he failed, he knew he would be lost.

He plucked the glasses from her nose, flung them to the floor. He took her in his arms and gave her the soul-jazzing tide-sweeping mind-bending deep-throated kiss he'd been saving all these lonely months.

Daisy broke it off first.

Superman opened his eyes.

She smiled. Her lips were all wet. "Took you long enough," she said.

And then it was just like the first time.

19 / Destino

ONE MORNING HE AWOKE to find Daisy's sleeping porch surrounded by white-faced monkeys. The trees were full of them. They made little mewling sounds, like a gathering of kittens and babies. They rustled and shifted away as he swung his feet to the floor. "Morning, guys," he said, scratching himself. "Don't be lookin' at me, I ain't done nothing to you."

He pulled on shorts and went out. A hard rain in the night had polished everything to a sparkle. At some ungodly hour he'd heard the wind blustering; he'd snuggled in tighter and gone back to sleep. Now he saw limbs down all over the garden, the stone birdbath toppled, a tree fallen across the path to the beach.

"Looks like we had us a little hurricane," he called. "Daisy?"

The monkeys meowed.

Normally she was up by now, painting faces in the yellow house, but sometimes she went to the beach for a swim before the sun got too hot. Superman heard someone rattling down the path from uphill. "Daisy, that you?"

"*Buenos días.*" It was Pito, thrashing through the weeds with his machete. Gyp dashed to him, wagging her whole hind end.

"Hey, old man, long time no see. Whatcha doing down here?"

Pito glanced up at the trees full of monkeys. "Was big starm last night."

"Yeah, I heard it. Looks like it was a hell of a blow."

"Now you fly," Pito said.

"What you mean?"

"*Como dicen los monos,*" said Pito. "*Después de la tormenta, se vuela. Vámonos.*"

"Yeah, absolutely," said Superman. "What can I do for you?"

"*Vámonos,*" he said. "Is time. Less go."

That's how Superman found himself stumbling along a path he'd never seen, up and around the flank of the south mountain, an hour's climb straight up while Pito beat the bushes for snakes. It drove him crazy that the old man was able to thwack through the steamy jungle without producing the first bead of sweat, while rivers poured down his own neck. "I wish you would tell me where the hell we are going."

Pito looked over his shoulder. *"Aquí. Ya."*

"Ya yourself," he complained. "I don't know why I . . ." His voice trailed off as he stepped around a clutch of butterfly palms into a magical place.

A waterfall sprang from a huge overhanging rock fifty feet up, tumbling, sparkling down a string of cascades to a shallow pool. This water was a milky, otherworldly blue, beyond turquoise, beyond aquamarine. It gave off its own light, filling the grotto with blue radiance.

The hairs on Superman's neck prickled up. The look on his face produced a rare smile from Pito. *"Preciosa, verdad?"*

"Sí," said Superman. *"Preciosa."* He dropped to his knees by the pool, and scooped up a handful. It tasted sweeter than water.

"You know what is *lágrimas?"* Pita made a sad face, wiped a finger under his eye.

"Tears?"

He nodded. "This is the tears of El Mago. You drink. Is good for drink."

"El Mago?"

"He sleeps in the mountane."

Superman sat back on his haunches. "Why'd you bring me up here?"

"You is impartant," the old man said.

"Yeah, I know, you been telling me that for a long time, and I'm really glad you think so, but—"

"Drink more." Pito reached behind a rock for a long-handled brass dipper.

"Thanks, I've had—"

"Drink."

"Well, if it makes you happy." He raised the dipper to his lips. If you could distill the color of a morning sky to a liquid, it would taste this blue.

"Destino," the old man said. "You know what is *destino?"*

Superman had heard the word in radio songs. "Yeah, it means 'destiny.' Fate."

The old man said, "This is the magic, what you say is the magic."

"I don't get it."

"No is magic. You gringo, you see magic but is, how you say, feet?"

"Fate."

"Fay-eet." Pito tested the word on his tongue.

"You telling me you didn't use magic to lift that plane up and fly it down the mountain?"

"Is the plane," he said. "Is the *destino* for one plane to fly. I helping the plane to find his *destino*."

"But it didn't fly. It crashed."

He shrugged. "*Destino.*"

"Well hell, Pito, if every damn thing is *destino,* what's the use getting out of bed in the morning?"

"*No sé,*" he said. I don't know. "Drink more."

"I've had plenty." Superman surrendered the dipper. "You better get some before Gyp drinks it all."

"Is not for me," Pito said. "Is for helping you find you *destino*."

"I'm trying real hard to understand here, but—"

"Wait. You unnerstand." Pito hid the dipper behind a rock. The strange glow of the water shimmered in his eyes. "You fly."

At the moment he spoke those words, Superman felt his knees lifting up from the ground. His whole body floated up, as if someone had switched off the gravity in the clearing. He found himself kneeling in midair, levitating, three feet off the ground. "Whoa!"

Gyp barked and waggled.

Superman waved his hands in the air, floating over onto his stomach, extending his arms like the comic-book Superman. Look, up in the air! Not a bird! Not a plane! He pressed his toes to the earth and pushed off. The ground fell away. He rose into the trees. "Hey hey hey! This is great!"

With no means of propulsion or steering, it was more floating than flying. He waved his hands and feet, swimming through thin air. He settled toward the glowing pool, imitating the astronauts' weightless somersaults in their capsule on the way to the moon. He drew his feet under and launched himself off the ground.

He shot up, up, batting branches aside, past the tops of the trees, straight on up past the overhanging rock, twisting in midair like a diver. Maybe he was dreaming, maybe something in that vivid water had sent him into this beautiful dream. He spread his arms and looked down to the green canopy sloping away from him, falling to the sea. He saw the beach, the gap in the trees at the Big House, the whole curve of the island, all the way across the channel to Gato Negro, where the waterfront was lined with dump trucks, bulldozers, tractor-trailer rigs. He thought: I am not dreaming trucks. I am flying for real. The old man is flying me with his eyes. The blue water is inside me, helping me find my *destino*. I am Superman. This is my *destino:* to fly.

He turned over, paddling hands in the air. He caught a breeze and rode it down to a branch, shoved off and went sailing through the arms of an oak. The only way to steer was to push off and float in a straight line until he ran into something. He scraped his arm on a branch, fell into a tangle of vines, and thrashed around until he found himself tumbling backward head over heels, bumping to earth at Pito's feet.

"Man, that is *fantastic.*" He sprang up again, gravity-free, floating six feet off the ground. Gyp barked and leaped. He snapped his fingers. "Come on, come on up!"

"Is only for good," said Pito. "If you use for bad, is no working."

"It's the water, right? There's something in the water." He swung around a branch and went sailing feetfirst toward the cliff wall. He kicked off a rock, ricocheted to another tree. In no time he was shooting around the clearing like a pinball, doing flips and loop-the-loops through the branches. He yipped and laughed and flew under the waterfall, drenching himself—floundered out of it, sailed backward, and found a tree with the back of his head.

He sank toward the ground, blinking at white dots of light.

"Is good," Pito said. "You fly good."

"It's better than good." He rubbed his head. "How the hell do you do it?"

"*Yo no. Tú.*"

Superman hovered on his back. This was better than any hammock. "You mean whenever I want to fly, all I have to do is just come get a drink of this water? This could come in handy. Do you know how much money you could make if you bottled this stuff?"

"Is no for money," said Pito, puffing up. "Always with you is the money. Money no is impartant. *You* is impartant. You fly. Unnerstand?"

Superman added crass materialism to his ever-growing list of character flaws. "No, man, there's a lot I don't understand. Why me? What's it for?"

"Sometime is no why," said Pito. "Sometime just *is.*"

Superman pushed off a rock, backstroking lazily through the air. This was so cool. He wished Ben Junior could see him right now. "Pito, what's going on over at Gato Negro? Looks like they're building something."

Pito said, "First coming a bridge. Then coming a war."

"War? What kind of war?"

"Now you learn. Later you know."

"Why you always have to be so damn cryptic? Can't you ever just say what you mean?"

"What means 'cryptic'?"

"You know, like, 'Now you learn. Later you know.' What the hell is that supposed to mean?"

"*Paciencia*," said Pito. "You wanting to knowing *todo*. But I not knowing. You has to learn. Is why you impartant."

"Why don't you fly, Pito?"

"*No es mi destino. Es el tuyo.*"

Superman did a back flip in the air. "So what's your *destino*, old man?"

"I living a long time," said Pito.

"Oh yeah? What about me?"

"You fly," he said.

"There—there—what you said? That's cryptic."

"*Sí.*" Pito almost smiled again, but caught himself.

Superman braced his feet on the ground and jumped into the sky.

20 / I Got Away Clean

I took a Greyhound bus to New Orleans, then a Trailways express to El Paso. Texas is a very wide state, with plenty of room for second thoughts. Twice I got off the bus intending to call home, at least let Cousin Katy know I was okay. I knew Mom would try to talk me into coming back, and I might be susceptible. . . . Twice I stood and stared at the pay phone until the driver said to get back on the bus.

My original idea was to get as far away from Opelousas, my mother, and the memory of Granny French as three hundred forty-five dollars would take me. If I found some trace of my father at the end of this road, that would be something important, something I did on my own. And then I could get started with my real life.

Let them suffer, as I had suffered. I would call when I was too far away to come back. I felt bad for Katy, who was probably worried about me, but not for my mother, who was probably not. When it sank in that I was really gone, Mom would surely breathe a sigh of relief and get on with her life.

The bus reached El Paso late afternoon on the second day. After all those miles of flat empty Texas, I was surprised to see a big city spread out among lifeless brown mountains. A chain-link fence zigzagged up and down dusty slopes. The city crept up to this side of the fence; the other side looked deserted. The man beside me said that was Mexico over there.

I took a city bus to the El Paso Civic Auditorium. The driver said the Statler Brothers concert was not until tomorrow night, was I sure I wanted to get off?

I don't know what I expected to learn from the Civic Auditorium, but this was my father's last stop before he flew off into oblivion. It seemed like the right place to start.

The bus roared away in a cloud of hot smoke. I walked across a huge parking lot, ten acres of asphalt without the first car on it. The building looked absurdly large, squatting in the middle of all that pavement with no one around—like a movie facade that would topple over if I pushed against it.

I found the walls to be of sturdy brick, with mirrored-glass doors that were locked all the way around. The building was encircled by a cordon of waist-high concrete pylons linked by ropes of chain. I perched on one of these chains, digging into my pack for a Nutty Buddy bar and the worn manila envelope stuffed with newspaper clippings.

In the years since my father's disappearance I had read these clippings hundreds of times, as if I might find a glimpse of what really happened in the white spaces between the lines. I pulled out a long investigative story, "The Last Flight of Superman Willis," by a man called Cy Hegborn of the *Fort Worth Star-Telegram*. I bit into the candy and scanned to the middle of the page:

> The star's final concert, in El Paso's barn-like civic auditorium, was much like the thirty-eight concerts that preceded it on the 1972 tour. The audience clearly enjoyed the show, recalling Willis to the stage three times for encores. But other members of the tour said the singer seemed depressed, not his usual ebullient self. Mike Witherspoon, a sound engineer at the concert, said Willis' performance that night was perfunctory. "I don't think he was having much fun," said Witherspoon. "He was worn out. He'd been on the road that whole year. But he was a pro. He knew how to act like he was having fun, even when he wasn't."

Behind me a man cleared his throat. I turned to find myself under the inspection of an old guy in a gray uniform with a MCKESSLE SECURITY patch. "There's no show tonight, son."

"Yessir, I know, I'm just looking around. You suppose I could take a look inside for a minute?"

"Auditorium's closed," he said, eyeing my backpack as if it might contain a deadly weapon. "You're not a vagrant, are you?"

"Nosir." I explained who I was, how far I'd come, why I wanted to look inside.

"We got a vagrancy law in this city," he said. "Better clear on out of here if you don't want the *police* to get you."

I showed him the clipping. He gave it a cursory glance and handed it back. "Like to hep you out, but a rule's a rule."

I said, "But couldn't you just—"

He patted his gun belt and told me to move along. His hearing aid squealed a demented radio tone. His gun was probably bulletless, like Barney Fife's gun. The man was all puffed up with his own importance, as if the safety of the citizens of El Paso depended on his ability to keep me out of the auditorium. By the time he told the story to his wife, I would have become a pack of hoodlums he'd chased away single-handedly.

I trudged across the parking lot. The guard's stare burned a hole in my back. Suddenly I sensed how large a place the world is, how few actual clues I had to my father's whereabouts. It was not going to be as easy as walking into the last place he had performed, and finding a map that would lead me to him.

I waited a long time for a bus. I stood in the shelter studying the map of El Paso. The sun fell behind the brown mountains, the city lights twinkled to life, and still I could see that old man eyeing me across the vast parking lot.

That really pissed me off. I'd been polite, asked permission, and said "sir," yet he treated me like some hippie out of *Easy Rider*.

"You're gonna die soon, you old bastard," I yelled, because I knew he could not hear me—but maybe the wind in El Paso carries voices farther than in other places. He started across the parking lot toward me.

He moved fast for an old guy. I saw a bus coming, a box of light fifteen blocks away. The guard would get to me first.

I considered sprinting off down the boulevard, losing myself in the warehouses on either side. Then it dawned on me how far I was from home, and how free. My life was a blank page, waiting for me to write the first sentence.

The guard huffed across the pavement. I heard keys jangling on his belt. If he had a heart attack it would be the second death on my hands in less than a week.

I stepped out of the shelter and started toward him with my arms out, as if in apology.

That slowed him up. "Did you—yell somethin'—at me, son?" he wheezed.

"Gosh, no sir," I said, crouching down, "I didn't say a word." Without warning I dashed straight at him, waving my hands to confuse him. I yanked the walkie-talkie off his belt and unsnapped the key ring.

He was old and out of breath. I was young and fast. I streaked across the lot, pumping my arms, looking back to make sure he wasn't fool enough to try to keep up. His walkie-talkie sputtered in my hand.

I had a moment of panic at the door when I realized there were about fifty keys on the ring, but someone must have been watching over me: the third key I tried was the one.

I slipped in, locked the door behind me, stuffed the walkie-talkie into a trash can. I ran down a long foyer to fling open the last set of doors.

The bang reverberated through immense darkness. This was a rectangular hall with sloping banks of seats and a platform stage at one end, a grayish half-light filtering through tiny windows at the roofline. The air smelled vaguely of beer. I ran across the vast floor, all charged up with my new recklessness. My tennis shoes echoed like elephant feet clomping up to the stage.

I ran downstage center, to the spot where my father must have stood. I imagined him there with a bar stool and a microphone, blinded by ranks of spotlights. I pictured the hall full of people, clapping and cheering.

In the distance I heard Barney Fife pounding on the door.

Running down the steps I had a flash of my father's life. He had filled up this huge space with people who cheered for him. I don't care how exhausted he was—that must have felt like a miracle, every time. He must have loved it. I did not believe he could have walked away from all that.

His disappearance was an accident. I knew it, now, for sure.

The magic key worked on the first door I tried. I stepped out into dusk. The back of the property was another vast parking lot, ending at a low ridge topped with scrubby bushes.

I took one step in that direction. A bank of floodlights blazed to life at my feet. An alarm bell shrilled.

For a long second I was blind. I stumbled back from the glare and turned to see my shadow projected a hundred times life-size on the auditorium wall. The light froze me in place with my arms out. I waved my hand to be sure that was me.

I was standing there waving my hand when I saw blue lights headed in from the highway. I hurdled the floodlights and tore across the parking lot.

Three cars full of cops screeched around to the front of the place. I scrambled up the ridge and crouched in the bushes to watch. Six officers jumped out, drew their guns, and ran into the building.

I cannot begin to describe the thrill I felt watching from that safe distance while they searched that auditorium for me. They searched a long time. I watched their cars spraddled out at the entrance, blue lights revolving. I knew I should slip into the canyon behind me and get out of there, but it was too fascinating to watch the trouble I had created.

Finally they emerged, six cops and old Barney, shaking his head and gesticulating. I ducked into bushes and found a trail running down the canyon, a long slope that came out at a chain-link fence and a wide creek, maybe twenty feet across. The fence was no problem. In five seconds I was up and over, wading the creek.

I hurried up the opposite slope, slip-sliding, my heart banging in my chest. The hill was crowned by a pile of smooth boulders. I climbed to the highest one and peered over to the parking lot. The cops had switched off their blue lights and were cruising out toward the boulevard.

I pulled the fat ring of keys from my pocket and flung it into space. I heard a *ching!* then the splash.

I sank to the rock, drenched with exhilaration. I was not about to call my mother and let her talk me into coming home. I was a guerrilla now, an outlaw, on a mission. I would do whatever I had to do.

This side of the creek was barren scrub. The factories and train yards and freeways all lay on the other side, the glow of streetlights contoured to the twists in the creek bed. It took me a while to connect this view to the map in the bus shelter, and to accept that creek as the Rio Grande. That is as puny and disappointing a river as you are likely to see. But that's just what it was, and that's how I found myself in Mexico.

I had always been a good and obedient boy, with a few minor exceptions, none of which could compare to the action I had just taken. That was a real gun on the old man's belt. How could I be so sure he didn't have a bullet, and wouldn't use it? That was a very stupid stunt. In fact, as I thought about it, it was amazing that I got away without being shot or thrown in jail.

But God, it was cool! I got away clean! I was no longer a good or obedient boy. A new door had opened up in front of me, and I had stepped through without hesitating.

When the sun came up I saw I'd been roaming the hills above a sprawling low-rise city on the Mexican side. My original plan was to spend a day or two in El Paso, getting a passport and poking around the airport for someone who might remember the night my father flew away. But that was before I told Barney my name and why I was here. For all I knew, breaking into the Civic Auditorium might be a serious offense in El Paso. The police might be looking for me. The airport would be the first place they would look.

Better, I thought, to stay in Mexico and keep going. I walked down into Juárez, found the bus station across the street from the cathedral. A man took some dollars and gave me pesos. I ate something from a cart on the street, some kind of pancake that made me queasy. Twenty minutes later I was jammed onto the first of many Mexican buses, heading south.

The bus was slow, hot, uncomfortable, but once my stomach stopped churning, I began to enjoy it. I was in a foreign country, for sure. People chattered in Spanish. I stared out at those arid brown hills, reveling in my foreignness.

There were three other Americans on the bus, two yackety college girls from Chicago making fun of everyone in their honking Midwest accents— "Oh my Gaad, that man looks like a bulldaag!"—and two rows ahead of me, a guy about my age, a slender longhaired teenager traveling alone. When the old lady beside me got off, this guy came back to sit with me.

We shook hands. His name was Jeff Wiesenblatt. He had dropped out of Oklahoma State and was on his way to South America to find himself. I told him my name was Jim, I'd had some trouble with the law in El Paso and had slipped across the border in the dark.

He laughed. "You're probably the first illegal alien ever to break *in* to Mexico."

He made me tell the whole story. I embellished freely. I had the Border Patrol roaming the hills with flashlights and dogs, while I crouched in the bottom of an abandoned water tank. Jeff was impressed. I discovered a certain talent for spinning a tale that I had not noticed before.

One of the Chicago girls got up on her knees, facing us. "Hey gize, we've got a bet. Are you brothers?"

We looked at each other, and grinned. I could see the resemblance— Jeff was thinner than I, but we were both hollow-chested, with longish dirty-blond hair and brown eyes. Jeff was Not Much To Look At, like me.

He went to talk to the girls, gripping the overhead pole with one hand while he swayed back and forth. By the time he came back, I had a plan.

The Chicago girls flirted with us awhile before they dozed off. Jeff and I regaled each other with stories of our wildest adventures. His mostly involved getting drunk and wrecking his parents' car. Mine were purely invented, and got better as the afternoon wore on. I told him I had been arrested at the age of twelve for climbing the White House fence and trying to throw a rock at Richard Nixon. I'd spent three years at a juvenile home until a visiting maestro heard me sing and offered me a voice scholarship to Juilliard. My mother was a psychotic murderess serving three back-to-back life sentences in a women's prison in California.

Jeff believed every word. I was amazed at how easy it was to become someone else, just by pretending.

Late in the day the radiator boiled over. Everybody got off the bus and spread out along the roadside while it cooled.

I volunteered to keep an eye on Jeff's backpack while he went to take a leak. The Chicago girls sat fanning themselves under a tree. No one saw my hand slip under the flap of Jeff's pack.

I found what I was seeking, and tucked it away in my pocket.

It was late, and Jeff was asleep, when the bus rolled into Monterrey. I mumbled "Later, man," and jumped off before the bus came to a stop.

The bus station was just the confusion I'd hoped for, vendors shouting, horns honking, crowds of hurrying people. I headed for a line of yellow cars with taxi lights, jumped into the first one, and sped off.

The driver spoke English. He said the airfield was five dollars, round-trip. I settled into the seat and pulled out my new passport. My name was Jeffrey Harold Wiesenblatt. Born August 14, 1962, in Miami, Oklahoma. The picture was not a good likeness of Jeff, and not a bad likeness of me.

Wiesenblatt. I would have to practice saying it.

In five minutes we were out of the city and zooming through dark hills. The dashboard was decorated with decals of women in lewd poses: one said WIDE OPEN BEAVER. The man drove very fast, slinging sideways on the curves, gunning down long pitted straightaways. He missed about eighty percent of the potholes and slammed through the rest. I was dazed by the strange landscape, lack of sleep, the sudden onset of my criminal tendencies. We bumped down a narrow lane onto a wide field. It took a moment to recognize the blue lights as a landing strip.

This place was to airports as the Rio Grande was to rivers.

"You catcheen a plane, main?" the driver said.

"No, I just need to talk to whoever's here."

"Well if you lookin' for sheet, you talk to me. *Me llamo* Jorge, what you name, main?"

"Jeff," I said. "Jeff Weezenblatt. Wysenblatt."

"You got money, Cheff?"

I thought a minute before answering. "Not much."

"You get some money, man, you talk to me. I get you the best. I give you my phone, it's my mother house, you ask for Jorge."

We jolted down the middle of the landing strip to a tin shack. A sign said BIENVENIDOS, which my *diccionario* translated as "welcome." A wrinkly old man came to greet us with the two shiny gold teeth in his smile. He pumped my hand enthusiastically and started talking a mile a minute.

I held up my hands in the international sign for "wait" and coaxed Jorge out of the car to translate. I told the little man I was looking for my father, who may have landed to refuel his Beechcraft Baron at this field on the night of July 14, 1972.

The old man shrugged and said, *"Hace mucho tiempo."*

"Is a long time ago," Jorge said.

I pulled out my clippings and pictures of my father and the airplane. The old man's face lit up. He cackled and pointed at the photo. "Superman!"

"That's right! Was he here? Did he see him?"

Slowly the story emerged. The gringo came down from the sky and introduced himself as Superman. Friendly gringo, *muy amable,* seemed to be enjoying himself, but also seemed totally lost. Bought a full tank of gas and left a two-hundred-sixty-dollar tip. Kept asking which way to the United States.

"He come from the north, from that way," Jorge translated, "but when he take off he fly that way." He pointed over my shoulder.

"He flew south?"

Jorge and the old man nodded, together.

"Did he say where he was going?"

"A los Estados," the man said. To the States.

Jorge translated what he said next: "Some men came around after, the Federales. The *señor* tell them what happened. He was afraid. He thought your father maybe is a *narco.*"

"A what?"

"Narcotraficante—a drog, how you say, drog smockler."

"Why'd he think that?"

"Because the money, main. And also he give him some sheet to smoke," Jorge said. "Then the Federales."

Some reporters had speculated that drugs had something to do with my father's disappearance, but I'd never believed it. Everyone knew he smoked a lot of pot, he and my mother both, like all the rock stars in those days. But they didn't sell it; why would they? They were wealthy consumers. They bought it and smoked it. The reporters had reached the same conclusion.

Jorge explained as we rattled away: the old man was nervous, didn't want trouble. He didn't like the Federales. He loved his grandchildren.

The taxi flashed over the hills, screeching through curves. All the way into the city Jorge tried to convince me to hire him as driver and guide. "Twenty bucks a day, man, you never beat that. I drive for you, I talk for you, we find you father real fast."

I was tempted, but at those rates I'd be broke in two weeks, and anyway Jorge was a lousy driver. We almost went off the road swerving to avoid a truck that came around a curve without lights. I gripped dents in the dashboard and decided to get back on the bus.

I rode one bus after another, down the long spine of Mexico, living on Cokes and candy bars, sleeping on the bus or at some hovel-hotel near the bus station, two bucks a night for all the noise and cockroaches you could stand. Sometimes, if I found a quiet room with a lady who cooked up generous plates of rice and chicken and tortillas, I'd take a day or two off the road to sleep and stoke up.

The crossing into Guatemala was the first test of my new identity. I held my breath while the sullen uniformed man glanced from me to the picture, and back again . . . then he laid the passport flat on the counter, hoisted a stainless-steel stamper, and with an emphatic *ka-chung!* welcomed me, Jeffrey Harold Wiesenblatt, to his country.

That experience made me overconfident all the way to the border of El Salvador. I sat for two hours while the immigration officer looked from my face to Jeff's picture, unconvinced. The bus went on without me. Eventually the man got tired of my sorrowful expression and let me through the gate. We played Chinese checkers while I waited for the next bus. I let him win.

Wherever I went, I showed people the bleached-out Polaroid snap of the island, twin cone-shaped mountains connected by a beach. They all shook their heads, until one day, in a tiny café in northern Nicaragua, the proprietor nodded. "*Sí,*" he said, "*la isla.*"

My Spanish was not good, but I knew *isla* meant "island." My heart took a jump.

"You know this place?"

He nodded.

"Where is it?"

He shrugged.

I asked if it was far or near, did it have a name? I leafed through my *Berlitz Spanish Handbook for Travellers* and held it out with my finger on the sentence: "Will you help me find this place, please?"

Again he shook his head.

"*Por qué no?*"

The man studied me while I ate my rice and beans. I ordered a second cup of coffee—that stuff down there is sweet and strong enough that one cup will crank up your pulse to about a hundred forty beats a minute. I turned upon that man my steadiest, most immovable stare, the stare I had learned from Granny French, who would have made a fine interrogator for the Gestapo if she hadn't devoted her life to sweepstakes contests.

The man came around the bar, sat down heavily beside me, unfolded a map. He put his stubby finger on a speck off the Atlantic coast of Nicaragua—all the way on the other side of the country, exactly opposite the direction I was heading.

"Isla Pescador," he said.

I tipped him three bucks and ran out into the hot afternoon, giddy with caffeine and excitement. At last I had a destination.

I looked up *pescador:* Fisherman's Island. I had no idea how long it would take to get there. Most of the people in these little countries were friendly, almost too eager to help. I hadn't met anyone who would admit not knowing the way to anywhere. They would stop whatever they were doing and walk five blocks out of their way to put me on the wrong track.

I spent day after day on buses trundling all over Nicaragua before I found one that was actually going east, all the way to the Caribbean coast. It was wartime in Nicaragua. Sometimes the bus would stop because some leaf or rock in the road spooked the driver, or a pack of soldiers wanted a look at the passengers. The drivers drove slowly and played their radios at top volume, as if to ward off evil spirits. There were millions of mamas, daddies, kids, and old folks in that country, and every one of them seemed to be going somewhere. At checkpoints, they formed a dutiful line beside the bus and submitted to the soldiers' poking and probing with a pained silence I tried to emulate.

One morning outside Tipitapa, I was standing in one of those lines when a tiny old Indian woman took offense at the young soldier trying to inspect the contents of her straw bag. She grabbed the bag away and began hitting the soldier with it, really pounding him about the shoulders with what sounded like a collection of pots and pans. The guy flung his arms up and darted out of her reach, to the delight of his *compadres* and the crowd.

The old woman was bent and wizened as an old cornhusk doll. An officer came forth to pacify her. She turned on him, swinging hard with her bagful of pots. He fled out of range. Soon she was surrounded by a circle of soldiers laughing as they approached, taunting *abuelita!* from all sides, "granny!" like kids playing a game. One of them sneaked up behind her, seized the bag, and dumped the contents in the road: a frying pan, a tea-kettle, three muffin tins, and a green submachine gun.

They ordered the rest of us back on the bus. I watched through the grimy window as the officer slung the old lady over his shoulder and carried her off down the street. We rumbled away. I turned my gaze inside the bus. I was the only one watching.

I spent twenty-nine hours on that bus, the *María Alejandra*. We passed two vast lakes and three smoking volcanoes. We bumped through miles of tangled forest and endless banana plantations on the slope to the Atlantic. People got off, but nobody got on. On the second day I got a seat to myself. We passed through some vast, empty country. I was the only passenger by the time we pulled into Boca de Pescado, a muddy village squatting around a lagoon at the end of the road.

The driver looked at me in the mirror.

"Gracias," I said, and got out.

Four ramshackle stores huddled around a mud intersection. An infection of shacks spread to the waterline. The green Caribbean stretched from the mouth of the lagoon. In the hazy distance, I saw the bluish line of an island.

The driver cranked the door shut. The bus wheezed away.

I went into the only store that was not locked up tight. An old Chinese man sat behind the counter. "Speak English?" I said.

He frowned.

I glanced at the shelves: a few sacks of rice, beans, lard, canned tuna, some dishcloths. I tried asking about Isla Pescador, but the man's Chinese Spanish was impenetrable. He glanced at the Polaroid and shook his head irritably, as if he had thousands of more important things to do. I thanked him and went out.

A black man came ambling down toward the rickety pier. I hurried up, dragging my pack. This man looked like the black folks back home in Louisiana. He smiled broadly, inspecting the faded snapshot. "Pescador don't look a ting like dot, mon, ain't got no heels."

"Are you sure?"

"Not less they growen since the last time I look." He walked me to the end of the pier. "Look. You see any heels on dot island?" He pointed to the flat blue line on the horizon.

"That's it?" My heart sank.

He nodded.

I waved the picture. "You've never seen this place before?"

"No, mon, not 'round ya. Look like a nice place. You goin' off da?"

I felt blood pumping through my temples. "I thought—I mean, this guy told me this was the place! Isla Pescador, that's what he said! I've been wandering around for a week trying to get here!"

"Hmm," said the man. "Well, look like here is where you got." He laughed, and climbed into his boat.

My first impulse was to go all the way back across Nicaragua, find the man who sent me here, and strangle him with my bare hands.

My second impulse was to have a look around Boca de Pescado, since I was here and surely would never come back. That took all of five minutes. I squatted on the stoop of the Chinese store to wait for the next bus.

A dim-eyed young girl in a Lynyrd Skynyrd T-shirt approached with a basket on her arm. She lifted a red-gingham napkin to reveal a nest of steaming-hot empanadas. I bought two and scarfed them down in four bites. Delicious. Stuffed with some kind of spicy ground meat. I called the girl back and bought four more.

"Tiene hambre," she said in a scratchy, old-sounding voice, like a three-pack-a-day smoker. She gave a little curtsy with my change.

I ate two and wrapped the others in a scrap of newspaper, for later. I saw my black friend walking from the pier to his shack. He and the Chinese man and the empanada girl seemed to be the only people in Boca de Pescado. I wondered how long until the next bus.

About thirty seconds later my ears started whistling. All the colors around me faded to gray. I stood up, stumbled two steps to the side, and fell over face first in the grass.

More than anything, this surprised me. I looked around to see if anyone had witnessed my embarrassment. I tried to pull myself up, and found that I couldn't. Way down in my belly came a rumbling warning, an immense molten force building inside, rising like lava through the strata of my body. Then everything exploded.

I lay in the grass a long time, racked by gusts of retching and shivering. The Chinese man came out on his porch and shouted at me. I raised my head to apologize. Another eruption caught me in midsentence.

He lifted my pack from the steps and flung it in the mud near my feet.

Lying there waiting for the next wave of nausea, I felt ants crawling on my arms. I was powerless to brush them off. The sickness swirled inside me, the keening in my ears. I thought: This must be the low point. Things have to get better from here.

A shadow fell over my face. I craned up. The little girl outlined against the sun, leaning down with her basket: *"Quiere más, señor?"* The smell of those pies wafted into my nostrils. I managed to turn my head in time to avoid puking on her feet.

She grabbed my pack and ran off behind the Chinese store, into the woods.

I lay there for hours, groaning and shivering. The girl didn't come back. That pack had everything in it: Jeff's passport, most of my money, the newspaper clippings . . .

In the distance I heard a bus. Somehow I dragged myself to the middle of the road. The driver slammed on his brakes. I lurched up the steps. It was the same driver who had dropped me off before. His hand came out for the fare, but when he saw my face he swallowed, handed me a plastic bag, and said, *"Pase."* I wobbled to the last seat, fell over, and died.

When I came back to life it was dark and the bus was full, some man prodding me to sit up. I shoved his hand away, hid my face, passed out again.

That night was a bad dream. At one point, some men lifted me up by my arms and put me off the bus. I hunched on a rough wooden bench, doubled over in the fluorescent gloom, holding a greasy newspaper packet between my knees.

The next bus grunted and heaved and whipped all over the road. I slumped against the window. The coolness of the glass on my face kept me alive.

Long stretches of time passed while I was unconscious. Somehow it got to be another day, and then a night, and we were bouncing through the rutted streets of Managua.

I was a frail, shaky boy tottering off that bus into the confusion of rush hour, the Plaza de la Revolución. The blare of car horns jangled with the razz of unmuffled motorscooters. Everywhere were buildings in rubble, winos crumpled in doorways, soldiers with guns, dirty children tugging my arm. Managua smelled like piss, French fries, diesel fumes.

I sagged against a cement post. I knew I should start asking around for the next bus, but I had no idea where to go. I had nine dollars, no passport, and one packet of deadly empanadas, which had clung to me, unaccountably, all the way from Boca de Pescado. The traffic made bouncy *boing-boing* sounds in my head. I was dizzy with exhaustion. Cars whizzed by, honking at me.

I heard a voice calling "Jim! Jim!" but I didn't know any Jim. My eyes were fixed on a storefront festooned with fat hanging bunches of grapes.

Those grapes drew me across the sidewalk. They were lustrous red, glistening with a sheen of pale dust. I lifted a bunch off a nail and gave the man a dollar.

A hand grabbed my arm. Immediately I felt worse. "Jim! Can you believe this? Small goddamn world, huh?" Jeff Wiesenblatt grinned at me. I nearly fainted. I must have reeled a bit. Jeff said, "Jesus, Jim, you look *bad*. What happened to you?"

He held on to my arm to keep me from falling—or from running? Did he realize I'd been traveling through Central America as Jeff Wiesenblatt? I had visions of angry embassy officials, deportation hearings, a Nicaraguan jail.

"I got sick," I said. "I've been on a bus. What day is it?"

"Thursday," said Jeff. "What the heck are you doing in Managua?"

I'd been going in circles, I explained, and somehow wound up back here. I didn't remember much of the last couple days.

I followed Jeff to a plaza with park benches. We sat. I ate a grape. The best grape ever.

I waited. When it did not kill me, I ate another.

I forced myself to eat one at a time, rolling the pulpy middle on my tongue and spitting out seeds.

"I just got here myself," Jeff was saying. "I got hung up in Mexico. All the lousy damn luck—remember that bus we were on?"

"Yeah." I dreaded what he would say next.

"Somebody ripped off my passport while I was asleep. There, or in the bus station in Monterrey. I had to sit in Mexico City for like a week waiting for my mom to send a copy of my birth certificate."

"You got a new passport?"

"Cost me like two hundred bucks, time it was over," he said. "Total bummer."

I bit into a grape. *There, or in the bus station.* He didn't know. I had to lose him at once and get out of Nicaragua. Find a bus to the south and get out of here.

But Jeff wasn't going to be all that easy to lose. Mine was the first friendly face he'd seen in weeks, and he was practically wagging his tail at the chance to speak English. He ignored my feeble protest and dragged me to a sidewalk café.

He drank beer. I drank coffee. Every sip of that hot milky brew brought a new surge of life through my veins. Jeff chattered on about his adventures in Mexico City, Acapulco, Guatemala, San Salvador. His adventures sounded like mine—bad buses, bad hotels, bad food, a good time overall. I sipped coffee and studied the destination signs on the passing buses.

"Listen, I'm starving but this place looks like Ptomaine City," said Jeff. "Wanna get something to eat?"

"I think these grapes'll do it for me. Want some?" He shook his head.

I had an idea. It was not a good idea, not a nice or kindly idea, but it was the idea I happened to have. I produced the newspaper packet. "Here, I just bought these on the bus. They're good."

He unwrapped the paper, took a whiff of two-day-old empanadas, and pronounced them satisfactory. "Sure you don't mind?"

"Help yourself."

"Thanks, man," he said, taking a bite. It was all I could do not to cry out "Stop! It's a trick!" but really he seemed to think they were tasty. He polished them off in no time.

Then I had only to make conversation for another minute or so before his eyes went all swimmy and he leaned way over in his chair. "Jeez," he said, "all of a sudden I don't feel so well."

"What's the matter?"

"I don't—I gotta . . . keep an eye on my . . ." He stumbled through a maze of steel chairs toward a door marked CABALLEROS.

As my fingers closed around the straps of his pack, I spotted a bus two blocks away, a sleek Greyhound-style bus with a bar of light that said COSTA RICA.

I tossed a quarter on the table and sprinted off down the avenue. I was truly sorry to do that to Jeff. He looked upon me as a friend, a fellow American. By the time he came to understand the true nature of our friendship, I would be long gone.

Maybe that was my father's hand on my shoulder, guiding me. I began to understand how you could lose yourself down here, how you could forget everything that happened to you before, and turn into somebody else.

21 / Concierto

BOUNDING DOWN THE TRAIL from the magic pool in slow-motion strides, Superman felt the drag of gravity returning. By the time he got to the beach he was earthbound again.

Over time, Pito said, he would learn to control it: the tears of the Mago in the mountain will help you learn what you secretly knew all along. If it is your destiny to fly, you will fly. You must use your destiny for the good of the people—or something like that; Pito's English was shaky, and Superman was too excited by his new power to pay much attention. He didn't really care why this particular magic had been revealed to him. It was enough to know he could fly through the air. The magic was not a trick. It was a real living part of the island. He had a knot on the back of his head to prove it.

He wanted to do it again!

Amelia had opened one door for him, and he had stepped through. And then Daisy opened another door, and then Pito. Every door led him into a new way of looking at life.

At least once a week he hiked up to the magic pool to drink the glowing water and fly through the trees. In the afternoons he swam in the ocean. Several nights a week he made love to a woman who was a bit stranger and more beautiful all the time. He gave his life over to flying, bodysurfing, the pursuit of Daisy. Somehow when he was doing these things the rest of the world just seemed to take care of itself.

The months slipped through his fingers, and turned into years.

The flying ability began to persist longer and longer between visits to the pool. He could control it in the daytime, but sometimes at night he'd wake up to find himself hovering over the bed, and he'd have to just drift on up to the ceiling and hang there like a bat until the feeling faded and he could sink down again. One time Daisy woke up while he was making his descent. It took quite a job of acting to convince her it was a dream.

He kept his flying a secret, even from her. He flew only in the clearing around the waterfall, and only below treetop level. Pito didn't tell him to do this—it just seemed the right thing to do with a gift of this magnitude.

Pito also didn't have to tell him a war was coming. He'd known it the first time he flew, that first glimpse of heavy machinery across the channel—the Magician quietly putting into action the plans that had so alarmed Amelia, years ago. *They say he wants to cut trees and take the top off that mountain and build something, I don't know what.*

Superman was beginning to believe what the monkeys and the old Indian had been trying to tell him: his presence here was no accident. Miss Emily made it seem he'd been lured here for the purpose of flying her out, but now he thought it was something larger than that. His disappearance had not been a random event. He had been brought here to fight for the island.

When the first rumors of the bridge swept through, the islanders rejoiced, thinking this would mean freedom: the wall would come down and they would be permitted to come and go like people anywhere. Like all slaves, they wanted to believe in the ultimate benevolence of their master; it gave them something to hope for.

Then a guardhouse went up on the waterfront at Gato Negro, and a matching guardhouse on the landward side of the island. The camouflage men issued identity cards to everyone on the island. The rejoicing ceased.

The island carried on its outwardly drowsy existence. Occasionally a corpse would wash up on the beach, an islander shot in an escape attempt. Or a man who got drunk and said too much would disappear, and you'd see his family at the beach every morning for weeks, keeping watch for a body that never washed up. Every so often the camouflage men staged a kind of war game, running back and forth in squadrons on the sand, flashing their guns. The islanders kept their heads down and stayed off the beach until it was over.

The place still looked like paradise, but Superman would never be able to see it that way again. Now he felt the dark force skulking behind all that natural beauty, the same force that blew his boat out of the water and brought the Electra down in flames. The Magician was still in his hideout atop the south mountain, controlling it all, making plans.

Superman always sought out the North Star on clear nights, and sent a good wish to his son, but it was an idle wish now. He could never go back.

He was not the same man. His life was in this place. He hoped Ben Junior would grow up not to hate him too much. He hoped Alexa was happy (but not too happy) with Jimbo. He hoped they were living good lives, but it no longer seemed like something that really involved him. More and more, he thought of his old life as a dream that had faded away in the daylight.

He stood straighter. He learned how to run again, how to play in the waves, how to spend a whole day doing nothing and go to bed feeling satisfied. He stopped punishing himself, and concentrated on becoming stronger.

Barges arrived and began to lay pilings. The bridge crept outward from both shores.

For six years the crews tried building that bridge. They'd spend months pouring pilings, a tropical storm would sweep through to tear it all down, and the next week they'd head out to start again. High tides swamped the barges; new barges appeared. Workers got disgusted and quit; busloads of new workers replaced them. Every few weeks Superman floated around the mountain to look down upon the bridge ends advancing, the army of worker ants carrying beams, supply boats crossing lines of white wake. He remembered when he used to gaze at this channel, longing for a way across. Now he knew how the Indians must have felt, peeping out of the trees at the first Spanish caravel, a beautiful vision of doom: *Go away. Leave us alone.*

He was an islander now. At last he had achieved the state he imagined for himself that long-ago night in his plane: a life without obligations, perfect freedom. He answered to no one. Every moment was his, to do as he pleased—except once a year, on August 24.

That was the night all the gringos trooped up the south mountain to the dance floor behind the chain-link fence for the Magician's birthday party. The famously disappeared were invited, of course, and a few of the prominent natives. Everyone got uncomfortably dressed up and said "Great to see you!" though they saw each other almost every day. The Jiménez Brothers played mariachi songs. A camera crew followed the guests around, videotaping their conversations for the invisible guest of honor.

People wandered out to look at the gardens, the pools, the two-story white stucco building with one door and no windows. Beyond the helipad were the barracks for the camouflage guys, who stayed out of sight on the night of the birthday party. Jimmy Hoffa brought barbecued chicken. D. B. Cooper chain-smoked and looked at his watch. Anastasia regaled them all yet again with the story of how she escaped the Bolsheviks and hid out with the Gypsies for twenty-eight years. Michael Rockefeller told his tales of the sex practices of the tribes in New Guinea, which never failed to send Frank into hysterics. Old Harry the magician wrapped himself in chains so everyone could watch him wriggle out of them. Usually it took half the party before he could shake them off and clamber to his feet, red-faced and spent, to a patter of polite applause.

Spike went around topping off glasses with Veuve Clicquot from the generous ice barrel in the corner. Rabbit stood off to one side in the shadows, smoking joints. The Sherman Brothers always performed "What's the Matter with Grandma?"—the skit that made them famous, the very skit that later killed their career when Lou muffed his line and Stu said "What the fuck is the matter with you?" on live coast-to-coast television.

Every year the Twins got drunk and made lewd remarks to the video camera, then everyone lined up to sing "Happy Birthday." Daisy blew out the candles.

Superman hated these parties, but he came because Daisy liked to dress up once a year with the hair and the lips and the whole total show, and just blow them all away. He liked to stand off to one side, watching her shine, knowing he would get to take her home as soon as she got a little drunk.

When he got loose himself he would feel his feet lifting up from the floor, and grab on to a table to keep himself grounded. Tonight he felt light as a bubble. The Twins had shed most of their clothing and were doing a slow-motion go-go dance to Stu Sherman's ukulele. Anastasia was asleep in her chair. D. B. Cooper danced cheek to cheek with Lou Sherman's wife. Daisy huddled with Michael Rockefeller in a corner, making fun of the other guests. Superman floated down the edge of the crowd.

"Great God, if it isn't the original sinner!" A big hammy hand came from nowhere to seize him. "Hello Superman, where've you been keeping yourself?"

"I've been right here, Rabbit. How's it going?" He did his best to avoid Rabbit, but sometimes Rabbit was just plain unavoidable.

"Just to look at you, now, just taking the first good long gander I have been granted in a very long while, I would say you are not merely flourishing, son—nay, the man is positively aglow. Island life agrees with you."

"What can I say?" said Superman. "If this ain't paradise, you can see it from here."

"Would you happen to be finding yourself in need of any spiritual advice, then, me laddie? I've got a whole new line of Red Dot."

"I don't think so, Rabbit. I'm halfway flying as it is."

Rabbit showed that line of tiny teeth. "You never fail to disappoint me, my son."

Just then a blare of trumpets, a dimming of lights, a glow of candles from the end of the floor. A crowd of guys in red shirts rolled out a cart with an enormous cake, the island sculpted in cake, green-frosting jungle and blue-frosting ocean, a chocolate bridge across the channel, a sea of candles blazing. In place of the summit of the south mountain stood an enormous sandstone-frosting pyramid.

Cries of "Daisy!" brought her forth to do her yearly duty. She looked into the video camera with that famous heavy-lidded pout, and blew out those candles in a way that gave every man in the room a thrill.

The lights came up and there was Frank at cakeside, looking respectable in his tuxedo. His hair was longer now, wavy silver and combed to the side. He was well over seventy, but you'd guess fifty-five; the years had been good for his looks. "Ladies and germs!" he cried. "Ladies and germs, may I have your attention! *Atención, por favor!* It is my great pleasure to welcome you on behalf of our host. He truly regrets his absence tonight." Ah so, Frank. Now playing hostess. "He's asked me to thank you all for coming, and to make the announcement we've all been waiting for."

"Put a lid on it, Frank," Stu Sherman yelled. He was bombed.

"The tux, Frank," Lou called, "what's with the tux?"

Frank ignored them. "What you see before you, my friends, is more than a birthday cake. One year from tonight we'll be celebrating the grand opening of a new, very private, very exciting hotel, right where we're standing. We all knew it would be something spectacular—and the Magician has not let us down. What do you say, folks, let's give a cheer for his most amazing creation yet, the fabulous Jungle Inn!" He waved his arm with a flourish. A few people clapped. Everyone stared at the cake.

Michael Rockefeller broke the silence. "An Egyptian pyramid in the New World? That's absurd!"

"Is he really gonna build that?"

"What've you got to do with this, Frank?"

"I'm executive director of the project," Frank said with a ruffle of pleasure. "I know, I can hardly believe it myself. But he's put his faith in me, and I'll do my best not to disappoint him. I hope you'll all join us to make this a big success. We're having a little get-together at my house to explain. Thursday at three. Everyone is invited."

What on earth could have gotten into old Frank? He'd never shown the slightest interest in the hotel business. Maybe the navigator had flown too long in the back of the plane. He must have always longed to sit in the pilot's seat. All the years in Amelia's shadow must have created the overwhelming desire to step out and do something big on his own, and now the Magician was giving him his chance.

The crowd sang a halfhearted "Happy Birthday" and dissolved into buzzing groups. Superman slipped up on Daisy. "What do you think about that?"

Her eyes shone. "I guess a year is long enough, if you really know how to live."

"Daisy, what's wrong?"

She squeezed his hand. "Nothing. I'm very happy for Frank. Get me a piece of cake?"

He got her the very tip of the pyramid, chocolate macadamia nut with caramel frosting. He took a piece of the bridge for himself.

Frank came up with a big hug for Daisy, a polite nod for Superman.

"Congratulations, Frank. Great idea. A pyramid. Too bad you're not going to be able to build it."

"I beg your pardon?"

"You can tell your boss from me—it's not gonna happen. He promised Emily he'd never do anything to ruin the island. We'll find some way to stop him."

Frank smiled. "Oh ho, goodness gracious, that is important news. Maybe you should tell him yourself. Speak into the microphone." He indicated the video crew, presently taping the Jiménez Brothers.

"Let me tell you how it is. If he tries to go through with this, there's gonna be a war."

Frank's smile faded. "What does that mean?"

"It means we're gonna get together and kick his ass." Spike stepped up, eyes blazing. "His days are just about over, Frank. You better be with us, because if you're not with us, you're against us. And you don't want to be that."

"I'm surprised at you fellows," Frank said, "agitating against our gracious host at his own birthday party."

"How much is he paying you, Frank?"

"Times are changing, Mr. Willis. There's a nice big ship coming in, and you can either get on it, or get your little boat swamped."

Rabbit spoke up: "Listen, guys, maybe Frank has a point. The man's got a bottomless wallet. I'm not sure how much good it would do to try and fight him. Maybe we should sit down and hear what he's got to say. It might not be the end of the world."

"Well said," said Frank.

Here came the Twins, all bubbly bright in their slinky blue cocktail dresses. "No talking business at a party!" cried Sandy.

"Anyone wanna dance?" said Linda.

"Hi, girls." Spike put his arms around them. "You want to help us stop this construction?"

"Sure, we hate it!" said Sandy. "What do we do?"

"Tell Frank here he's full of pure horseshit."

"Frank," said Sandy, "you're—I'm not gonna say that, Spike!"

"You know, children," said Frank, "you'd best think carefully about whose side you're on. See you Thursday. . . ." He went off to mingle with his admirers.

Daisy stared into the middle distance. Superman squeezed her hand. "You okay?"

"Take me down to the beach," she said. "I want to get really drunk and dance on the beach."

He kissed her in front of everybody.

THERE WERE CAMOUFLAGE men guarding the Big House, and the walkways were paved now with black volcanic stone, but the courtyard and pool were just as Superman remembered. Huffing Peruvian flute music floated across the water from the pavilion where Amelia used to dine in the rainy season. All the canvas shades were down.

His entrance brought a burst of light that turned all heads from the screen.

"Here he is," said Spike.

"Mr. Willis." A familiar voice. "We wondered what happened to you."

He blinked in the gloom. Two dozen people sat around a long table, watching a slide show. Most of the crowd from the birthday party was here, and a few islanders.

Superman inched down the wall to stand behind Spike and the Twins.

On the screen, a helicopter on a lighted landing pad dissolved into a sketch of an extravagant spa-and-pool project: thermal tubs arranged on a gentle slope, glass-walled saunas and steam rooms, blue-and-gold-striped cabanas like something from the Arabian Nights. The artist had sketched healthy-looking people in relaxed attitudes, a wall of bamboo waving blurrily in the distance.

"You can see we're taking advantage of natural thermal sites, which is another energy savings," said Frank. "You can't tell from this picture, but the spa is designed to recirculate about eighty percent of its water. We'll use the overflow for landscaping."

A ripple of approval spread down the table.

What a beautiful world Superman saw projected on that screen!—luxurious suites, slide-away glass walls, limitless views of the sea, waiters smiling upon handsome couples. The show was an artful mix of stock photographs, floor plans, and artists' renderings, the projectors synchronized so that each image dissolved into the next, accompanied by that *puff-puff* Peruvian flute and Frank's earnest narration.

His seersucker slacks, red suspenders, and bow tie gave Frank a kind of ornery stateliness, like Mark Twain without the mustache. Lined along one wall were several young native guys in a red-polo-shirt-and-slacks uniform, Frank's handpicked staff. Not a homely one in the bunch. The Aztec youth was one of them. Pito was there, too, leaning against the wall. He gave a nod of greeting. Superman smiled.

A young woman at the table thought he was smiling at her. A pretty, thirtyish blonde, a bit pinned up and stuffy-looking in her schoolmarm tortoiseshell glasses, she didn't take kindly to a smile from a stranger. She put her nose up and turned to the screen, as if to suggest that he do the same.

"Fourteen suites in all," Frank was saying, "ranging from the standard at twenty-eight hundred per night to the four-level Presidential Suite, five thousand five hundred all-inclusive." He clicked to a sketch of a huge room with a stage. "An interior elevation of the ballroom. We'll be able to handle events up to two hundred people."

Superman was wondering where on earth Frank had learned to talk like this when the schoolmarm spoke up. "I think we can guarantee somewhere in the neighborhood of ninety percent occupancy," she said. "You simply don't see these kinds of amenities, not in Hawaii or even the better end of the Caribbean. You're staking out new territory in the upmarket here."

"Exactly," said Frank. "Every suite will have several spectacular views."

Superman spoke up. "How you gonna arrange that, Frank? Considering you're building on a mountain full of two-hundred-year-old trees."

"It's a matter of pruning. We'll trim from the top. Of course some trees will have to come down, but we intend to plant three for every one we cut."

"Great," said Superman. "And in two hundred years they'll grow back."

"Hey Superman," Rabbit said, "you're out of order."

"Rabbit's right," said Sandy. "We agreed to watch Frank's presentation before we discuss any problems."

"Hey, okay, I was late," Superman said. "Sorry." He pressed against the wall and watched.

The flutes tootled. A slide showed a well-dressed couple arm in arm on a balcony, gazing out at their spectacular view. The next slide was the same couple, the camera pulling back to take in more of the pyramid. The camera zoomed back, and back, until the couple was a speck on a distant balcony and the main structure was revealed in its pyramidal splendor, crowning the summit of the mountain.

"Once you come to the Jungle Inn," said a warm whispery voice on the soundtrack, "you'll never want to leave."

The screen faded to black. The flutes struck a low note, and held it. Two of Frank's lads sprang to turn up the lights.

A light smattering of applause traveled round the table. Only the schoolmarm and the polo-shirt guys clapped with any real enthusiasm. Spike rolled his eyes at Superman. Linda yawned.

"As you can see," Frank said, "we're trying for something special here— an *experience*, not just another hotel. I want our guests to have the time of their lives. And everyone on the island can be a part of that—can't they, Melanie?"

"That's right, Frank." She touched the bow at her collar, and glanced at her notebook. "Our industry surveys show a high correlation between the satisfied vacation consumer and what we call the 'local ambience' of the destination. That's a term we can argue and discuss ad infinitum," she said, preening a bit, "but it boils down to this: will the natives be friendly to our guests?"

"That depends, doesn't it," said Sandy, "on how the 'natives' are treated. Quid pro quo."

"Frank, who is this woman?" said Linda.

"Oh, sorry," said Frank, "I thought everyone had been introduced. This is Melanie Llewellyn of Destination Strategies, out of San Diego. Melanie's a special consultant on the project."

"You're not actually *paying* her," said Sandy.

Melanie spoke for herself: "My fees are between myself and my client, but if you want to know whether I'm worth it—most definitely."

"Ooh, I bet you are." Linda crossed her legs.

"My job is to help a developer allocate resources to produce a satisfied customer," Melanie said. "In a cost-intensive location like this, customer satisfaction is key. Frank agrees with me that involving the community is crucial to maintaining our ambience level."

Superman heard mutters from the Spanish-speaking end of the table. "Could you talk a little slower, please?" he called. "Not everybody here speaks your kind of English."

"Oh, goodness—sometimes I forget where I am." She gave him the smile she'd withheld during the slide show, and turned to address the islanders as she might a class of third graders: "If . . . I . . . speak . . . too quickly . . . please tell me. *Dígame.*"

Superman said, "You want to get the community involved in this project, to bring up your ambience level or whatever, right?"

"Precisely," said Melanie.

"I'm sure Frank has told you we're all against it."

"Of course you are. You live in a beautiful place. It's logical that your first reaction to any development would be negative. Our job is to turn those 'no's into 'yes'es."

"A smile is just a frown turned up-side down," sang Spike, and Superman jumped in with the harmony part—"muh friends—lemme tell you again"—and before you knew it they were off on a finger-snapping doo-wop chorus of "Smiling Faces." "Someti-himes . . . ohhh, they don't tell the truth!" Soon they had everyone laughing and clapping along.

Melanie patiently smiled, tapping paper with pen. Frank looked irritated, but he was too well known for bursting into song on all sorts of occasions to raise an objection.

Melanie jumped in—"Frank didn't tell me we had all this musical talent on the island. You guys want a job in the nightclub?" This effort was greeted with the polite chuckle it deserved, and landed Melanie back in control. Superman gave her ten points for spunk. It had been a while since he'd watched a real American go-getter at work.

"Seriously," she said, "we'd like to propose a system that has worked well at some of our islands with smaller populations. We call it our Ambassador program. We're inviting everyone at this table to become an Ambassador for the Jungle Inn. These will be paid positions, now—not enough to make you rich, but then we're not asking you to do any work, either."

Frank beamed from the head of the table, like Daddy Warbucks.

Lou Sherman said, "You're gonna pay us?"

"For what?" said his brother.

"Who cares for what?" Lou said. "How much?"

"One hundred dollars a month," said Melanie.

"Each?"

"Each."

"For what?"

"All we ask is that when you meet our guests, you treat them as friends. Have fun with them, be helpful and friendly—as we know you would anyway. We'll pay you to help create good word of mouth. We want you to make this the friendliest vacation spot on earth."

"They're gonna pay us to be nice to people," said Lou Sherman.

"I'm not sure I can do it," said Stu, "even for a hundred bucks."

"I've got something else in mind for you fellas," said Frank. "When we finish this construction we're going to throw a grand-opening extravaganza like you've never seen. I definitely want the Sherman Brothers as headliners. Along with the comeback performance of Superman Willis." He winked at Superman.

"I thought he was dead," said the lovely Melanie Llewellyn.

Superman smiled. "He's retired."

"You hear that, Stu?" Lou was excited. "Headliners!"

"It's second billing, don't be a putz," said Stu.

"All Ambassadors will have full use of the hotel and spa facilities, and we'll be organizing special events . . ." Melanie turned to Catalina with a warm smile, and glanced at her notes. *"Queremos que todos ustedes se sientan aquí como en su casa,"* she said. (We want you all to feel as if our home is your home.)

Catalina grimaced at this display of intercultural hospitality. *"Sí, pero esta es nuestra casa, gringa más fea,"* she said. *"Y ustedes quieren cortar todos nuestros árboles."* (Yes, but this *is* our home, you ugly gringa. And you want to cut down all our trees.)

The islanders murmured assent. Melanie chattered on about the projected payroll impact on the community, estimated dollar values of infrastructure improvements, on and on yak yak until her words were bouncing off Superman's ears like foam-rubber balls. But he noticed how everyone had perked up at the mention of money.

Sandy took up a pencil and began scribbling numbers on a scratch pad.

"We want you on our side," said Melanie, "and we're willing to pay. It's good business for everybody. Life is so much more pleasant when we all get along." Superman saw sweat beads trickling down past her ears.

"So when do we get paid?" said D. B. Cooper. "I'm flat busted."

Clearly Frank thought he could buy everyone at this table for thirty pieces of silver, and it was beginning to look as if he might be right. The whole setup gave Superman the willies: the fresh-faced corporate sweetie with her slide show, the boys in red shirts lined up along the wall with their hands folded left over right; the silent servants serving coffee and cinnamon cookies. No doubt about it, Frank had this place humming like a machine.

Sandy said, "I'm not a *business*woman, Frank, but you'd be spending thirty thousand a year just for this . . . Friendliness Insurance. How can you possibly afford that?"

Frank said, "Melanie?"

"No, Frank," said Sandy, "I asked you, not her."

"We've heard enough from her," Linda shot.

"People, people." Frank held up his hands. "Please. One at a time."

"Let me handle this, Frank," said Melanie.

That was the wrong thing to say. Linda picked up her Jungle Inn scratch pad and sent it sailing across the table, where it struck a glancing blow off Melanie's shoulder and fell to the floor.

Melanie gaped as if she'd been hit by a meteorite. "How dare you assault me with a—with a scratch pad!"

"Ladies, please," Frank said. "Melanie has my full confidence. We're offering you all a good deal, if you're not too thickheaded to take it."

Spike's eyes glittered. "You trying to buy us off, Frank?"

"Certainly not."

"What would you call it?"

"A goodwill investment," Frank said—ah: there it was: the sign Superman had been waiting for: Frank's ears reddening as he struggled to hold on to his temper. "Damn it, can't anybody see what we're trying to do here? We're bringing all sorts of improvements to the island, we're pouring in millions and actually trying to create some kind of future for this place— and all I hear is flak from you lazy, ungrateful people."

"Frank . . ."

"What have you ever done for these people, Spike? Have you ever created a single job for anybody?"

"No, Frank, I'm not a captain of industry, like you. I just live here."

"Don't forget, you live here because you're allowed," said Frank.

There: he had flung his threat on the table for everyone to see. Take the money and shut up, or get out. It went without saying that no one was allowed out.

Stu Sherman didn't take long to decide. "If the man wants to pay me to be nice to his guests, I say thank you, Frank, where do I sign."

"Ditto," Lou said.

"Yeah, guys, don't you think you're coming down a little hard on Frank?" That was D. B. Cooper.

Most of the gringos spoke up to say they might have concerns on a few issues, but mostly they thought the Jungle Inn was a swell idea and they would be happy to serve as Ambassadors. Unconditional surrender without a fight.

That is how craven we've become, Superman thought. You can buy anyone with a slide show, some cookies, a hundred bucks a month. These people are *dying* to sell out. He felt himself floating out of his chair. He locked his feet around the legs.

"I can't believe this!" Sandy burst out. "Frank, I say the hell with your stupid pyramid! Have you lost your mind? Don't you see this would be a disaster? This is exactly what Emily was trying to stop. It goes against everything that's good about this place."

"The owner of this island is approaching us all in good faith. Your neighbors seem willing to admit at least the possibility that we can work together. I must say, I'm encouraged by what I'm hearing."

"Well you can count me out," Sandy announced. "And you can shove your hundred dollars where the sun don't shine."

"Hear hear," said Linda.

"I'll apply you girls' share to my favorite charity," Frank said. "Hysterical Women in Desperate Need."

Superman got up. "I don't need to listen to any more of this. You all stay if you want. I've heard enough."

He pulled back the curtain, stepped into the courtyard. He stood waiting for the scrape of chairs, the murmur of everyone coming to their senses. He heard a couple of scrapes. Sandy and Linda came out, followed by Spike.

"That's it?" said Superman.

"The few, the proud," said Spike.

"Where's Daisy?" said Linda.

"She said she'd meet us at the beach," he told them. "She doesn't want to get involved. She has a bad feeling about this."

"Me too," said Sandy. "But we have to do something. I'll talk to her."

They went down the black-stone path, past ranks of camouflage men. Linda performed a dead-on imitation of Melanie Llewellyn. "How dare you attack me with a—with a *scratch paaaaaad!*" rolling her eyes like the Bride of Frankenstein. They were laughing when they reached the fork in the path.

Superman said, "What do we do now?"

"What do we ever do?" Spike said. "Let's go have a drink."

LA DISCOTECA WAS PACKED with islanders dancing and drinking, kids running wild. The people faced west out of habit, looking out to the dark sea. No one was thinking about what was happening on the other side of the island.

Midway through his third margarita, Superman realized he had been looking at the problem through a very small keyhole. There were only a few gringos on the island, but there must be three hundred natives, not counting a passel of children—a whole army of brown people.

That's how he thought of them still, after all these years: the brown people. He had tried to make friends with some of them, but always there was a certain unbridgeable gap. No matter how hard he listened, how many hours he spent poring over his *diccionario,* he couldn't understand more than half of what they said. When he summoned the nerve to venture a phrase or two in Spanish, they always laughed, whether he was trying to be funny or not. He knew all their names: Carlos, Beto, Cinthia, Álvaro, Mariela, Alejandra, Juan Carlos, Jorge, Susana, Dennys, Pepino and Quique and Ronaldo and Estefan, Isabel, Lita, Cecilia, María Elena, Paco and Flaco and Merlyn, Memo, Diego, Manuel. He always waved and smiled, and said *hola,* and they did the same. But he'd never been inside any of their houses, never invited them to his. He had lived among these people for eight years without really knowing any of them.

It was like Alabama when he was a boy, the white people had Negro "friends"—former maids or gardeners, usually—but each side kept to its own, out of suspicion and habit. On this island, the two worlds spoke two languages, so the division ran deeper. Superman knew the island people looked at him the same way: just one of the gringos.

But now he needed to talk to them. He needed them to listen, without laughing at him.

He told Daisy he'd be right back, just up to the house for something. He jogged home, grabbed what he'd come for, and set off again down the beach. He didn't want to be out of breath when he got there, but he knew that if he stopped to think about what he was going to do, he would never do it.

A strong breeze came up the sand, surf pounding, a thunderstorm flashing its cannons far out at sea. Superman slung the Gibson over his shoulder and walked through the coconut grove, into the lights and the salsa music, along the back of the bar. He felt his heart pounding, just as it used to pound when he made the long walk from limo to stage.

Freddy the bartender looked up in surprise: gringos never came behind the bar. Superman crooked a finger. Freddy put his head down, listened carefully, and went off to seek permission.

Superman stood between beer coolers, out of the path of the whizzing bartenders. The windows were three deep in people, clawing past each other waving hands, thrusting money, and shouting for beer. From behind the bar, the mock airplane in the ceiling looked almost real, even with strings of pineapples and onions dangling from the wheel strut.

Señor Rodríguez, Presidente y Gerente General de la Restaurante Discoteca Amor Y Mar Y Sol Y Blues, was a rotund mustachioed man in his fifties, a dead ringer for the old *caballero* in the picture next to Einstein's. "*Qué necesitas, Señor Bang?*" he said—that was how the islanders pronounced "Ben."

Superman explained. First the man smiled at his awkward Spanish, but then he grew quiet and listened. At last he shrugged and said, "*Por qué no?*" They shook hands.

Superman stepped out past the kitchen. The Gibson was out of tune, but it didn't matter; the monotonous *whanka-whanka* of the salsa made everything sound off-key. Standing in the shadows, he felt his nerves jumping. He was about to do something he had sworn never to do: stand up to sing, unprepared. There's no greater risk for a performer, no quicker way to turn off an audience, than to bumble through something, learning it as you go along.

But he had to get their attention. He knew only one way to do that: stand up and sing.

When the DJ switched off the salsa, the people on the dance floor cried "Whooo!" as if they were going over the top of a roller coaster. The mirror-ball kept twirling, the colored spotlights rotating, but the sudden wave of quiet left everyone stranded in the middle of the floor, dazed and a little deaf.

Superman moved through the dancers, dragging the bar stool Freddy had lent him, holding up the guitar to keep from skewering anyone.

At one end of the platform was a space big enough for a bar stool. The grinning DJ came around with a microphone stand. *"Concierto! Pura vida!"*

Superman heard a shout from the vicinity of the bar: "Aw *right!* Yes!" Spike came charging to a table down front. "Man, it's about damn time!"

Daisy and the Twins swam upstream through a crowd of disappointed dancers headed off for beers. The people at the outer tables filled the silence with talk.

Superman settled on the bar stool. Gyp curled up at his feet. The DJ clicked the mike button and murmured "Pow, pow, pow, *hola hola,*" testing for feedback and squeal. There was plenty of both. He nodded and went back to his panel to focus the spotlights on Superman.

"Buenas noches . . ." Superman's voice boomed from speakers all around. "Test test testing, one two three four . . . hey folks, sorry to stop the salsa, but don't worry, there's always more where that came from." He strummed a chord, making a last effort to tune the D string while he searched his mind for the words to "Contigo en la Distancia."

It was one of the old mournful *romántica* ballads he had learned from the late-night transistor radio. "No Me Platiques Más," "La Barca," "Estrellas en Sus Ojos," "Inolvidable" . . . these songs were slow, and simple enough that even Superman could understand the lyrics, full of kisses, embraces, lips, and mouths and hearts and souls, the kind of words you couldn't use in an American song because they would laugh your cornball ass off the stage. "Contigo en la Distancia" was his favorite:

> *No existe un momento del día en que pueda apartarme de tí*
> *El mundo parece distinto cuando no estás junto a mí . . .*

He saw faces lighting up. The crowd drifted closer. He sang softly, slowly, feeling his way through the *español,* lingering on the breaks in the lovely, lost melody. The words were full of longing, obsession, a dreamy inconsolable quality:

Más allá que tus labios, del sol y las estrellas
Contigo en la distancia, amada mía, estoy.

Beyond your lips, beyond the sun and the stars, across the distance, I am with you, my love. As he reached the last of the verse, he looked up from his guitar into a sea of smiling men and teary women. The dance floor was jammed with couples swaying along. Superman tapped his foot through the guitar break, and repeated the last two verses in the high register, in the manner of old César Portillo de la Luz himself.

The last note brought a big solid roar of applause going all the way back to the beach, drowning the sound of the waves. Superman had not heard that roar since his last concert in El Paso. It thrilled him down to the spaces between his toes.

"Thank you," he said. *"Muchas gracias! Muy amable."*

They wouldn't stop clapping. Spike jumped up and down, yelling "Ho! Ho yes!" Daisy smiling and crying, the Twins blowing kisses . . . even Jimmy Hoffa looked impressed. Only Gyp snoozed, unmoved by the uproar.

Superman bent to the mike. "Thank you, folks. That's the only one I know in Spanish, so you'll just have to bear with me—"

He strummed three hard whacks on the guitar, the loopy guitar intro line, and then off into "Superman's Revenge":

> *When he's up in the sky, do you know how he feels*
> *Not a bird, not a plane, just a man of ideals*
> *Watching people go bad in their usual way*

It was like flying, like riding a bike. He had known how to do it all along. He hadn't lost it. He would never lose it.

For the first time since the Flor-A-Bama Lounge he was using his music not to make money, but to *communicate*, to break down a wall between himself and these people—to make them stop what they were doing and listen to him. And it was working. They flooded in from the beach and all corners of La Discoteca, pressing up to the back of the crowd, dancing and clapping along.

> *You better run—it's time for*
> *Superman's revenge*
> *Superman's revenge*

They cheered and whistled and made the floor tremble. Superman's voice sounded good—and why not? He'd been resting it for eight years. He stayed in the groove, didn't give them time to stop clapping. He said, "Okay, here's a song about Jesus," and set off into a *gong-ding-gong-a-langy* syncopated cowboy strut:

> *Talkin' to the dog*
> *You keep trying to tell him what to do*
> *Just a stupid little dog*
> *But he's wearing the same gold watch as you*
> *If you ain't got time to stop what you're doing and give that dog a bone*
> *Then you won't be seeing JEE-sus when he calls the dogs back home.*

Applause mixed with hoots of laughter from the gringos. Superman soaked up the feeling: like a heroin addict who's been clean for eight years, wrapping the cord around his arm and plunging in the needle, relaxing into the familiar exultation, his heart surging with relief while a voice in his mind shrieks *Oh God! What have I done!*

But it was too late for second thoughts. The drug was in his veins. He wanted to sit on that bar stool all night and play every song he knew, to keep the excitement going. Now he remembered: this is the juicy part. You separate yourself from the audience—get up on a stage, single yourself out with lights, make them stand and listen in the dark—and if you do the job right, you forge a bond with every person in the room. Your reward is a surge of approval that washes over you like the warmest softest wave in the sea.

He hooked his toes in the bar stool to keep from floating away. He'd almost forgotten what sent him up there in the first place, an urge that had nothing to do with applause or the wonderful surprise on Daisy's face.

"Thank you, folks," he said, "okay! Enough! *No más!*" but they kept clapping and whistling. He grinned. "Thank you, thank yewwwwww . . . *muchas gracias.* Okay. Thanks a lot. Listen, I want to say something—"

" 'When Time Stands Still,' " Spike bellowed, waving the flame of his cigarette lighter. " 'Take Me Anywhere but Heaven'! 'Statutory Romance'!"

"Hey Spike, shut up and come up here a minute, would you?"

Spike glanced behind him, as if there might be some other Spike.

Superman nodded: yes, you.

The people demanded an encore, clapping in rhythm, like football fans. Spike made his way through the ranks.

Más allá que tus labios, del sol y las estrellas
Contigo en la distancia, amada mía, estoy.

Beyond your lips, beyond the sun and the stars, across the distance, I am with you, my love. As he reached the last of the verse, he looked up from his guitar into a sea of smiling men and teary women. The dance floor was jammed with couples swaying along. Superman tapped his foot through the guitar break, and repeated the last two verses in the high register, in the manner of old César Portillo de la Luz himself.

The last note brought a big solid roar of applause going all the way back to the beach, drowning the sound of the waves. Superman had not heard that roar since his last concert in El Paso. It thrilled him down to the spaces between his toes.

"Thank you," he said. *"Muchas gracias! Muy amable."*

They wouldn't stop clapping. Spike jumped up and down, yelling "Ho! Ho yes!" Daisy smiling and crying, the Twins blowing kisses . . . even Jimmy Hoffa looked impressed. Only Gyp snoozed, unmoved by the uproar.

Superman bent to the mike. "Thank you, folks. That's the only one I know in Spanish, so you'll just have to bear with me—"

He strummed three hard whacks on the guitar, the loopy guitar intro line, and then off into "Superman's Revenge":

> *When he's up in the sky, do you know how he feels*
> *Not a bird, not a plane, just a man of ideals*
> *Watching people go bad in their usual way*

It was like flying, like riding a bike. He had known how to do it all along. He hadn't lost it. He would never lose it.

For the first time since the Flor-A-Bama Lounge he was using his music not to make money, but to *communicate*, to break down a wall between himself and these people—to make them stop what they were doing and listen to him. And it was working. They flooded in from the beach and all corners of La Discoteca, pressing up to the back of the crowd, dancing and clapping along.

> *You better run—it's time for*
> *Superman's revenge*
> *Superman's revenge*

They cheered and whistled and made the floor tremble. Superman's voice sounded good—and why not? He'd been resting it for eight years. He stayed in the groove, didn't give them time to stop clapping. He said, "Okay, here's a song about Jesus," and set off into a *gong-ding-gong-a-langy* syncopated cowboy strut:

> *Talkin' to the dog*
> *You keep trying to tell him what to do*
> *Just a stupid little dog*
> *But he's wearing the same gold watch as you*
> *If you ain't got time to stop what you're doing and give that dog a bone*
> *Then you won't be seeing JEE-sus when he calls the dogs back home.*

Applause mixed with hoots of laughter from the gringos. Superman soaked up the feeling: like a heroin addict who's been clean for eight years, wrapping the cord around his arm and plunging in the needle, relaxing into the familiar exultation, his heart surging with relief while a voice in his mind shrieks *Oh God! What have I done!*

But it was too late for second thoughts. The drug was in his veins. He wanted to sit on that bar stool all night and play every song he knew, to keep the excitement going. Now he remembered: this is the juicy part. You separate yourself from the audience—get up on a stage, single yourself out with lights, make them stand and listen in the dark—and if you do the job right, you forge a bond with every person in the room. Your reward is a surge of approval that washes over you like the warmest softest wave in the sea.

He hooked his toes in the bar stool to keep from floating away. He'd almost forgotten what sent him up there in the first place, an urge that had nothing to do with applause or the wonderful surprise on Daisy's face.

"Thank you, folks," he said, "okay! Enough! *No más!*" but they kept clapping and whistling. He grinned. "Thank you, thank yewwwwww . . . *muchas gracias.* Okay. Thanks a lot. Listen, I want to say something—"

" 'When Time Stands Still,' " Spike bellowed, waving the flame of his cigarette lighter. " 'Take Me Anywhere but Heaven'! 'Statutory Romance'!"

"Hey Spike, shut up and come up here a minute, would you?"

Spike glanced behind him, as if there might be some other Spike.

Superman nodded: yes, you.

The people demanded an encore, clapping in rhythm, like football fans. Spike made his way through the ranks.

Superman took the mike off the stand and handed it to him.

"What are you doing? I can't sing."

"I'm done singing. I want to talk to them. I need you to translate."

Spike nodded. The corners of his mouth went up. "Give 'em hell," he said.

Superman just stood there while the clapping died to isolated pockets. Then he began to speak. La Discoteca fell quiet: his voice and Spike's amplified translation, the beat of the surf, the *whap-whap* of a ceiling fan out of balance.

He asked a few questions: Do you know who owns this island? Who owns the trees? The monkeys? The ocean? The air?

He stood quietly while Spike translated, phrase by phrase.

Maybe you think nobody can really own those things, he said. You think they can't be bought and sold, like rice and beans. But you're wrong. One man owns them all. He is selling you out, as fast as he can. And you're helping him do it.

The crowd began to mutter and stir.

I'm a gringo. You stand here and listen to me sing, and you clap for me, and I appreciate that, I really do. But you're clapping when you don't even know what I'm singing about.

Maybe you've heard about the new hotel on the mountain. You've heard it means everybody on this island will have a good job, everybody's gonna get rich, if you just play along and do what they tell you. Things will loosen up, you'll be allowed to come and go. And maybe that sounds good to you. But that's because you don't understand what it means.

There's only one man on this island who's going to get rich. Already he's richer than you or I can ever dream of being. He has no intention of setting you free.

He will do whatever it takes.

He will cut down the trees.

He will blow the top off the mountain.

The Magician owns this island. Every monkey, every lizard and bird. You sold it to him.

And what I want to know is—did he buy the people, too? Does he own all of you? Miss Emilia told me once that you are his slaves.

Spike glanced a warning over his shoulder, but Superman said, "Go ahead, Spike. Word for word."

Spike obeyed. When he spoke the word *esclavos*, the mutter took on an angrier buzz.

"I just got here a few years ago," Superman said. "But this is your home. Are you gonna help him destroy it, or help us find a way to stop him?"

The room fell silent. Direct confrontation was not the native style. Superman knew he had really insulted them when the crowd parted to reveal Señor Rodríguez, El Presidente of La Discoteca, in a towering rage.

He spoke in forceful gusts of rapid-fire Spanish, his eyes flashing. Superman caught a phrase now and then—*orgullo de la gente,* the pride of the people, and *trabajos nuevos,* new jobs—but he couldn't quite make out whether the man was condemning him or agreeing with him. Spike tried to translate but couldn't keep up, finally lapsed into silence and gawked along with everyone else as El Presidente worked himself into a full-throated arm-waving rant, his fists smashing down on a table, beer bottles flying.

The crash of breaking glass brought a huge cheer from the assembly. Superman felt a flash of remorse: what have I wrought?

"He says the gringos have always sold them out," Spike said, "always stolen from them, worked them like slaves, and for nothing. Says it's fine for you to get up and sing your song, and ask your . . . impertinent questions, but you're just like all gringos, there's something you want. You seem like *buena gente,* good people, but the gringo never says what he really wants."

"What should I do?" said Superman.

Spike shrugged. "Sheez, I don't know. You started this."

Superman took a deep breath and told them exactly what he wanted. The translation was greeted with an uneasy silence.

El Presidente faced him down with a fierce, testing glare, as if they might get down on the floor and wrestle—then he broke out in a broad grin, raised his arms, and came forward to clap Superman on both shoulders. *"Qué buen' idea,"* he said. (What a good idea.)

"How do you say it in *español,* Spike?"

"Huelga," said Spike.

Superman put his fist in the air and cried *"Huelga!"*

The answering shout brought Gyp up from a sound sleep, barking.

22 / *El Mango Jesús*

THE BUS DRIVER PLAYED slow, dreamy love songs on his cassette player. The music seemed to lift us up on soft wings and fly us over the potholes.

It was just past dawn when we pulled up at an open-air café on the Costa Rican border. I hoisted Jeff Wiesenblatt's pack and followed the sleepy passengers down the steps. We lined up for the once-over from the customs officials. The man barely glanced at Jeff's picture, and waved me through the gap in the fence.

This was Costa Rica: a simple chain-link fence at the border, a green valley tamed into neat fields and fencerows, pastures speckled with cows. Across the road was a schoolyard full of children in white shirts, blue trousers and skirts. A mural decorated the wall around the playground.

The other passengers headed off for coffee, but that mural called me across the road. It was crude and beautiful: fantastic figures of dolphins and whales, swimming turtles, soaring birds, jaguars, snakes, trees laden with globy red fruit, troops of silly-faced monkeys. But what really caught my eye was the middle section, a landscape of green jungle leading down to a wavy blue ocean, and, just offshore, a small island with two cone-shaped mountains.

Twin mountains, connected by a swaybacked ridge and a wide strip of beach.

The schoolkids were kicking soccer balls, leaping, chasing, chattering, filling the air with their noise, as if to celebrate my discovery.

I approached a plump older woman standing at the corner of the yard, a teacher surveying the uproar with an air of benign neglect. "*Señora?*"

She smiled at me. "*Sí, mi amor.*"

"Do you speak English?"

"*Ay, no, amorcito.*"

"*La isla,*" I said, pointing down the wall. "With the two mountains. *Dónde?*"

She shook her head in puzzlement.

I made hand signals for her to follow me, and she did, stepping out of the gate to see where I was pointing—the center of the mural.

"*Ah, la isla,*" she said. "*Qué linda, verdad?*"

"Yeah, but where is it? *Dónde está?* In Nicaragua?"

Her sour expression told me what she thought of Nicaragua.

"Costa Rica?"

"*Más abajo.*"

I flipped through my Berlitz: *abajo:* below. "Panama?"

"*No, Panamá no.*" Her eye roved the playground. She spoke in a clear, expressive voice that was accustomed to addressing the young and ignorant, so I was able to follow what she said. The island was not really part of any country. The natives called it Isla del Mago. It stood off the Pacific coast near the border of Costa Rica and Panama, a remote region known as El Indio, the Indian. Apparently there were old disputes over which nation controlled El Indio, but the area was too remote to cause much of a fuss. *La tierra de nuestros antepasados,* she called it. The land of our ancestors. At least that's what I think she said.

As she strolled away I looked up *mago:* magician. Island of the Magician. It gave me a little tingle.

Behind me I heard a shout: "Jim!"

Oh God. I turned. There he was, pressed against the fence at the end of the schoolyard.

I could have easily turned away, climbed back on that bus, and kept going. I thought about it, I really did. But there he was, looking at me, trapped behind a fence in Nicaragua because I had given him bad empanadas and fled with his pack.

I thanked the *señora* and walked down the wall to the fence. "Hi, Jeff."

His eyes burned. "I think you've got some things of mine."

"You're right."

"That was a shitty thing to do," he said. "I've been sick all night."

"Sorry. I needed your passport."

The bus driver honked. I hurled Jeff's pack over the fence, and ran for the bus.

He caught up with me in the bus station in San José. He didn't say anything, just went to the end of the line for the bus to Corcovado. I took a window seat. He sat three rows behind me. For the next twenty-one hours his eyes bored holes in the back of my head. We went through the Tala-manca Mountains, down the Pacific side of Costa Rica, across the jungles of Corcovado and into the kingdom of El Indio. No word passed between us. When the bus stopped for mealtimes, Jeff went off by himself and sat staring at me.

Probably you've never heard of it, but El Indio considers itself a country apart from all others. There's even a border station, a shack with a roof of palm thatch, and a flag, a bright-blue field with a sea turtle and a monkey facing off from opposite corners. A stone-faced old Indian man boarded the bus, looked us over, bowed deeply, and beckoned us through.

We rolled through wave after wave of jungle mountains, valleys of trees so old and gigantic that no sunlight filtered down to the earth. Every once in a while, the bus stopped at a village, but mostly we saw virgin jungle and the treacherous road.

I was jammed in between a man with a cage full of chickens and a woman with two squalling babies, so I didn't see the horse before we hit it. The people in front had plenty of time to scream while the driver slammed on his brakes and the bus fishtailed all over the road and then *wham!* broadside into the horse. I was wedged in too tight to go anywhere. Jeff Wiesenblatt sailed over my head and landed on the seatback three rows in front of me.

The force of the impact spilled a baby into my lap. I grabbed it and held on as the bus shuddered and slumped to one side. I didn't know what we'd hit. It felt like a wall. The baby made a hiccupy gasp and wailed louder. The air in the back of the bus filled with flapping chickens and feathers and the groans of those who had bumped their heads. The mother snatched the baby as if I might try to make off with it.

Jeff was bleeding from a nasty gash in his thigh, apologizing profusely as people climbed up on the seats to let him out.

The bus emptied slowly from the front. After weeks on buses like this, I knew that when anything happens, it is the God-given right of everyone on the bus to get off and have a look for himself. I grabbed Jeff's pack and followed the herd to the exit.

That horse didn't look big enough to have stopped a whole bus. It lay on its side in the dirt, eyes open, legs sticking straight out. It was dead, but the bus had suffered the worst of the visible damage: windshield cracked, front end mashed in, a flattened tire. The driver surveyed the damage with a stricken expression.

This was a souped-up school bus, blood red with silvery trim, psychedelic scenes painted down both flanks (sunsets, peacocks, busty girls in bikinis), and a name inscribed in flame-tipped letters: EL MANGO JESÚS.

Jeff sat on a rock, bleeding. No one was paying him any attention. His face was whiter than the Jockey shorts he pressed against the wound, trying to staunch the flow. Blood trickled down his leg, down his sneaker, and into the dust.

I went over to him. "How you doing, Jeff?"

"Oh, I guess I'll make it." He squinted up at me. "It's a lot of blood, but it could be worse."

"You're better off than the horse," I said. "Does it hurt?"

"Not so bad. You know, in Oklahoma we have fences to keep the damn horses out of the road."

"Brought you your pack," I said. "You better keep an eye on it. Somebody might try to swipe it."

"Yeah, fuck you," said Jeff.

I couldn't argue with that.

I went to the driver and asked him how long he planned to stand there looking at his bus.

He glared as if I'd spat on his shoe.

I strained to be polite. I pointed out the widening stream of blood on Jeff's leg, the waxy pallor of his face. I cast a glance toward heaven, and a glance at my watch. My nonverbal skills were improving. The driver understood, and was not at all pleased.

"*Ay, Dios,*" he said, posing his hands under his chin, as in prayer. "*Dame la paciencia!*"

Probably I should have apologized, but Jeff was in danger of bleeding to death, and the driver was more concerned about his bus.

"You want him to die?" I said, cranking my voice up a notch. "You gonna stand there twiddling your thumbs like an idiot, or you gonna get him to a doctor?"

The word "idiot" stiffened the driver's chin. "*Hale,*" he said.

I flipped through my Berlitz. *Hale* was Central American slang for "get out of here."

"I'd just love to *hale, señor,* I really would," I said, "so why don't you just start the bus and let's all *hale?*" I made sweeping gestures toward the bus. I mimed turning a key, placing my hands on a steering wheel, driving away.

The driver went off like one of those Fourth of July fireworks that spins slowly at first, throwing a shower of sparks, then faster and faster until it's a whizzing circle of fire, lifting off and shooting skyward where it explodes with a crackly *bang!* He shook his finger in my face. He pawed at the dirt with his shoe. He laid out a string of curses that would have blistered my ears if I'd understood even one of them.

Jeff got to his feet and hobbled toward us in an effort to break up the argument. He took about five steps before his face turned white and he fainted.

The driver left off yelling and joined the rush to his side. No one had been the least bit impressed by Jeff's bleeding, but that dead faint really got them on their feet and moving.

The driver helped carry him to the bus. They laid him across the front seat and went at him with smelling salts from the first-aid kit. Everyone climbed aboard. The driver started the engine and maneuvered around the horse, back onto the road. Jeff stirred. We rolled off thumping on the flat tire.

A kind-faced woman helped Jeff fashion a tourniquet from a leather belt. I was impressed with his ability to remain calm while bleeding.

At last, a village. We all piled out in front of a house. The doctor came out, a young guy in boxer shorts, yawning, scratching his belly. He took one look at Jeff and whisked him inside.

The driver recruited four men to help place the jack and change the tire. I went over to help, but one surly glance backed me off.

I knew that if I hadn't spoken up, we might still be squatting back there in the road staring at a dead horse, and probably at a dead gringo. I waited for someone to congratulate me on my quick thinking. No one did. I moved to the steps of the house, where some of the younger passengers were talking and smoking. They got up and went into the street.

You are the stranger here, I told myself. You lost your temper. This is not your country. Be cool.

At last the doctor stepped out to hold the door for Jeff and his crutches. Jeff wore a big painkiller smile and a gauze bandage that encased half his leg. I don't know what pills that doctor gave him, but he looked to be having a great time. The passengers applauded. Jeff giggled and made his way to the bus.

The driver finished hammering the fender back from the tire. Everybody piled on. As I passed the front row, a hand snaked out to grab me. "Hey, hey, you saved my life, man! I'd still be bleeding back there if you hadn't stuck up for me! Siddown!"

I sat. Jeff was one mighty happy and forgiving guy. He flung an arm around my shoulders and said I had saved his life, we gringos have to stick together. He was really soaring.

He asked where I was headed. Isla del Mago, I said.

"I read about that. It's private, I think—some kind of estate. Why there?"

I told him I was looking for somebody. Jeff said maybe he would go there, too, take a few days off the road to heal up. "Eighteen stitches and I've never felt better in my life," he said. "It's all your fault, you son of a bitch!"

He went from giddy to unconscious in two minutes, slumped against the window with a string of drool hanging from his lip.

I was happy to have saved his life, to make up in some small way for what I had done to him.

The driver turned on his radio: equal parts static and salsa. We groaned through twists and turns and switchbacks, laboring for an hour to the top of a mountain, only to look out upon the next valley, the next mountain. We went places a bus shouldn't go, where the road was half washed away and we teetered on the very brink, setting off landslides with our tires. We crossed churning white rivers on creaky bridges held together with baling wire and the prayers of the passengers, who made the sign of the cross before each one.

El Indio was spectacular country, clouds clinging to the sides of jade-green mountains, waterfalls spilling past bends in the road, giant ferns and blooming shrubs crowding the shoulders. But it was hard to enjoy the scenery when a new and terrifying death seemed to lurk around every curve.

Jeff was still comatose when we trundled over the top of the last mountain to a stunning glimpse of the blue Pacific, stretching out to infinity. I shook his arm: "Wake up, I think we're here."

We descended a steep grade. A sign said BIENVENIDOS A GATO NEGRO above a stick drawing of a grinning black cat. I saw a grassy field full of semitrailer trucks parked at odd angles. Blocks of great oaklike trees sheltered stucco cottages. The road curved past a soccer field, a little white church, and a row of clapboard stores to the waterfront, where it ended in a milling crowd.

I helped Jeff down the steps. He was groggy, confused. I got him over to the seawall and propped him up on his pack.

A multitude clogged the entrance to the unfinished bridge stretching over the water to the island. There was some sort of disturbance, raised voices.

I walked away, down the gritty gray sand. I didn't allow myself to look until I had the Polaroid snap in my hand. Then I held it up, side by side with the real thing.

The cone-shaped mountains were a perfect match. The beach must be on the other side. A rush of joy swept me like a fever, left me breathless, jangling, floating on air. Here was my first glimpse of the place I had imagined for so very long. In that first moment the view repaid me for the years of waiting, the countless miles and hours it took to get here. I pumped my fists in the air and did a little dance, right there on the sand. The bus roared away.

PS you should see this place.

Okay, Dad. I see it. I'm here. Where are you?

23 / Groundbreaking

SINCE THE BIRTHDAY PARTY Daisy had been crying a lot, for no reason. She stayed in bed all day, or kept to herself in the yellow cabin. Superman walked across the garden, up the steps. He heard . . . a radio? Someone singing?

The door was hooked from inside. "Daisy? Are you in there?"

What was that sound? A soft crooning . . . crying? He tugged at the door. "Daisy?" The hook felt as if it would give to one—good—*yank!* And it did.

All the stone faces were down off the walls, as if an earthquake had struck the cabin. Daisy hunched on her knees in the second room, humming "That Old Black Magic." She held a stone face on her lap, a slender Asian-looking creature with purple eyes and white speckled lips.

She dipped a rag in the bucket and rubbed the face, smearing the paint. That was turpentine. She was wiping the face off the stone.

She had already wiped off about a hundred of them, to judge from the heaps of smeared stones around her.

Superman spoke in a whisper: "Daisy. What are you doing."

She dipped the rag in the bucket, and swabbed at the rock.

He knelt beside her. "Look, you're ruining them. They're beautiful. What are you *doing?*"

She turned with a distracted smile, as if Ben were a silly child who could not be expected to understand. Her cheek wore a smudge of bright red. "They're all wrong," she said. "I know how you hate them. What a stupid waste of time."

"What do you—I don't hate them! Jesus, after all the work you put in, to come out here and . . . what the hell is the matter with you?"

"Don't yell at me."

"I'm not yelling!"

"I see how you look at them, and you're right. I'm not blaming you. It's not your fault."

"Daisy, don't do this." He took the stone from her hand.

She reached past him for an egg-shaped soldier with looming white eyes. "If you want to help," she said, "stop looking at me that way." She swashed the rag in the bucket and bent over the stone.

Superman got up. "Are you drunk?"

"No."

"Did Rabbit give you more of those pills? I've told you to stay away from him."

"You're not my mother."

"I wish you would tell me what's wrong."

"I'm probably crazy. They always said I was." She wiped away the soldier's eyes. "Everything's wrong, Ben. It's never going to be right. You're brave to try and fight it, but you won't win. It's stronger than you. More people will die. Don't you understand? Our lives here are over."

"Daisy, you haven't seen the way the islanders have thrown themselves into this! They're on fire with this thing! Come with me, I'm going over to the barricade. You'll see."

"I have work to do. I can't leave these behind. I can't stand the thought of people laughing at me."

"Come on. You need to get out."

"No, *you* need to get out. Get out and leave me alone. You're always here, always hanging around. You never give me a moment to myself."

He sighed. "I'll be back in a couple hours. I love you."

"I have work to do," she said, almost to herself.

SUPERMAN SCANNED the passengers stepping down from the bus, Gato Negrans returning from San José and a sprinkling of tourists: plump older couples, a group of well-dressed Latinos, a slender American boy on crutches, and the shaggy-haired kid who helped him down the steps.

Their expectant half smiles turned to confusion when they saw the crowd blocking the bridge. This was the fourth week of the *huelga*, a word which meant "strike" but had grown to encompass the barricades, the walkouts and picket lines—the whole joyful spirit of resistance that had seized the island. Jimmy Hoffa had stepped in to organize the *huelguistas*. For twenty-three days, no bridge worker had been allowed to approach the gap in the middle. Boats trying to land on the island were turned back by beach patrols. On Day Eighteen a helicopter touched down at La Discoteca to pick up a stranded bridge crew, and was driven back into the sky by a pack of children throwing mangoes.

A twelve-foot wall of bamboo blocked the Gato Negro entrance to the bridge, fat yellow poles laid end to end, interlaced with barbed wire. To get around it you had to climb over the side, hang from a beam, swing your legs over the water, shinny up a post, and jump to a railing.

Superman was relieved to find the *huelguistas* on the other side as numerous and determined as ever. It felt like a street party—salsa on the transistors, families picnicking, old ladies holding umbrellas for shade. It was well known that the strikers were letting their friends pass the barricade at night. For twenty-three days Gato Negro had been the scene of tearful reunions, family members who hadn't seen each other in years. The men huddled around their command post, the covered bed of a pickup truck, replete with walkie-talkies and coolers of beer. A banner drooped from the superstructure of the bridge: NUESTRA ISLITA PARA NUESTRO PUEBLITO. "Our little island for our little people."

The blockade might not stop the Magician, but at least it was costing him a ton of money. Three bridge crews sat idle at full pay in Gato Negro, with sixteen backed-up tractor-trailer loads of materials for the Jungle Inn. A fleet of work barges rode uselessly at anchor in the channel.

For the first time, Superman thought he smelled the possibility of victory. He had never dreamed the islanders would take up the crusade with such determination, that they would stick it out through long days and nights, booming rainstorms, steamy hot afternoons. The *huelga* was theirs now—once Hoffa got them organized, they appointed their own group leaders and rotated assignments. If they could stay strong just a week or two more, Superman believed, the drivers would turn their trucks around and drive away, the bridge crews would pack up and go home. The Magician would have to surrender.

At least that's what he tried to persuade the *huelguistas* around the pickup truck, in his best broken Spanish. If it's a real emergency, he said, somebody needs to go to the *clínica,* let them pass. Otherwise, no exceptions. If you let a few people out, the whole wall falls down. We have to cause maximum irritation. We have to be strong. *"Con fuerza!"*

They laughed, and clapped him on the back—*"Tranquilo, Bang, tranquilo!"*—relax!

He munched a slice of watermelon and spit seeds on the ground. A wiry young man with thick eyeglasses came to report two gringos seeking permission to cross to the island.

All eyes turned to Superman.

He shook his head. *"Nadie."*

They're just kids, the young man said. One of them has a bad leg. *No puede caminar.* He can't walk.

"He can ride back the way he came," said Superman. *"No excepciones.* We're not here to open the place up to tourists."

The guy shrugged and went to deliver this news.

The men around Superman grew solemn. They hadn't expected him to turn his back on a gringo. Everybody knows gringos stick together.

A week or two more, he told them. Stay strong. We're going to win.

He shook hands all around and climbed the railing at the barricade. It was harder going back this way—you had to swing like a trapeze artist and thrust your legs into space to reach the little ledge. It would have been easier just to fly around the bamboo wall and float across the gap, but people were watching. He seized the rail and pulled himself over.

The breeze off the water picked up, whipping his hair.

It struck him that he had just stepped off the island for the first time since he crashed the Baron. He could have climbed on that bus and kept going. The thought had not even occurred to him.

Escaping this place had once been his obsession. Now, when it was as easy as stepping on a bus, he hadn't even thought about it. He found himself quickening his step toward home, toward Daisy.

Suddenly his whole life had come down to the problem of defending the island against a force he could not see. He knew it was hopeless, like trying to defend the ocean against the influence of the moon. But he felt compelled to try, for the sake of Amelia's memory and the magic he had found in this place, for the sake of the monkeys and the islanders living under an evil spell. This seemed like the most important thing he could do. Even if he had never made promises to Amelia, if no one had ever tried to kill him, if he'd never met Daisy or learned how to fly, there was something fundamentally wrong with the systematic destruction of a beautiful place.

Superman was happy here—finally happy, after a lifetime of searching. His conversion was complete. This island had stripped him of his things, one by one—and had given him everything in return: love and magic, a new peace, some ideas on the nature of God, a measure of forgiveness for his sins.

And now somebody wanted to destroy all that. It was too much to think that the club of the famously disappeared could remain a secret on an island aswarm with tourists, although Daisy said she could make herself disappear in the crowds on Fifth Avenue whenever she wanted. A scarf and a pair of big Italian sunglasses, no one will know who you are.

The barricade at the island end of the bridge was manned by women and children and dogs, Gyp among them. The women waved Superman through, calling *"Cántese!"* Sing!

He smiled, and waved. His eyes fell on a chrome-yellow jeep honking its horn across the road, a familiar old jeep with shiny new paint and a logo: THE JUNGLE INN. At the wheel was Frank's Aztec boy, Raúl, in a red polo shirt.

Superman said, "Are you honking at me?"

"Frank wants talk to you."

"What about, the weather?"

"La huelga."

Superman got in. Gyp scrambled over the fender, into the back. Raúl zoomed past the silent earth-moving equipment, the bridge workers' shantytown. Maybe this yellow jeep was a white flag. Maybe Frank was ready to surrender. It was possible, but somehow Superman didn't think so. Not yet.

He found Frank in the shade of the gazebo, holding forth on a futuristic cordless telephone with a retractable antenna—the first telephone Superman had seen in eight years. Raúl disappeared into the house. The soundtrack to *Oklahoma!* poured from the windows.

Superman walked to the brink of the terrace. In the light of a late afternoon, with the clouds flashing gold and the ocean rolled out like a sheet of glass, he could not take his eyes from the ugly straight line of the bridge, jammed like a syringe into the exposed flank of the island.

Frank raised his voice: "Why do you ask me, if you don't want my opinion? I've got someone here. I'll call back." He clicked off the phone and stood from his chair. "Mr. Willis. Sorry to make you wait. Thanks for coming."

"Always glad for a ride up the hill."

Frank was looking very nautical, white slacks and a red shirt printed with blue anchors. "Please, sit! What can I get you? Cocktail? *Cerveza?*"

"Nothing, thanks."

"Oh *por favor.* It's after five. What do you say, *limonada con vodka?* That's what I'm having."

"Nothing."

"I saw you having a look at our bridge," Frank said. "What do you think?"

"I walked across it today. Nice view from the middle. You know they're having a little party on the other side."

"So I've heard . . . I don't know how you've done it, Mr. Willis, but you've managed to turn the laziest, least aggressive people on earth into a fairly effective little army. My congratulations." Frank sipped his drink. "I never really saw you as the leader type. Always thought of you more as a loner."

"I didn't do anything," Superman said. "I just pointed out a few obvious items, and the people took it from there."

"Oh no, you're very smart, playing to their strength. They're masters of the art of doing *nada*." He indicated a telescope on a tripod. "I've seen them over there, swaggering around with their walkie-talkies. Their girlfriends are probably impressed, but I'm not."

"Frank, you're wrong about these people. They're not lazy. They're just not in as big a hurry as you are to screw up this island. For once they've decided to stand up for what's theirs."

"Call it off," Frank said. "Call it off now. Go talk to whoever you need to talk to, say whatever you have to say, but I want it stopped."

"Oh, Frank." He sighed, and shook his head. "You know I can't do that. Tell your boss to go pick on some other island."

"Let me tell you a true story, Mr. Willis." Frank straightened in his chair. "When they built the first atomic bomb, the Americans had a secret debate on how to drop it on Japan. Should they use it without warning, as they wanted? Or should they drop it in some remote place, as a demonstration? Finally they decided to drop leaflets over Hiroshima with an ultimatum that said, 'Something horrible is going to happen if you don't surrender at once.' The problem was, they'd been dropping leaflets like that for years, and nobody even picked them up anymore, they just swept them into the gutter. And so eighty thousand people were incinerated."

"That's a very interesting story, Frank."

"Well, it would be, if you'd lived in Hiroshima. If you got an ultimatum like that and didn't take it seriously."

"Is that what this is, Frank? An ultimatum?"

"Think of it as a leaflet floating down from the sky. If you don't call off this silly *huelga*, people are going to get hurt. And I won't be able to stop it. I'm just managing this project, I have nothing to do with security."

"What, you got a nuclear bomb? Where is it?" Superman peered under his chair, and the table.

"This is no joke, Mr. Willis. I'm giving you the chance to prevent a disaster. You've spent time with these savages—can you tell me what it is they really want? Pito doesn't seem to want to tell me."

"Stop building the bridge. Give up the hotel. Give them back their island."

"That's absurd," he said. "The island does not belong to them. Of course we know we should make some sort of gesture. We understand they have to save face—they can be downright Japanese about that. What if we built them a community center? You know, swimming pool, tennis courts . . . ?"

Superman had to smile. "Polo field?"

"Or a school. We could build a little school for the kids. Wouldn't that be adorable, a little red schoolhouse down by the bridge? I know just the spot."

"Give it up, Frank. You can't buy these people." Even as he said it, his heart began to sink. Promises of swimming pools and schoolhouses were just the sort of thing that might send the *huelguistas* home in a good mood, thinking they'd won.

Frank's ears glowed. "I'm trying to negotiate in good faith, Mr. Willis. I'm under quite a bit of pressure here, and you are being very difficult."

"You could join up with us, Frank. Help us keep the island alive."

"Don't be ridiculous."

"Do you think you can destroy it and nobody's gonna say boo? Is that what you thought?"

"Nobody's destroying anything," said Frank. "This is private property. The man has a right to build whatever he wants. Now call it off."

"Frank. I *can't*. You don't get it, this has nothing to do with me now. I'm not leading these people. Hoffa's out of it. This is their fight now. If I told them to quit when they're ahead, they'd laugh in my face."

"You think they're ahead?" Frank's eyes narrowed. "Obviously you have no idea of the force you are up against."

"It's you and a few loyal *employees* against the whole island. You're outnumbered, Frank. How can you win, unless you just kill everybody?"

The phone made a burbling sound. Frank pressed a button. "Yes." He listened a minute. "Are you sure?" He put the phone on the table faceup, the red light still aglow. "Well, that's it, then. It's on your conscience. The bridge will be open in a week, and we're ready to break ground for the hotel. Will you tell them to call it off?"

"No."

Frank turned his chair to face the south mountain, picked up the phone, and said, "They're not moving."

For a moment the world held its breath, then a bright flash bloomed low in the trees on the south mountain, an erupting geyser of earth and a percussive wave like fifty thunders, a great rolling RHOOOOM that knocked Superman back in his chair. The ground shuddered. Whole trees tumbled end over end through the air. A cloud of earth billowed up, widening as it climbed. The roar traveled over the channel to the mountains on the mainland, and came back a threatening rumble.

Superman opened his mouth to say *Holy Mother of*—but another flash, another blast wave, stuffed the oath down his throat. The charges were chained together in sequence, one every ten seconds. The air filled with blue smoke, trees blown to toothpicks, a fine dirt falling like rain. Each blast wave met a returning echo.

And here came the monkeys, flying through the treetops like a fast-moving wind, not squeaking or chirping or screaming. Fleeing for their lives.

Frank said, "Well. That seems to have worked. I'll call you back." He punched the antenna into the phone. "Mr. Willis, you'd better get those people away from the bridge."

24 / *The Doctor's Dinner*

I SAW THE FLASH and a puff of dense smoke and thought, *Jesus a volcano!* then the sound of an explosion split the air. The crowd screamed. I pulled Jeff aside to keep him from being trampled in the rush to the seawall.

The first screams had barely died when a second earth-cloud bloomed from the mountain, followed by the "ohhh" of the crowd, and another thunderous roar.

People shook their fists at the island.

I got Jeff up on his crutches and moving toward the barricade. No one was looking at us. In my restless pacing I'd seen three or four guys slip over the railing and pop up on the far side of the barricade. Now I hurried Jeff to that spot.

I saw how to get across the gap, how to swing to the opposite ledge—but there was no way Jeff could follow.

A third blast wave rolled through, and a fourth, too well timed to be anything other than man-made explosions. I found it more than strange that someone had chosen to celebrate my arrival by blowing the top off of Isla del Mago.

Jeff peered down at the green water.

"Think you can make it?" I said.

He shook his head.

I waited for him to say "Go on without me," but he didn't. Three guys converged on us out of nowhere. They grabbed us and hustled us off the bridge, shouting, shoving. I shook off their hands and went to join the crowd watching the mountain explode. Jeff crutched along after me.

The blasting went on for long minutes. Each explosion sent a fresh dust cloud boiling up, a thunder peal rolling over the water. People glared at Jeff and me as if we were somehow responsible.

"Who the hell is shooting off bombs?" Jeff said. "My guidebook says this is supposed to be a peaceful country."

"It's dynamite," I said. "They're blasting. These people don't like it. Looks like that driver dropped us off in the middle of a fight."

"Man, I think you're right. When the hell is the next bus out of here?"

"I'm not going anywhere," I said, "except across that bridge." This was a statement of fact, not the kind of bragging I'd been doing so much of lately. I had come too far to think of taking even one step in the other direction. No barricade, no mile-wide stretch of water, could keep me off that island. I was more determined than anyone present. I would sit right here until they got sick of looking at me. Then I would walk across that bridge to find my father.

I sat down cross-legged and leaned on my backpack, to wait.

Jeff said, "I think maybe I can talk to them," and hobbled off toward the blockaders. They were drinking beer, shouting curses at the cloud drifting away from the island.

In place of the cone-shaped summit was a flat, treeless spot. The sun was a dusty red circle sinking past a wall of smoke.

Jeff offered a pack of Marlboros around. Six of the strikers accepted, so then he had to go around with his lighter. When he had them all puffing, he tried telling a joke. Their laughter carried over the street, but it didn't sound friendly to me, more like mockery. Someone asked him a question. Jeff leaned one crutch against the other and bent to take something from his pack—a Polaroid camera. He backed up three paces, waving the guys at the edge closer to the middle. Everyone put on wide toothy smiles. The flash went off. They gathered around to watch the picture develop.

When Jeff got clear of the crowd, he looked down at the spot in the dirt where his backpack had been.

He sputtered and fumed, shouting, waving his arms in the air. A crazy-eyed guy came dancing out in front of him, snapping his picture with an imaginary camera, laughing hee-hee-hee.

Jeff took an off-balance swing and crashed on his side in the dirt.

I ran to him. He pushed me away. "Did you see who robbed me?"

"It happened too fast." It hurt to watch him pull himself up on his crutches.

His face was pale red, like watery tomato juice. "Goddamn idiots! Why are they laughing?" he cried, turning on them. "You think this is funny? You go to *hell!*"

The men smirked and nudged each other.

"Come on, guys," I said, "that's not fair. Give him back his pack."

They glanced at each other, unimpressed.

"Give me back my money and my passport, you *idiots!*" Jeff stormed. *"Idiotas! Idiotas!"*

I wished I had left him on the bridge and scooted on around that barricade. I could have been on the island by now.

"Okay, fellas," I said, "come on, now, somebody here's bound to speak English."

The goofus who did the photo-dance said, "I speaking Eenlish, main! What thee hell? Fock you, main! Hee-hee-hee."

The others thought that was funny.

"You speak English?" I said. "Then tell your buddies to give back his stuff, or we're gonna . . ." What? Call the cops? Send for the U.S. Marines? My threat petered out in midsentence. The local cops were in plain view, fat guys in khaki shirts eating rice and beans off paper plates. "Who's in charge here?" I said, flipping through my phrase book. *"Dónde está el jefe?"*

The men shook their heads, bemused. A young man with thick eyeglasses stepped out of the crowd, the same one who had already denied us permission to cross. "My name Marcos. I speak Eenlish a little. Wha's the prolem?"

Jeff whirled on him and started yelling, which didn't help. I steered the guy to one side. He explained what I'd already gathered: this was a general strike, a total blockade, nobody allowed on or off the island. They were trying to stop a gringo from building something on that mountain.

"That's fine with me," I said, "but you *gotta* let me in. I came all the way from Louisiana on the bus. Do you have any idea how far that is?"

"I sorry," he said. "Nobody pass."

Jeff stood in the intersection, glaring at the blockaders. Every few seconds he would let fly with another round of expletives. The crowd paid less and less attention. Night settled around us like a cloak. A stiff breeze came in from the sea, rustling the palm trees.

"If you let us in," I told Marcos, "I'll come back and help you with your blockade. I promise."

"Sorry," he said. "Tell your friend is no good, speaking loud."

"He's not my friend," I said. "I just met him on the bus. Come on, let me back there—just me, okay? We won't tell anybody. I'll be gone before you know it." This was a betrayal, but what choice did I have?

Marcos clapped his hand on my shoulder, and smiled. "Hey, gringo, go home."

I didn't care for that condescending smile: like the attitude of that pompous old security guard in El Paso, it started a clock ticking in my ear.

I pried his hand off my shoulder. "You listen to me," I said. "You have *no* right to keep me here. My father's out on that island, okay? And he's sick. He's got a heart condition. He needs me. Do you understand what I'm saying? He might be dying. He might be dead already. And if that's—you listen to me!—if I get there and find out that's happened, I'm coming to find *you*."

He began to stammer: "Oh no, is not only me, is all of the peoples of the island, all the peoples working together . . ."

"No." I stared him straight in the eye. "I don't care about them. It's *you* I'm coming to see." I poked my finger in his chest. "That's a promise. Do you understand?"

"Wait." He went off to consult the men at the pickup truck.

I was shaking with righteous anger, terribly afraid of what I had done. If there truly was justice in the universe, I would arrive on the island to find I had killed my father with my preposterous lie. I had summoned up the most unspeakable possibility and put it out as the truth, for my convenience.

What if it came true? What if I got to the island to find he was dead?

Now it would be my fault, for imagining it. All these years I had kept up the dream that he was alive on a mysterious island, waiting for me to come to his rescue. But now, with the island in sight, I had shattered the dream. The first time you truly imagine someone dead, their death becomes a living presence in some corner of your heart. I knew I had done a bad thing, for which I was already sorry.

Marcos returned with Jeff's pack—stripped of all but five bucks and his passport—and told us we would be escorted past the blockade, by special vote of the committee and so on. My story had turned the trick.

I waded through the crowd. Everyone had heard about my ailing father, I could feel it in the nods of the men, the old ladies patting my arm as I passed. Way deep in the callous part of my soul, I was pleased at having deceived them.

"Jim, this is great!" Jeff hustled along on his crutches. "What did you say to them?"

"Just shut up and keep moving." Marcos led us past the barbecue grills, past a pile of children sleeping on rice sacks, a crowd gathered around a radio. Six or seven teenagers lay stretched on the pavement of the bridge, gazing up at the stars.

I shook Marcos's hand. "Marcos, really—I appreciate this."

"Con mucho gusto. I am hope is okay, your father."

"Thanks," I said, hating myself. "I hope so too."

Marcos went back to his friends. I walked to the edge of the gap. In the dark, the water looked to be five hundred feet below us. "Jeff, you're going to have to do this without your crutches."

He said, "Oh, no, no." We studied the leap to be made. I was afraid the blockaders might change their minds. Finally Jeff announced he would rather climb the superstructure spanning that end of the bridge, a route that looked twice as perilous to me as swinging across the gap. Jeff thought it would be easier with his leg.

Handing me the pack and his crutches, he stumped over to the incline, braced his good foot, gripped the beam, and hunched up a few inches at a time, like a rock climber, huffing and swearing. Up he went, all the way to the top of the bridge, pulling himself onto a crossbeam.

After this display of nerve, I had no choice. I hoisted the crutches on one shoulder, slung his pack on my back, and went up after him.

"Sure is high up here. . . ." I held on tight, trying to swallow my fear. From this altitude I could see the gap in the bridge, the blockaders spread out like a carnival through the intersection. People pointed me out to their kids. Straight down was the barbed-wire tangle of the barricade and, below that, dark water.

I forced my eyes up. The steel beam of the superstructure stretched out before me, lengthening, shrinking up slender as a tightrope. I crept on all fours to the beam on the other side. "Okay, Jeff, this was your big idea. Let's do it." With a deep breath for courage, I stood up.

The wind was now gentle, now blowing harder. I held out my arms to the sides and took a step, rocking in place side to side, mentally welding the soles of my shoes to the beam. Another step, arms out, wobbling, and another . . . I reached the first crossbeam and sank down to grab on with both hands.

Jeff inched along on his butt, dangling the bad leg over the side. "I don't know why the hell I'm doing this," he said. "I don't even want to go to this island."

"Hurry up and let's get offa here." Fixing my eyes straight ahead, I willed myself to a standing position. The beam was exactly twice as wide as my foot. I tried imagining an eight-inch stripe painted down the middle of a parking lot. I felt a quiver through my shoes: waves bashing the bridge supports far below.

I held still to let Jeff catch up. In the distance I heard a grumbling of engines, and beyond that a rhythmic sound, indistinct at first, *whumpa-whumpa-whumpa* growing louder as two stars on the eastern horizon grew brighter.

A brilliant column of light shot down from the larger star, casting a circle on the water, and from the second star a second column of light.

The helicopters panned their lights over the water, roaring so low overhead that their hurricane wind threatened to blow us off the bridge. I clung to the beam. They swept over, circling around to hover at the end of the bridge, blasting the crowd with their lights and the deafening wind.

The bridge vibrated underfoot. I turned toward the island and saw forty, maybe fifty men in camouflage, waving guns, pouring across the gap, running for our end of the bridge.

The blockaders scattered like ants from a kicked-over anthill, lawn chairs and umbrellas scudding over the pavement, children wailing for their mothers. A grill toppled, spilling bright fire into the street and sending up a whirlwind of sparks. The helicopters bathed the scene in unnatural light.

Jeff sat paralyzed by this spectacle. My shouts were lost in the awesome noise of the choppers. I decided to abandon him—no, that's wrong; I didn't decide or even think about it, I just went. I raised up and loped along that beam as fast as my hands and feet would carry me. The crutches clanked against my leg. From the crowd of running men I heard a *pop-popping* like firecrackers.

I did not look back until I reached the end of the beam. A herd of soldiers poured onto our end of the bridge, firing into the air.

I yelled for Jeff.

This time he heard me. He set out down the beam, humping along on his butt, six inches at a time.

The first line of camouflage men attacked the bamboo wall with axes and picks.

"Get up, damn it!" I cried. "Get up and run!"

Jeff jerked up the bandage to get his foot on the beam. From forty yards away, I saw his face twist in pain. He raised up on all fours just as the soldiers kicked down the barricade and swarmed off the bridge. Again the *pop! pop!* lights winking from gun barrels as the men charged ahead, shooting their guns straight up, whooping, celebrating. Bullets clanged and whizzed past my ears. I drew myself into the smallest possible ball, wrapping my arms over my head.

I was watching through the space between my elbows when a bullet caught Jeff in the side. He straightened up, flung his arms out. Another one hit him in the leg and knocked him off the bridge.

I died fifty times while Jeff fell through the air to an insignificant splash, far below.

The bridge shuddered under the weight of men running. I held fast to my perch and prayed for them to stop shooting. They charged out into the streets of Gato Negro.

I rode the incline of the beam like a skateboard on the soles of my shoes, landing hard on my hands. Another pack of soldiers came crunching across the bridge toward me.

I scrambled to the rail, shucking Jeff's backpack and crutches. I must have kicked off my shoes, too, although I have no memory of that, nor of climbing the rail and leaping into the water. The next I knew I was fighting up for air, bobbing in waves much larger than they had seemed from above. The water was salty, warm as blood.

And then a blinding light, a furious wind tearing the tops off the waves—a helicopter lowering over us. I thrashed over to Jeff, got his arms around my neck, got his face out of the water.

The chopper stayed right on top of us. It was like trying to swim through a tornado with a dazzling blue sun hovering ten feet overhead. Jeff slipped off my back and rolled over in a dead man's float.

I cradled his chin in the crook of my arm, frantically sidestroking toward shore. At last my feet touched bottom.

It took forever to haul him up onto those rocks. The helicopter turned its light away as if it couldn't bear to watch. In the sudden quiet I heard someone crying, "Don't die, don't die." It was me. It just seemed so unfair. I had robbed this guy twice, and then saved his life, and now he was going to die on me. Black blood pumped from a hole in his side, and another hole in his thigh.

I don't know where the strength came from, maybe it was one of those adrenaline surges you read about, or maybe I was that strong. I got my head under him and lifted his long, limp body on my shoulders, stumbling across boulders to the seawall.

In the middle of the intersection, a ring of camouflage men surrounded the strikers.

"Somebody help me!" I staggered toward them. "Somebody, please!"

They whirled on me, leveling guns—I lived my own death in that instant, the bullets punching through my body, I felt how it would feel to fall and die on this spot—but they did not shoot. Jeff's blood streamed down my chest.

Marcos stepped from their ranks. "There is doctor, a *clínica*—" The guns swiveled to face him. He kept walking.

The soldiers shouted in Spanish but Marcos just kept walking, leading me past the guns and the terrified people and the lines of men fanning out along the bridge approaches.

In my exalted state I believe I could have carried Jeff to Oklahoma, if that's what it took to save him. We passed a cantina, a row of darkened houses. People pressed to their screen doors to watch us.

A white cinder-block building, a painted red cross. We pushed through a crowd of casualties, old ladies with twisted ankles, kids with bloody cuts, a man with his left arm hanging down grotesquely. The people got out of our way when they saw Jeff's blood all over me.

A fat girl in white stood in the door of the little building, furiously chewing gum, her arms folded across her bosom as if to keep the whole world at bay. Somehow the sight of that human rampart just drained the strength out of me. I sank to my knees, rolling Jeff onto the grass.

Marcos went to speak with the girl, and came back. "We wait."

"What do you mean, wait?"

"The doctor have his dinner," he said. "He come soon."

"What?"

He nodded.

"He's eating *dinner*?"

"*Sí* . . ."

"Are you crazy? Go *get* him! This guy is *dying!*"

"Is no good speaking loud," he said. "The doctor come soon." He settled on the grass, and patted Jeff's shoulder.

Jeff stared up, making shallow sounds like a dog panting. . . . I don't know if he saw me. Probably there was nothing I could have done. Probably it was too late even if it had not been the doctor's dinnertime.

I did not want to think about the fact that I told Jeff to get up off his butt and *run!*

I had wanted so much to be like my father: invulnerable. I had set out to find him and prove that I, too, was a man of steel. I thought I could resolve conflicts, save lives, make the world safe for humanity. I even thought I could keep Jeff Wiesenblatt from dying.

I was wrong.

It was not like Granny French, who died all at once. It took Jeff a long time. His eyes turned dull before he stopped breathing. Then he stopped, and I saw once again what death looks like: nothing. The absence of life, and that's all. No living person can hold that still.

The doctor stepped out of the house beside the *clínica,* wiping his mouth with a napkin.

The camouflage men picked me up, one on each side of me, and marched me out of there.

25 / Daisy

You know why I'm here, don't you, Daisy.

Does it have to be now?

I'm afraid so.

I thought we had until the next birthday.

Plans have changed. Circumstances beyond our control.

But that was the agreement, we could stay until the grand opening.

The decision wasn't mine. He can't stand this uncertainty. He wants to move this phase of the project along.

Where is he sending us?

You know I can't tell you. That's why you have to sleep first. So you can wake up in the new place.

I don't like them looking at me. Tell them to go outside.

Hale, Flaco. Espérese afuera.

I'm not ready to go. Why can't he build his damn pyramid somewhere else?

We've had wonderful lives here, Daisy. We should be grateful that we got to stay this long. You know the rules. You know what we agreed to. He has another use for this place now. We have to move on. We always knew this day would come.

When will you bring Ben?

Everyone will come along in a week or so.

Ben can fly, you know. He flies in his sleep.

I heard something about it. How are you feeling?

Sleepy.

That's good. Can I get you anything?

Lipstick.

You don't need it. You're lovely. Maybe you should take the pills now.

I don't want to.

You don't want me to use a needle, do you? Of course not. Wait—there you go. Good. Did you swallow them both?

Yes.

Now lie back and close your eyes, and think of the prettiest sunset you ever saw. That's good. Close your eyes. Relax.

Rabbit?

Yes, Daisy.

Is it really a nice place?

It's beautiful. I've seen pictures. You're going to love it. It's nicer than here.

I feel so sleepy.

That's good. You just go on to sleep. You just step through that door, and I will meet you on the other side.

Rabbit, please turn off the tape recorder.

Just as soon as you're asleep.

26 / Trust the Monkey

THE CICADAS WERE SILENT. The cheep of the crickets sounded meager, uneasy. The island still trembled from the force of the explosions. Restless birds fluttered among the trees. Superman smelled dynamite in the air.

Before he reached the top of the cliff he saw the glow reflected in the palm trees, heard the popping and snapping, the ominous roar. "Oh Jesus, no!"

He scrambled over the top to the spectacle of Spike's little house burning, sheets of bright flame leaping up to the sky. The heat blanched Superman's face like noon sun on the hottest day of the year, and then hotter, and he could go no closer. He smelled gasoline. Burning palm fronds detached themselves and wafted into the air on a column of heat.

Another trapdoor yawned beneath him. He plunged down, descending another level toward an infernal zone. *Christ they will kill us all!*

And then he thought: Daisy.

He did not stay to watch the fire.

He ran down the beach. Two jeeps full of camouflage guys roared past toward La Discoteca.

All the lights in both cabins were on. Gyp did not come bounding out to greet him. Superman stopped on the trail, heaving for air, just short of the pool of light from the yellow cabin.

The scene was too still.

He sprang to the porch, the screen door ajar. He'd yanked out the hook himself. "Daisy?" Her stones lay in heaps on the floor. She had wiped off every last face.

He ran to the pink house, the door standing wide open.

He stepped into the kitchen and found Gyp on her side, her mouth open in a smile, a red corona of brains spattering the floor around her head.

The scene on the sleeping porch was a masterful piece of work, authentic in every detail. Daisy lay facedown across the bed, naked, legs akimbo. Eyes open, staring. Empty pill bottle just out of reach. Fingernails grazing the floor.

Superman sank down beside her. He felt as if his head might explode. Her hand was cool. He wanted to cry but the tears would not come. After a minute or twenty minutes he got up to look for some way to cover her, a sheet or something.

In the center of the kitchen table, he saw a cassette recorder in a brown leather case.

The tape was rewound and ready. Superman pressed PLAY.

You know why I'm here, don't you, Daisy.

Does it have to be now?

I'm afraid so.

Superman sat listening until the tape recorder clicked off.

Then a strange electronic burbling behind him.

A telephone. The handset of a cordless telephone, in plain sight on the bedside table. Daisy didn't have a phone, but there it was. Her killer was calling right now.

Superman slid out the antenna, and pushed a button that said TALK.

"There you are." A familiar voice. "I've been waiting for you."

"Rabbit, you son of a bitch. Why did you do this?"

"Do what, Superman? Shoot the dog? Kill the movie star? It's all in a night's work, my son. Did you get a chance to listen to the tape?"

"Why?"

"She knew why. I'll explain it to you."

"I am coming to fucking *kill* you."

"Oh now, Superman, calm yourself. I don't think you really grasp the particulars of this situation. You're way outnumbered. Why not come up to Frank's and we'll talk? We can work something out. It's all over now. Your little *huelga* is over. Nobody wants to hurt you."

Just then a piece of the door frame flew off and struck Superman's ankle. He stared stupidly at the chunk of wood, thinking, *What in the world?* then it dawned on him. All the lights on. The black night outside. The phone to bring him to the sleeping porch and hold him there.

He dove for the floor.

A line of holes splintered across the wall; *pop! pop!* from outside; the ghost-breath of bullets flying past his head. He crawled on all fours to the kitchen.

He started for the door—*no, wait*—grabbed a teakettle from the stove and flung it out the door ahead of him. Bullets plashed and rang. The kettle skip-bounced off the porch, riddled with holes.

Pressing flat to the wall, he eased his eye past the doorsill, scanning the shadows beyond the fountain.

A shadow shifted right. Superman ducked another burst of gunfire.

He was weaponless, trapped in a house with one door.

Then he remembered the bats.

He wriggled on his belly to the center of the kitchen. In one motion he made the jump shot and slammed his fist against the trapdoor, which flew up clattering into the attic. He fell back, launched himself a second time, seized the rim of the hole, *Don't shoot me don't shoot my legs please,* heaved himself up.

There were no bats. He ran to the end of the house, kicked out the window, and fell back at the sound of gunshots. He ran to the other end and hurled himself through the glass. The roof of the porch collapsed, spilling him in slow motion to the bushes.

In a second he was up and running hard down the path. His life depended on running: he ran. He heard someone thrashing along behind him.

No use running to the beach: no cover there.

There was nowhere to go but up.

He ran straight up the knobby root, catapulted to the first branch, and dragged himself into the crotch of a huge old strangler fig.

Rabbit hurried by, scanning the path with a blunt-nosed submachine gun.

Superman froze. He forced his own cells to merge with the tree. Don't look up, Rabbit. Don't . . . look.

Rabbit trotted underneath. "Oh Suuuuupermaaaan, ally ally oxen free!"

He kept going.

Superman's breath leaked out through his pores. He crawled out the limb, looking for a way down. He'd let weeks go by since his last trip to the waterfall. *This moment* was why he had learned to fly—this chance to save himself—and he'd taken his power so much for granted that he wasn't even prepared to use it.

The sound of Rabbit returning sent him scuttling back to his hiding place.

Not Rabbit. Four or five camouflage men, carrying guns.

I am part of this tree, Superman prayed. If you look up, you will see only a tree.

One of the men glanced up then. Their eyes met—the man's eyes passed over Superman. He jogged off after his friends.

Superman climbed limb to limb, higher and higher. So this is how it ends, he thought. Mountains exploding, houses burning, camouflage men roaming with guns. How stupid I've been with my busy little half-assed *huelga!* You people are professionals. You're *good* at this.

He remembered how he'd shrugged off Frank's warnings. He felt a black gorge rising in his throat: stronger than hatred, more powerful than a ton of dynamite, able to leap cone-shaped mountains in a single bound. Look! Up in the tree! It's . . .

Superman.

He wanted to cry but the tears would not come.

Someone laid a hand on his shoulder.

The shock nearly toppled him from the tree. He gasped and slid sideways, clutching the limb, whirling to face the enemy.

A solemn white-faced monkey regarded him from the next branch up, one hand over its mouth in imitation of his reaction. It made a little mewling sound. Its face was a white mask surrounded by black fur, the eyes glittering an even darker black. The expression was quizzical, pensive. Superman felt sympathy from those eyes—pity, almost.

He had never been this close to a monkey. It smelled like an unwashed dog.

It reached out one small black hand and tapped him lightly on the shoulder—tap!—then shrank back to await his reaction.

He did not move.

"Rrr," said the monkey.

He heard men running both ways on the path, shouting Spanish. He put his lips together and puffed three notes, so soft they would never travel past the monkey's ear: C-A-F!

The monkey blinked, reached out again—tap! tap!—then drew back to scratch at a flea. Its face was ancient, faintly disapproving.

Superman whistled soundlessly: C-A-F!

"Urm?" came the soft meow. The monkey loped a few steps along the branch, and turned. "Mrrn?"

Superman had the distinct impression that he was expected to follow.

More monkeys rustled in the branches below. They had sneaked in to fill the tree with their soft whimpers, the swish of leaves.

One of the running men stopped with a shout: *"Vea! Allá! Allá!"* then the stutter of a gun, a pulse of blinking light. Something tumbled from the tree and hit the ground with a thud.

The tree came alive with shrieking monkeys.

"Car'epicha, maje, 'way puta, tu 'stás matando monos!"

The men laughed and turned their lights on the dead monkey.

"Cállense! Vámonos!" They ran on.

The monkeys screamed and chattered, shaking the tree—all but Superman's monkey, which ran down the branch to him. This time its tap had the weight of impatience. It dashed away three steps, turned back—come *on!*

Superman raised up on his haunches and walked hand over hand down the limb. Another limb curved in from the big sycamore-looking tree across the path. If he'd ever given it any serious thought, he would have been certain that a full-grown man cannot walk through the top of the jungle. There cannot be a roadway of sturdy limbs interlocking in a meandering line forty feet above the ground. But he trusted the monkey. The monkey showed him the way. The other monkeys screeched and fanned out through the trees. Superman's monkey lagged back, cantering only as far as the next limb, waiting for him to catch up.

He shinnied down trunks and inched to the end of teetering branches . . . there was always another branch there, just strong enough to hold him, or a thick vine hanging down like a climbing rope. He passed through a grove of giant old robles with limbs so fat and gently sloping that he was able to rise up and walk without holding on.

A flickering glow ahead—fire in the trees?—no, the dance-floor lights of La Discoteca.

Superman groped for handholds, slowly working his way through a grove of bay trees. The monkey dashed ahead with effortless grace.

From this height, La Discoteca was a sprawl of tin roofs, a flash of colored lights. Everything seemed normal. Couples strolled in from the beach. A table of islanders laughed over bottles of beer. You would never guess there were people dying, houses burning, men with submachine guns running around shooting.

A vision of Daisy flared in his eyes—that most beautiful woman, left to die in such a way.

And his friends, all of them. Dead. Everyone who got up from the table and walked out on Frank's little meeting.

There was evil afoot in this place. He saw the pattern in these random acts of murder, all the way back to Emily. Each death had been designed to round out an individual destiny.

Emily died in a plane crash, as the world had always assumed.

Daisy died facedown on a bed in a bungalow, with an empty pill bottle beside her hand. Spike died smothered in flames.

All of them victims of a joke, an unimaginable act of cruelty—a joke you could understand only if you knew why they were here.

He would find some kind of revenge for them all.

The monkey meowed, and capered away.

Superman had no choice but to follow.

PART THREE

PART THREE

27 / *Like Father, Like Son*

"TELL YOU SOMETHING, brother, this place wasn't always like this, the violence and everything," said the man with the Big Smith overalls and the glittering eyes behind gold-rimmed glasses. "It used to be great. We had all the great ones here—we had Amelia Earhart, son, I mean we had *everybody*. This place was paradise. A place you could come to disappear completely. Then some people decided to make trouble, and it threw everything out of whack."

"You're not listening to me!" I was practically screaming. "They *killed* the guy. Don't you think somebody will care about that? I mean, shouldn't we report it?"

"Report it to . . . ?"

"I don't know, the police, or the embassy or somebody."

"This kid, this Jeff was . . . American?"

"Yeah."

"Oh well, hell, relax. Uncle Sam can handle it. You've attracted enough attention for one night. You want another one of those—what the hell is that, anyway?"

"Tom Collins," I said. "Yeah, why not." I was on a mission to drink every thought of Jeff Wiesenblatt completely out of my mind. I'd ordered the only cocktail with a name I could remember, and it was good: Hawaiian Punch with a splash of lighter fluid. I don't know why Rabbit had rescued me, but I was broke and he was buying, and this was a better ending to the evening than I had imagined just an hour before.

By the time the soldiers marched me across that bridge, Jeff's backpack and crutches had been swept away with every trace of the assault. I walked between two camouflage men, my head high, trying to seem unafraid while scenes from *Midnight Express* flickered through my head. I tried to bribe the men with my Timex; they laughed and steered me to the back of a black

Land Cruiser. They drove me over the mountain to this disco on the beach, where the lights and noise distracted them from whatever fate they had in mind for me. They parked to one side of the dance floor, shouted at me to stay in the car, and went to get beers.

It was hot in the car, but I shivered in my damp jeans and T-shirt, bare feet. At that moment my determination had dwindled to nothing. I was sure that the low point of this journey was still ahead of me. In the back of that car, peering out at the people drinking and dancing, I wished desperately to be anywhere else.

The big man in overalls spotted me and wandered over to the car. "Whatcha sittin' in there by your lonesome, sonny boy? Come join the party!"

"They told me to stay here," I said through the glass. "I think I'm under arrest."

"Naah, don't mind those guys," he said. "Come on out. They're friends of mine, I'll make sure they don't mess with you. Come on, let me buy you a drink."

I resisted at first, thinking, Yeah well it ain't your butt in this sling here, but he kept at it until he coaxed me out of the car.

My captors sat around a concrete soda table, showing their guns to some girls. When they saw me walk by with the big guy they waved, as if we were old friends who hadn't seen each other in a while.

He said his name was Rabbit. He went off on this riff about the Lord and the sins for which I would never be forgiven unless I made some effort to redeem myself. He put on this pseudo-religious act as a way to throw you off guard but he was some kind of scammer; you could smell the scam rising up off him like cologne. It occurred to me that if I poured my drink in the sand every time he glanced the other way, he would keep buying drinks for us both, and when he was good and drunk I might find a way to scam a few bucks off him. I took a couple of sips to allay his suspicions. "Amelia Earhart," I said. "That's amazing."

"You think I'm putting you on," Rabbit said, "but it's the God's truth. If you just sit there and listen to me, I can prove it."

"No, gosh, I believe you—it's just kinda hard to believe, you know?"

He eyed my glass. "Son, you're awful thirsty to be so damn skinny."

I clinked my glass against his, as they do in the movies. "Cheers."

"Good for you," he said, raising two fingers to the bartender. "We need some new blood around here, the locals are all lightweights. Drink up, son, your first night's on me. The ol' newcomer reality shakedown."

"Thanks, Rabbit."

A telephone bleeped. He reached into his pocket and drew out a cord-less handset. "Yeah." He listened a minute. "Well how should I know? That's what they're here for, Frank. Calm down. We won, okay? How far can he get? I'll call you back." He clicked off. "Tell you, son, I hate these things," he said, waving the phone. "Pretty soon they'll implant a microchip in your skull when you're born, and the bastards'll track us wherever we go."

"What kind of work do you do, Rabbit?"

"I'm a scientist," he said, "a freelancer. Actually I'm semiretired; I'm on a project for a client here. I'm doing some interesting work with organic preservation."

Overhead I heard a rustle, an animal passing through the trees. Rabbit said it was probably a monkey. I hurried to the beach to look up, but I couldn't see anything.

My knowledge of the world had widened in my weeks on the road, but nothing had prepared me for the jungly splendor of Isla del Mago. That place has the heaviest air I've ever breathed—it smells green, green and wet and fairly sour, like the stem of a dandelion rubbed between your fingers, like mounds of moist grass in the sun, flavored with flowers and the salty sea. Even at night, with the spine of the island looming dark black, you could smell all the green in the air.

My few sips of liquor had already made me light-headed, but hadn't done anything to wipe the image of Jeff from my mind. Once more I had stared death in the face, and once more I felt implicated. I knew I would probably have to take on a load of guilt about it—if you thought about it in sequence, I was more or less directly responsible for Jeff's death—but mainly I felt very glad to be alive and out of that Land Cruiser. A great curving beach stretched away from my feet. Long lines of white surf top-pled over with a satisfying crash. The night sky was full of moonlight and cottony clouds. I stretched out my arms to the cone-shaped mountains, and turned to the lights of the disco.

Rabbit had set up two shots of a golden liquid, with lemon and salt, on the bar. He kept his steady gray eyes on me while I tossed it down.

The liquor burst and spread through my chest like burning gas. The lemon only made it burn hotter. Chaysus! Mm. I shook my head, *blrlrlrlrl-rlrlr.*

"Here, son, this'll put out the fire." He slid a fresh Tom Collins across the bar.

I gasped for air, a fish with a smile on its face. "Man! What was *that?*"

"You never had tequila? Well hell, this calls for a celebration! Freddy! *Dos más!*"

Rabbit kept drinking and drinking, and it didn't seem to change him, made him perhaps a bit jollier, louder. He was clapping me on the shoulder and telling me how Jimmy Hoffa got a special five-spice flavor into his barbecued chickens. "Secret Chinese ingredient," he said. "Sonofabitch must've brought a ton of that stuff down with him."

"Did you ever hear of a guy called Superman?" I said. "Superman Willis. His real name was Ben."

Rabbit's eyes flashed. "Rock-and-roll singer?"

"Yeah . . ." I straightened.

"I remember, what was it—didn't he die in a plane crash or something?"

"His plane disappeared in 1972. You never saw him around here?"

His brow wrinkled from the effort to recall. "Not that I know of. We've had just about everybody else, though. I assume you've heard of John F. Kennedy."

"I think Superman Willis might have landed his plane on this island," I said.

I couldn't decide if that flash in his eyes meant he knew something, or he was just miffed at having his line of bullshit interrupted. "What's the deal, you a big fan of his?"

"I'm his son."

"No kidding." He looked at me with new interest. "Really. Superman Willis was your father?"

"Yep." I felt pleasantly woozy, and strong.

"So what, you came down here looking for him?"

I nodded. "How long have you been here?"

"Forever. You know, now I think of it, there was a guy came through a while back, claimed to be some kind of musician. I don't remember anything about a plane, though. Where'd you hear that?"

"He sent me a picture of this island."

"Oh yeah, when was that?"

"A couple of years after he disappeared."

"That was what, seven, eight years ago? I was here then. He was a pretty big star, wasn't he?"

"He's a bigger star now," I said. It was true. My father's disappearance had firmly cemented his legend. *Superman's Final Revenge* was the ninth-best-selling album of all time, gaining on Bing Crosby's *White Christmas*. Somewhere in Los Angeles a pile of money was growing.

"So that was your old man, huh? Amazing. You came all the way from—where'd you say? Mississippi?"

"Louisiana."

"You came all this way looking for him? How in hell did you get here?"

"On the bus."

Rabbit whistled. "I bet you're worn out from a trip like that. Let me give you a little spiritual advice, my son. Something to liven up your evening."

"Like what?"

He put out his fist. I opened my hand. He dropped in a shiny yellow pill the size of an aspirin, with a red dot in the middle.

"What is it?"

"Red Dot Forty-Four," he said, "the end product of an intensive twelve-year program of research. The closest you'll get to heaven on earth, at least for tonight. Go on, take it. It's good for you."

Now, my mama didn't raise no fool—she was a bit of a fool herself, but then aren't we supposed to be getting smarter with each generation? I wasn't about to swallow a pill handed to me by a stranger in a Central American disco. "Thanks," I said, tucking it in my shirt pocket. "I'll save it for later."

"You better go on and take it, pretty unstable in this humidity."

"That's okay—I wouldn't mind another drink, though, if you're still buying."

He grinned. "Smart kid," he said, "smarter than—than when I was your age. Never take candy from a stranger. All honesty, though, the stuff's clean, no kickback. You'll have a great time. Ask anyone about ol' Rabbit. I'm one of the good guys."

"Maybe later," I said. "I just got here."

The lights flashed and rolled, the music thumped out again through buzzy speakers, the dance floor came alive with people bobbing and spinning. Two hours before, I was kneeling beside Jeff in the doctor's front yard. Now I stood at the epicenter of a raucous party, staring at the full-scale, life-size mock-up of an airplane mounted in the ceiling behind the bar.

The plane was painted Pepto-Bismol pink. Strings of pineapples and onions dangled from the wheel strut. The shape of the nose resembled a plane I had seen before.

"Be a mortal shame for you to come all this way and go back empty-handed," Rabbit was saying. "Listen, a friend of mine's building a hotel on the mountain, incredible five-star place. A pyramid, of all things. They're always looking for sharp kids like you. You think you'd be interested in a job?"

"Yeah, maybe . . ." I slid down from the bar stool. "I gotta pee. Where's it at?"

"Just go out in the jungle," he said. "Hurry back, son. I think you and I need to talk business."

Around back I found a rickety ladder already leaned against the eave, as if someone was expecting me. I hurried up and tramped across the roof, ankle-deep in palm fronds and rotten coconuts, to the spine of the plane. I swept the trash aside with my foot, clearing a space around the fin-shaped skeleton.

This was no mock-up—this was a real airplane that had broken apart in a crash. Someone had painted the nose section pink, mounted it over the bar, and used panels from the tail to patch a hole in the roof. Rubbing my shoe on the algae scum, I uncovered a block number: 4.

In the throb of the music no one heard my shout, heard me fall to my knees and begin scrubbing in a frenzy with both hands.

494AD.

I hurried down the ladder, trembling with excitement. I went into the bushes and tried to pee, but my hands were too shaky to manage the zipper. Coming back into the light I saw I'd smeared brown algae all over my jeans.

My father was on this island. He had been here, at least. That was his plane.

Rabbit knew that. He was lying. He'd tried to conceal his surprise when I mentioned the name, but he was not a good actor. Probably he knew the whole story. Why would he lie about it? Must have a good reason.

I decided to proceed with caution, play along, stick close but not too close to Rabbit. Find out what in hell was going on here.

"What happened to you?" Rabbit said.

"I slipped. It's muddy back there."

"And you're kinda tipsy, my son. Whatcha say, one more? Aw come on, you still look thirsty to me."

And that's how Rabbit got me thoroughly drunk for the first time in my life. He kept trying to talk me into that pill—"Come on, son, *trust* me!"— but even in my elevated state I knew better than to trust any man who says that. I went out on the dance floor and thrashed around to the Clash "Rock the Casbah," dropped the pill on the floor, and pretended I'd lost it.

Rabbit acted irritated for a minute but got over it. He told stories of the old days, the faded celebrities who came to this island to live out their lives. I told tales of my journey from Opelousas. Rabbit was easy to like. He laughed at everything that was remotely funny. As the party began to wind down, he said I must be a really good kid, coming all this way to look for my dad. Saddest story he'd heard in a while. He knew a place where I could spend the night, free, even have a little shack to myself.

The last part of that evening is unclear. We walked a mile or ten miles down the beach, then straight up a mountain, a slick path through tangly jungle. Twice I had to stop to throw up. We came out in a landscaped clearing, a high pink wall glowing under soft lights. I was drenched with sweat, barely able to stand.

An old Indian man led me to a bamboo hut with a soft bed, white sheets, a real feather pillow. I fell on that bed and slept without dreams.

The next morning was like waking up in heaven. I found my clothes laundered and folded at the end of the bed. A woman with a face like a statue led me to a gazebo on a cliff overlooking the ocean, and brought breakfast on a silver tray.

The channel was swarming with barges, machinery trundling back and forth along the bridge, men scurrying. The assault on the bridge, Jeff's long fall, my whole nightmare journey, seemed miles and years from this peaceful scene.

Rabbit came out cradling a cup of coffee, followed by Frank, the old guy in charge of building the hotel. Frank looked me up and down in a rather personal way, and asked what kind of work I could do. Did I have experience?

Of course I did—I had assembled dozens of airplane models, for one thing, I'd made an A-minus in Chemistry II, and I was stage manager of the Huey P. Long senior production of *All the King's Men*—but I didn't tell him those things. I lied and said I'd worked the front desk of a hotel in New Orleans. That seemed to satisfy him.

"We've had some labor problems," Frank said, "but that's over now. We're working double shifts to get back on schedule. Grand opening is August 24. You're not afraid of hard work, are you?"

"No, sir."

"Excellent. We'll start you on a crew. If you do well, maybe a better job when the hotel is open. You don't have work papers, do you? If you see somebody that looks like immigration, be sure to duck." I would live with the workers on the site, he said. My starting pay would be one hundred dollars a week.

I was used to Granny French's grudging five- or ten-dollar allowances. That sounded like a huge lot of money. "Gosh, what can I say? Thanks."

"Don't tell the others how much we're paying you. If you have any problems, you come talk to me."

These people were deadly serious about their hotel. Within a week of breaking the blockade, they had that bridge finished and open to traffic. Truck convoys roared across all night and day, bringing ever more tons of material.

This was my first time near a construction site, but I was a quick study, and did a great job of sucking up to the foreman. I lit his cigarettes, laughed at his terrible jokes:

Q. What's coyote ugly?

A. A girl so ugly that the next morning you gnaw your arm off to get out of there without waking her up.

Within a week I was supervising my own crew, eight native guys digging trenches and pushing wheelbarrows. All day I stood around telling them what to do in my pidgin Spanish. At the end of the day I ate a huge plate of rice and beans, went to my little tin shack, fell into my hammock with a copy of *501 Spanish Verbs Fully Conjugated,* and slept the sleep of the gainfully employed.

On Saturday nights the whole island turned out at La Discoteca. On Sundays my crew and I took our hangovers to the beach. We played in the waves and hissed at girls walking by—*tsst tstt, chica rica!* Their indifference was lovely.

Slowly I began to fall under the island's spell. Every inch of the beach was alive and in constant motion. Seashells ambled across the sand, propelled by invisible crabs. Sea turtles crawled up at night to lay eggs. There were huge butterflies with electric-blue wings, three kinds of monkeys, ten billion birds that sent up a rippling curtain of song at the first gray of dawn. At noon the sun was a blast furnace, pouring molten light from the sky. At night the sea breeze was sublime.

I never stopped looking for him. Once I thought I saw him in a gang of drunken gringos at La Discoteca, but when I got close it was not him. The man saw me staring. I nodded and kept going. Always I traveled a circuit from the bar to the beach, under the coconut trees, along the back of the dance floor, on around to the bar, never stopping, always looking. The guys on my crew thought I was cruising for girls—they told me to quit looking and just *pick* one.

I never saw him, but I felt his presence. I gathered his story in pieces, one offhand conversation at a time. I was careful whom I asked—the natives, mostly, and only after I had picked up enough Spanish to understand what they told me.

My father crashed his plane on the beach in front of La Discoteca. Badly banged up in the crash. Recuperated in the Big House with Frank and an old lady, La Doña Emilia. In recent years he'd been healthy, and happy, with a taste for the local moonshine and a ready smile everyone seemed to enjoy. He had a girlfriend, a beautiful *gringa* called Daisy. He played guitar, and sang like an angel. Once he performed an impromptu concert that made the whole island fall in love with him.

And then came the trouble, the *huelga*, the end of the *huelga*, and they'd never seen him again.

A lot of people disappeared that night, they said. Troublemakers. Gringos. The woman called Daisy. A burned boy called Spike. A pair of identical twins, lovely girls who were the illegitimate daughters of some American politician. Ronald Reagan? No. Someone else. Richard Nixon? That was it.

All those gringos burned their houses down and disappeared, in one night.

Nobody liked to talk about that night. The islanders were still afraid. Only a few men in camouflage stood guard at the bridge, but they might as well have been a thousand. There was no talk of protests or blockades. The Jungle Inn was a great thing for the island, a *great* thing—they'd always thought so. A few gringos had tried to stir up trouble, but that was over. No sense dredging it up.

Whenever I had one of these conversations, I would turn to find Rabbit a few feet away, pretending not to listen—sometimes Frank's brawny gofer boy Raúl, or one of the other polo-shirt guys from the Big House. They conferred on their cordless phones. I knew they were watching me.

Money flowed onto that island like water from a bottomless well. Enormous prefabricated concrete wall panels came across the channel on barges. The construction site took on an aspect of grandeur, like one of those Cinerama shots in a Cecil B. DeMille movie, the pharaoh's ten thousand slaves building a pyramid, men sweating and struggling against immovable forces as far as the eye can see.

First we leveled that mountain with dynamite. Every morning my crew joined the pick-and-shovel gangs creeping across the section to be blasted. Our job was to hack out cavities for the dynamite. In the afternoon, when the explosives guys finished setting the charges, we would gather on the rim of the crater to watch them blow.

One afternoon we were on the northwest rim, shoving and splashing each other from the spigot while the explosives guys moved about in the pit, making final placements. My crew was trading insults with Juan Carlos's crew. Suddenly Juan Carlos let out a shout and fell down. I was marveling at his overreaction when the wave of scalding air knocked me to my knees. By the time I picked myself up, the site was a cauldron of smoke and premature explosions, men screaming, running for their lives.

Faulty timing switch, the head engineer explained the next day. Circuit breakers must have failed. Linked charges fired off in a string. Maybe static electricity . . . five men dead, thirteen injured. Human error strongly indicated.

For a week, all blasting was suspended. My crew was pulled off pouring concrete to dig five graves. They didn't like that at all. I pitched in with a shovel myself, and we finished the job in silence.

They gave us a raise. The blasting went on.

A freak wind came from nowhere on a clear day and flattened every tin-sided hut in the workers' camp. We spent two days sorting out clothes and belongings, hammering our shacks back together from the pieces we found.

Tools disappeared, or were found strewn through the jungle, tossed into mudholes. An epidemic of flat tires swept the fleet of supply trucks. Ten crates of dynamite disappeared from the shed. A barge sank in mid-channel on a clear, windless night. My crew unloaded a semitrailer with two hundred cartons of what was supposed to be floor tile. I noticed the cartons seemed light; I thanked God for their lightness and didn't say anything, but the foreman pulled up the flap on a carton and found they were all full of white athletic socks.

Odd things, crazy things. An army of spiders invaded the showers. Bulldozers exploded and burned. Clothes vanished from clotheslines. A yellow Jungle Inn jeep rolled off a cliff when no one was looking. A *machetero* went to open a storage shed and was met with a cresting wave of paint, fifty gallons of sky blue pouring over the doorsill.

Shipments arrived with forged purchase orders: three thousand copies of *Good Housekeeping* magazine, eight hundred cases of Maybelline Jungle Red nail polish, a refrigerated truckload of cinnamon rolls.

One morning at breakfast, I tasted something slightly off about the orange juice. By noon the mountaintop was a vista of misery, long lines of pale men knotted up in front of the latrines, awaiting their turn. Those unable to wait fled to the edges of the jungle. I heard some fairly significant muttering among my crew, but when they got to muttering like that I couldn't make out a word.

At last the hole in the ground was as big as we could make it, and we began filling it in. The giant crane swung its head, lofting I beams into place. We stuffed long hollow pipes full of a grayish claylike plastic, something to do with earthquake protection. Cement mixers rumbled all day. Welders ran around touching the corners of the grid with their blinding blue lights. Thirty of us would gang up on a huge concrete panel, lifting and straining a wall into place. In six months we transformed that flat mountaintop into a steel-glass-and-cement pyramid, twelve stories high.

I liked the guys on my crew, and I enjoyed watching the pyramid grow from that hole. It was nice to come home at night and flop in my hammock, knowing I had earned twenty bucks from the sweat of another man's brow. The foreman job was easy. The beach was beautiful. I was on my own, doing fine.

And every day I was coming closer to him.

Sometimes I told myself he was dead, but I never really believed it.

Maybe he'd discovered I was here, and had moved on. After all the energy I had put into missing him, wishing for him, searching for him, it was unsettling to think that he might not have missed me, might not want to be found. In all my years of wondering, that was the one scenario I had never let myself imagine.

He had lived here eight years, getting on with his life as if I never existed, as if my mother and I never meant anything to him at all. He had walked away from us, forgotten us, thrown over his whole life. Okay, maybe we weren't much, but we were his family. What kind of man would do that? I wondered. What kind of idiot son would waste his time searching for a father like that?

Either he was dead, or gone, or else he wanted nothing to do with me. But even if he didn't love me—even if he *hated* me—you would think he could have picked up a phone and made one call. In eight years he had never bothered.

Just as I'd never bothered to call home in the months since I left Opelousas.

That particular thought nagged me all one afternoon. Even the participles of the verb *hacer* (I make, I made, I have been making, I could have been making) would not make the thought go away. I walked to the *teléfono público* at the guardhouse by the bridge and waited while a young girl carried on lengthy love chats with three different boys in succession. By the time I stepped up to the phone I had almost lost my nerve.

Is this what happened to my father? Did he get this far, put his hand on the phone, and lose courage? That wasn't a crime, was it—losing your nerve?

I huddled against the booth, waiting through a series of staticky clicks, a widening hiss, and a string of operators who said "One moment, please." At last I heard the familiar guttery double-ring of the Opelousas exchange.

Way down at the end of that tunnel of sound, I heard my mother's hello.

"International operator with a collect call for anyone from Benjamin, will you accept?"

"Why of *course* I will!"

"Go ahead, please."

"Hi, Mom."

"Benny? My God, is that you?" *Is that you?*

"Yeah, it's me." I heard her voice echoing back, and my own tinny echo: *Yeah, it's me.*

"Jesus, Benny, this is so weird, it's like, telepathic—I was just thinking about you! Where are you? You sound like you're on the moon." *On the moon.*

"I'm in Central America." *America.*

"Central—sweetie, I've been so worried! Why'd you run off like that? I called the police but they wouldn't do anything. It's not considered running away if you're over eighteen." *You're over eighteen.*

"I'm okay," I said, "spending a lot of time on the beach. I've got a job now." *A job now.*

"Where are you? When are you coming home?" *Coming home?*

"I don't know." *I don't know.* "Not yet." *Not yet.* "Look, there's some people waiting to use the phone. I just wanted you to know I'm okay." *I'm okay.*

No one was waiting.

"Wait, don't hang up! Just tell me where you are, sweetie, please?" *Sweetie, please?*

"I'm looking for Daddy." *For Daddy.* "He came here. I'm sure of it now. I haven't found him yet, but I'm getting close." *Close.*

For a moment I thought we'd been disconnected, but then I heard her little cough, and the echo. "Poor Benny, I had no idea you still missed him so much. I miss him too, you know? Every day. I guess I could have paid a little more attention to what was going on with you, huh?" *Huh?*

"Forget it, Mom. I gotta go. I don't know when I'll be back. Just don't worry, okay?" *Okay?*

"Benny, I think this is something we can work on, the two of us—"

She was still talking when I hung up.

28 / Her Real Life

ALEXA TOLD THE OPERATOR she had to know the location of whoever had just called her collect from Central America. Yes of course it's an emergency. The woman tried to give her some line about federal regulations, but Alexa climbed on her broomstick and whizzed a few circles around that woman's head and got put through to a nice supervisor who tapped on her computer and said the call originated from a place called Isla del Mago.

He came here. I'm sure of it now. I haven't found him yet, but I'm getting close.

Alexa wrote the words "Isla del Mago" on a legal pad.

Benny's voice on the phone left her breathless. She had tried so hard not to say the wrong thing, whatever that was, but he hung up on her anyway. Alexa seemed to have this effect on people. She got on their nerves, even the people who loved her. She never meant to do it, but this problem had followed her around all her life. She thought maybe eight years in Casa San Jacinto would have helped, but it only seemed to have gotten worse.

At least she was no longer as crazy. Still irritating, perhaps, but a thousand times less crazy.

When you've been as crazy as Alexa used to be, when you've spent years trying to act normal while dozens of hideous little men are shrieking in your ears, rubbing their nasty fingers on your face, lifting your eyelids to peek in at you trying to sleep—come ON, Alexa, wake UP, it's time to go to the PARTY!—it can come as quite a relief when the mental health professionals finally declare you insane and take you away.

All the stupor-inducing needles in the world will not make the little men any less terrifying or real, but at least, knowing you are in an institution, you can begin to understand that the whole world has not lost its mind—only you, and these people in here. The little jabbering men exist only in your head; they are not out there inflicting themselves on all those normal-looking people walking around. Thinking you're crazy is scary enough, but thinking that you might be the last sane person on earth, and the earth really is infested with these squat little shoulder-sitting creatures no one else seems to notice—now, that is the path down which true madness lies. That is the path that can lead you to the twenty-four-hour Rexall, reaching up among the Wilkinson Swords for a packet of old-fashioned Gillette safety blades.

Alexa would not have tried to kill herself if she'd been able to think of some other way to silence the vile little men. For her earlier self she had a kind of easy regard, a fondness tinged with nostalgia. She would never have done any harm to that earlier person, who was innocent and rather sweet, if sometimes inclined toward unwise decisions. But that person had ceased to exist a while ago.

It might have been easier to look in the yellow pages under "Mental Hospitals," dial the number, and sit quietly waiting until they came to take her away. But Alexa could never have made that call on her own. The illusion of sanity was her last layer of armor, the last thing she could ever surrender.

She put on her nice yellow silk panties with handmade satin-lace trim, and the matching bra. She made sure the house was full of people, the downstairs reeking of Jimbo and his bong-smoking friends. So there was a chance, at least, that someone would find her.

She tried to set a certain mood with candles, and sandalwood incense. A warm bath, a beer, and some pills—blue ones and red ones. Billie Holiday on the stereo.

Among the shampoo bottles at the end of the tub she placed a pair of silver picture frames: Benny's fourth-grade school photo, all cowlicks and freckles, and a snapshot of the happy family teetering on the rim of the Grand Canyon, the year Benny turned four. A friendly tourist snapped the picture for them. Ben's long arms wrapped them all together, keeping them safe from the hazy vastness behind them; three faces pressed cheek to cheek, smiling in the certainty that they will never fall.

The little men hunkered in the soap dish, splashing down from the shower curtain, sliding *wheee!* down the slick end of the tub.

"Now I think I'm just gonna have to say goodbye to all you boys," Alexa said, sinking back in the water. "It's been interesting, but I don't think I can take any more."

A troop of them scrambled for the Gillette packet. Alexa snatched it up and scattered them with one swipe of her arm. They were slippery little devils. They had no substance. You could smack your hand down on one of them, squashing him to nothing, and he would just pop up again somewhere else. More than once Alexa had thought: If you could teach them to behave, these guys would make terrific pets.

But always there were more of them, and their mission was to drive her insane. She was determined to outwit them. She hoped being dead would be better than living like this: more peaceful, anyway.

She scanned Benny's school picture for some sign that he would understand what she was about to do. He grinned: Look at me, Mom! Look at me!

Her husband would never understand—but if Ben Willis had ever paid one moment's attention to anyone but himself, he could have seen that something was wrong with his wife. He would have noticed how distracted she was, trying to carry on normal conversations while the little men yanked her earrings and jibber-jabbered their disgusting nonsense.

She could never quite believe Ben was dead. She loved him so much, wouldn't she have felt *something* when he died? If he was still alive and out there somewhere—if he had run off and left her to slide into chaos by herself—well then, let him suffer. He didn't deserve to know why.

Poor Billie, always down in the mouth. Cheer up, girl.

Alexa slipped a thumbnail under the paper tab, and pulled up. Candlelight glimmered on the edge of the blade. Its symmetrical design made it a pleasant thing to hold between two fingers.

Ignoring the howls of the wicked little men, she made the first incision. The blood eased out along a thin dark line and pooled up in a tear, which went *plop!* in the water and billowed down, an inverted mushroom cloud.

Jimbo found her, saved her, packed her off to Casa San Jacinto. While Alexa was still under sedation he cleaned out the bank accounts and disappeared. She spent the next eight years trying to discover how things ever came to such a pass.

HER REAL LIFE BEGAN the night of October 14, 1959, when the outgoing Opelousas High homecoming queen handed her a bunch of red roses and placed the tiara on her high, lacquered hair. Alexa had spent most of her teenage years feeling homely, gawky, unworthy. She and Betsy Campbell had entered the pageant on a mutual dare, and spent their time mocking the stuck-up girls who were sure to win. Alexa (who was still

Doris French at the time) went grimly through the paces of rehearsal, expecting the worst. Her father had raised her to believe that people who expect the worst are never disappointed. But then sometimes, as she found out, life walks up and hands you a bunch of red roses.

The band played "The Tennessee Waltz." In the high-ceilinged gymnasium, the applause reverberated like the roar of thousands. Alexa wept not from happiness, not from anything as simple as that, but from the knowledge that her father was wrong: people who expect the worst are doomed to get it: life is full of possibilities for beautiful girls, and Alexa had somehow become beautiful. Anne Marie Snodgrass might be a better citizen, Betsy Campbell's grades were as perfect as her teeth, but Alexa was the winner, the official most beautiful girl in the school. She felt wonderful and awful, embracing those poor losers. Her tears of regret were only slightly more authentic than their sobbed congratulations.

On her way out of the gym, Mr. Timmons from the hardware store sidled up. "Honey, did you realize you made the rest of those girls look like barking dogs up there?"

"Oh now," she said, "that's not very nice—I mean, Betsy Campbell—"

"Trust me," he said. "Barking, howling dogs." He offered to sponsor her in the Miss Cottonseed Oil pageant in St. Martinville the following weekend, and that's how Alexa found her calling.

Before she was through she would be Miss Cottonseed Oil, Miss All-Dixie Tractor Pull, Miss Natchez Pilgrimage, Miss Bon Coeur Motor Speedway, Miss Louisiana Farm-Raised Catfish Fillet—thirty-eight local and regional titles in all, every midlevel pageant between Vicksburg and Beaumont—leading up to her triumph in the big auditorium at Lafayette, where she competed three times for the title of Miss Southwest Louisiana against a flock of gorgeous dark-skinned Cajun girls who hated her for her radiant blondness.

Alexa was rarely the most beautiful girl in the pageant, but she had learned to carry herself in a way that seemed to hypnotize judges. She strolled down the stage with her head high, a queen among mortals, imaginary tiara sparkling in her golden hair. She'd learned all the tricks from the pageant magazines: Vaseline to make the teeth sparkle, hot candle wax to strip off unwanted hairs, an underwire bra for extra support in the swimsuit competition.

Her talent was Dramatic Recitation, a poetic monologue she had written from the point of view of a tree. "I see the people passing beneath my spindly branches in the chilly months of winter," it began, "and yet they do not know that I see." The rest of it was just about that bad, but it was mercifully brief, and nobody ever said anything about it. She wore a gauzy costume and performed in a green spotlight, waving her arms like branches in the wind.

At her interview, the judges pitched a slow lob down the middle: "In view of the armed conflicts now going on around the world, what would you do if you could be head of the United Nations for one week?"

Alexa fixed her eye on the judges, mostly old balding fat men, and said, "I would put all the atomic bombs on a rocket, and shoot them into outer space. And then I would declare all-out war on Communism."

And the new Miss Southwest Louisiana is . . . Miss Opelousas, Doris Marie French!

After that, there was no place to go but New Orleans, the Miss Louisiana pageant, the gateway to Atlantic City. In the weeks leading up to that night, trying to starve off a few pounds, Alexa experienced her first hallucination: a vivid waking dream of herself perched on the back of a big red convertible, the queen of all America. That was the first time she remembered wondering if she might be a little bit crazy.

She cast that doubting voice out of her mind: the voice of her father, old Leland "Don't Get Your Hopes Up" French. Watch me, you sour old ghost—I am getting my hopes up, and I am going to win this thing.

Her mother had been mostly indifferent to Alexa's pageant career, but she warmed to the prospect of having Miss Louisiana for a daughter. She spent two months' wages on the glittery blue sheath from Roth's for the evening-gown competition. "Who knows, Doris," she said, "maybe it's time for your ship to come in. You want to look good if it does."

Alexa loved her for that.

Her mother wanted to organize carloads of supporters to come to New Orleans and cheer, but Alexa said it would distract her from the job she was going to do. "You can listen on the radio, Mama. Some of the girls bring cheering sections, but I don't think the judges like it."

"Whatever you say," her mother said. "I would hate to miss seeing you win."

"If I win, you can come to Atlantic City with me."

They grinned at each other, and hugged. That was a happy night.

Alexa's first taste of New Orleans was the noisy hotel in the French Quarter, where drunks roamed the streets and the buildings slumped against each other. She fluffed her bouffant, squeezed into the dotted-swiss dress she'd chosen for the Get Acquainted Reception. The ladies of the Lafayette pageant committee flooded into her room, clucking and fussing until they had redone her makeup and changed her into the gray-check tweed suit with the string of realistic pearls.

The ballroom was a haze of cigarette smoke and perfume, crammed with girls and their pageant committees and a sprinkling of older men whose job seemed to be standing about leering at the contestants. Instantly Alexa identified them as judges, and made a beeline toward them. For the next hour she charmed and chattered and flattered and smiled, moving gracefully from one to the next, simpering, laughing, listening, nodding, pretending to be scandalized, pretending not to be, turning compliments back on their givers. The Lafayette ladies backed off to watch her in action. She was a regal presence, a head taller than any other girl in the room, completely at ease, seemingly oblivious to the effect she was creating. She was perfect.

And then she let her eyes wander up from the shiny head of Mr. Sammy Rubino, who was talking about his chain of Italian restaurants.

A young man was staring at her.

He was the most beautiful man she had ever seen. He was twenty-one, maybe, twenty-two. Just the most gorgeous bright-brown puppy eyes, sending out a wave, a warm defining vibration, so much stronger than any other eyes in the room. Alexa found herself gazing into those eyes, gazing really deep, all the way through to the person inside. The hubbub of the room faded to a pleasant hum. Those eyes sought her out, and he smiled and that smile just went flying into her like the sweetest silver arrow that ever flew from a bow.

She let her gaze fall to the top of Mr. Rubino's head. He was saying something about cheese: only real mozzarella on his pizza pies, you wouldn't believe some of the things people try to pass off as cheese. She said, "That's really interesting," while thinking, My God, who is that beautiful guy. She felt his gaze like a heat lamp on the side of her face. For a long, magnificent moment Alexa forgot who she was, why she was there, everything she'd ever wanted. She fell in love. Just that fast.

He stuck out among the tuxedos in his faded Levi's and flip-flops, his blue ink-stained work shirt. He might have been a hotel employee sent in to fix the air-conditioning, *sure is hot in here.* . . . But no, he was somebody. The ladies of the pageant committees flocked around him, sending forth glissandos of laughter at his witty remarks.

How dare he turn that soul-stroking smile on any other woman? In those first moments of seeing him, even before she knew his name, Alexa felt the first pang of jealousy.

And so it had been ever since.

His name was Ben Willis, they said, up-and-coming folksinger from Alabama, emcee for the pageant's big night. All week the other contestants flirted with him at rehearsals, thinking he might have some influence with the judges. Behind his back they said he was cute, but didn't he have any decent clothes? Alexa kept her thoughts to herself. She tried not to stare at him, but it was like trying not to look at the only candle burning in a darkened room.

At the Friday dress rehearsal the girls were made to sit quietly in the auditorium while Ben Willis ran through his performance for the light crew. He seemed so comfortable up there, so much at home in his own skin, guitar propped on one knee, brushing back his shaggy hair with his thumb, waiting patiently while the technicians fiddled. He strummed a few chords and sang in a voice soft as water:

There's the moment when you see her standing there
All the sunlight in the world is shining down upon her shoulders
And the wind is making music in her hair,
And the world you thought you knew is something better,
    something newer,
She's my candy girl
My true love song
The only one I see
And now I don't know
If it's right or wrong
But she's the one for me.

His eyes sought her out in the opening lines. He sang the song just for her, just the two of them here in this room. Alexa felt herself growing luminous, watching him. Girls on both sides turned to stare at her.

She forced her gaze down to her hands, but then she couldn't help it—she had to look up again. He was still singing to her. The blush overtook her whole body.

Her life had brought her to this place: everything she had worked for, everything she had dreamed, every moment of hoping and striving had led her to her big chance, tonight. And here she was ready to throw it all away and fling herself at this stranger. He knew it. He was doing this on purpose. He knew the power in his eyes, knew she'd never been in love at all, she'd never even believed about love when she read it in books. Her heart was a small cool thing waiting for the first human touch, and God help her, if that man ever touched her she would never stop burning.

His song ended, to wild applause from the girls. Alexa stumbled over their knees, up the aisle, downstairs to the ladies' lounge. She splashed water on her face, and sank trembling to the plush green fainting-couch.

What is happening here, Doris? Get hold of yourself! What would the judges think if they'd seen you run out that way?

She stood to face her reflection: breathless and rumpled, wild-eyed, as if she'd been kissing him instead of just watching him. Upstairs, the recording started up, the shouts of the choreographer, the *clackety-clack* of tap shoes as the girls went to work on the big song-and-dance number, "Saturday Night in Old N'awlins."

You are not in love with anyone, Alexa told the mirror. You are going to be Miss Louisiana.

She put herself together and went back to the rehearsal. Ben Willis was nowhere in sight.

She was in her hotel room surrounded by Lafayette ladies in a last-minute cloud of hairspray when the knock came, a bellboy with a dozen roses, a long box of chocolates, a note: "Be my candy girl?—love ya, Ben W."

That rattled her all over again. This wasn't just a silly one-way crush, a product of her overheated imagination. He knew who she was. He sent roses.

"Would y'all mind giving me just a minute?" she said.

"Honey, are you all right?" said Mrs. Bouchard. "Look at her, doesn't she look kind of pale to you? Doris?"

"Aw, she wants to call her sweetie," said Mrs. DeShields.

"I just need to catch my breath for a minute, okay? It's been such a busy day."

"Of course—girls, come along, let's give her some air."

The door clicked shut. Alexa dialed the front desk, and shortly heard three rings.

He picked up. "Yeah, hello."

"Is this Ben Willis?"

"Yeah."

"Well, this is Doris French."

"Who?"

"Doris French. Miss Southwest Louisiana."

"Oh"—his voice suddenly warm—"right, hi. Hello. God, I'm glad you called."

"Mr. Willis, what are you trying to do to me?"

"What do you mean?"

"Well, here I am trying to win this pageant," she said, "that's the only reason I'm here, just trying as hard as I can, and I can hardly breathe for you staring at me. All week. And today, the way you sang that song and all the girls looking at me, like—like—I don't know what. And now this, these flowers, and the candy . . ."

"Hold on," he tried.

"I don't know why you picked me," she went on, a good head of steam now, "but I wish you would pick on some other girl. This pageant may seem like nothing to you, but it's important to me. I'm not going to let you make me lose."

"Hey, Doris French, would you shut up for one minute?"

The words shocked her to silence.

"First off, I haven't sent you any flowers or candy. Somebody is playing a joke on you."

"Oh, sure," she said, her heart sinking.

"And in the second place, Miss Southwest Louisiana, I wish I had sent you flowers. And candy. And diamonds and a big ol' mink coat. I'm sorry for staring at you, I can't help it. You're the prettiest girl out there. If I was a judge, you'd have already won. You're the most beautiful thing I've ever seen, okay? My confession."

"You didn't send these?" She touched the red velvet petals. "But who would—your name's on the card."

"Sorry," he said. "I'm not the type."

"But you have been staring at me."

"We've been staring at each other, right? This week started out to be a huge drag, but then I saw you."

"Well, it's an awful distraction," she said, clinging to her anger in the face of the warm glow of his voice, the curtain of heat hovering so near she could thrust her hands into it. "I'm sorry if I . . . if you didn't . . ."

"Listen, what are you doing tonight? After the show."

"Well—I don't know," she said. "It depends."

"On whether you win?"

"Oh, I'm gonna win. In spite of you."

"Good for you," he said. "I like your spunk. There's a guy that plays stride piano in a club uptown. Professor Longhair, the best. We could eat oysters and go hear the second set."

"I'll be busy tonight. You just keep your eyes to yourself."

"I can't promise anything," said Ben Willis. "Good luck, Doris. See you there." He hung up.

The Lafayette ladies whisked her into a taxi, a bumpy ride down rain-driven streets, then the backstage buzz of the auditorium, tight-faced girls jostling for space at the mirrors. The illusion of camaraderie that had prevailed all week dissolved in a show of tense nerves and icy courtesies. Girls broke down in tears, stamped off in a fit of temper. Flocks of pageant ladies chattered and got in the way.

Alexa stood off by herself, absently touching her hair, reliving his voice on the phone. His voice curled up inside her and made her all warm.

She took her place in line behind Miss Natchitoches.

"Heard you got roses, Doris," said Miss Ponchatoula.

Miss Natchitoches cracked up, and other girls down the line. They'd all chipped in for the candy and flowers, one of those little jokes contestants play on each other in the spirit of sisterly fun.

Alexa kept the smile on her face, Ha ha ha, look at me I'm Miss Congeniality! Nothing can touch me! I'm going to win!

The curtain went up. The orchestra played. Ben Willis looked uncomfortable in his rented tuxedo, reading jokes off index cards in his hand.

Alexa paraded in swimsuit and heels, glided along in her gown from Roth's, hop-skipped and lip-synched through "Saturday Night in Old N'awlins." She performed her monologue in her gauzy green costume, whirling and swirling in the wind. "The breeze that blows softly and warmly through my branches will carry my leaves away, when autumn begins to fall," she intoned.

Ben was waiting in the wing, a big grin on his face. "You make a great tree," he said. "Did you write that yourself?"

"Don't make fun of me."

"Who's making fun? You were great."

"You look just as silly in a tux, anyway."

"Why, thanks."

She tried to brush past but his hand stopped her—just his fingers, lightly, on her arm. Oh God. The touch she had dreaded. She felt it as a thrill, a mild electric shock. "Please . . ."

"Please what?" His lips, very close to her ear.

Their eyes met—dear God, it was nice from a distance, but up close it was a whole different magnitude of feeling. He dazzled her, that's what he did, he cast a spell on her right there beside the curtain pulleys backstage at the Saenger Theater.

"Please go away," she murmured.

"Let's go together. Right now. You and me."

"Go where?"

"Somewhere close. I really want to kiss you and I don't want to stop."

"And what about tomorrow?"

"I'll kiss you some more."

That was the moment Alexa lost the pageant—she lost it all at once. Everything she had done in her life seemed inconsequential compared to the prospect of kissing this man. She kissed him. She didn't flee with him right then, although that was the strongest of the urges besieging her. As it turned out she'd have been just as well off; she didn't even make the top ten. She wasn't even disappointed until very much later, when she thought back on it. She went off with Ben Willis to a club called Tipitina's. She went off and married him, that's what she did, and things were never quite as fine after that.

She loved him. She never stopped loving him from the moment she first glanced over the head of Sammy Rubino and saw him, as the Beatles said, standing there. As soon as they were married she began to get on his nerves. She didn't mean to do it, but she could feel it happening. She devoted herself to loving him with the same single-minded energy she'd brought to her pageant career. She drove him away with the intensity of her devotion. She tried to turn herself into what she thought he wanted, a fun party girl, the model wife of a rock-and-roll star. She tried to make friends with the guys in the band. She got pregnant and had Benny, and that worked for a while—Ben adored the baby, so he had to spend time with Alexa. But then his career went crazy and Alexa went crazy right along with it.

Deep down, she thought, Ben really did love her, but sometimes he hated her too. It shocked her to find that love and hate could live together in a person like that. Sometimes she could feel the two feelings coming off him simultaneously. She did too many drugs and spent too much time thinking about how she had given up the title of Miss Louisiana for this man who did not even want her around, except as an ornament on his arm at a party. The little men began to whisper in her ear.

She embarked on a campaign to make herself important to him. She even joined the band, knowing she could not sing a lick, because she thought he might stop hating her if somehow she could fit herself into the one thing he truly loved. That led to the worst humiliation of her life, in a studio in Pasadena, and the awful feeling that he had never loved her at all.

She left him, that time, but of course she went back. She couldn't help it. She was addicted. She thought things were getting a little better between them—then Ben disappeared, just went off and left her cold turkey.

Without him, she no longer had any idea who she was. She found herself hating him at the same time she loved him. For the first time she understood how these emotions could live together. The hatred did not diminish the love, only made it stronger and harder to bear. The little men came to sit on her shoulder. Alexa fell to pieces. It took eight long years and a thousand boxes of Little Debbie Snack Cakes to put herself together again.

I haven't found him yet, but I'm getting close.

Maybe she should leave it alone. Much as she hated to admit it, Benny was old enough to take care of himself. Let him try to find his dead father, if that's what he needed to get on with his life. Alexa was making great strides right here in Opelousas. She was actually living on her own, without him—something she never thought she could do.

Late that day, though, her hand found its way to the phone. She dialed up the Globe Trotters Travel Agency, run by Betsy Robicheaux, formerly Campbell. "Betsy," she said. "This is Alexa Willis. Doris French."

"Oh my God, girl, how are you? I heard you came back, I've been thinking about you!" Betsy said. "What can I do for you?"

"I've been thinking about a little vacation," Alexa said.

29 / The Cave

THE MONKEY LED Superman to the big black rock jutting from the cliff above the magic pool. He had floated past this rock fifty times and never noticed the subtle fold in the surface that concealed the entrance to a narrow tunnel. He crawled up into the mountain on his hands and knees. The tunnel opened into a spacious room lit by the blue glow of a spring, the magic water welling up with such force that the surface bulged like a crystalline eye. Luminous water spilled down a chute to the waterfall.

The cave was the perfect place to disappear. In the daytime sunbeams entered through skylight holes in the rocks. There were dozens of small green lizards, well-made jumpy lizards with intelligent heads on slender necks, like wee dinosaurs. Sometimes they hopped on Superman's face while he slept. He never killed one on purpose.

He bathed in the pool and drank deeply of the glowing water. Every evening at dusk he floated up to the purple-flowering *orgullo de la India* tree at the top of the cliff, and went off for his midnight ramble along the treetop highway. He furnished his hideout with things he picked up on his nightly forays: machete, battery-operated lamp, blankets, a pillow, a wine-glass, a plate. He ate whatever he managed to find or steal. He slept on the flat rock, or floating just over the rock. All day he sat at the mouth of the tunnel, listening to the waterfall. On clear nights he prowled the roof of the jungle, looking for some way to satisfy his deep craving.

Revenge. Even the word sounded sweet, much sweeter than "justice." Justice would end with Rabbit and Frank and the Magician going to jail, spending the rest of their lives regretting their crimes. Revenge sounded better—blinding agony, hideous screams, vengeful laughter in the dark.

There was something missing, though, some ultimate point that escaped him. Revenge means paying back those who have done you wrong by doing them a thousand times worse. Revenge cries out for an answer from its victim, a confirmation that he knows why this terrible thing has been done to him. He sees you taking revenge, and in that lies its satisfaction, and its fatal flaw. You are reduced to the level of your oppressor. In taking revenge, you become what you hate.

True revenge would involve something subtler—a random act of God, maybe, lightning striking, a tree falling, or something so beautifully planned and executed that the victim never even knows what hit him.

Before you can gain true revenge, you must first understand your enemy, and there were large gaps in Superman's understanding. In his night of panic after he found Daisy on her bed, he didn't realize that not only Spike and the Twins had disappeared, but also Jimmy Hoffa, Her Highness Anastasia, Michael Rockefeller, D. B. Cooper, the Sherman Brothers . . . Only later, eavesdropping from the trees above La Discoteca, had he learned that the whole collection had vanished, all in one night. Simply ceased to exist. All their houses were burned to the ground.

The war was over. The Magician won. Superman was left to fight on alone.

His eyes filled, but he seemed incapable of giving in to his tears. Sometimes he would remember something tangible about Daisy—the way she licked her lips before a good round of kissing, the way the corners of her eyes crinkled when she smiled—and he'd have to cover his face with his hands.

It was so lonely to be the only one mourning her. To the rest of the world, she'd been dead a long time. They'd known her as a movie star, slightly disturbed; they didn't know what a warm, sexy, half-crazy, deeply beautiful woman she turned out to be. Superman worried that he was doing a poor job of mourning, a shallow and wavering job, these sudden outbursts of dry, choking grief followed by a numbness that dulled him like novocaine.

He mourned the Twins with their identical souls—and oh, Spike. Old poor Spike. His mama burned him to make us all think he was ugly, but we knew it, Spike, we knew how beautiful you were.

Down inside, Superman knew his mourning was as good and deep as anyone's, even without tears. He loved his friends. He would love Daisy forever. He loved her in a way he never loved anyone: wild, fast, intense, without words, without stopping, for so many nights now that he could not imagine his life without her.

Why did she have to die?

Maybe the monkeys had brought him to this place to find an answer.

He was not the man he used to be. The old Superman would have slipped across the channel, jumped the first bus out of Gato Negro, and gotten the hell out of Dodge. But now he could not do that. He had to keep fighting until there was no fight left in him. Until his true revenge was complete, or he died trying to get it.

He made a list:

1. 10 k. roofing nails
2. 20 8-oz. bottles ipecac
3. 40 bottles Visine
4. 100 m #45-gauge copper wire
5. 3 m cotton batting
6. 5 gal gasoline
7. 20 wine bottles (empty)

He set his mind to the problem of assembling these items and hauling them back to the cave without disclosing himself. He had to assume that every human being on the island would turn him in without blinking an eye.

He heard a sound from the mouth of the tunnel, a scrape of shoe leather against rock.

He lunged for the lamp switch—the fluorescent went dark but the red flasher kept flashing. He stuffed it under the blanket and dropped to a crouch, groping for his machete.

Whoever it was had to get on hands and knees to squeeze through the tunnel. That gave Superman about five seconds to get up on the rock and press flat to the wall, inching along the ledge just above the entrance.

A head poked through, someone standing—

Superman raised the machete. He was preparing to bring it down with all possible force when a soft voice said, *"Hola."*

He gasped. She screamed. He dropped the machete with a clatter. She covered her head with both hands. He fumbled for the lamp, flipped the switch, swung the light around to find Catalina shrieking, waving her hands—Don't kill me!

Jesus. He would have, too. One second more and he would have cleaved her skull like a coconut.

The knowledge of what he had almost done tumbled him back with a groan. Catalina was weeping, down on her knees collecting the cans spilled from her basket.

"*Lo siento,*" he said, "*lo siento, Catalina, 'sculpe, 'sculpe, una gran sorpresa.*" I'm sorry. I'm sorry. A big surprise. He didn't know how to say "You scared the shit out of me."

It took a while for her to stop crying and Superman's heart to quit hammering. She crept over to show him what she'd brought: sardines, tuna, olives, crackers, brown bread, rice and beans, tortillas, lemon cookies.

"How'd you know I was here?"

"*Perdón?*"

"How *sabe usted* that *yo* is *aquí?*"

"*Los monos me lo dijeron,*" she said. The monkeys told me.

He would either have to trust her or find a new place to hide. He was not disposed to trust anyone. Catalina had never had a nice word for him, why should she want to help now? This might be a trap.

He tightened his grip on the machete. "Who sent you here?"

"*Cómo?*"

"Who . . . sent . . . you . . . *aquí.*"

"*Los monos, como te dije,*" she said, irritated at having to repeat herself.

"I don't believe you," he said. "*No te creo.* You're working for the Magician, aren't you—I know what you're up to! You get out of here now before I . . ." He waved the big blade at her.

She shook her head in disgust. "*Qué idiota más tonto. Baja eso!*" You stupid idiot—put that thing down! She snatched the machete from his hand, tossed it *clang!* to the rocks at his feet. "*Estoy aquí para ayudarte, hijo de puta!*" she cried—I'm here to help you, son of a bitch! She lit into a hand-waving tirade in which the word *idiota* was a prominent feature. Superman stepped back, and back, until she had him up against the wall of the cave with her finger wagging in his face.

He had to trust her, at least long enough to get her out of here. He dodged her finger and started in again with the *lo siento*s.

"*Escuche,*" she said. Listen. She spoke slowly, in the patronizing over-pronounced Spanish she might use to address a dim-witted person. You are important, she said. The monkeys say you are important. I don't know why they would choose an *idiota más tonto* to deliver us from these *gringos horribles,* you're no more than a *gringo horrible* yourself, but you are the one. The chosen. *El elegido.* The monkeys knew when you came. They told us to save you. To keep you here. Why do you think we fed you and bathed you and cooked for you? Because we like you? No. We hate you. Because we are your slaves? No. In our hearts we are free people. It's because the monkeys chose you.

The frankness of this outburst caught him off guard. Of course he'd known Catalina hated him, but she'd never said it to his face.

"*Ahora viene la guerra,*" she said. Now comes the war.

"I thought it was over," he said. "I thought we lost."

Catalina rolled her eyes heavenward. Are you a fool? Don't you see what they're building right over your head? While you sit here, doing nothing! It's why we saved you. Don't you remember the questions you asked, that night at La Discoteca? I ask you the same—are you going to just sit here and let them kill this island? "*Papi dice que's el diablo,*" she said. "*Él dice que están construyendo una casa para el diablo.*" Papi says they're building a house for the devil. "*Es la profecía,*" she said.

"*Profecía.* What *profecía?*"

Pito learned it from his *abuelo,* his grandfather, who learned it from his own *abuelo. Cuando a la gente no le sirva el mono, al mono no le servirá la gente.* When the man has no use for the monkey, the monkey will have no use for the man.

Superman made a skeptical sound. "You want to help me? That's why you're here?"

She nodded.

He rummaged through the blankets for his list. "Get me these things. Leave 'em someplace where I can get at 'em—the big tree with yellow flowers, by the pool there? There's a big rock behind it. Do you know which one I mean?"

"*Sí, no soy estúpida.*" She folded the list, glanced up with a glimmer in her eyes—wait! What was that? Could it be? An actual glint of affection from Catalina, the Heart of Stone?

"You help?" she said suddenly, a stunning burst of English. "You help *mi Papi?*"

"Yes," he said. "I'll help your Papi. I'm glad to know he's still in the fight. I don't know what we can do. Maybe we can fuck 'em up somehow."

The wall of stone melted. Catalina rushed forward with her arms out— a hasty embrace, lips brushing his cheek—then pulled back with her eyes demurely down, as if they'd engaged in a passionate kiss.

"Ah-ha! We're not all the same, are we, Catalina. We're not all *idiotas más tontos.* Some of us are okay. Come on. Admit it. You like me."

She grimaced. "*Tú eres el hombre más feo del sistema solar,*" she said. You are the ugliest man in the solar system.

He laughed. "Oh, yeah? Come on—give us a kiss." He pooched out his lips and made kissy sounds.

Catalina said "Poof!" as if she'd never encountered such witlessness. But he knew the truth now. He followed her to the mouth of the tunnel, reached out to pat her hand. "*Gracias,* Catalina."

"*Con mucho gusto,*" she said. "*Bang.*"

And they became friends, at long last.

Catalina kept him well fed while he learned to move along the treetop highway as swiftly and quietly as any tree-dwelling creature. A quarter moon lit the path around the fringes of the mountain to a giant mango tree, the closest vestige of jungle to the construction site.

If it is spectacular to flatten a mountain and build a twelve-story pyramid, the Jungle Inn was a spectacular thing. It was immense, and what was more amazing, it was *there.* The top of a mountain is a very large thing to replace. God and nature and magic are mighty and inscrutable forces, and look how easily they'd been defeated by four hundred workers with dynamite and earth-moving machines! In one day, between sunrise and sunset, those men cut a swath wide as a football field down the side of the mountain, just to clear out a view. They piled up the trees, sprayed the piles with diesel fuel, and set them on fire. The trees smoldered for days.

Superman saw one or two things he could do.

He started with small actions, psychological warfare against the workers. Summer-camp stuff: swiping clothes from the line, spiking the water supply with ipecac one day, Visine the next. (Ipecac for the dry heaves, Visine for the squirts.) He seeded the road with roofing nails. He sneaked up on a yellow jeep, leaned into the bumper, and rolled it off a cliff. He strung wire between trees to unhorse the *motociclista* message carriers zipping uphill to the hotel.

Catalina brought a stack of Jungle Inn purchase orders. He had fun filling them out, and she mailed them off for him.

He did not intend to hurt anybody. His idea was to harass them into giving up and going away.

Anyone glancing up could see him rambling along in the starlight, under the brilliant moon. He was amazed to discover how rarely people look up. They walk around with their heads down all the time. They never glance up unless they think something is about to fall on them.

Superman remembered when he was that way. Now he was sensitive to the darkness, supertuned to the slightest sound. Now he saw how many of the hanging branches were snakes.

The next night, floating around the coconut gap above La Discoteca, he noticed a yellow jeep parked at an angle. He saw the camouflage guy slouched at a table, his back to the jeep, wrapped in conversation with one of the party girls *de la playa*. In two minutes the girl was on her way to a night in the arms of the law, and Superman was the proud owner of a bolt-action rifle with telescopic sight and a full ammo belt.

He didn't intend to kill anybody, but he was not about to pass up a chance to defend himself.

He sighted through the scope of the rifle, plotting a night's activities from the safe remove of the mango tree. He learned to blow a transformer with one rifle shot. Yellow trucks came every morning to repair the damage, but by then he'd be back in his cave, dreaming of a really big bomb.

The men kept building. Nothing stopped them, or even slowed them down much. The island did its best to resist the pyramid, as it had tried to shrug off the bridge. Superman saw the hand of God, or nature, or Pito, in the big wind that came from a clear sky and scattered the workers' shacks. The freak chain reaction that killed five men on the dynamite crew. The plagues of spiders and ants and stinging wasps, the near hurricane that blew through in May, flattening all the royal palms, shattering every window on the western face of the building.

But the Magician's force was greater. Every evening at sunset when Superman floated up to the *orgullo de la India* to begin his night's prowl, the first thing he saw was that great unnatural monument squatting above him on the mountain. From this distance, in the last moments of daylight when the sun posed at the apex, the Jungle Inn actually looked rather impressive.

Scary thought. Superman shook it off. That thing was the physical representation of a man with too much money and a monumental opinion of himself.

He heard voices near the site where the dance floor had been torn up for the spa. He crept around the mango, pushed off, and set sail for a wide-limbed roble. His silent landings were improving. He worked his way around the tree until he was looking right down on them.

"I don't know why you blame us," Frank was saying. "We've done everything just the way you instructed." He sat with his hands on his knees, tensely regarding the speaker box on the table.

Rabbit stretched his feet as if he hadn't a care. "He blames you because you're in charge, Frank. God knows why he blames me. I'm just doing my job."

"I blame the whole miserable lot of you," said a tinny voice from the box. "I've never seen anything go to hell quite this fast. Who's in charge down there? Is anyone in charge?"

"I'm in charge of my department," said Rabbit. "We're ahead of schedule. You're gonna be happy with what you see."

"Frank?"

"We're two days off schedule, and we've already made up three days this month. We'll be ready. Everything's under control."

"Then why have I got the goddamn U.S. ambassador on the phone telling me about riots out there?" A deep, rotund voice, the hint of a drawl.

"There were no riots," said Rabbit. "There was a strike months ago, and we broke it as per your instructions. Minimal casualties. We've got no trouble now. The construction looks great, you're going to be impressed."

"It makes me uncomfortable when people tell me how impressed I'm going to be."

"Come see for yourself, then," said Frank. "Rabbit's right, it looks terrific."

"What about all this sabotage? You've got a twenty-million-dollar project held up by one guy, this crazy singer out roaming around in the woods with a gun?"

"He's not holding us up," said Frank, "and he isn't alone. He has help."

"Who's helping him? I thought everyone else was accounted for, Rabbit, didn't you say that?"

"We got 'em all, a clean sweep. I've got the list if you want to see it. We don't know who's with him, probably a native or two. He's pretty good at keeping himself hid."

"What are you doing to find him?"

"We're making regular sweeps," Frank said. "Everyone's keeping an eye out."

Superman smiled, on his high branch.

"We'll round them up," Frank went on. "Right now I'm frankly more concerned about the menu for opening night." Good old Frank.

"I don't want them rounded up," said the box. "I want them eliminated. No more delays. I've made plans for that night and I will not have interference, do you hear me?"

"Loud and clear," Rabbit said. "This connection is amazing. Where are you, anyway?"

"Goddamn it! Don't make me come down there and straighten this out!"

"Try not to worry so much," Rabbit said. "It's not good for your health."

"Who said that?" the box demanded. "Frank, was that you?"

"It was Rabbit," said Frank.

"What I meant," Rabbit said, "is you're getting all worked up over nothing. Frank's right. Everything's under control."

"Brother Rabbit," the box said, "instead of worrying about my health you might look to your own. You might find it in danger with that mouth as big as all outdoors."

"I will take your advice, sir."

"And Frank, cowering in the corner."

"I'm here," Frank said, trying not to cower.

"Find this man and finish it."

"We'll flush him out," Frank said. "I've got something he wants. He doesn't even know I have it. Kind of an ace up my sleeve."

"Don't get fancy, Frank. Do as I say. I'll call back tomorrow, same time." The box clicked.

"Well, that wasn't so bad," Frank said.

"Oh, no," said Rabbit. "He's royally pissed."

"You didn't help with that 'try not to worry so much.' What was that? Are you out of your mind?"

"I was trying to make him laugh. Sometimes it works."

"It didn't work."

"Find heem, Frank," Rabbit said in a Peter Lorre voice. "Find heem, and feenish eet."

Superman was dying to know what particular ace Frank might have up his sleeve, but rather than press his luck he floated out of the roble and made his way back to the cave.

The rifle improved his method for destroying heavy machinery. The main idea was to keep ground time to a minimum—get out of the tree, do the setup, and get the hell back in the tree before the big noise brought people running. He placed a bottle of gasoline on the ground beside the dozer tread, ran a twist of gas-soaked muslin up to the fuel tank, and sprang back up to his tree. One clean shot burst the bottle, set a spark off the gravel, and blew the whole thing to smithereens while he made a leisurely escape.

But always there came another bulldozer, another dump truck, another convoy of workers. Superman was a gnat biting at the hide of a great unstoppable beast. His desperation grew in tandem with his confidence.

He began taking chances.

One night he decided to blow two backhoes at once. He placed his Molotov cocktails and had just inserted the fuses when he heard voices. He melted into the ground, swallowing the urge to breathe. The footsteps crunched closer. He molded himself into the tread of the backhoe. The camouflage men walked right by him. One of them actually lifted a foot to step over the bottle—and kept walking, oblivious.

Superman fled up the tree, squeezed off two shots and watched both backhoes go BOOM! The men came running back, shouting. If they heard anything over the explosions, it would have sounded like triumphant laughter, high in the trees.

Superman shouldered his rifle and kept climbing, planning hoping trying and sometimes succeeding, but mostly making very little difference.

For months he had clung to nonviolence like a good civil rights–loving liberal, but his heart was growing harder. Catalina was right: these people were killing the island. When would it be time to start killing the people? In the lonely afternoons he paced circles in the cave, trying to think of some way to win. He thought of Robert E. Lee at Petersburg, the last winter of the war: outnumbered, surrounded, clinging desperately to a hopeless cause in the face of a vastly superior foe. His only hope was a bold stroke in some unexpected direction—one brilliant all-out offensive thrust, throwing everything in, a fight to the finish.

Of course Lee tried that, and wound up at Appomattox. Probably he should have surrendered that winter, and saved himself a terrible spring.

Superman couldn't quit while he still had a chance. It simply wasn't in his nature. He lusted, he thirsted, he needed revenge.

Truly, he thought, it was the strongest emotion. Stronger than love, or thirst, or desire, stronger even than ambition, which had always served as the divine spark in Superman's soul. When someone hurts someone you love, you cannot sleep until you have tasted the suffering of that man.

At dawn he was back in the mango tree, reviewing the actions of a busy night: another jeep over the cliff, three transformers blown, fourteen tires slashed. He had done his best, but morning revealed business as usual, new tires for the jeeps, new transformers for the poles. The Jungle Inn was complete, except for a million details. Even from a distance he could feel the grand-opening buzz in the air. Foremen ran around trailing herds of painters and carpenters. Gangs of workers planted palms, unrolled sod, poured last-minute sidewalks. Waiters practiced their tray-handling maneuvers on the tennis court. Red polo shirts buzzed around in yellow jeeps, dispensing advice.

Here it was, the realization of the Magician's dream: a great pyramid soaring into the sky, crowned by a silvery tip. A pyramid from Disneyland. It was breathtaking in its scale, its haughty massive disregard for its surroundings. A flag flapped crisply on a pole near the entrance: white letters JUNGLE INN on a field of navy blue.

I will own that flag, Superman vowed. I will take that flag down from its pole.

He raised the rifle, scanning the windows of the south wing—a girl on a ladder hanging curtains, a boy drawing a squeegee down the window, a large woman laughing, leaning out, calling to a man in the garden below.

He drew a bead on the laughing woman, panned down to the man, centering the crosshairs on his skull. Bang, you're dead.

Some movement caught his eye—he swung the rifle and by glory if he wasn't looking at Mr. Frank Napier, general manager of the Jungle Inn, leading a herd of polo shirts to the swimming pool.

Well. Hello, Frank.

Superman could end it right here, right now. Just squeeze the trigger and put an end to Frank. Instant death. Boom. That would qualify as justice. But was it revenge?

No. Frank wouldn't suffer. He would never know what hit him. He waved his arm, sharing his wisdom with his young colleagues, who formed a line and stood listening with their hands behind their backs.

Superman shifted his aim to the right, the young man opposite Frank. The back of his head filled the scope. Streaky blond hair, longish.

That would ruin Frank's day. If he saw one of his young employees' heads blown apart, right in front of him.

That would be some revenge.

Superman put his finger on the trigger.

He could kill. He could do it.

The target shifted—he found it again and centered it, bracing his arm against the limb to steady his aim.

One pull of the trigger. Boom. Take that, Frank.

The target moved, stepping back, turning—oh no. His face. There was his young honest open American face. His smile melted Superman's heart, at two hundred yards.

Superman lowered the rifle.

His hands were shaking. He leaned his head against the tree.

He could have done it. He could have killed the boy. The Jungle Inn was a bad thing, an unforgivable crime against nature, but there was not one thing about it that scared Superman as much as the knowledge that it had almost turned him into a killer.

30 / The Last-Minute Rush

FRANK WAS A NERVOUS WRECK. He hated the landscaping at the pool—wanted all those expensive roses yanked up and replaced with "something beautiful, something tropical," he said. "For God's sake, this is not Pasadena." The color of the retaining wall leading up to the helicopter pad, he said, looked like something that might have come out of a baby. Anything wrong with forest green, as called for in the plans? He even hated the clever signs the sign painter had posted everywhere, cutout metal frogs with cartoon balloons, croaking directions to pool, spa, clubhouse, lobby. "What is this, the Frog Inn?" he complained. "Who ordered these signs? They're ridiculous. Get rid of them."

He marched back and forth waving his arm. In his haste to come down and throw his weight around, Frank had left his house wearing pink puff slippers with rabbit ears and rolly eyes. When I saw my boss glance down at those shocking-pink feet, I had to turn around and smile the other way.

My boss nodded yes, of course Frank, right away Frank, whatever you say. I saw the blood simmering behind his eyes—we were in a desperate race, thirty-six hours before a chartered cruise ship full of invited guests would arrive for the grand opening, and here was the Big Boss telling us to undo everything we'd spent the last two days doing. Frank didn't often interfere, generally he was a kind of figurehead who went around nodding and smiling, and left the complaining to the people under him. But now he was pissed off, live and in person, and you never saw a bunch of subbosses get down and grovel with more gusto.

They sent us running in all directions to carry out orders. For a month I'd been working inside the hotel in a red polo shirt, preparing to become a front-desk assistant night manager. The red shirt with the Jungle Inn logo was much envied among the boys of my former crew; it marked you out as a house servant, as opposed to a field hand. In the last-minute rush, though, even us polo-shirt types had been pressed into service painting walls, unloading trucks, hauling crates of food to the restaurant freezers. My boss sent me with a hand truck to find forest green paint.

Down the ramp I went, into the gloomy basement, stacked floor to ceiling with boxes of sheets, towels, soap, kitchen supplies, barrels of cleaning solvent. I was amazed by the sheer quantities of *stuff* that went into a hotel, and then there was one whole wall of the stuff no one had ordered: ball bearings, toasters, teething rings, antibiotics.

The paint room was all out of forest green, but the guy said I might find some in the utility room on seven. The freight elevator was occupied, and the guest elevators with their expensive purple-mahogany paneling were off-limits to hand trucks. Tucked away at the side of the elevator core was a private express elevator to the eighth floor, the first level of the Presidential Suite. Usually a guard stood by this door—the penthouse was a restricted area—but today no one was around. I decided to ride up to eight and bang the cart down one flight to seven, by which time the freight elevator should be free.

For such an imposing structure, the Jungle Inn wasn't all that huge inside—the ballroom and public spaces occupied the lower levels, and of course the floors get radically smaller the higher you go in a pyramid. There were only fourteen suites in the whole place. The least expensive was three thousand dollars a night. I found it impossible to believe there were fourteen people in the whole world who could get a good night's sleep at these prices, but the rooms were incredible split-level suites with built-in streams and waterfalls and slide-away walls, rare birds in cages, priceless paintings, closed-circuit TVs that rose up from the floor, massive Egyptian-style furniture, sweeping views of the sea. Each suite would have its own staff of servants.

I rolled the cart into empty silence, the eighth floor. I'd imagined a more lavish version of the suites on the lower floors, not this stark white emptiness. No furniture, no interior walls, just a white shiny floor, and something I'd never seen: a spiral escalator.

If it had been a normal staircase, I might not have felt compelled to abandon my hand truck and investigate. I had to have a look at the ingenious mechanism, which seemed to operate on the principle of a screw. I stepped on. The whole spiral revolved, lifting me up as it turned.

I stepped off in a white room with one door, a mural of the Sphinx buried up to its neck in sand. I tried the knob. The door was open. It led to a hallway, which led to another hallway and switched back on itself, branching, forking. A maze. I wished for a bag of crumbs so I could leave a trail.

I followed three or four blind alleys before I came to a door sheathed in sandstone, elaborately carved with hieroglyphs. I pressed my hand against it.

The walls and ceiling in the little chamber began to pulse with red light.

This place was spooky. I was not supposed to be here. I fled back through the maze to the escalator. The spiral reversed direction and carried me down. What kind of place was this, where the escalator knows which way you want to go, where you follow a maze to get in, where you touch a door and the walls start blinking?

The elevator door slid open. "Ah, wouldn't you know," Frank said, "young master Willis is exploring! Just the fellow I've been looking for."

I was surprised he remembered my name. We hadn't spoken since the day he hired me. "I was trying to find forest green paint."

"Of course you were. How'd you get past the guard?"

"There wasn't one."

"So you thought you'd come up and have a look around? You knew this area is restricted?"

"Well, yes sir—I was on my way down. . . ."

He took my arm, steering me into the white empty room. "I wouldn't hear of it. This gives us a chance to catch up. How's the job going, Mr. Willis Junior? Are we treating you right?"

"Sure." I thought about it and added "sir," thought some more and said, "Thanks for asking."

"I hear you're doing a fine job. Don't think we're not paying attention. We've been keeping a close eye on you. Perhaps you've noticed."

"No, sir," I lied.

"Young fellow like you will always have plenty of opportunities. We're impressed with your focus, your drive, your ability to get along with the men on your crew."

"Just trying to earn my pay," I said, "sir."

"No, no. Real dedication. Positive attitude. We've kept up."

This was not the spluttering general who'd been raging at us a few minutes before. He had managed to swap his pink bunnies for huarache sandals. We stood at the glass wall, the whole island spread out at our feet. "How long do you plan to be with us, Mr. Willis?"

"As long as you want me, I guess." *As long as it takes to find him. I'm close now. I feel him sometimes, watching me. I turn around—nobody there.*

"Rabbit tells me you came here to look for your father."

My stomach clenched like a fist. "Do you know where he is?"

"I haven't seen him in months," Frank said. "But he's here."

A shiver ran through me—he's here! He's alive!

"If you'd seen him," Frank said, "would you tell me?"

"The minute I see him, we're on our way home."

"What makes you so sure?" Frank said. "He's been here for years. Nobody stopped him from leaving."

"Then where is he?"

"Well now, *that's* the sixty-four-thousand-dollar question! I think he's very close by, but I'm not about to chase through the jungle to find him. There's no gentle way to put this, son—your father has gone *off*. How well do you know him?"

That was a good question. "He's my father," I said.

"Did you ever know him to hurt anybody?"

"Of course not."

"You probably know we had some local resistance to this project. Your father was an instigator. Things didn't go his way. He snapped. He turned dangerous. He's even killed people."

The only killing I'd seen was Jeff Wiesenblatt shot off a bridge by an army of camouflage men. "I don't believe you. Who did he kill?"

"His comrades-in-arms. His dear friends. He swayed them at first, until they realized what a stupid game he was playing. They came over to our side. So he killed them. It was so sudden. We were all friends before that . . . he was happy here. He always said he . . ."

"What?"

"He was glad to get away from his obligations."

Out of everything Frank had said, that sounded the most likely to be true.

"We know he's got a gun, he's behind all this vandalism," Frank went on, "but he's not alone. He can't possibly be in all these places at once. Are you sure he hasn't tried to contact you?"

"You've been spying on me. You know he hasn't."

"It does seem odd, though. Doesn't he like you?"

"He doesn't know I'm here."

From the way his eyes lit up, I thought maybe I shouldn't have said that.

"Doesn't know? But Rabbit said he sent for you."

"He sent me a picture of the island. A long time ago . . . in a bottle. He didn't know I ever got it."

Frank said, "Don't you think he'd want to see you?"

"Well—sure. That's why I'm looking for him."

"Why didn't you talk to me? We could have looked together. I told you the door was always open."

"Rabbit lied to me from the start," I protested. "He said my father never even came to this island. I thought you knew where he was and you didn't want me to find him."

"So who's been spying on whom?"

"I'm not—I didn't—"

"You've been upstairs already? What did you see?"

"Look, why don't I just take off," I said, edging around him. "It's been great working here."

"Don't be silly, you can't leave now! The party's tomorrow night. We're all going to have fun. We've earned it, we've worked hard. Come along—there's something you need to see."

He steered me up the escalator. Ignoring the door to the maze, he inserted a needlelike key into the Sphinx's right eye. The side wall slid away to reveal a freight elevator hung with gray quilted pads.

I'd helped build this hotel, and I'd never known of any elevators other than those in the central core. There were whole sections of the building I hadn't seen since the girders were laid and those parts walled off. Frank held the door. "After you."

"I really oughta find that paint," I tried.

"It can wait." He took my arm and marched me into the elevator. Short of knocking him down and running, there was nothing I could do. The car jerked, and began to descend. I heard faint Muzak, the same Rodgers and Hammerstein loop that played throughout the public spaces.

"We think your father will probably try to crash our party tomorrow," Frank said. "He won't be able to resist the temptation. Nobody wants to hurt him, but we can't let him go on disrupting things. Now we have bait for the trap."

"What trap?"

The doors slid open. "After you, Willis Junior."

I stepped out.

Frank stayed in. The elevator slid shut.

I was trapped in a small chamber with one door and cinder-block walls. The door had no knob, just a square window latticed with steel wire.

An electric *clack!* followed by a pneumatic *pfssssh!* The door swung open.

I stepped into a dark, cool room full of machines. Creedence Clearwater Revival blasted from hidden speakers, "Bad Moon on the Rise." This was some kind of laboratory with the lights down low: shiny white tile, racks of twinkling machines, parallel rows of bullet-shaped capsules topped with oval glass domes, computer monitors glowing soft green. Two men sat watching a bank of tiny TV screens, flickering scenes from cameras hidden all over the grounds of the Jungle Inn. One monitor showed a freeze-frame of me pressing my hand against the carved sandstone door.

Through the smoked glass I saw the next room, four figures in green surgical masks hovering over one of the steel capsules. The glass dome stood open on a hinge.

I recognized the bushy beard and gold-rimmed glasses. Rabbit saw me, and waved. "Be with you in a minute. Don't touch anything."

I had the vague sense that I was here against my will, but I didn't want to press the point, in case I was wrong and he let me go with a lecture on unauthorized snooping. I wandered over to the row of capsules—sleek, streamlined, machined from stainless steel, about six feet long, a cross between an Airstream trailer and an iron lung. They were empty, I thought, until I saw lights blinking on the one at the end, and found myself gazing down through glass at a nice-looking woman with blond hair and a pug nose that blunted her prettiness. A red sweater, a short white skirt, bare feet, cherry-red toenails. She appeared to be sleeping. Her hands were folded in the classic pose.

> *Don't go a-round to-night*
> *Well, it's bound to take your life*

I pressed my hand to the glass. I stared at that woman, willing her to breathe. She did not breathe. She was dead. How could it be? She looked so alive—her skin dewy and fresh, her face relaxed in a subtle smile. I'd seen death. It looked nothing like this. She appeared to be having a pleasant dream, one eyebrow arched ever so slightly. But no living person can hold that still.

Suddenly I did not want to be here. Whatever they were doing, I did not need to know more about it. I could think of no good reason a hotel might be in the business of keeping dead people in stainless-steel capsules. Getting the hell out of here seemed like the right idea, but the electric door had long since clicked shut.

Rabbit came in just as I found the red button that opened it. "Hey hold on there, son, don't be in such a rush to slide out of here just when ol' Rabbit is trying to renew our acquaintance! What's your hurry?"

"I don't think I'm supposed to be here. But I didn't see anything."

"Oh really? What didn't you see? Did you not see Linda down here, looking positively radiant? Come on, have yourself a good look! Don't be shy, son. Very lifelike, don't you think?"

I stared down, terrified. I managed to nod.

He clamped a heavy hand on my shoulder. "Looking at her, would you say she's alive?"

I shook my head.

"Aw now, you disappoint me, Junior. This is Nobel-quality work—you're not showing the proper appreciation. You are looking at a breakthrough, my friend, the greatest leap forward in the retardation of organic decomposition since the discovery of formaldehyde. What you're seeing is a woman who's been deceased for forty-three weeks. She's not frozen, she's at sixty degrees Fahrenheit."

"How did she die?"

"That's not important," said Rabbit. "What's important is the state of preservation."

"How do you—what did you do to her?"

"I've managed to synthesize an oxidization inhibitor that's long-term reliable in carbon-based organisms," said Rabbit. "It wasn't easy, but look at the results! The inhibitor reduces the natural tendency to decay. We replace the fluids with a stream of inorganic solutions, and keep her out of the oxygen. She'll still be looking this good fifty, a hundred, years from now."

"But wh—why are you doing this?"

"Just think about it, son! If you can stop the human body from decaying, doesn't that kind of change the whole picture on death? You don't have to bury your loved ones, you can keep 'em with you, looking as good as when they were alive. The possibilities are endless."

"You're—you use this to make money?"

"Oh no, this is strictly science. For the good of mankind, I assure you. Others will probably try to capitalize on it, but my passion is for the empirical result. My boss is a collector, you know. I'm kind of a curator."

"You killed her to do this—this experiment on her?"

"We're long past the experimental stage," said Rabbit. "What you're seeing is the state of the art. Come look at Sandy."

He led me to the capsule in the other room. The glass lid was down.

Inside was a woman who looked so much like the other woman that I gasped out loud. They were exactly alike. This one wore a white sweater and red skirt. Bare feet. Red toenails.

"Is that magnificent?" Rabbit said.

"What is she, a . . . a clone?"

Rabbit grinned. "Identical twins. We've had to do a little manipulation of the facial muscles—it's quite a challenge to keep them looking so much alike." He rummaged through drawers while I tried to keep from staring at the dead woman who looked so alive.

The guys from the TV console moved into the doorway. Rabbit turned with a syringe in his hand, a cotton ball impaled on the needle. He started toward me. "This will only sting a little. . . ."

I ducked him and collided with the men in the door. They seized me. I kicked and scratched and clawed and tried to outscream Creedence Clearwater. One man held me pinned while the other yanked up my sleeve to expose my arm.

Rabbit came with the needle. He was right, I hardly felt it at all.

31 / The Law of the Jungle

SUPERMAN DANGLED HIS FEET in the glowing blue pool and let the lizards scamper over his hands.

He felt light-headed, queasy. That was the biggest scare of his life. He had been ready to kill that innocent kid just to see the look on Frank's face. Was there anything he would not do?

He had to get out of this war. It was making him crazy.

He'd always considered himself a peaceable man. Where did it come from, that urge to shoot a kid? Why had the weapon in his hands felt so much like an opportunity? Superman took a look inside his own soul, and found a killer lurking in there: a predator perched in a tree, taking aim at a human being. He felt it as a craving, as basic as breathing, as natural as cupping his hands for a drink of glowing blue water. It was not a game, it was real, those were real bullets in the rifle. Superman held the power of death in his hands. Every muscle in his body strained to use it.

That smile stopped him.

That smile.

He could not shake the image. There was something so haunting about the way the boy turned just in time to smile into the crosshairs, and save himself.

He saved Superman, too.

Imagine your life after something like that. Always you would see that smile in your dreams. Once you crossed that line you would never be the same. You might even kill again, if that's what it took to erase that smile from your mind.

A man is just an animal with a wilder animal chained up inside.

From a distance, Superman looked like a peaceable man. From a distance, the jungle looks peaceful, too, but when you are up in its trees watching, you see a thousand small murders every day. An army of ants feeds on a moth, beneath a tree that is slowly being strangled by a philodendron, upon which sits a scarlet macaw waiting to swoop down on a dragonfly. From the high branches of the *orgullo de la India* you see ten billion plants striving, twining, pushing their neighbors aside, snaking their arms out, sticking their heads past each other up into the sun, fighting to compete, to overwhelm, to prevail.

The urge is within us: eat or be eaten, kill or be killed, prevail or die. Old Mr. Darwin has laid down the law. Surely the better angels of our nature are appalled by what they see.

Superman thought he had uncovered the greatest mystery years ago, when he realized that everything in the universe is connected, God is contained in all things—but now he saw the dark side of that equation. Evil is in all things, too. Even within the heart of a peaceable man. We're connected by life, and by the urge to destroy life. Once a child learns he can kill, he kills—maybe just a snail, or a worm, maybe he learns that civilized people do not kill everything smaller or more helpless, and he hides the urge until he grows up and joins the army and takes up killing as an occupation. Or grows up thinking himself a peaceable man, until one day he finds himself in a mango tree with a rifle.

Superman knew this was why he lost his power. He had always been careful to observe Pito's instructions: use the power for good. Fantasize about revenge all you want, but if you use the power for bad, it won't work anymore. The moment Superman aimed that rifle at that innocent kid, he felt his whole body grow heavy. His perch in the tree became instantly precarious. He abandoned the rifle and stumbled back down the treetop highway, inching along, clinging to branches he used to take at an easy lope.

His foot missed a branch and he plunged twenty feet to the ground, snapping off limbs as he fell. It knocked the breath out of him and sent him limping back to the cave.

He lay down beside the glowing blue spring, drank his fill, and sat back to wait for the sensation of lightness to return. He thought he felt something, took a couple of exploratory hops. Nothing. He forced himself to drink more. Okay, I'm sorry, I used the power for bad—actually I didn't, but I started to, I wanted to, damn it, and this is a hell of a moment to find out that the penalty is the same as if I had.

Grumbling wouldn't change anything. It was no longer his *destino* to fly. He had misused his power and lost it, and he would just have to accept that. His friends were all dead, but evil was still alive on the island. He would still have to fight.

He pulled his feet up from the water. He blinked, and looked again.

His feet were not there.

They were *there*, he could feel them, but he was looking at the place where his feet should be, and he saw nothing.

His feet seemed to have disappeared.

The portion of his legs that had been underwater was invisible. His legs simply faded into thin air. He wiggled his toes. He kicked one foot against the other. It was as if his feet had gone to sleep, but instead of losing sensation they had lost the capacity to reflect light.

He laughed at the illusion: Red Dot flashback? A trick of the light? Brain tumor? It was not a happy laugh.

He drew in his leg and pounded the fleshy place in midair where he could feel, but not see, his ankle.

You have to learn to think in terms of possibilities, Ben. You're absolutely impaled on what you already know.

Maybe I'm having a stroke, he thought. Maybe this is the onset. Any minute the side of my face will begin to sag.

He flexed his feet this way and that, trying to see some reflection, some ripple in the air. Nothing. He turned the beam of the flashlight upon his invisible feet. The light passed through to the floor.

Well now, he thought, this is physically impossible, so it must be a trick of my brain. Something strange is happening here. Maybe I'm having a stroke. Probably I have a few minutes of consciousness left. I should try to find someone to help me.

But really, he felt just fine. From his head to a point midway down his shins.

It isn't in the people. It's this place. It has its own power. Anyone can drink from the well.

If a man truly wants to disappear, this is where he can come to do it.

Is that what I want? he wondered. Is that why I came here after all, to go on and disappear the rest of the way? Is that my real *destino*?

It might have certain advantages.

Superman took off his clothes and immersed himself in the pool.

32 / Grand Opening

WHAT A GLAMOROUS SCENE that was, the white cruiseliner glittering in the bay, the great pyramid lit up and shining, searchlights raking the sky with slender fingers, helicopters buzzing in like dragonflies. Superman had never imagined such a night in the jungle. Ladies glided by in elegant gowns. Servants in white jackets carried trays of champagne. The walkways were outlined by candles in blue stained-glass boxes. The Jiménez Brothers blatted away on a garishly bright strip of lawn, "Guantanamera," what else?

You had to hand it to Frank, and the power of money: exactly a year had gone by since the pyramid first appeared on the Magician's birthday cake, and here it was a reality, swarming with people. In one year Frank had built this monstrosity from scratch, and for tonight he had shipped in this celebration by air, land, and sea—all the food, the guests, the entertainers, the whole shebang from the searchlights to the French crystal flutes and champagne: Veuve Clicquot, someone said. Ver-y nice.

Superman slipped unseen among the white tents in the gardens below the pyramid's north face. The guests nibbled shrimp as they drifted from tent to poolside, between an imposing pair of Sphinxes flanking the entrance. Mostly they looked like Americans, with a sprinkling of Germans, Frenchmen, Latinos. Predominantly older folks, although there were some glamorous younger couples, too. You could tell they were rich by the tasteful hum of their conversation. Superman thought he recognized a few minor show-business types, but he might have been imagining things.

He was intensely conscious of his nakedness among all these well-dressed people. If you wish to disappear completely, he had discovered, you must go into it naked. Clothes do not disappear. The evening was plenty warm enough, but the urge to cover himself was no less profound now that he was invisible. His hands kept straying to cover his frontal zone. That didn't do a thing for the backal zone, which was hanging out for all to see, if anyone had been able to see him.

He had no idea how long the effect would last. He had kept himself submerged in the glowing pool all afternoon, right up till the last possible moment, then dried off and hurried up the mountain to the grand opening. He strolled undetected through the ranks of camouflage men at the gate, and joined the flow of celebrants among the tents, between the Sphinxes, up the grand staircase to the lobby.

Towering over the interior was the glittering sarcophagus of the pharaoh Khafre, gazing down with a neutral expression. The pharaonic theme was carried throughout the hotel, scarabs and black granite obelisks, papyrus mats, zigzag Nile-pattern carpeting. Even the cocktail waitresses wore those Cleopatra bangle-fringe things on their hair.

A handsome woman looked straight through Superman to repair her mascara in a mirror. She must have felt him there, but she made no sign. You don't often get to see how people's faces change when they think no one's watching: their eyes turn vacant, their features shut down, you can see them thinking about themselves. He waved his hands in front of her face. Nothing. She craned around to look at the side of the mirror, and nearly kissed his cheek.

Another thing about being invisible: you can't tell quite where you are by looking. You have to do it by feel, trying to guess the right amount of space to leave between you and everything around you. More than one guest murmured "Excuse me" to thin air.

If Superman had known how to do this disappearing act when he was nineteen, no woman in a skirt would have been safe. As it was, he had to resist the temptation to have fun with his new power, which despite the nakedness factor had definite advantages over the old one. He had a job to do. He would do well to keep his mind on it. Any minute he might turn back into a pumpkin.

He moved with the crowd up the stairs on plush, wine-colored carpet. The mellow tones of the Jerry Vale Orchestra poured out through the doors of the ballroom. Jerry himself stood at center stage, silver-haired and prosperous-looking, crooning "Sunrise, Sunset" while his string players sawed at the air. The air-conditioning system struggled against a mist of cologne, cigarette smoke, human exhalations. Jerry Vale mopped his brow.

Superman drifted through the audience, inspecting the old-money tuxedos, the ladies' gowns of tropical-weight linens and silks. A video crew turned its lights on a pair of excited partygoers, who gushed about the Jungle Inn. "So tasteful!" they said. "Out in the middle of nowhere!"

So this was why the Magician had declared war on the islanders, closed out his collection of the famously disappeared, blown the top off the mountain, and built a pyramid—so a shipload of wealthy, boring people could come sip champagne and admire him for it. It was such a pompous, overblown, horrific gesture that Superman could not resist the first opportunity that presented itself: Melanie Llewellyn, elegant in black crepe, her hair done up in a twist, about to cross paths with a waiter and a full tray of glasses. Superman stuck out his foot and sent the guy into a spectacular slow-motion pratfall. The glassy crash caught Jerry Vale in the most sensitive moment of his tune. The waiter got up with a withering glance for Melanie. A wave of laughter passed through the house.

Superman hopped up onstage and went to stand in front of Jerry Vale. He noted how Jerry's nose hairs quivered when he hit a high note. After a few moments he had to admit that making faces is not all that much fun when no one can see you.

He followed Jerry's microphone cord to the soundboard at backstage left. He distracted the soundman with a tap on the shoulder, unplugged the mike cord, and stuffed it down in a forest of wires.

The orchestra played on. Jerry kept singing "Little Green Apples" without realizing no one could hear him. The soundman scrambled among the wires. Superman turned every knob on the board to the full-on position, electrifying the ballroom with an ear-rending feedback screech.

The orchestra whanged to a halt. Jerry Vale glared at the soundman, who was batting frantically at the control board. As soon as he turned a knob down, Superman would turn it up again. The man's eyes widened. He took a step back and went into a defensive crouch, as if the soundboard might attack him.

Jerry Vale stomped over with his mike in hand—"Would you please tell me what the fuck is going on back here?" He didn't see the invisible hand that had plugged him in again. His words went out live. The audience roared.

After that, Jerry found it impossible to recapture the mood of "Little Green Apples." He tossed off a quick rendition of "Happy Days Are Here Again" and stormed backstage shouting how quickly he planned to fire whoever had booked him into this godforsaken Third World hellhole; he might not be Top 40, but he hadn't sunk THIS low, not YET!

The Sherman Brothers hustled past him to the stage. Their shiny suits bore the creases of fifteen years in a suitcase. Lou Sherman had shaved his head to a GI flattop to re-create the look that made him famous. He was the dumb, crew-cut clown, while his brother Stu was the hipper, smarter one, with a swoopy sixties-style late-Beatles hairdo that was actually a rather crawly-looking toupee. "Well gee, Stu" had been the expression of the moment for about three weeks in 1967, shorthand for "I haven't the slightest idea."

"Let's hear a big round for Jerry Vale and his orchestra!" Stu cried. "Weren't they great? Unbelievable. Beautiful."

Lou struck his patented dummkopf pose. "Gee, Stu, Jerry said a bad word."

"Oh yeah, Lou, what word was that?"

"He said 'fuck.' Did you hear him say that?"

"I don't know that word, Lou. What does it mean?"

"Well . . . well, gee Stu, I'm not sure I know either." Lou scratched his crew cut.

"If you don't know what it means, how do you know it's a bad word?"

"Well . . . well, gee, Stu, it *must* be bad. Whenever Mama used to say it, Daddy'd get so scared he'd run hide in the bed!"

That brought a mild laugh from the audience, and a bemused grimace from Stu. "Lou, that word can get you in a lot of trouble. You better watch out who you say it to."

"I said it to my teacher, Miss Pringle," said Lou.

"You—you did not! Good grief, what did she say?"

" 'After class, Mr. Sherman,' " he reported in a high teachery voice.

"Well that's very interesting," Stu deadpanned, "but I don't think these people want to hear about you, Lou, just look at 'em. All dressed up with someplace to go—the grand opening of the magnificent Jungle Inn. Isn't it marvelous? Let's hear a round of applause for all you very special people."

The guests applauded themselves politely.

"Happy Halloween, Stu," said Lou.

"It's not Halloween, this is August. Halloween's in October."

"Well, gee . . . why's that guy wearing a costume? Look, over there—it's Superman."

"Superman?" Stu's eyes widened. "Where?"

"There, in the corner."

A spotlight wandered the heads of the crowd, settling on a well-padded Superman in cape and tights, with a rubber mask to top off the illusion. He clasped his hands over his head like a victorious boxer and turned side to side, acknowledging the applause.

Suddenly he was surrounded by young men in red polo shirts. One of them snatched off the mask to reveal—

Freddy. The bartender from La Discoteca.

They laughed. It was a joke for the locals. They'd gotten together to work Superman into their act. Very funny. Ha ha.

"Superman!" cried Stu. "Good to see you, buddy, where've you been? We thought you flew the coop!"

While this was going on, the real Superman was climbing a rope ladder to the flies. He took a position above center stage, took hold of himself, and began squeezing out single droplets of urine, which plopped fatly in the middle of Lou Sherman's crew cut.

Lou touched his head, shifted over a step. Superman crept along the catwalk, refining his aim.

Lou stammered over his line, glanced up angrily into the lights. "I think it's raining in here," he ad-libbed.

"What are you talking about?" Stu snapped. "That's not your line."

"Something's dripping on my head."

"You're supposed to say 'I have superpowers too.' "

"I have superpowers too," said Lou.

"Oh yeah? What kind of superpowers do you have?"

"Well, gee, for one thing I have X-ray—dammit!"

"What is the *matter* with you?"

Lou sniffed his hand. "I'm not kidding! Somebody is peeing on my head!" He craned up into the lights.

"Jesus, Lou, what is this?" Stu screamed. "Are you gonna melt down on me here? Don't do this to me again, goddamn it, I warned you . . ." He made a threatening move toward his brother. "Say your line!"

Lou said, "Ah, you go to hell," and then Stu was all over him, hitting him *pop!* with his fist, the two of them slamming to the floor, tussling, rolling.

The audience pressed up to the stage for a better look.

Superman shook off the last invisible drop, and went back to the ladder. Climbing down he spotted the old Indian in the shadows, quietly watching the chaos. He sneaked up to whisper in his ear: "Pito. Don't turn around. It's Ben."

Pito didn't jump, or flinch. He kept his arms folded, his eyes toward the stage. "You go now," he murmured. "No is safe for you here."

The Shermans rolled across the stage in a death grapple.

"Don't worry, nobody can see me."

"You go," the old man said. "Is bad here. Something bad is happen." He turned to find himself talking to an empty space. If ever there was a moment when you would expect the old man to look surprised, this was it. He just blinked. "*El ojo,*" he said.

"What?"

"*El ojo del Mago,*" he said. The eye of the Magician. "You was to swimming in there." It wasn't a question. There was sadness in the old man's eyes, as if Superman had done something he would regret.

"You didn't say anything about swimming. How long you think it'll last? I've been this way more than an hour."

"*No sé,*" said Pito.

A bunch of polo shirts were trying to separate the Sherman Brothers, who lunged at each other to catcalls from the audience.

"Well, I mean—it *is* gonna wear off, right?"

"The tears of the Mago is to drinking. Not to swimming. I no tell you to swimming. That is for other kind of *destino.*"

"Oh Jesus! Now you tell me!" Superman swallowed his panic. "Listen, old man, you gotta help me here. I can't do this all by myself. Now there's ten crates of dynamite under a brush pile by the big mango tree, the southwest corner."

"No!" Pito's whisper was harsh. "You no learn *nada.* You want to kill. Is not for kill. Is for to live. Is why we fight."

"No, I—listen. I *know,* I understand now. I don't want to kill anybody. Everything you said about using the power for good—that was all true. I blew it. I can't fly anymore. But we have to do something. I'll run 'em all out of here. You go get that dynamite."

"I do something," said Pito.

From behind came a rustle, a piercing cry like the shrillest bird in the jungle. An incredible bird-woman swept past them onto the stage, yipping and yapping. Lupe "Chita" Malanota was a rare vision: great feathery headpiece, slinky beaded halter top from which her bouncy bosoms threatened to spill, fishnet body-stocking, seven-inch platform heels. Chita had built her career around those voluminous breasts and that shrill birdy voice. She was a favorite of the late-night talk shows, where she could be counted on to wiggle in her chair and make vaguely obscene remarks in her comical Puerto Rican accent. Now she burst out with a string of *ay-ay-ay*s and chased the Sherman Brothers off the stage, arching her jet-black eyebrows and stamping her feet like a flamenco dancer.

"Guuuuude ebeneeen!" she howled to the audience. "My name eess Cheeeeeee-ta! Ay-ay-ay-ay-ay-ay-ay!"

The rhythm players of the Jerry Vale Orchestra set up a galloping bossa nova. Chita shimmied and shook dem hot gazangas and got the audience up on its feet dancing—not an easy task, after the dispiriting exit of the Sherman Brothers.

Superman couldn't think of a thing he'd rather do than unfasten the hook-and-eye clasp that stood between Chita's famous breasts and her audience. But she looked like a nice hardworking girl, under all that makeup. Had he really come here to embarrass her? Is that what his war had come down to? Chita twitched and jittered, snapping her fingers, bouncing those boobs at least once personally toward every man in the audience. She was singing, but not really. It didn't matter. She looked sensational swooping around that stage, waving her shimmery wings.

Superman set off instead to blaze a trail through the ballroom—a candle tipped over, men jumping and swatting; a tablecloth jerked suddenly from a table, flapping in air before draping itself over the heads of two old ladies, who screamed; waiters colliding head-on, trays of chicken wings flying, a row of bottles sailing off the bar *smash!* into a wall. People tripped and stumbled and fell. The ballroom began to look like a wrestling match with two hundred contestants.

Superman worked his way down the room. He licked his finger and stuck it in a woman's ear, producing a shriek that stopped Chita in the middle of an *ay-ay-ay!*

"Ju trine to rune my ack, beech?" she bellowed from the stage. "Ju wannu come up here and sheck you fat ass, come on up! Come *on!* Ju see who wannu payu fadat! No fucken body, dass who!"

Just when it looked as if Chita was going to go the way of Jerry Vale and the Sherman Brothers, the band galloped into "Tequila." Chita went on with her show. The fat lady gathered herself with a snort and marched out, taking six irate friends with her.

This was Superman's plan of attack: create such an uproar that the party fell apart and these innocent people fled back to their boat. Then find some way to do some real damage to the Magician's creation.

Chita gave up the stage, and the orchestra swung into a medley of 5th Dimension hits. Superman skulked down the wall. He couldn't believe the blasé attitude of these partygoers—he'd expected his tour of the room to send them all shrieking into the night. What does it take to frighten people these days?

The scariest thing in the room was the orchestra's rendition of "Aquarius." When at last the moon was in the seventh house, and Jupiter aligned with Mars, the trumpets swung into a something-big-is-about-to-happen fanfare. Spotlights wandered the room and settled on a dazzling figure in white, mounting the steps to the stage.

In every way she was an extravaganza: two-foot-tall powdered wig, spiky eyelashes batting in a field of white makeup, ropes of diamonds glittering upon a powdered bosom, jeweled lorgnette in her hand, her great swirling gown a dazzle of rhinestones. She was Marie Antoinette. She was fabulous.

She was Frank.

She swept to center stage and stood with head modestly inclined against an outbreak of cheering. Frank had gone all the way, at long last: he had shaved his mustache. His blue eyes gleamed with pleasure. He was the Queen, center stage in his castle, being cheered by his subjects. It might have been the finest moment of his life.

Except that he had an enemy somewhere in this room. And that enemy had certain advantages of which Frank was not aware.

He seized a microphone. "Good evening, friends! Hello! *Buenas noches! Bonsoir! Bienvenidos!* How the hell are you tonight?" The crowd roared hello. They were having a good time now. All that expensive champagne was kicking in. "Let them eat cake!" he cried, twirling to show off his gown. "Off with their heads! Let them eat cake!" The audience roared.

"No, but seriously—welcome, my friends." He paused a moment while the crowd simmered down. "This is such a special night for me, I can't tell you. For years, one man had a very special dream of this place, a dream beyond what any of us could have dared to dream. He envisioned the finest hotel in the world, where the finest people could come to share the wonders of our beautiful island. He handed that dream off to me, and now— here we are! Can you believe it? I know it's real, but for me it's just . . . it's pure magic. Thank you so much. Thank you. Off with your heads!" He curtsied, waved his lorgnette. "I understand we've had some . . . *interesting* entertainment so far. I know you're going to be very excited about our next performer, a lady who really needs no introduction ... ladies and gentle-men, the Jungle Inn has the great honor to present to you now the one, the only, the first lady of popular song ..."

The Jerry Vale drummer struck up a roll. A spotlight flickered into the wing, illuminating a small mousy woman in a brown knit midi-dress. Her hair was brown. She looked like a secretary in an insurance company. She came onstage with a flick of her hand and a big toothy smile, as if expecting a standing ovation. Nobody knew who she was until Frank said—

"*Damas y caballeros* . . . Miss—Helen Reddy!"

Life is full of surprises.

The audience applauded with some enthusiasm, but if anyone had taken a vote, Marie Antoinette would have won in a landslide.

Superman could not stop himself. He jumped up onstage, sauntering past Helen on his way to the soundboard. She smelled nice: French per-fume. She had the eyes of a scared little mammal.

Pito was nowhere around. Superman put his lips to the soundman's ear and said, "Bogey bogey bogeyman gonna gitcha if you don't get up right now and RUN!"

The man did just that.

Superman eased into the chair, unplugged Helen's microphone, plugged in a mike for himself. The orchestra swung into the opening bars of Helen's most famous anthem, the song that had held the number-one spot on the Billboard Hot 100 for ten consecutive weeks, spoiling Super-man's one and only best shot. Once more he knew there must be a God, something about the universe and how it's all connected: was this not the finest opportunity of anyone's life? He leaned to the microphone and, in his deepest baritone, sang the song that made Helen famous:

> *I am woman, hear me roar*
> *In numbers too big to ignore. . . .*

He didn't know the words to the verse, but he made up some good ones. Helen looked puzzled by what was coming back from the monitors, but she kept singing, and the orchestra played on. They couldn't hear the waves of laughter pouring over the footlights.

> *I am woman, hear me bitch*
> *Buy my record, make me rich*

The audience laughed harder as the song went along. Helen was visibly startled by the blast of applause at the end. She spoke in a soft flat Australian accent. "Thank you all so much, what a nice warm welcome, I hope you like this next chune."

The musicians struck it up. Superman let Helen sing it to the chorus, then switched on his mike:

> *Delta Dawn,*
> *Please take off what you've got on*

It wasn't as good as "I Am Woman," but the audience loved it. About halfway through the chorus, Helen Reddy got this frozen look and stopped singing. She tapped the bandleader's shoulder. The music died. The two of them came looking for the soundman.

Marie Antoinette swept back onto the stage, leading a boy by the hand. A skinny, dazed, hungry-looking boy, maybe eighteen, with long streaky hair and a blank look in his eyes. Sweat-circles under the arms of his red polo shirt. His face was pale, almost waxy.

Frank led him trembling to the spotlight at center stage.

Superman knew that boy. That was the boy. The one he almost killed. The one who smiled into his rifle scope and saved both their lives.

Something about that boy made the crowd very quiet.

Frank tapped the mike. "All right, well, hm!—we'll bring Miss Reddy back out in a moment, but first I wanted you to meet one of our most valued employees here at the Jungle Inn. Son, say hello to the folks." He gave the boy a little push.

"Dad?" A small voice echoed through the room. "Are you here? Daddy?"

"What's your name, son," Frank said, "tell 'em your name."

"Ben."

"Ben what? Go ahead."

"Willis."

"That would be Ben Willis Junior?" Frank said.

The boy nodded. He turned his face to the light.

It was not possible, but yes it was.

"We're hoping Mr. Willis Senior will favor us with his presence," Frank said, "if he would be so kind."

"Daddy, don't do it. It's a trap. They—"

Frank jerked his hand. The boy fell silent, took a wobbly step back.

Superman knew that boy. He had almost killed that boy.

He walked to the center of the stage, and looked close, to be sure.

Something broke open inside him. He reached out, put his arms around the boy. He tried to say "I'm here." His voice failed. A painful tingling swept over him, like the blood rushing back into a limb that has been asleep, and then everyone in the ballroom saw Superman naked and weeping, with his arms around his only son.

33 / Bedlam

SO THERE I AM ONSTAGE lights pulsing like flashers on a police car, someone gripping my hand *Mom? Is that you Mom?* pulling me into the lights in front of all those people, my ears roaring *ga-WHAAW, ga-WHAAW*, a great mournful foghorn sounding in the middle of my brain. The horn has been moaning like this for twenty-three hours now, twenty-three years. *That's enough Mom they don't want to hear any more from you.* Wait, that's not Mom. That's Marie Antoinette. The lights pulse in time with my blood.

Look at all these people! Are they real? Hard to say.

For the longest time Rabbit and his friends left me slumped in a chair in the room of stainless-steel capsules. I was not tied or restrained in any way. I knew I could get up and walk out of there, if I could convince my muscles to obey the commands of my brain.

I shrank down very small and walked up my arm, through my ear, into my brain. I introduced myself to the people who ran the departments: they sat at computer consoles like the people on *Star Trek*, monitoring my body functions. They said there was nothing they could do until the drugs wore off.

Real people in surgical scrubs came to take my pulse.

Then suddenly it's later and a lady in glittery diamonds pulls me up by the hand, to an elevator, through a crowd to the stage. *Mom is that you?* She is murmuring into my ear, telling me what to say.

We stand on a stage. The foghorn is moaning *ga-WHAAW, ga-WHAAW*. Marie Antoinette pulls me into the light. "Say hello to the folks." She gives me a shove.

"Dad?" DAD DAD DAD DAD DAD DAD

"Are you here?" HERE HERE HERE HERE HERE HERE

"Daddy?" DADDY DADDY DADDY DADDY DADDY DADDY

Tell 'em your name, son, says Marie Antoinette. Tell 'em your name.

I tell 'em and tell 'em and tell 'em. My voices echo back to me. I have so many voices. There are lights in my eyes but only one light so pale blue and beautiful that it makes me want to cry. It shines through the holes in my eyes.

Marie Antoinette is asking questions. I remember who she is what they said why they want me here. I cry "Daddy, don't do it! It's a trap!"

Marie jerks my arm.

I stumble back, on the verge of collapse. Someone wraps me in his arms, holding me up. No one is there, but I feel his pressure, the warmth, I smell the faintest trace of . . . Old Spice? I close my eyes. When I open them again, a man has his arms around me. He is naked. Crying.

Who are you?

Men in camouflage swarm around us. The man cries "Ben Junior!"

Oh Lord God Almighty, nobody calls me Ben Junior.

That man is my father.

The soldiers drag us off the stage. "Ben Junior!" He is alive. I have found him. We have found each other.

They haul us apart, hustling us down opposite walls past the crowd milling, straining to see. The orchestra strikes up a song. Helen Reddy comes out to sing. This must be a dream. I saw her sing once before, at my father's memorial concert. And now here she is to welcome him back from the dead. Her voice pierces the foghorn in my brain:

> *She was forty-one ga-WHAAW*
> *And her daddy still ga-WHAAW*

All at once the doors swing shut *ka-chung.* We are trapped in this place.

I look up, searching for that special blue light, but instead I see fog spreading out on the ceiling, curling downward toward us. This is not fog hissing out of sprinkler nozzles in the ceiling. This is not fog.

Now I can smell it—sweet, like almonds—and so can the people around me, a woman faints at my feet or maybe it's the white pearly mist curling down from the ceiling. Screams and flying glassware, a sudden surge of people trying to get out. The traffic reaches an ominous pitch near the doors, grunting and shoving. Some men take up a table as a battering ram. The doors are strong. People cough and cover their faces with napkins.

A tiny *plash!* of breaking glass, high above us in the mullioned windows, another *plash!* and the panes begin to shatter *plash! plash!* down the row smashed in by tiny fists.

Small reddish monkeys pour through the jagged glass chattering, screeching, followed by big black monkeys with angry white faces cantering down the curtains, leaping onto chandeliers, vaulting tables, shrieking, pouncing on shoulders and necks and the hairdos of ladies. One set of doors gives way. A stampede begins.

The fog streams out through the broken windows. Someone plants a firm hand on my head and shoves me under a table. *Please, sir, are you the Wizard of Oz? I just want to go home.*

I crawl across the floor. A great herd of feet thunders by, the foghorn *ga-WHAAW* and the bitter chatter of monkeys.

An old Indian helps me up. I know this man. He put me to bed once, in the bamboo hut behind the Big House. I stay close behind him. The ballroom swirls like a circus, chandeliers crazily swinging, people stumbling around with monkeys on their heads. Ten or twelve red monkeys caper across the stage. Helen Reddy abandons her microphone and flees to the wings.

The human river dissolves in panic as it reaches the doors: the floor slimy with frogs: mottled brown frogs as big as your hand, tiny green frogs, red frogs, bright-yellow poison-arrow frogs, a sea of frogs croaking, hopping.

The frogs open a path for the old Indian. I follow him down the frog-carpeted stairs, across the frog-hopping lobby.

The steps outside are seething: the fleeing guests slide on smeared frog remains. A woman staggers by with a monkey latched onto her neck, her mouth open in a soundless scream. Searchlights flash in my eyes. The foghorn makes a terrible groan.

"The *monos* is come," the old man is saying. "Is the *profecía*."

A voice behind me says, "Ben Junior, give me your pants."

My father. A Jungle Inn flag wrapped around his waist.

"My pants?"

"You're wearing underwear, right?"

"Y-yeah, but—"

"What's the matter with you? Are you—look at him, Pito, look at his eyes. What'd they give you? Did they tell you what it was?"

"Red Dot," I say. "Red Dot Ninety-nine."

"Aw Jesus, you must be freaking out. Okay, now, stay calm, it'll be okay, it may take time to wear off. I've been there. Just hold steady, and give me your pants."

I do as he says. He ducks behind a bush and returns with the flag draped around his shoulders, sucking in his stomach to keep from popping the button on my shorts.

His skin is wrinkled, deep brown from the sun. His face is different, the bones rearranged, a scraggly beard. His nose crooks to the left. He has the eyes of a man who has lived too long in the woods.

"My God," he says, "they were trying to kill everyone."

"The *monos* is open the windows," says the old Indian. "Why you no fly?"

"I can't, Pito. I can't do it anymore. I lost it." My father turns to me, stares at me, hard. "It's good to see you, son."

"I know what they're doing," I tell him. "We have to stop them."

34 / *This Is Not a Drill*

AFTER THE FIRST SHOCK of recognition, this boy looked nothing like the boy Superman had carried around in his head all these years. Ben Junior was six feet tall, skinny but strong, with real muscles in his shoulders and arms. At first glance he resembled the hungry young man who once got up at the Flor-A-Bama to sing a Hank Williams song.

Here they were together in this place, fighting on the same side. Superman never dreamed it was possible. He'd spent years regretting the mistakes that brought him to the island, pondering the flaws in his character, examining his navel with all the self-centered attention he had once given to his career. Meanwhile his son had grown up and come all this way to find him. It was a hell of a lot more than he'd ever done for his son.

The boy's eyes were popping. He couldn't stand still. Said he'd been here for months working on the construction crew, looking for Superman. He tried to explain what he'd seen before they seized him and shot him full of drugs, but it came tumbling out all confusion—something about Frank, and Rabbit, and a hidden laboratory, women under glass. . . .

"It's okay, son, just show us. Can you show us where?"

He led them against the tide of fleeing partygoers, down a ramp to the basement. For the moment, the Jungle Inn lay exposed. The camouflage men had fled the monkey-and-frog invasion ahead of the first ranks of little old ladies. Superman's heart was pumping. This was the chance Lee never had at Petersburg, the chance to fall upon a distracted enemy and win the greatest upset victory of all time.

The boy led them up to an empty white room, a spiral escalator, a mural of the Sphinx, a maze of corridors, a stone door sheathed in hieroglyphs. Pito placed hands on the door. The walls and ceiling pulsed red. The door swung open.

They stepped into a dim tunnel. The door closed behind them.

The tunnel forked. "Which way?"

"I don't know," the boy said, "I didn't get this far."

Pito led them to the right. The tunnel made a series of sharp twists and switchbacks, and let out in the white empty room they'd entered first.

They went up the spiral again, through the maze, through the sandstone door. They followed the left fork down twisting turns—and came out again in the empty white room. This place was a hall of mirrors, a maze leading back to its beginning.

"Maybe we took a wrong turn," said Ben Junior.

"You took the turn I wanted you to take," boomed a voice from the top of the escalator. The spiral hummed and revolved, bringing with it a tall, elderly man in a gray suit and red bow tie. "Dapper" was too small a word for him; he was the personification of outsized seventy-five-year-old elegance, a big rangy man with every white hair in place, his mustache perfectly trimmed, a white orchid in his lapel. "I wanted to meet the people who ruined my party."

Pito's eyes flashed. "Is you."

"Yes, Pito, is me. Your English hasn't improved, but you look well. How on earth is little Catalina?"

"Is big," said Pito.

"And you're the one they call Superman." The man extended his hand. "How do you do. Howard Hughes."

Superman shook the hand, repeating the name to himself. "The Magician. It's you."

Hughes laughed, a dry rattle. "I haven't worked any new tricks in a while now, but yes, that's what they call me in these parts. We used to have a real magician on the island. Did you ever get to meet him?"

"A little old guy," Superman said. "His name was Harry."

"Houdini. Amazing fellow. We should all live to be a hundred and four."

Superman's head was spinning—Jesus! could this really be—as in Jane Russell, the Spruce Goose, Hughes Aircraft, RKO Pictures? Billionaire, recluse, builder of hotels? The Magician?

Of course.

The Errol Flynn handsomeness of his large, rectangular face was undiminished by the deep lines of a mottled, sun-battered complexion. He spoke with a slight Texas twang, an air of confident power, though he looked somehow pale and sickly beneath his age spots. Superman remembered all the things he'd ever heard about the Magician, and saw in a flash how they could add up to this man—right down to the fact that no one ever dared mention his name. That was a powerful name.

"It can't be," said Ben Junior. "Howard Hughes is dead."

"That doesn't count for all that much around here," Superman said.

"No, but really, he is. He went insane. He had ten-inch fingernails and stringy hair and he had to wear a diaper. After he died, some used-car salesman wrote up a fake will and tried to get his money."

Hughes smiled. "This is your son?"

"His name's Ben."

"What's wrong with his eyes?"

"Your people have been playing around in his head," Superman said. "You drugged him and locked him up to get to me. I'm the one that's been fighting you, Mr. Hughes. I didn't know you were such a coward. If you wanted to get to me, you didn't have to mess with an innocent kid."

"I'm not innocent," Ben Junior said.

"Yes you are," said his father.

"And of course *you* could have come to me," said Hughes, "instead of blowing up bulldozers and hiding in the woods, or wherever you've been keeping yourself. I know all about you, Superman, I know everything you've done. Did you think I couldn't afford a few bulldozers? Did you really think you could stop me with your little pop-gun campaign?"

"I still think so," said Superman.

"You have no power, and Pito's is weak. Mine is stronger now, isn't that true, Pito."

"*Sí.*" Pito stared at his feet.

"Did he take you to the waterfall, Superman? Did you find your *destino?*"

"Yeah. Twice."

"He took me the first time I came here. As a matter of fact, Pito sold me this island—for how much, Pito? Twenty-four dollars and a handful of beads? We drank from the blue pool. I found my *destino.* Would you like to know what I found?"

"What's that?"

"I was born to be a king," said Hughes. "Chosen by the gods to be a ruler of the earth. This wasn't my idea. Pito started me down this path. Now I've done it, Pito, are you proud of me? I've fulfilled my *destino.*"

"You is bad man," said Pito. "You kill many peoples."

"A king has to do that sometimes. Otherwise you run the risk of your subjects running amok."

"Are you telling me this was all Pito's idea?"

"He led me to the first realization," said Hughes. "I didn't really grasp the full implications until I went to Giza in the fifties. I was standing at the northeast corner of Khafre's pyramid and suddenly I knew I had lived there before. You have to understand, my natural father was taken from me when I was a very young man. It might have destroyed me. I always felt as if . . . I could have done something to save him. But then I realized there was no use mourning him. He wasn't my father at all. He was only a mortal. In one flash I realized why I'd bought this island, why the gods gave me this incredible capacity to accumulate money—I'd always wondered, you know. The way it just flowed into my hands. Come to find out I'm the reincarnation of Khafre, son of Khufu. This was revealed to me. I was born to rule the world. And to build a pyramid in celebration of my ancient father."

He volunteered this information in a matter-of-fact tone, as if confessing that he used to be a member of the Rotary Club. Superman had never heard anything quite so demented coming from such a reasonable-sounding man. "Mr. Hughes, I don't care who you think you are, it doesn't give you the right to go around killing people. For whatever crazy idea."

"No, indeed," he said, "I took that right upon myself. I've never found it necessary to play by the rules. I was granted a lifetime exemption by the gods. It's a hard fact of life, Superman. Some lives are worth more than others. If I'd played by the rules, do you think I'd be the richest man on earth?"

"Well—"

"You think this is a crazy idea, but you see, I *don't care* what you think. I have my own idea of who I am. Oh, I can hear 'em all saying there goes old Hughes again, off on one of his nutty schemes, now he's decided he's King Tut. And maybe it *is* nuts—but so what? I have eight billion dollars! I can afford to humor myself. Can you even conceive of such a figure? Can you begin to imagine the kind of power that gives you?"

"Yeah, the power to cut down trees and build a monument to yourself."

"More than that. The power to live out your dreams, to buy anyone you desire. I've bought kings and presidents and women, the most beautiful women on earth. I bought a man to act out my death for the entertainment of the public and my board of directors. I bought this island and everyone on it. No one stands in my way. Least of all you. I could buy you like that." He snapped his fingers.

"I don't think you can, Mr. Hughes."

"People are cheap. Amelia? I paid the Japs a hundred thousand in gold.

They threw in Frank at no extra charge. Your old friend Mistress Monroe? Fifty thousand and one call to the L.A. county coroner. Anastasia I gave ten thousand, I think. Kennedy was a favor for an old friend. Jimmy Hoffa paid *me*. I've assembled the finest collection of human beings in the world, and all together they didn't cost as much as one cut-rate Renoir."

"You bought them," Superman said, "and then you killed them."

"It was all in the bargain. They were as good as dead before they ever got here. They all had one thing in common—they were too famous. They came here desperate, nowhere else to go. I gave them new lives. They knew it wasn't forever. They agreed to my terms. I supported them for years. I gave them privacy, luxury, everything they ever wanted."

"In return for what?"

"Come with me. I'll show you." Nothing in this man's demeanor would give him away as a lunatic. If anything, he was a bit too neatly put together, as if striving to project an illusion of sanity. They trailed him up the escalator, which he explained was his own design, after a Leonardo da Vinci sketch for a flying machine. He played the genial host, leading them through the maze to a seeming dead end, a hinged panel into a passageway that led to a widening staircase, red lights pulsing in the walls.

"Do you know anything about the kings of Egypt, Superman?"

"I would've never picked you out as one of 'em, if that's what you mean."

"When the king is laid to rest, he's surrounded by his most precious possessions, including all his wives and courtiers, his most famous subjects. He spends his life collecting the most storied, honored people in the kingdom, and together they travel to their reward. I always found that a terribly attractive notion, the idea that all the interesting people would cease to exist when you do. It eases the pain of going, somehow."

They entered a round chamber with a red ceiling, throbbing like a beating heart. The wall sank silently into the floor, and they were in a large dim room, surrounded by rows of stainless-steel capsules with oval domes of glass. Each capsule stood in a column of light from above. "This is my springboard to eternity," Hughes said. "If the gods are pleased with what I've done, I should be back in about three thousand years."

"Mr. Hughes," Superman said, "what the hell?"

Ben Junior said, "This is what I was trying to tell you."

A great triangular space at the peak of the pyramid, a trophy room filled with gleaming humming caskets, people under glass. The collector's collection. There must have been a hundred bodies laid out in rows along the points of a six-sided star.

One capsule stood empty on a raised dais at the center. It was easy to guess who that was for.

The first corpse looked very much alive, if a bit overdressed, a pin-striped suit with a pearl stickpin in the lapel. Slicked-back hair, a wide bull-dog face. On the glass by his feet the plaque said JAMES RIDDLE HOFFA, AMERICAN LABOR LEADER.

"I met him through Momo Giancana," said Hughes. "Jimmy was a good man in his heart, but a tough son of a bitch when he wanted something."

There was Anastasia, peaceful in repose, an antique gown of seed pearls and lace, a spray of perfect white lilies. The plaque said HER ROYAL HIGH-NESS ANASTASIA, EMPRESS OF ALL THE RUSSIAS. Superman moved down the row.

Hughes watched his face with satisfaction. "Our friend Rabbit is a mir-acle worker, isn't he? You almost expect them to sit up and talk."

"You brought them here," Superman said, "so you could mount them like trophies. For this sick idea of yours."

"They're mine. They belong to me." Hughes reddened under his spots. "They *gave* themselves to me. They died without pain. Don't you see this is the greatest honor I could give them? I'll inherit their fame and carry it with me to the next world. Let me tell you a secret, young friend. I've gath-ered up all the money and notoriety anyone could want in this world, and it isn't enough. I want more. I want to be famous forever. The Egyptians are the only ones who ever figured out how to do it. They would have appreci-ated me. It's only in our time that the grand gesture has gone out of style."

Pito knelt beside a capsule on the next row, his face pressed to the glass. Superman glimpsed the cracked leather of a flight jacket, a flash of silver hair. "Oh hell, Pito, no wonder her coffin was so light. She wasn't in it."

Amelia was unchanged: the faintly superior smile, the determined set to her jaw. "Tonight she is sleeping," the old man said softly.

Superman walked down the points of the star. He found all the missing ones, the Twins, Rockefeller, D. B. Cooper, the King of Siam, Madame Olgova—oh God, poor Spike. Alongside the bodies of his friends were older corpses in advanced states of decay, sinking husks with plaques: Chaplin. Churchill. Disney. Auden. Will Rogers. Nijinsky. These dusty piles of sunken-in clothes were the remains of great men. The Magician was more than a collector: he was a grave robber, too. He had two Barrymores, two of the five Dionne quintuplets, the infant Charles Lindbergh Jr. At least that's what the plaques said. Superman would never know if those were really the people in there.

At the end of the row he saw a white dress, a gold rope knotted at the waist. The dress was cut low in front. Red lips. A cloud of platinum cotton-candy hair. She was too beautiful to be dead. She looked as if she might lick her lips and yawn, and open her eyes.

Superman could not take his eyes off her. This was as close as he would ever be to her again in this life. She looked so perfect, so alive. . . . He wanted to lift that glass dome and crawl in there and lie down beside her. Maybe that wasn't true love they had shared, but it felt as wonderful and all-consuming as love, and it made him a better man. It damaged him to see all her heat and electricity reduced to this static display, a butterfly trapped under glass, but for some reason it was not frightening to see her like this. He was glad she was still beautiful. She would have wanted that.

"You see why we can't wait around for natural causes," Hughes said. "You have to start the process immediately to get these kinds of results."

Superman grabbed him by his lapels and slammed him against the glass. "That one over there is for you, right? Why don't we go ahead and put you in it?"

"Take your hands off me," Hughes said. "You can't hurt me now. You've destroyed yourself."

Superman tightened his grip, full of the urge to kill, fully aware that he would never be able to do it.

"I have a fast cancer, an untreatable bone disease," Hughes said, "and an arrhythmia of the left ventricle. The doctors lied to me, they're all frauds, but I know the truth now. I'm dying. And you're going to die with me." He shook off Superman's hands. "The sequence has already begun. There's no way to stop it. All the entrances have been sealed."

"What the hell are you talking about?"

"There's a framework of titanium tubes along the base and the four axes of the pyramid. The tubes are packed with plastic explosive. The detonator's controlled by a remote computer. It's counting down now. Why do you think no one stopped you coming up here? I was waiting for you."

"What means this?" said Pito.

"It means this building is an explosive device. Very soon we'll all be returning to our original state, as we were just after the Big Boom. We'll be atoms again."

"You're crazy," said Superman. "You're bluffing."

"No, it's true," stammered Ben Junior, "I mean, my guys and I, we packed stuff in the tubes. We didn't know what it was."

"It's my time to die," Hughes said, "and I intend to do it in the most spectacular fashion. I've done everything I was put here to do—for this time around, anyway. Tonight is the night."

"Let's get out of here," Ben Junior said.

"No," Hughes said, "you're going with me. You ruined my birthday. It was so carefully prepared, I had half the Fortune 500 gathered in one room. We were all supposed to go together. Can you imagine the headlines? But you chased them off with your stupid monkey tricks. Shame on you. I see that look on your face, Superman. You think I'm evil. I'm not evil. I'm *you*. I'm what you set out to be. You wanted to be rich and famous, didn't you? You got a good taste of it. Surely you can understand a man trying to go all the way."

"I never hurt anybody," said Superman—a lie, of course, but what were his piddling crimes compared to the crimes of this man?

"And you never got very far, either, did you? Although I suppose you did all right for yourself. Look at the one on the end. I saved it for you."

The casket was empty. The plaque said BENJAMIN "SUPERMAN" WILLIS, AMERICAN FOLKSINGER.

"Do it," Superman said. "Blow us all up, you crazy old man. You don't have the guts."

"We talk," Pito said. "Is no good to die."

"That's what I say," said Ben Junior.

"You go." Pito waved his hand at Superman. "Both you go. We talk."

"I have nothing to say to you, Pito," said Hughes, "and no one is leaving the building."

"If you want to die," Superman said, "just kill yourself and leave us out of it."

"I don't want to die," Hughes said. "Damn it, do you think I want to? Imagine—*me* dying. I'm not even old! Look at me! I should have fifteen, twenty years left. I've bought the most expensive doctors in the world! My father died when I was nineteen, Goddamn it! What the hell use are doctors if they can't keep one man alive?"

Superman saw real pain in his eyes, and the fragment of a possibility. "Maybe you'll get better," he said.

"No. The condition is irreversible."

"People get better," he said. "It happens."

Hughes shook his head. "I know what you're trying to do. It won't work."

"You pathetic old man." Superman gave in to a swell of indignation. "All that money, that power—it's useless to you. Grand-opening night, up here all alone, too frightened of people to even come down and meet your admirers. Watching it all on TV, by yourself. You can buy anyone, but you haven't been able to buy yourself even one friend, have you? No wonder you're dying. What have you got to live for? You *had* to build yourself a monument because you know there's not a chance in hell anyone would build one for you."

"Dad, look," Ben Junior said, faintly. "This is Marilyn Monroe."

"I know, son. Go on out of here now. Go downstairs."

Hughes gazed down through the glass. "We had five wonderful years together. She made me feel like a young man again."

It was all Superman could do to keep from using that bow tie as a garrote. "You're lying," he said. "You never even met her."

"Of course I did. She was mine for five years."

Superman didn't think he shoved hard enough to knock him down, but Hughes fell and even slid a few feet on the floor. Superman was upon him instantly, jerking him to his feet. "Don't *talk* about her!"

"Back off." Hughes produced a small blue-metal pistol from his jacket. His hand trembled.

Superman backed off.

The steel-blue eyes glittered. "I'm sending a video to the States. Twenty years of birthday parties, a little tour of this chamber, and the story of the Jungle Inn, right up through the grand-opening boom. And it will be quite a boom, I promise. They'll never forget us. I just wish I could be there to see it." He waved the pistol. "Do you want to go first?"

"Is no good to die," Pito said.

"Oh shut up, you old fool." Hughes backed to the capsule at the center of the room, fumbling with his free hand to lift the glass dome. "You're right, Superman. This life has been lonely. But I'm not bitter. We all have to go sometime. At least I'll have a chance to come back."

"Son, get out of here." Superman kept his voice even. "Run. If he points that gun at you I'll kill him with my hands."

Pito focused his gaze on the gun.

You could see the boy trying hard to make sense of it all, his eyes darting from one to the other. "No, you come with me."

"Go! *Hurry!*"

Ben Junior ran for the stairs.

Hughes turned—the gun flew from his hand, *ping!* off a glass dome, and clattered to the floor.

"Ah, Pito, your power's not so weak after all." Hughes lunged for the gun. He moved fast for an old dying man. He got his hands around it. Superman stared into the little black hole.

A stern voice came from the walls all around: "Please evacuate the hotel. This is not a drill. Please evacuate the hotel. This is not a drill."

Hughes glanced at his watch. "Right on time."

Superman grabbed for the gun—knocked it to the floor, scrambled over and got it. When he turned, Hughes was climbing into the capsule, stretching out on his back.

Superman waved the gun. "Shut it off!"

"Nothing I can do. For every action there's an equal and opposite reaction."

"Please evacuate the hotel. . . ."

"Go away. Leave me in peace." Hughes pulled down the glass dome, adjusted the orchid in his lapel.

"This is not a drill. . . ."

He folded his hands, closed his eyes. One old man who missed his father too much, who didn't get enough love in his life—a life that was the envy of half the human race.

Superman glanced at Pito. They bolted for the door, down the stairs, through the maze. They came out in the white room. Ben Junior was pounding the glass wall with the blunt end of a fire extinguisher. "The elevator's dead. There's no stairs on this floor. Help me!"

". . . evacuate the hotel. This is not a drill. . . ."

"What the hell, son, we're eight stories up!"

"Would you just *help?*" Ben Junior swung the holy hell out of that canister. The glass cracked, and shattered. Superman grabbed his son's arm to keep him from falling out. Together they peered over the precipice.

The glass wall fell away at a fifty-degree incline—a steep slope, not much better than a straight fall.

Sometimes a man has a smart choice and a stupid choice. And sometimes he has no choice at all. Superman kicked out the last shards of glass.

"Please evacuate the hotel. This is . . ."

"Don't think about it," said Superman. "Hold on to me."

He sent his mind back to the taste of the magic blue water, the feeling of springing up into the sky, free of gravity. He put one arm around Pito and the other around his boy, and launched them from the window.

It wasn't flying, really, more like floating. His power was not as strong as before, but strong enough to keep them fast in his arms. Together they slid down the wall of glass, taking hits off ridges and crossbeams, sailing straight and fast, but not too fast, slowed by Superman's returning power of levitation as if by a parachute, eight stories down to a soft crash landing in a bed of daylilies.

They picked themselves up and ran. They were almost to the perimeter fence when Superman realized Pito was not with them. He turned.

The first flash bathed the mountaintop in scalded bright light.

The ground rolled. The asphalt driveway rippled like the ocean. Ben Junior went down on one knee.

The mountain erupted in light, sixteen explosions in a chain reaction. The pyramid toppled in on itself, a collapsing exploding volcano.

35 / *Superman Reconsiders His Obligations*

THE BRIDGE WAS JAMMED with refugees streaming toward Gato Negro, families with their belongings piled on wheelbarrows and wagons. Here and there a pickup truck laden with old people crept along at the same pace as the people walking. Kids skipped out in front, elated to be awake at this hour. Their parents looked grim, exhausted. While the gringos were up on the mountaintop dancing to the Jerry Vale Orchestra, the islanders had been quietly packing up, fleeing the troops of rampaging monkeys. The arc-vapor lights on the bridge cast their faces in shadow. Now and then a rumble from the burning remains of the Jungle Inn.

Pito and Catalina came out of the crowd, wheeling a cart.

"Oh thank God, old man, I didn't think you got out!"

"Detrás de tí," Pito said. (Right behind you.)

"Por lo que recuerdo, él cada vez es más feo," said Catalina. (Every time, he's uglier than I remembered.)

"Aw, Catalina, you know you love me." He waved a hand at the bridge. "Where are they going?"

"Is the *profecía,*" Pito said. "The *monos* having no use for the man. Tonight the Mago is waking. He is angry. We go to waiting."

"The Mago?"

"He sleeps in the mountane. Tonight he is waking." He pointed across the channel at the mound of bright fire crowning the summit of the south mountain. "He is taking the iseland again, for the *monos.* For the *animales.* So they can be freedom."

"What are you gonna do?"

"We wait here. In some time the Mago is sleeping again. The *monos* is come to forgetting. Then we go home."

Ben Junior stared at the shuffling column. "Who are all you people?" he cried, breaking the wild-eyed silence that had gripped him all the way down the hill. "Where are you going?" He grinned, a goofy version of the sweet smile that had saved his life. "Look at 'em, don't they look silly with all that stuff on their heads? Why is everybody going the same *way*?"

"Try to calm down, son, keep your voice down. It'll wear off soon."

"Don't tell me what to do," the boy snapped. "Who are you, anyway?"

Superman said, "Ben Junior . . ."

"Don't *call* me that!" He shoved him away. "Nobody calls me that! My father's *dead!* You're not my father!"

"You know what? It's real hard to believe, but I think I am."

The boy's voice flattened. "Then where have you *been* all my life."

"I've been right here," Superman said. "Trying to get home to you."

"That's bullshit. You could've come home."

"It was complicated."

"You could've called, or . . . got on a bus, but you stayed. You forgot about me. Get your hands off me. You're *dead*."

"What do you want me to say? 'I'm sorry' sounds kind of weak."

"Yeah, it does," the boy said. "You fell in love with her, didn't you?"

Superman said. "I tried to come home to you, Ben. For a long time. A bunch of different ways. I got trapped, but I never stopped thinking about you." He glanced over the heads of the refugees, over the superstructure of the bridge: the North Star. For years he had bounced the same wish off that star. Tonight the wish had come true, his son was beside him.

But it was not the way he'd imagined. Always in his dream Ben Junior was a little boy rushing into his arms, a blaze of love. Not this mouthy teenager with his eyes rolling around in his head.

Don't blame him. Rabbit messed around in his brain, to get to you. "How on earth did you find me?"

"You sent me a picture."

Superman shook his head. "A picture?"

"In a bottle. You wrote a note on a piece of your shirt."

Superman had forgotten it the moment he tossed it from the plane. He felt a smile breaking out. The best shirt a man ever had. "You mean you *got* it?"

The boy didn't smile. "You look different now. You don't look like the picture."

"It's been a long time. You look different, too."

The boy wandered out of the river of people, to the railing. He stood staring down at the water. "I met this guy Jeff," he said. "He died here. It felt like my fault. That happens to me a lot."

Superman touched his shoulder. "I always wanted to come home to you, son. At first I couldn't, I was hurt. Then I tried, but—they stopped me. After a while, I got to thinking about what went wrong between me and your mother. And I realized it was all my fault. I was no good for her. You were both better off without me. So I gave up trying to leave. I wasn't a good father, I know. I had a lot of other things on my mind."

"That's what *she* said. She spent the last eight years in a loony bin trying to find herself. Then she came home and said, 'Oh, sorry I missed your childhood, but I'm feeling a lot better now.' "

"Your mom?"

"I guess you forgot her, too."

"I didn't know she—I thought she was with her, her . . . husband."

"Jimbo? They got a divorce the same week she married him. She flipped out at your funeral. Jimbo stole all your money. She went off to Crazy Land. I never saw her again till Granny French died."

"I didn't know she died, son. I'm sorry."

"Everybody in Opelousas thinks I killed her."

A wave slapped the bridge piers.

"Why do they think that?"

"She was hurting. She wanted me to do it. I thought about it. I didn't do it, but I . . . I thought about it. I could have done it. Then she died. And it was my fault. So I came to find you. I thought you might understand." He turned, his face shining with tears. "When you died I was so mad at you—God! I hated you so much for making me miss my piano recital. I thought it was my fault you died, 'cause I hated you so much."

Superman swallowed the stone in his throat. "You should never have had to carry all that around with you, Ben. I swear, I did try to come home. I didn't try hard enough."

The truth was that his son had ceased to exist long ago, replaced by the imaginary boy he carried around in his head. Superman had made a new life in this place, he had let himself be swept up in his lusts and obsessions and wars, while the other world went on with its meaningless spin. He hadn't stopped to think that Ben Junior might be living an actual life of his own, that the sturdy slender boy might have grown into an almost-man who feels real grown-up guilt, love, pain, sorrow.

He never dreamed that his boy might still love him enough to come all this way to find him.

"I can see through you," said Superman Junior.

Superman stuck his hands in his pockets. "I imagine you can."

"No—I can see through to the other side of you. That is so weird."

Superman looked at his hand. He was just the slightest bit transparent.

"It's the drugs making you see things," he said softly. "It'll wear off soon."

They joined the last line of refugees over the bridge. Islanders and their worldly goods jammed the streets of Gato Negro. Ben Junior wandered to the seawall to stare back at the fire on the mountain.

Superman pulled the old man aside. "I'm disappearing again."

Pito looked him over. *"Sí, señor."*

Catalina said: *"Pareces mejor así."* (You look better that way.)

Superman said, "Isn't there something I can do?"

Pito shook his head sadly. "Is the *destino*," he said. "After the fly, you . . . disappear."

Superman thought of all the ways he might have died since he came to this place: smashed up in the crash of his plane; drowned on the beach his first night with Sandy and Linda; bashed on rocks in the down-plunging river; burned alive in the orange-and-green boat; swept out to sea by the current; crashed again in the Electra; shot in Daisy's house; blown to bits in the pyramid. Every time, something had brought him safely past the darkness.

There had to be a reason. God (or Pito, or magic, or fate) had kept him alive so he would be here when his son came to save him. And now the same force had decreed that it was time for him to disappear.

A yellow jeep made its way slowly through the mob on the bridge. At the wheel sat Frank in the blackened remains of Marie Antoinette's ball gown, Rabbit shirtless in Big Smiths, bellowing people out of the way, turning to yell: ". . . but no, you had to get all fancy and build the damn Cairo Hilton! I tried to tell you it wasn't a real hotel!"

"How dare you try to put this on me," Frank shot back, "after you dragged me into it! How was I supposed to know what that lunatic was doing? I spent a year of my life! You're the one who was helping him—"

"Why don't you both just shut up?" That was Melanie Llewellyn in the jump seat, her hair down around her shoulders, the elegant black dress in tatters.

Superman stepped in front of the bumper. Frank had to stop, or run him over. Frank stopped. "Mr. Willis, you have to believe me. He handed me the plans for a hotel, and I built it. That's all. I never knew what he meant to do."

"Oh for pity's sake, Frank, you're in this up to your eyeballs," said Rabbit. "At least pretend you're a man and admit it. A hotel with half a ton of plastique in the foundation? Get serious."

"That wasn't my department."

"You were afraid, just like I was," said Rabbit. "You knew he was crazy but you were afraid to say no."

"I didn't know he intended to gas us all and blow up the place. No sir, I did not."

"Don't look at me," Melanie said. "I'm just a consultant."

"Doesn't matter, does it, folks?" Superman thumped the hood with his fist. "He's gone. They're all gone. He gave us a tour of his little museum. I got to see your handiwork, Rabbit. Very impressive."

Rabbit raised a snub-nosed machine gun. "Stand out of the way."

Superman straightened. "Gonna shoot me? Go ahead. You afraid of me? You think I'm looking for a little *venganza?*"

"Let's go, Frank," said Melanie.

"Yeah Frank, drive on. Forget Amelia. Forget Daisy. And Spike. And the rest of them. Go on ahead and have yourself a nice life, Frank. I hope the three of you will be very happy together." He stepped aside, made a sweeping motion with his arm: proceed.

"Mr. Willis. I didn't kill anyone. I did what I was ordered to do. Mr. Hughes sent a man down to work on the Electra. The starboard engine was supposed to malfunction on the taxi run, so you'd both have time to get out. It went off too late. It wasn't my fault."

"But you knew it was going to happen."

"If I'd tried to warn you, he'd have killed me. He was a powerful man."

"Not anymore."

"No." Frank glanced over the water, toward a low, wavery star growing brighter. "I suppose the joke's on us. I must say you were very unkind to Helen Reddy."

"That wasn't me, Frank, that was the monkeys."

The star hammered across the channel, a helicopter shining its light. It swept over the bridge and circled back, blasting a hole in the crowd on the street.

Ben Junior stared up at the light. "It's pretty," he cried.

"Rabbit, what did you do to my boy?"

"He's a good kid," said Rabbit. "It was just a little something to liven up his evening. He'll come around in a week or two."

"Get us out of here, Frank," said Melanie.

Frank pressed the accelerator, edging ahead. The helicopter settled on a stretch of glittering pavement.

Superman put his arms around his boy.

Pito said, "You happy to see you son."

"Yeah, real happy."

"Mebbe he is liking to know my Catalina?"

Superman turned. Pito kept a very straight face. "I don't know, Pito, he's a little old for her, don't you think?"

"Is okay," Pito said. "Catalina, she is a leetle young, too."

"Pito, you knew a long time ago this was gonna happen. The monkeys told you. You could've stopped it."

"Is needed the bridge, for the peoples to leaving," the old man said. "Is needed you fly, for to wake up the Mago. And you son, for to show us the way."

The helicopter's hatch popped open in the hand of a slightly plump woman with long shapely legs. She struggled to hold on to her big floppy hat in the downwash of the blades. She peered at all the people with their cartloads of things.

"Mom?" Ben Junior hesitated, then started forward. "Mom!"

"Benny?" She opened her arms. "Surprise!"

They came together. Superman hung back, watching. Alexa had put on twenty pounds; it had softened the sharp edges of her figure. A few lines around the eyes could not dim the Miss Southwest Louisiana radiance of her smile.

The boy led her over. "Mom, look who I found."

Alexa blinked, and stepped back. "Ben?"

"Yeah, it's me. I thought you were afraid to fly."

"I got over it." Her eyes filled. "You're alive?"

"It looks that way."

"But—what's wrong with you? My God. You're *faded*."

"Yeah, I know."

She made a little shrug of her shoulders, as if she wanted to embrace him but wasn't sure. He made the nod that told her it was all right. All these years later and still they could speak without talking. He took her into his arms. She was crying.

A commotion arose in the helicopter, Rabbit waving his gun at the pilot, Melanie strapping in, Frank climbing aboard with a brown suitcase and a platinum wig in a plastic bag. The pilot revved his engine. The chopper lifted up from the street.

"Hey, wait a minute!" Alexa cried. "Where does he think he's going? That's my helicopter, I paid for a round trip!"

The chopper raced across the channel, circled once over the burning wreckage of the pyramid, and flew off due south.

Pito said, "This you wife?"

"Pito, this is Alexa."

Pito fished among the clutter on Catalina's cart and came up with a knob-headed walking stick and a sky-blue short-sleeved shirt, neatly folded to display the ink stains under the pocket. He handed these things to Alexa. "You keep," he said. "For goodlock."

36 / Friendly Skies

THEY RECLINED IN the shaggy seats of first class. A movie called *Animal House* played on an overhead screen. The stewardess brought champagne and smoked almonds.

Superman rested one hand on his walking stick. He wore dark glasses, black gloves, a Panama hat pulled low over his eyes. It was blowing his mind to be up in this sleek metal tube hurtling through the stratosphere toward the good old U.S. of A. He had almost forgotten the smell of jetliner air: cool, airless, filtered of everything but a faint ineradicable odor of lasagna.

Ben Junior got bored with the movie and went back to check out the girls in coach class.

"Okay, well, you loved her," Alexa said, picking up where they'd left off. "But would you say you were in love with her?"

"Yeah," Superman said. "I would have to say that." His new policy of total honesty made him uncomfortable about half the time, but still it felt better than lying.

"Oh. Well. That makes it harder, if you really were."

"Yeah."

"Did you love her more than me?"

"Different," he said. "She was different."

"Prettier? Smarter?"

"Just different, Alexa."

"Do you think you might conceivably forget her someday?"

"I kind of doubt it," he said. "But that doesn't mean we can't try to see . . . you know, how it goes with us. Without taking its temperature every five minutes. Right now it feels great, you know? I didn't really expect that. I thought you would hate me, or I would hate you."

"Well, I can't compete with a ghost," said Alexa. "I wouldn't even want to try."

"You're married to one, looks like."

"You are getting harder to see." She shook her head. "If you disappear completely, I won't be able to keep track of you."

He smiled. "That's one good thing."

"Did you spend a lot of time thinking about me, Ben? Or did you just forget me?"

"Some of both. It's funny, I wondered the same thing about you."

"Oh, I never forgot you one minute. I was too mad. I kept having this feeling that you were alive, you were out there somewhere living it up while I was going crazy. And, hey—you were."

"I wasn't exactly living it up," he said. "Not all the time. Listen—do you remember the time you tried to sing with the band?"

She cast her eyes down. "Of course."

"I read what you said about me at the Hollywood Bowl, and I'll tell you, you were right. That was the meanest thing anybody ever did to anybody."

"It sure as hell was," she said.

"I've been sorry since the minute I did it. But I never even told you. I was a bastard to you, Alexa. I don't know if I'm all that much different now, but I can give it a try."

"You're different, all right."

"You think so?"

"You never used to be sorry for anything."

"That's true," he said.

"You remember that time I married Jimbo and he stole eight hundred thousand dollars from us? I was sorry for that, too."

"Yeah, I bet you were."

"We're lucky, though. We're not poor. You're bigger than ever. There's a lot of money. Did you know that?"

"Ben Junior told me," he said, "but it doesn't seem real." He pinched his lip. "I don't know what I think about chasing after all that again. I've got a kind of different perspective on things. Getting famous does weird things to your head, you know? It just doesn't seem that important to me now."

"What would you do with yourself?"

"I don't know, maybe try to write a few songs for Ben. Have you heard him sing?"

"No."

"Well I have. In the shower. Jesus, what a voice. Amazing. You should hear—" He hushed as a little man in a brown suit went past to the bathroom, and Ben Junior came back to his seat. "See anything cute?"

"*Nada.* You'll never guess who's back there, though."

"Who?"

"Remember the video crew? All three of 'em are back there doing tequila shots."

"Do tell."

"Yeah, and look what I found in the overhead compartment." From his shirt he produced a manila envelope, from which he drew a videocassette. The label said HH—MY OWN STORY.

Superman turned it over in his hands. "Where did you learn to steal?"

"Mexico," Ben Junior said.

"What is it?" said Alexa.

"Home movies." Superman turned it over in his hands. "What do you think we should do with this, son?"

"We could throw it away."

"I think that's an excellent idea. Course there's no law saying we can't have a look at it first. Do you know where we can get hold of a machine that plays these tapes?"

Ben Junior rolled his eyes. "Of course, Dad, it's called a VCR. Everybody's got 'em now."

"Oh forgive me, Mr. Up to the Minute."

"Let me see your hand."

Superman pulled the glove back an inch.

"It's getting worse," the boy said. "You're almost gone."

"I know. I think the altitude makes it worse."

"It figures, I finally find you and you start disappearing all over again." Superman Junior pulled on his earphones and turned his eyes to the video screen.

Superman grinned. The kid was a natural smartass, just like his father.

The LAVATORY OCCUPIED sign blinked off. The plastic door swung open, and Superman found himself looking into the eyes of a little old Mexican man in a brown suit, a luxurious tie, creamy ivory fedora. The man grinned, showing two shiny gold teeth. "Bienvenidos," he said. He brought his hand up to lift the hat, just so, a salute as he passed Superman on his way to the back of the plane.

37 / Superman's Revenge

THE EL PASO CIVIC AUDITORIUM sold out within ninety minutes of the first announcement on the *Today* show. Details were sketchy. The concert would go live nationwide on an exclusive NBC simulcast starting at seven central, eight eastern. "Certainly one of the more interesting comeback stories in the history of pop music," said Bryant Gumbel.

"Certainly is, Bryant," said Jane Pauley. "And now Connie Chavez is going to show us some great ways to spruce up summer suppers with chicken on the grill. Connie?"

"I can't get over this thing," Superman said, punching the remote. Since his first encounter with a remote-control TV-VCR, they'd had a hard time prying him away from it. He made the tape go *zzp zzp* in reverse and there was Bryant Gumbel again: ". . . more interesting comeback stories in the history of pop music." *Zzp zzp.* ". . . comeback stories in the history of pop music." *Zzp.* ". . . pop music."

"Give me that thing." Alexa grabbed the remote. "Your son's nervous, can't you see he's nervous? Say something to him."

"*Tranquilo*, son, you're gonna be great." Superman got up from the chair. "Don't you hate that word 'comeback'? Makes me sound like Judy Garland."

"She's dead," said Alexa, "and anyway, you're bigger than she was, at least for tonight."

Superman Junior pressed his nose to the plate glass, staring down at the mob swarming the auditorium doors, the white trucks with peacocks on the sides filling the parking lot of the auditorium. He wore a silvery space suit and glittering ruby-red boots.

Superman wrapped an arm around his shoulder. "How 'bout it?"

"I don't know. I'll probably puke or something."

"I wouldn't let you go out there if I didn't know you were going to be great."

"But what if I puke?"

"Ben. Listen to me now. Are you sure this is really something you want?"

"I think so. Yeah."

"If you want to change your mind, you still can. Just say it."

"It's too late. Look at all those people."

"Never too late for anything. You taught me that." He leaned to kiss his son on the cheek.

Ben Junior rolled his eyes, but let his father kiss him.

"You're a natural, Benny," Alexa said. "Listen to your dad, if you don't want to listen to me."

"Mom . . ."

"Alexa, you're freaking him out."

"I know, I'm sorry," she said. "It's this diet, it makes me so jumpy."

"I don't know why you're starving yourself," Superman said. "I like you better with meat on your bones. You're a lot nicer than when you were skinny."

"Thank you," she said, "I think."

A coded knock at the door: *Ba-ba-BUM ba-ba BUM.* Barney Kleber rushed in, so excited it seemed he might start throwing off sparks. "Unbelievable! I have never seen anything like it. I just told Barbara Walters to take a hike! Do you know how I have dreamed of this day?"

Superman smiled. "I can only imagine."

"ABC has a crew in the air from Dallas, they're begging us to hold off till nine. Of course it's out of the question, Brokaw goes live with the satellite feed in five minutes. This thing has taken on a life of its own."

"How exciting," Alexa said. "I'm going on down, make sure nobody gets my spot. Benny? Break a leg, sweetie. Don't worry, I'll be right there watching you."

"Thanks, Mom."

She kissed him, and went out.

Superman said, "It used to drive me nuts when she watched me sing."

Ben Junior said, "I don't mind."

"You're a better man than I. You really want this, don't you?"

He nodded. "I do."

"Okay, Barney, what do we need to do here?"

Barney lit into a string of things that had to be decided *right now.*

Ben Junior wandered to the window, pressed his face and hands to the glass.

Superman half listened, yeah, Barney, sure, you decide. The kid was still a little strange, anyone could see that. Red Dot Ninety-nine had never quite worn off. He was moody, dreamy-headed, always going off to meditate with his eyes closed. Maybe this concert was not such a good idea. "Son? You okay?"

"I'm fine."

"What are you doing?"

"Talking to the people who work in my brain."

Superman glanced at Barney, who arched his eyebrows, Are we sure about him? "What are you telling 'em?"

"Not to let me puke." He opened his eyes. "Are we ready to go?"

"Let's do it." Superman cinched the belt of his white satin boxer's robe, and pulled the hood over his head.

A&M Records had sealed off the nineteenth floor of the Hyatt El Paso. Barney's elevator key let them ride unmolested to the basement. A service tunnel led under the parking lot to the auditorium. When it came time to choose a location for this show, there had never been any question that Superman would pick up where he left off. At long last he would give his El Paso fans their money's worth. A hollow roar echoed from the far end of the tunnel.

"Dad?"

"Yeah."

"Were you ever afraid before you went on?"

"Every time, son. Every goddamn time."

"Are you afraid now?"

"Not so bad. I'll have you up there with me. Look, if you ain't afraid, you ain't *alive.*"

"Well, okay," said Ben Junior, "I guess I'm alive."

Superman grinned. He knew the boy would be great. Never had he heard a voice like that: an angel. Like Superman's voice through a finer, rarer kind of horn. Ben Junior was younger, better-looking, with a three-octave range and a sweeter contralto than his father ever had. He could be a much bigger star. It was his *destino.* All he needed was a little push.

Superman still wasn't sure that stardom was something he would wish on his only son—but he would be there to watch him, to guide him. To let him know it was okay to quit, anytime. Your only job is to do what you have to, to save your own soul. Just stay sane. Don't forget who you are. You can survive, and who knows? It might even be fun.

They ran the security gauntlet into the frenzy of the darkened auditorium. Spotlights panned the crowd, a sea of people leaping and jumping, pounding their fists in the air.

"Don't look," he shouted into the boy's ear. "Think of this as a very noisy piano recital."

The lights focused on center stage. The crowd's roar threatened to bring down the roof. Superman followed his son up the steps. He felt the roadies trying to peer inside the shadow of his hood.

The lights went out, all at once. The crowd screamed for mercy.

Superman Junior walked downstage center to the microphone.

"Ladies and gentlemen," the announcer said, "please welcome Benjamin Willis Junior."

A dense column of light shone down upon this handsome slender boy in his silvery suit and red boots. The ovation carried an air of polite disappointment.

Alexa's smile lit up the stage by the speaker tower.

Superman Junior raised his hand, and waited for the crowd to fall silent. Only his father was close enough to see that hand trembling.

The boy sang the first line in a clear, soaring voice that filled the farthest reaches of the hall.

When he's up in the skyyyyyyy . . .

He held that note a full two bars. The band struck an ominous chord.

Do you know how he feeeeeeeeels . . .

The tone never wavered, the clean vibrato lifting up over the heads of the audience, changing their minds about him. He went up a note:

Not a bird, not a plaaaaane . . .

Now there was a thundering of drums, a riser levitating through the darkness at the back of the stage.

Just a man of ideeeeals . . .

The crowd saw the drummer on his throne, shrouded in a white robe, his sticks flailing, a blur of motion. The crowd went wild.

Watching people go bad . . .

The drummer got to his feet, never missing a beat of his wild tattoo.

In their usual way . . .

Rockets burst from the stage frame, belching sparks and white fire. All the lights came up at once. The crowd saw the boy in the spacesuit, the guys in the band, and behind them, on the riser, the drummer shrugging out of his robe.

A blue shirt danced in midair. A sky-blue shirt with inkstains, a hand-sized piece of cotton missing from the tail.

You could see the man wearing the shirt, faintly, if you got very close and used one strong light from the side, but the people in the audience and at home in their living rooms saw only a blue shirt, dancing in air.

A roar died in ten thousand throats. In the silence, Superman grabbed his sticks, smacked one-two-three on the rim, and kicked off into pure rock and roll. Ben Junior leaped into the air.

> *You better run—it's time for*
> *Superman's revenge*
> *Superman's revenge*
> *Superman's revenge . . .*

Superman didn't know how long the world would stay interested in an invisible rock star, and he didn't care. He was up here for fun now. He still loved playing the music, but he no longer felt the need to be a star. It was his boy's turn for all that.

Superman's only remaining ambition was to enjoy the rest of his life, no matter how much or little time that might prove to be. The best revenge, as it turns out, is no revenge at all. The best revenge is to sit back and watch the bad people of the world topple under the weight of their own badness, with no assistance from you. The best way is to live your own life, win your own victories, be as good as you can, love the people you love, let the world surprise you with how magical it can sometimes be. Seek out your *destino*. Take the signs as they come, read them if you know how.

Leave it up to God to sort the good from the evil, to deal with each according to his own kind. That's his job, after all, and when humans try to interfere, we almost always get it wrong.

Superman glanced to the speaker tower. Alexa glowed with pride, her long blond hair swaying in time with the song. She's a different woman now, he thought, better even than when I first fell in love with her. And I'm a better man. Maybe it will work this time.

It felt different, being with Alexa again.

It felt different, sitting there at the back, playing drums, singing harmony for Superman Junior.

It felt just fine.

PERMISSIONS ACKNOWLEDGMENTS

Grateful acknowledgment is made to the following for permission to reprint previously published material:

Jondora Music: Excerpt from "Bad Moon Rising" by John Fogerty, copyright © 1969 by Jondora Music. Reprinted by permission of Jondora Music.

Hal Leonard Corporation: Excerpts from "Smiling Faces Sometimes" by Norman Whitfield and Barrett Strong, copyright © 1971 by Jobete Music Co., Inc. All rights controlled and administered by EMI Blackwood Music Inc., on behalf of Stone Agate Music (a division of Jobete Music Co., Inc.). All rights reserved. International copyright secured. Reprinted by permission of Hal Leonard Corporation.

Peer International Corporation: Excerpts from "Contigo en la Distancia" by César Portillo de la Luz, copyright 1952 by Peer International Corporation, copyright renewed. International copyright secured. Reprinted by permission of Peer International Corporation.

Andrew Scott Music and Helena Music Company: Excerpts from "The Impossible Dream," words by Joe Darion and music by Mitch Leigh, copyright © by Joe Darion and Mitch Leigh. Reprinted by permission of Andrew Scott Music and Helena Music Company.

Warner Bros. Publications U.S. Inc.: Excerpt from "Everything's Coming Up Roses" by Stephen Sondheim and Jule Styne, copyright © 1959 by Norbeth Productions, Inc., and Stephen Sondheim, copyright renewed. All rights administered by Chappell & Co.; excerpts from "Louie, Louie" by Richard Berry, copyright © 1957 (copyright renewed) by Windswept Pacific Entertainment Co. doing business as Longitude Music Co.; excerpt from "Lovesick Blues" by Irving Mills and Cliff Friend, copyright 1922 (copyright renewed) by EMI Mills Music, Inc. All rights reserved. Reprinted by permission of Warner Bros. Publications U.S. Inc., Miami, FL 33014.

Gone for Good

MARK CHILDRESS

A Reader's Guide

A Conversation with Mark Childress

Q: You've described this novel as "Latin American magical realism meets Southern Gothic." Can you elaborate on what that means to you?

MC: I've been fascinated by modern Latin American fiction since I first read García Márquez, Borges, Cortázar and the other great ones in a class at college. They took what my Southern Gothic heroes like Faulkner and O'Connor had done and added a kind of direct magic to the mix. *Gone for Good* owes a lot to both schools—the Southerners, for their history hauntedness and love of language, and the Latin Americans, who showed us that literally anything can be real if the writer can make the reader believe it. In some way, Superman Willis is like a Southern writer who suddenly finds himself lost in a García Márquez tale.

Q: You've called the American obsession with celebrity the "religion and scourge" of our time. Why do you think that need for celebrity—both the need to feel close to our celebrity idols and the yearning to be celebrities ourselves—affects so many of us?

MC: Maybe because going to the movies is more fun than going to church. That sounds flippant, but isn't meant to be. Television, pop music, and the movies establish an extremely powerful intimacy, but only in one direction—you feel close to the people on the screen or the radio, but they don't even know you exist. There's something very comfortable and weird about that.

Q: Of all of the celebrities and mysteriously disappeared people living on Isla del Mago, who would you most like to meet and why?

MC: The cool thing about writing fiction is, I don't have to choose. I got to meet all of them and to live with them for a couple of years. Writing a novel is like inviting a bunch of odd people to live in your head for a while. Sometimes you get tired of them and wish they'd go away, but mostly it's a lot of fun in there. That said, I'd really love to spend an afternoon on the beach with Daisy.

Q: **What writers or artists have inspired your work?**

MC: All of them, especially those who lived to a ripe old age. I'm inspired even by the ones who made art that I don't personally like, because they faced down the odds against artists and went on and did it anyway. My most direct inspiration has come from my friends who are writers. They lead by example and instruct me with kindness.

Q: **How is the Magician's search for fame in *Gone for Good* different from Lucille's in *Crazy in Alabama*? Both were willing to kill for it, but the Magician is the ultimate villain and, with all her faults, it's impossible not to be charmed by Lucille. How does that desire for glory become so destructive?**

MC: I guess they're both addressing the same question from wildly different angles, which is: Is it possible to become immortal? Fame is about the only way anybody can achieve immortality these days, aside from the odd saint—and even candidates for sainthood have people campaigning for them full-time. Destructiveness enters into the picture when the drive for immortality becomes more important than the living, breathing people around you.

Q: **Is there a particular music legend from the seventies that inspired the story of Superman?**

MC: There's a list of clues early on in the book for the astute reader. I think he would have been friends with Jim Croce and Joni Mitchell and Jackson Browne and others of their generation, but I wanted to write about somebody who was his own man.

Q: **After being abandoned by his parents, Ben Jr. is saved by Granny French. Like Willie in *V for Victor* and Meemaw from *Crazy in Alabama*, she is a quirky woman who is** very easy to love. Are these women unique to the South?

MC: I doubt it, although the way they talk and act may be particularly Southern. I don't know why variations on that grandmother keep showing up in my fiction. My own grandmothers were very different from each other and from these characters. All I know is that old people have a large impact on young children—at least they did on me. The very old and the very young share a secret language.

Q: Can you talk about the striking contrast between the humor and tragedy in your books?

MC: Life would be impossibly tragic if we weren't able to laugh at it. And a life of nothing but laughter would come to seem silly and empty if there wasn't always something darker lurking ahead down the road, something to laugh in the face of.

Q: How did you decide upon the personalities behind the famously disappeared? Did you research their personas and quirks or create identities that seemed to fit the facts of their personal histories?

MC: For me, writing a novel is a much more intuitive process than, say, writing a newspaper article. I never know what's going to happen when I sit down to begin a novel. So it's not really a question of "deciding" or "creating" anything, other than a setting and a kind of mood. If everything's working okay, the people walk onstage and begin speaking and acting on their own. They really take over. When I'm dealing with real people, as in *Gone for Good*, I'll go back after the first draft and read up on things, to see if I've got anything glaringly wrong.

Q: You moved to Costa Rica several years ago. Why do you feel so connected with the tropics?

MC: It's peculiar—the first time I stepped off a plane in the airport at San Jose, I felt like I was at home. Didn't speak much Spanish, didn't know a soul—but I felt completely at ease and was instantly charmed by everything and everyone. Maybe it's all those years of reading the Latin American magical realists. I had visited the region in the pages of their books, so it felt familiar to me.

Q: **Do you prefer to write at a particular place or time? Any set routine?**

MC: It takes me a long time to write a book, two or three or four years, depending. The only way I've found to get it done is to start in the morning and write until I don't have anything left to say for that day. First I like to have a big cup of coffee and read over what I did yesterday, and then I jump right in with both feet.

Q: **One reviewer compared this novel with *Alice in Wonderland* and *The Wizard of Oz*. Ben Willis truly changes when he crashes out of his normal life into entirely different circumstances. This is also true of Lucille and Peejoe in *Crazy in Alabama*, Leroy Kirby in *Tender*, Stella in *A World Made of Fire*, and Victor in *V for Victor*. Do you think it's extreme situations and different surroundings—falling down the rabbit hole—that force us to grow?**

MC: But isn't every novel the story of a character in extremis? A story in which something changes forever and will never be the same? I think that's the stuff of fiction—an interesting character thrust into an impossible situation. I'm a big fan of large novels with lots of people to whom lots of interesting things happen. No one ever grew by staying in the same place their whole lives, with the possible exception of Eudora Welty.

Q: **Your books are all very different from each other. If there are any common themes throughout your work, what do you think they are?**

MC: 1. The aforementioned grandmother.

2. Be careful what you wish for, you might get it.

3. Don't be afraid to do something strange once in a while, just for the hell of it.

Q: **What do you want people to get out of your books?**

MC: I hope they have a good time, and keep turning the pages, and maybe laugh out loud once or twice, and maybe feel a little sad, too, and be sorry when it's over, and tell their friends to read it.

Q: **What's next?**

MC: Who knows?

Mark Childress was interviewed by Steven Gutierrez, a freelance writer living in New York City.

2. Be careful what you wish for, you might get it.

3. Don't be afraid to do something strange once in a while, just for the hell of it.

Q: **What do you want people to get out of your books?**

MC: I hope they have a good time, and keep turning the pages, and maybe laugh out loud once or twice, and maybe feel a little sad, too, and be sorry when it's over, and tell their friends to read it.

Q: **What's next?**

MC: Who knows?

Mark Childress was interviewed by Steven Gutierrez, a freelance writer living in New York City.

Reading Group Questions
and Topics for Discussion

1. Before crashing into the island, Ben was feeling disenchanted with his fame and success: "His life would be perfect, he thought, if he could disappear right now. . . ." Why do you think fame and music stopped being fun for Ben? What kind of story would he have had if he had not gotten lost?

2. When Ben realizes that he has no choice but to land his plane in the water, he thinks of all the things he wishes he had and had not done. He takes photos of himself and the island and writes a note to Ben Jr., briefly thinking of communion as a child and his father and his son's smile. You are in the same situation: What do you do with the few moments before you crash?

3. Consider the voices that tell the story. The chapters about Superman are told through a narrator and refer to Superman in the third person. The chapters about Ben Jr., however, are told through his own voice. How does this affect how we feel about the characters? Do you feel closer or sympathize with one more than the other? How does the narrator's voice relate to Superman? Is it Superman speaking to himself, the author, or something more?

4. After Amelia's death, Ben has an epiphany about God and life on the island: "God is the frog, the spider, the firefly with twin headlamps. . . ." Daisy immediately notices the difference in him. How does Ben make this spiritual change? Does this come from realizing his past failures? From letting the nature around him finally affect him? From the Red Dot that Rabbit gave him? Have you ever had realizations like this? If so, what caused them, or allowed them?

5. After Daisy and Ben were together for the first time he had the urge to run from her because he needed to stay focused on getting back home: "Every waking moment would be given to adoring her, inhaling, imbibing her. She would become your addiction, the thing you did with your life." Later, he accepts

his place on the island, a life with Daisy, and stops trying to get off the island: "The months slipped through his fingers, and turned into years." In a sense, he was right in that loving her did trap him. Is that always the case with love? Was he being true to himself by running away from her or by being with her—or both?

6. If you could spend time with one of the mysteriously disappeared, who would you choose and why? Whose character's presence surprised you the most? Were Amelia's and Daisy's personalities what you expected from knowing their pasts?

7. Fame controls most of the people in this story. The Magician was willing to sacrifice people for the immortality he thought fame could give him. Do you think you can live on through fame? What does this story say about superstardom?

8. How does celebrity affect your own life? Would you want to be famous? If so, could you avoid the unhappiness it caused some of these characters? How important are celebrities to you personally? How much do you know about them? Do you think our culture is overly obsessed with famous people? Why or why not?

9. Considering how little his father was involved in his life, why do you think Ben Jr. felt a need to find him? Do you see similarities between the two characters?

10. We see Alexa only through Superman or Ben Jr. until nearly the very end of the book. How did your feelings about her change after reading chapter 28, "Her Real Life"? Do you think her husband or her son understands her well?

11. Consider this conversation between Ben and Daisy:

> "But everything they told us is a lie!"
> "Welcome to the real world, Ben. Where've you been keeping yourself? People don't want the truth. They just want confirmation of the lies they've already heard."

If you, like Ben, were faced with incredible conspiracies, dead people, and magical powers, would you be able to adjust? Would you be able to believe what was happening? How do people learn to accept the impossible?

12. Do you think Ben's reunited family will stay together?

13. Considering the fairy-tale aspect of the book, what would you say the moral to this fable is?

Praise for Mark Childress

V for Victor
"A speeding bullet of a book . . . In this adventure story the hero, Victor, is sublimely lost, a celebrated ragamuffin like Huck Finn."
—*The New York Times Book Review*

"Fantastic, extravagant . . . Thoroughly charming."
—*The Boston Globe*

A World Made of Fire
"That rarest of finds, an unsentimental coming-of-age story, the novel is also an engrossing mystery. . . . We couldn't ask for more."
—*San Francisco Chronicle*

"A wonderful and powerful novel . . . Mark Childress is a novelist of astonishing gifts."
—Pat Conroy, author of *The Prince of Tides*

Tender
"*Tender* is more than just a fine novel; it is a big, all-American, Technicolor dreamboat of a book, as vital and intense as anything I've read in the last ten years."
—Stephen King

"Haunting . . . An evocation of an American phenomenon and the time and place that nurtured an ascent to glory. Childress gets everything right."
—*The Los Angeles Times Book Review*

Crazy in Alabama
"Something that nobody has ever written before . . . Childress plays out his two hands here, civil rights and husbandicide, like a master playing out a fancy game of double solitaire."
—*The Washington Post Book World*

"Triumphant . . . It is a measure of Mr. Childress's skill as a novelist that he soon had me eating out of his hand. . . . This novel seems not only fresh and original but positively inspired."
—*The New York Times Book Review*

"If Flannery O'Connor and Stephen King had written a book together, this would be it. Hilarious and scary!"
—Fannie Flagg, author of
Fried Green Tomatoes at the Whistle Stop Cafe

© Jerry Bauer

About the Author

MARK CHILDRESS was born in Alabama, grew up in the Midwest and the South, and was graduated from the University of Alabama. His articles and reviews have appeared in the *New York Times*, the *Los Angeles Times*, the *San Francisco Chronicle*, the *Times Literary Supplement*, *Southern Living*, and the *Birmingham News*, among other publications. He is the author of three children's books and four previous novels, *A World Made of Fire*, *V for Victor*, *Tender*, and *Crazy in Alabama*. He lives in Manuel Antonio, Costa Rica.

T E N D E R

In *Tender*, novelist Mark Childress has redefined the American epic. He takes us on a wild ride through the last three decades as his fictional hero, Leroy Kirby, makes his meteoric rise to stardom, from the poverty-stricken child of an overprotective mother and absent father to an icon who stands for everything American—a role that will ultimately consume him. After reading *Tender,* you will never think about the South, fame, or rock-and-roll the same way again.

"A BIG, ALL-AMERICAN, TECHNICOLOR DREAMBOAT OF A BOOK . . . THIS IS A GREAT NOVEL."
—Stephen King

"HAUNTING . . . AN EVOCATION OF AN AMERICAN PHENOMENON AND THE TIME AND PLACE THAT NURTURED AN ASCENT TO GLORY. CHILDRESS GETS EVERYTHING RIGHT."
—*Los Angeles Times Book Review*

Available in bookstores everywhere.
Published by The Ballantine Publishing Group
www.randomhouse.com/BB/